The Avenging Angel and the Spy

THE HIDDEN HEARTS
BOOK TWO

SUSAN CARROLL

OLIVERHEBERBOOKS

The Avenging Angel and the Spy Copyright 1991, 2025 © by Susan Carroll

Previously titled: Rendezvous

Cover Design: Dar Albert

Published by Oliver-Heber Books

This title was previously published

0 9 8 7 6 5 4 3 2 1

One

~~~

E scape was impossible. The carriage careened through the ruts of the dirt road at a bone-shattering pace, the slope of the French countryside flashing by in a blur of green. But the sounds of pursuit could be heard clearly. The shouts of the soldiers and the thunder of their horses resounded above the rattle of the coach windows, the clatter of the iron-rimmed wheels.

Within moments the carriage would be overtaken. The four occupants of the berline realized this even before the coach began to slow. They knew the exhausted team pulling the heavy vehicle could no longer maintain such a pace. Late afternoon sun glinted through the windows, casting shadows upon the apprehensive faces of a slender seventeen-year-old boy and the careworn woman clutching a little girl close to her side. When the sound of a musket shot cracked through the air, the child buried her face in her mother's skirts. Outside, the whipping mane of the lead soldier's mount edged into view. The rider hurled abuse at the coachman and the postboy, then bellowed out a command to halt.

Madame Coterin's arms tightened about little Sophie and she exchanged a frightened glance with her son, Phillipe. Both of them looked instinctively toward their companion, who was seated upon the leather seat opposite—a tall woman garbed in a high-waisted gown of black silk, her features obscured by a veil.

Even though her expression was masked, Isabelle Varens conveyed to the Coterin family an appearance of calm and collected wits.

"It will be all right," she said in unmistakably English accents, her voice as cool and silvery as a clear mountain stream. "The important thing is to allow me to do the talking and not to panic."

Isabelle reached with seeming casualness for a miniver muff stowed beside her upon the seat. Only she knew with what tension her fingers crooked around the pearly handle of the pistol strapped within the fur's depths. The familiar rush that she always felt at the scent of danger coursed through her: part fear and part exhilaration at the thought of confronting the enemy, besting him.

Another shot rang out and the coach lurched to a stop, which nearly tumbled them all from their seats. The French soldiers surrounded the berline in a swirl of dust and bluecoats, sweating horses and glinting sabers. Belle could hear the postboy's terrified cry. One of the militia cursed her coachman, and Feydeau answered back with Gallic fervor.

Young Phillipe shifted his brown frock coat and groped for the hilt of his sword. Stretching out her hand, Belle stayed him with a warning shake of her head just as the coach door was wrenched open. The beefy shoulders of a soldier filled the opening, the sword he brandished forcing Belle back against the faded velvet squabs.

"Be still," he growled. "Don't any of you make any sudden moves."

Madame Coterin shrank deeper into her corner, her sobs mingling with her daughter's. Phillipe's face paled. Using his thin frame, he attempted to shield his mother and sister.

"What seems to be the trouble, monsieur?" Belle asked. Her voice sounded slow and even, completely out of tempo with the quickening of her blood. She undid the leather strap that held the pistol and readjusted the muff so that she could level her unseen weapon at the man's stomach.

"The trouble is, my fine lady, Sergeant Emile Lefranc does not take kindly to having his orders disobeyed." The soldier puffed out his chest and thumped it with his fist. "When an officer of the Elboeuf militia demands a carriage draw rein, that command had best be obeyed double quick."

"What right have you—" Phillipe managed to choke out before Belle cut him off.

"Indeed, sir, we intended no disrespect." Behind the curtain of her veil, she assessed the burly man, resplendent in his royal-blue coat with scarlet facings and yellow epaulettes, the silver galoons of a sergeant upon his sleeve. Probably recently enlisted and fiercely proud of it, likely to be overzealous, was Belle's conclusion. And beyond him, although she could not see to count them, Belle reckoned that the sergeant must have at least a half-dozen men at his call. She relaxed her grip on the pistol. The threat of force was not the answer to wangling her way out of this one. Her safety and that of the Coterins would depend entirely on her wits. She was not even sure as yet what these soldiers wanted.

Playing for time, she pretended to shudder "Surely, sir, you can have no reason for terrifying innocent women and children."

She noted Phillipe stiffened with indignation, but any gallant action he might be contemplating was hindered by his mother, who now clung to him as well as his little sister.

The sergeant's sword wavered as he retrieved a crumpled sheet of parchment from his pocket and flashed it at her with an air of swaggering importance. "My orders are to stop any suspicious-looking vehicle and search it."

Belle tried to read the document, but glimpsed little beyond the date before the sergeant snatched it back. Fructidor, the Year XI or, Belle thought, September 1802 to the sane world outside of revolutionary France.

"We shall be only too happy to cooperate," Belle said in her sweetest tones. With slow deliberation she raised her veil. The sergeant froze, his eyes widening, his lips nearly pursing into an appreciative whistle. Belle had no difficulty imagining what he was seeing: the eyes, melting blue, seductive; the cheeks, high, fine-boned; the ringlets, golden, the complexion, creamy, subtly shaded with rose; the lips, carnellian, tempting. She had oft studied her reflection in the mirror, not out of any vanity, but more in dispassionate evaluation of the beauty Fate had seen fit to bestow upon her, a weapon that could prove more effective than the pistol she carried.

The sergeant had already forgotten himself enough to lower his sword. His manner was somewhat less blustering as he said, "Forgive me, madame. But I must ask to see your passport."

"Certainly," she murmured. As Belle withdrew the paper from the purse tied to the belt of her gown, Madame Coterin sucked in her breath, but the sergeant took no notice. His eyes remained fixed upon Belle. She forced herself to remain unperturbed as she handed over the passport.

The sergeant unfolded the paper. Stroking his chin, he made great show of examining the document. As the seconds ticked by, Phillipe drummed his fingers upon his knee. Belle sought to give him a reassuring smile. After all, the passport was one of the best forgeries English pound notes could buy.

But her own anxiety heightened when the sergeant stepped back and summoned one of his men. The two soldiers drew a few steps from the coach, their heads together in earnest consultation.

"*Mon dieu*," Madame Coterin wept. "They know! They have discovered—"

"Hush!" Belle whispered. Her neck muscles tensed as she strained to hear.

"Madame Gordon, sir," the second soldier was saying, "traveling with her daughter and two servants."

"Oh. Oh, of course." The sergeant harumphed, then muttered something about the sun having been in his eyes.

Belle stifled an urge to laugh as she realized what had been wrong. "Nothing is amiss," she whispered to Phillipe and his mother. "Only that the sergeant cannot read."

But they had no chance to relax before the sergeant returned to the coach door. "You are Madame Gordon?" he asked, his eyes making a more thorough inspection of Belle, lingering on the bodice of her gown.

"That is so, sir," Belle lied.

"An English lady traveling alone?" His voice held a faint note of censure.

"Alas, sir, I am recently widowed. Since your great general Napoleon has been so gracious as to declare a peace between our two nations, I thought to visit France as so many of my countrymen are doing. In the gaiety of Paris, I might forget the good husband I have lost."

"But you are heading away from Paris, madame."

"True." Belle permitted her gaze to rake over the sergeant's bulky form with just the right combination of shyness and bold admiration. "I have done enough forgetting."

The sergeant's cheeks waxed red. He returned the passport, removed his cockaded hat, attempted to smooth his coarse windblown hair, then straightened the hat upon his head again. While he was so flustered, Belle pressed home her advantage. Resting her hand upon his sleeve, she looked him full in the face and coaxed, "Perhaps, Captain—"

"Sergeant, madame. Sergeant Lefranc of the Elboeuf militia."

"My dear Sergeant Lefranc, perhaps if you would tell me exactly what you are searching for, I could be of some help to you."

The sergeant's arm quivered beneath her touch. "Deserters, madame. Deserters from the army."

Deserters? Not a certain royalist spy who most often went by the name of Isabelle Varens? Not the family of the Chevalier Coterin, the agent recently caught pilfering Consul Napoleon Bonaparte's private dispatches?

5

Phillipe gave an audible sigh, and if Sergeant Lefranc had been gazing at Madame Coterin, he would have seen the relief she could not disguise. But the soldier's stare never wavered from Belle, and she schooled her features most carefully.

"Dear me!" she said. "Deserters! How very dreadful."

"Indeed it is, madame. But you would be astonished at how oft the country folk protect such rogues. That is why we need to stop every coach to be certain no one is hiding them."

"As if I would do such a thing." Belle heaved a tremulous breath. The sergeant's interested gaze followed the rise and fall of her breasts. "I despise such cowards who slink away, leaving brave men like you to face all the danger."

Sergeant Lefranc shuffled his feet, an embarrassed smirk on his face. "Well, 1 can see I made a mistake. Please accept my apologies, madame. Although it was most suspicious—the way you attempted to avoid being stopped."

"Not at all, sir. You see, I have heard horrible tales of your deserters, how they prey upon the countryside like marauding brigands. When I saw the blue coats, I had no notion who might be after me, and being but a defenseless female ..."

Belle allowed her lashes to drift downward, all the while watching covertly for any sign the sergeant might disbelieve her.

But the man was only too eager to agree. "Of course, Madame Gordon. Such journeys are indeed hazardous for a lady with no male protector."

It was fortunate, Belle thought, that the sergeant did not see the way Phillipe flushed and glowered at him.

"Perhaps," Sergeant Lefranc continued, moistening his lips, considering there are these deserters prowling about, my men and I should provide you an escort to your destination."

Although Belle greeted the suggestion with concealed dismay, a spirit of mischief also stirred inside her. Ever since the Revolution had first swept through France, she had had more than one occasion to escape to the coast, but she had never done so decorously escorted by a contingent of the Revolutionary Army. Yet when she caught a glimpse of Madame Coterin's face sick with apprehension, Belle suppressed the devilish impulse to make even more a fool of Sergeant Lefranc than she already had.

She graciously refused his offer, assuring him that she did not mean to travel much farther that day. When he continued to press her, she silenced him by saying, "And I have no wish to get you into difficulties, sir, by drawing you so far away from your garrison."

The sergeant stopped in midsentence, clamping his lips together and looking uncomfortable. It was just as she suspected, Belle told herself. The good Lefranc had already exceeded his authority by traveling even this far from the town of Elboeuf. After a few more weak protestations, he was content to take his leave of her, pressing a kiss upon the back of her hand before closing the coach door. The sergeant remounted his horse and signaled to her coachman that he was free to continue.

Belle heard Feydeau spit out a final oath before whipping up the horses. As the coach lumbered into movement, a heavy silence settled over the interior, a silence that remained unbroken until they saw the last of Sergeant Lefranc and his farewell salute.

"Insolent dog," Phillipe muttered, glaring out the window.

"He was but carrying out his mission," Belle said.

Madame Coterin released the death grip she held upon Sophie long enough to cross herself. "Thank the Bon Dieu."

"Not God, Maman," Phillipe said. "We must thank Mademoiselle Isabelle." His eyes lit up with admiration. "Never have I known any other woman possessing such sangfroid, such courage."

I was simply carrying out my mission," Belle said. But that was not true, she thought. She was being paid to spy upon the French army, to gauge the extent of military preparations in France, not to rescue the Coterin family. She would likely receive a blistering communication from Victor Merchant regarding her deviation from duty. Ah, well. Belle shrugged. She would consign it to the fire as she did with all the unpleasant notices from her employer.

"In any case," she said aloud to forestall further compliments from Phillipe, "we stood in no danger. Luckily the sergeant was not looking for us."

"Lucky indeed!" Phillipe's face clouded. "For all the protection I provided, sitting there like a great lump. I should have—"

"You should have done exactly what you did. Kept quiet and kept your head. You behaved most sensibly."

The bitter set of Phillipe's mouth showed that he was unconvinced by Belle's words. She thought it best to let the matter drop, but Madame Coterin chimed in, scolding her son.

"Oui. We want none of your heroics, I beg of you, my Phillipe. It is bad enough to have lost your poor papa to this accursed folly. I will not see the Revolution consume my boy as well."

Phillipe flushed with mortification.

"According to your Consul Bonaparte's decrees, the Revolution is over," Belle said dryly.

"The Revolution will never be over." Phillipe's hands clenched. "Not until the monarchy is restored, the killing of King Louis avenged, not until his brother is seated upon the throne—"

"*Tais-toi*, Phillipe!" his mother cried. "You grow to sound more like your papa. I cannot bear it. I care not who governs France. All I want is peace, to keep my children safe."

It was a prayer many French mothers had voiced during the endless years since the mobs of Paris had pulled down the Bastille stone by stone, since Dr. Guillotin's grim invention had been erected in the Place de Grave, since the streets had flowed with so much blood even the horses pulling the tumbrils of the condemned had reared back in fear.

Fresh tears coursed down Madame Coterin's cheeks. Belle leaned across the seat to take the woman's hand in a strong clasp.

"And so you shall keep them safe, madame. I promise you. It is not much farther to the coast. By nightfall we shall be crossing the channel to England, a new life for all of you."

Madame Coterin stiffened. Belle sensed the rebuff and withdrew her hand immediately. She understood only too well, she thought with some bitterness. Madame might be grateful to Belle for the rescue, but Belle was, after all, a spy, scarcely an occupation any decent woman would pursue.

Madame Coterin sniffed, struggling to compose her features. "I beg your pardon. It is not my custom to carry on so. But I am so very tired."

"Of course," Belle said. "You should try to rest. It will not be long before we reach the next posting station."

Madame nodded. She sagged back against the cushions, gathering her little girl up in her arms. A strange child, the little Sophie, Belle thought. So quiet one often forgot she was there, even her weeping muted as though she had learned at a tender age, if one must cry, it was best done as silently as possible.

Belle's gaze traveled to each of the Coterins in turn, Sophie, her eyes overlarge in her wan face, Madame Coterin, her dark hair prematurely streaked gray and Phillipe, the squaring of his slight shoulders doing little to hide the fact he felt just as frightened, just as lost as his mother and sister.

Damn Laurent Coterin to hell, Belle thought. Although she and the late chevalier had both worked for the same network of royalist agents, Coterin had been an amateur, a hopelessly incompetent spy. He had been arrested on suspicion of intercepting Napoleon's dispatches, and easily convicted because Laurent had put his notes in the old Julius Caesar code, a cipher so simple a child could break it. The chevalier had crowned his folly by getting himself shot in a botched escape attempt from prison. But in Belle's eyes Coterin's most unpardonable sin had been implicating his innocent family in his activities, while never making any provision for their safety in the event of his being discovered.

"Is the sun in your eyes, mademoiselle?"

Belle was startled out of her reflections by Phillipe's voice. "I beg your pardon?"

"You scowled so just a moment ago. I thought the sun might be bothering you. I could draw the shades if you wish."

"By all means. If you want to announce to the world we have something to hide."

"Oh. Of course not." The young man gave her a rueful smile. "How clever you are, mademoiselle, to think of such small details."

It was one of the reasons she was still alive, Belle thought. But she merely returned Phillipe's smile and lapsed into silence. Despite the rough sway of the carriage, Madame Coterin and her daughter managed to drift into a sleep borne of exhaustion.

Their journey, which had begun when Belle had met them with the coach in the Rouvray Forest outside of Paris three days ago, had been an arduous one, though not as eventful as Belle had anticipated. They had only been stopped once and that by Sergeant Lefranc. But the apprehension of being overtaken had been in itself nerve-racking, that and the additional distress caused by one of the carriage poles snapping outside of Rouen. But soon, Belle prayed, very soon she would bring this mission to a successful conclusion.

Unable to relax, Belle stared out the window at the gentle monotony of the Norman country-side, the flat meadows dotted with cows, here and there the gray stone of a farmhouse or an apple orchard, the trees laden with ripening fruit. No grand, breathtaking vista, and yet the scene was somehow more satisfying with its aura of peace, of normalcy. She watched the sun setting behind a wheat field recently harvested. As the fiery orb bathed the sky in a glow of rose and gold, a rare sense of tranquility stole over Belle.

She would have liked to have clung to the feeling, but was disturbed all too soon. The leather seat creaked as Phillipe shifted and cleared his throat. Reluctantly she dragged her gaze from the window and realized the young man was staring at her, likely had been doing so for some time.

The last rays of the sun caught the shine of his beardless face, the brightness of his eyes. Was he regarding her perhaps a shade too tenderly? Belle had caught such an expression on his face more than once, but she kept hoping that she only imagined what it portended.

When she caught him staring, the boy averted his eyes. He coughed again. "I was wondering, mademoiselle—"

"Yes?" Belle's tone was not encouraging.

"Well ..." Phillipe swallowed. "I was wondering. How did a lady like you became involved in this dangerous work? Indeed, I envy you. Such an exciting life you must lead."

"Too exciting sometimes," Belle said, eager to evade any questions about her past.

"Your friend Baptiste in Paris says you are the best royalist agent working in France today. He said that during the Terror, you helped so many aristocrats hide and escape, it is no longer safe for you to enter the city."

Belle made no comment, but she tensed. She had indeed once come close to losing her life in Paris. If she closed her eyes, she could easily conjure up chilling images of her confinement in the Conciergerie, the walls of that dread prison enfolding her like a tomb. But it was not fear of death or of being arrested again that kept her from Paris so much as fear of her own memories, some bittersweet, but most the stuff of nightmares. The City of Light for her had become a city of darkness.

"Baptiste told me you helped smuggle arms to aid the Catholic uprising in the Vendee," Phillipe continued. "He said that men call you the Avenging Angel."

"Baptiste talks too much." Belle mentally cursed her fellow agent. How she hated that foolish nickname. She had not gone to work for the royalist cause because she cared a fig whether the deceased king's fat brother Louis XVIII succeeded in reclaiming his throne or not. It was because the royalists paid her well and she had despised the violence of the revolutionaries who had overrun France. She was no one's avenger and certainly no one's angel. Only the insouciant Baptiste, presuming upon old friendship, had ever dared call her that to her face.

"Have you been a royalist agent for a long time?" Phillipe asked.

"Oh, a long, long, long time," Belle said, hoping to remind him that she was nearly ten years older than he.

Her hint appeared to go wide of its mark, for Phillipe bent forward, his lips parting in a shy smile. "I am so glad you are crossing the channel with us." He paused, and then asked in a voice that cracked, "Dare I hope, mademoiselle, that you will come and call upon me and Maman after we are settled in Portsmouth?"

Belle suppressed an urge to tell him she doubted his mother would welcome such a visit. An adventuress in her home was the last thing the respectable woman would want in other circumstances.

"We shall see," she said. She realized that even this vague promise was a mistake. Phillipe's face lit up, and she had the impression that if he had dared, he would have reached for her hand to kiss it.

Calf love, Belle thought. She had seen the symptoms of such infatuation far too often not to recognize it, and in males older and wiser than Phillipe. It never failed to astonish her—that she could inspire such devotion so quickly in men. Her gaze turned to her reflection in the carriage window.

Beautiful, she had oft heard herself proclaimed. Was it only she that noticed the hint of hardness that had developed about her mouth, the world-weary expression in her eyes?

Such flaws had obviously escaped Phillipe's notice, for when Belle turned back to face him, his gaze appeared more openly adoring than before. This was a complication she did not need. She liked the boy. To her, young Phillipe represented all that had been best in the old regime of the French aristocracy, the charming manners, the good breeding, the sense of honor. She had no desire to be the first to break his heart.

"Mademoiselle," he asked, "have you—have you—"

"Have I what?" Belle prompted, although she dreaded what might be coming next.

"Have you ever been in love?"

"Oh, aye, many times." Belle laughed. But the boy looked so wounded, she regretted her flippant reply. She surprised herself by adding softly, "No, in truth, only once and that was enough."

Phillipe gave her a speaking glance. "Truly," he said, "once is enough."

Fearing what he might say or ask next, Belle decided the only way to escape his questions and longing looks was to feign sleep. She forced a yawn. Murmuring her apologies, she nestled her head against the squabs. As she closed her eyes, she heard Phillipe's deep sigh.

With difficulty, Belle forced herself to relax and pretend to doze. She was far too vigilant to drift off in actuality. In any case, Phillipe's recent words would not permit her to do so. His innocent question echoed through her head. "Have you ever been in love, mademoiselle?"

Only once.

Her reply carried her back to a time when she had been as young as Phillipe, but far older in experience even then. Yet for one sun-drenched day in spring, she had felt as innocent, as trembling with hope as any maiden.

The path through the village of Merevale had been strewn with May blossoms, crowded with the peasant folk who had come for a glimpse of their young lord's English bride. And the heat ... as though it were yesterday, Belle could feel the sun's rays beating through the white crepe of her gown, the lace pinniers of her bonnet hanging limp against her neck.

But it had been cool inside the nave of Saint-Saveur. With her eyes tightly closed, Belle could still envision the lofty rib vaulting of the roof above her head, the tall windows of the lantern tower, the stained glass spilling a quiltwork of colored light upon the altar.

There had stood the newly consecrated Pere Jerome, garbed in his vestments, his youthful face aglow with the excitement of performing the marriage sacrament for the first time, his voice quivering as he had put to her the question.

Would she, Isabelle Gordon, pledge to honor, obey, and cherish forever Jean-Claude de Varens?

Belle recalled how she had turned to gaze up into the face of the young man at her side. With painful clarity, she pictured Jean-Claude's solemn face, the waves of his light brown hair, his mist-gray eyes giving the impression of one always lost in a dream.

She had promised to cherish him forever, and he had echoed her vows, stooping to brush a chaste kiss upon—

Belle wrenched her eyes open, forcing the image back behind the closed doors of her mind. There were no forevers to be found in the France of 1789. The Revolution had destroyed things more sacred than her marriage vows. St. Saveur was no more. Rechristened the Temple of the Enlightenment, the colored glass had been shattered, the golden candlesticks looted, the stone before the altar stained with Father Jerome's blood.

And the last time she had seen Jean-Claude- Belle pressed her fingertips against her eyes.

"Mademoiselle?"

She did not at first notice the touch on her wrist, it was so butterfly soft.

"Mademoiselle. I think we are approaching the posting station." The tug at her arm became more insistent.

"What?" Belle lowered her hand to meet Phillipe's concerned gaze. "Oh, yes. The posting station."

When she glanced out the window, she saw that the sun had set, the glass pane curtained with the purple haze of twilight. The occasional flicker of a lantern marked their approach to Lillefleur, a hamlet of thatch-roofed cottages with the spire of a church set in their midst.

"You looked so distressed a moment ago when you first opened your eyes," Phillipe said. "Did you have a bad dream?"

"No. I never have dreams anymore."

Belle composed herself. By the time she turned back to face Phillipe, she had shaken off the memory of Jean-Claude. Gripping the back of her seat, she braced against the jolt as the carriage trundled along the rough lane leading through Lillefleur.

Madame Coterin and her daughter were startled awake. Sophie whimpered and Belle could hear the child's frightened breathing like a small creature cornered in the dark.

"There is nothing to fear," Belle said. "We are going to stop to change the horses. It will not take long, and then we will be on our way again."

Sophie ducked her head and burrowed deeper against her mother. On the outskirts of the village, the carriage halted in the yard before a row of long, low stables. Belle could hear the postboy scrambling from his perch on the box, the ancient Feydeau alighting at a slower pace. The coachman's gruff voice rang out, greeting the station's ostlers and giving them his commands.

Presently, he stuck his grizzled head inside the coach door. "The change, it take twenty—maybe thirty minutes," he said.

"So long," Madame Coterin faltered.

"My fault, it is not." Feydeau leveled a fierce look at Belle. "What more is to be expected when you do not send the outriders ahead to bespeak the horses."

The lack of outriders had been a source of contention between Belle and Feydeau at the outset of the journey, Belle insisting that outriders would only serve to call more attention to their carriage.

"Twenty minutes is fast enough," Belle told the old man. "Though you might see what you can do to hurry them on a bit."

"Merde!" Feydeau said, but went to do as she suggested.

Belle bit back a smile. Feydeau might be surly and his speech as vulgar as a Petit-Pont tripe vendor, but Belle had worked with the old man enough to know that he could be depended upon, capable of keeping a sharp wit in case of any unforeseen disasters.

Belle did not foresee anything going wrong, not on the fringes of this quiet village. The wait proved not so much nerve-racking as it was tedious. Phillipe fidgeted in his seat, and Sophie tugged at her mother's sleeve.

"I am so hungry, Maman."

"Hush, Sophie," Madame Coterin crooned.

The child subsided at once, but Belle could see her thin shoulders tremble. Sophie spoke so seldom, and Belle could not recall her ever having asked for anything. These past few days the child had borne fears and discomforts that would have set many adults to whining, and she had every right to complain of being hungry. The last of the provisions that had been brought with them had been consumed early that afternoon. When Baptiste had packed up the hamper for them, he had not expected it to take so many days to reach the coast. Never venturing farther from his beloved Paris than the fringes of the great Rouvray Forest, the little Frenchman was obviously unfamiliar with the conditions of the roads this far from the city. The French had been so busy these past years shrieking for liberty, equality, and brotherhood, no one had troubled about anything so mundane as filling in the ruts.

Belle lowered the window glass, the cool evening breeze fanning her cheeks. She poked her head out the window and looked for Feydeau. The old man was busy lighting the coach's lanterns. He would likely snap her nose off if she sent him to find food. Belle glanced back at Sophie's wan face. Surely it would not be such a great risk if she were to alight and purchase something for the little girl at the posting inn.

Belle gathered up her muff and announced her intention, but as she pushed open the coach door, Phillipe piped up, "I shall escort you, mademoiselle."

"Thank you, Phillipe. That will not be necessary."

"But I cannot allow you to venture alone into a vulgar place like an inn."

Belle stifled a sigh. If the boy only knew how many 'vulgar' places she had been obliged to enter alone in the course of her life.

"Please, Phillipe. I should feel much more comfortable if you remained safe— Er, that is, I think your mama and sister need your protection far more than I do."

"That is so, Phillipe." Madame Coterin clutched at her son's sleeve. "You listen to what Mademoiselle Varens tells you."

"But—"

Phillipe was still protesting as Belle leapt nimbly to the ground and closed the coach door. She strode away from the carriage, hoping that Madame could keep the boy's gallantry in check for the short time her errand would take.

Noting one of the ostlers ogling her, Belle lowered her veil. She buried her hands in the muff, comforted by the feel of her pistol secured by its leather strap. The evening air was brisk, the sky overhead beginning to sparkle with stars, the moonlight more than adequate to illuminate her way across the stableyard.

The posting inn stood just beyond the stables, its sign bearing the words *Soleil d'Or* creaking in the breeze. As Belle studied the half-timbered frame structure with its jutting second story, she doubted the Golden Sun had ever merited its name.

The wood showed signs of dry rot, the shutters hanging half off their hinges. The candles' glow beyond the dirty panes appeared dim and uninviting, but Belle had frequented far worse establishments. She shoved open the heavy oak door and entered.

The atmosphere was hazy with smoke from the logs crackling in a stone fireplace that was not drawing properly. Most of the rush-seated chairs were empty except for a toothless old man who hunched over a table, swilling something from a mug. He appeared to be deep in conversation with a plump woman wearing a soiled apron. Seemingly, the only other person present was a lanky youth clearing the remains of a roast chicken off one of the rough-hewn tables. But Belle was startled by a burst of male laughter.

Muffled, the harsh sound came from somewhere above her. Her eyes followed the course of a rickety stair to the gallery on the second floor, the doors to the rooms beyond swallowed by darkness.

"Can I be of some help to you, madame?"

The woman's question snapped Belle's attention back to the main floor of the inn. She was scrutinized by three pairs of eyes, their expression not hostile so much as wary.

"Yes," Belle said. "I should like to purchase some food for myself and my traveling companions."

The chair scraped on the uneven brick floor as the woman heaved herself to her feet. Twisting her work-worn hands in her apron, she approached Belle.

"Don't got much left. Only some bread and cheese."

"That will do," Belle said. "And some of your good Norman cider if you have it."

The woman nodded and disappeared through a door at the back. More noise echoed from the floor above, the sound of shattering glass followed by raucous laughter.

The old man calmly refilled his cup. Although the boy shuddered, he kept on with his work. By the time the inn's hostess had returned bearing a straw basket, the laughter had increased in volume.

"You are having a rather convivial gathering here tonight," Belle said.

"Mmmpf," the woman mumbled. She cast a nervous glance toward the stairs and thrust the basket at Belle. Packed inside was a crusty loaf of bread, a creamy slab of Pont-l'Eveque cheese, and a brown jug.

Balancing her muff atop the basket, Belle began to count some coin into the woman's calloused palm, when one of the doors above them slammed open.

Belle's head jerked upward in time to see a girl burst onto the gallery. Raising the hem of her homespun cotton dress, she bolted sobbing for the stairs. Hard after her came a strapping soldier, his blue coat unbuttoned to the waist, revealing a hairy chest.

Although he swayed drunkenly, the soldier caught the peasant girl before she descended the first step. He hauled her roughly against him.

"What's your hurry, ma petite? You can't be tired of our company so soon."

"Ah, please, monsieur. I beg you. Let me go."

The soldier knotted his hand in a length of the girl's hair and began dragging her back toward the room. Cold fury surged through Belle. Her gaze flicked to her companions, but the boy had bolted for the kitchen. The old man affected not to hear, while the woman tensed and muttered, "I told 'Ree not to go flirting with the likes of them."

Belle took a half step toward the stairs, then stopped. It was none of her concern, she told herself. She had enough to do making sure the Coterins reached safety.

She heard the drunken soldier give vent to a loud oath. Glancing up, Belle saw that the girl had managed to wrench free. Gaining the stairs, the peasant maid fairly tumbled down them in her effort to get away. Still cursing, the soldier staggered after her.

"Isabelle, when will you learn to mind your own affairs?" Belle sighed to herself. Not tonight it seemed, she thought as she positioned herself at the bottom of the stairs. When the soldier charged past her, she thrust out her foot and tripped him.

The huge man crashed headlong, upending a table and sending a candlestick flying. The girl escaped out the back. Belle could hear the old man and the hostess draw in their breath as though fearful of what would happen next.

"So clumsy of me," she said, staring down at the soldier's sprawled form. "My apologies, sir."

She moved quickly toward the door, but the soldier was not as drunk as she had supposed. As she reached for the latch, she could hear him regain his feet. With a snort of rage, he hurled himself at her.

His weight knocked her against the door, jarring both basket and muff from her hand. Pinned by his bulk, she could scarce move, too tangled in her skirts for a well-placed kick.

Belle's heart thudded with apprehension as the soldier thrust his coarse, unshaven face but inches from her own. The reek of sour wine assailed her even through the layering of her veil.

"Perchance you need a lesson in not being so clumsy, hein?"

She had no chance to speak before his hand shot up, gripping the edge of her veil. He jerked hard, ripping the delicate silk and wrenching the bonnet nearly off her head.

He studied her exposed features, the angry red ebbing from his cheeks. When Belle saw the lust flare in his bloodshot eyes, she struggled to squirm free.

"Easy, m' beauty. Old Jacques's not going to hurt you. Maybe you'd just like to step upstairs and raise a glass with me and my comrades."

Belle kept her voice cool. "Another time, perhaps. I'm in something of a hurry."

The soldier let out a huge guffaw. His arms closed about her waist, his grip tightening. Belle suppressed an urge to claw at his face. Against this huge bear of a man, such distraught tactics would never prevail. She glanced across the room. The old man stared fixedly into his cup, the hostess wringing her hands in her apron. They were no more capable of helping Belle than they had the peasant girl. During the Revolution, most folk had learned to spare themselves by looking the other way when trouble came.

Belle wrenched around, seeking her muff. It had tumbled beside the basket contents near the door. The soldier half-lifted

Belle off her feet, pulling her toward the stairs. Above her she could hear the voices of his brutish companions raised in an obscene song. Once the soldier succeeded in carting her up to that room, Belle knew she was lost.

As he moved to heft her up over his shoulder, Belle flung her arms about the soldier's neck. Yanking his head downward, she crushed her mouth against his so hard she thought she would suffocate. The taste of his sour breath made her stomach churn, but she continued the savage embrace until he jerked his head back.

"Damn!" he panted. "You're a right passionate little bitch."

"I'm a widow. It's been a long time since I've had a man. All the young strong ones have gone off for the army."

He slackened his grip and wound an arm about her shoulders. "Come upstairs, then." He chuckled. "I'll show you several strong fellows who just unenlisted."

Deserters. Of course, Belle thought. That explained the furtive attitude of the inn's hostess. Damn Lefranc. Where was the swaggering sergeant when she really needed him?

She had no choice but to deal quietly and efficiently with this drunkard herself. Belle stiffened her frame, hanging back as the soldier attempted to propel her up the first step.

"What's the matter?" she taunted. "Don't you think that you would be man enough for me?"

The deserter flushed beet red. "Show you who's man enough."

But with a deft movement Belle ducked from beneath his arm.

"Not here," she said, forcing a coy laugh. She could handle the man far better if she could get him outside. Here she ran the risk that he would be missed and joined by his friends at any moment.

Managing to evade his groping hands, Belle darted forward and retrieved her muff. The soldier grunted with frustration and seized her about the waist with a bruising grip.

"Out back," she said. "There's a barn with a hayloft,"

"Let's get on with it, then." Yanking her with him, he flung open the door and pulled her through it, his breath hot upon her cheek.

After the stifling atmosphere of the inn, Belle welcomed the cool darkness of the yard. Although sickened, Belle pretended to sigh with pleasure when the soldier pressed wet kisses against her neck. As they staggered around the side of the building, his hand pawed at her breasts.

Belle set a slow pace, wriggling her fingers inside the muff toward the pistol, then rejected the notion. The noise would be too great, and she had an aversion to shedding blood unless absolutely necessary. Besides, the stream of moonlight had just revealed to her a much better weapon.

Stacked neatly beside the inn was a cord of wood, one particularly stout log balanced on top of the load. It would serve. This fool's head was not that thick.

But she needed to act quickly before the aroused drunkard tried to take her in the dirt beside the vegetable patch. He already strove to hike up her skirts.

Hiding a grimace of distaste, she braced one hand against his hairy chest to hold him off. "Oh, dear. I seem to have dropped my purse."

"Forget it. Can find it later."

"But I have twenty golden *louis* inside."

The hand tugging at her gown hesitated. "T-twenty?" He moistened his lips with greed. "Did you say twenty gold pieces?"

"Yes, if you could only get down and help me look—"

"Take your filthy hands off her!" The piping voice rang out.

Both Belle and the deserter turned to stare at the slender figure who had crept up behind them. Phillipe looked absurdly youthful, his face taut with anger, the sword wavering in his hand.

"I said get away from her, you cowardly dog." The boy advanced closer. "Prepare to defend yourself if you are even half a man."

Belle stilled a groan. She tugged at the soldier, attempting to draw him away from Phillipe. "Pay no heed to him. He is just a foolish boy."

But the deserter shook her off with a vicious laugh. He faced Phillipe, drawing his own weapon. The man's mouth widened into a wolfish smile. "Why, you strutting bantam. I'll cut you in two."

Phillipe trembled, but held his ground.

"No!" Belle cried. She attempted to step in between the two men, but the soldier's arm lashed out, knocking her aside. She lost her balance and fell heavily to the ground. Before she could roll over, she heard the horrible rasp of steel against steel.

Struggling to a sitting position, she saw the deserter beating back Phillipe's blade. Whatever the Chevalier Coterin had taught his son, it certainly could not have been how to use his sword. Even drunk, the deserter was more than a match for the boy. The man easily slipped past Phillipe's guard and nicked the boy's cheek.

So much for handling this matter quietly, Belle thought. She shoved herself to her feet. Drawing the pistol from its place of concealment in the muff, she cocked it.

"Stop!" she commanded. "Both of you. Put up your swords."

But with one deft movement, the soldier sent Phillipe's weapon flying from his clumsy grasp.

Belle took aim at the soldier. "Hold or I'll shoot."

The man didn't seem to hear her. Like a beast, crazed by the scent of a kill, the soldier drew back his sword. Phillipe flung up his hands, bracing himself.

Belle fired. The report of the pistol was deafening, the shot reverberating through the still night air. The soldier wavered, his sword arm yet upraised. He blinked, staring down at the flow of crimson splashing down his chest. Then the man staggered, collapsing into a heap at Phillipe's feet.

Belle froze, but only for an instant. She ran to Phillipe's side and caught him by the sleeve. "Back to the coach. Hurry!"

But Phillipe didn't move. His face white, he stared at the fallen soldier, then at the smoking pistol in her hand.

The shutters of a window above them banged open. Another soldier thrust his head out, his blue coat outlined by the light shining behind him.

"*Qu'est que c'est ca?* Jacques? Is that you?"

"Come on!" Belle wrenched Phillipe, nearly setting him off balance. He snapped out of his trancelike state.

Both of them tore off running and stumbling through the dark. The distance back to the stableyard seemed endless. Belle's heart hammered, her lungs aching by the time she drew within sight of the carriage. She cried out with relief to see the new team hitched in the traces, Feydeau pacing in a fit of impatience.

"Where the devil—" the old man started to growl.

"Get us out of here," Belle gasped.

Although Feydeau glared, he moved quickly to obey. Belle all but shoved Phillipe into the carriage. She scrambled up after him, slamming the door shut just as the coach lurched forward.

As the vehicle swayed into movement, Belle reached for the pouch stuffed in the corner of the seat.

"What—what—" Madame Coterin started to wail.

"Be quiet!" Belle drew forth some powder and shot, struggling to reload in the semidarkness of the jouncing coach. Between Madame's praying and Sophie's whimpers, Belle strained to hear the outcry of pursuit.

When the pistol was loaded, she scooted to the coach window and peered out. The village of Lillefleur had receded into darkness, the night quiet except for the rattle of the berline. No tocscin rang from the church steeple to alert the countryside, no gallop of mounted riders took up the chase,

The minutes ticked by, marked by the rumble of wheels putting distance between them and the posting station. Holding a handkerchief to his injured cheek, Phillipe also glanced out.

"Why is no one coming after us?"

"Probably because the people of Lillefleur know how to tend their own business better than I do," Belle muttered. As for the deserter's comrades, likely they had been too drunk.

Belle's fear gave way to anger at herself for taking such a stupid risk by leaving the coach in the first place, and anger at the guileless young man seated opposite her. The moonlight accented Phillipe's pale face as he regarded her gravely.

"You killed that man," he whispered. "You shot him down and never looked back."

"If I am not mistaken, isn't that what you intended to do?"

"I fought him honorably, in a sword fight—but to use a pistol like that! It wasn't fair."

"What was I supposed to do? Let him butcher you? If you had stayed with the carriage as I ordered, the killing would not have been necessary."

"I came to look for you because you had been gone so long. Then I saw that man dragging you away. I only wanted to defend your virtue."

"What makes you think I have any virtue to defend? I went with him of my own choice."

Phillipe flinched as though she had struck him. His lips moved, but no sound came. The look in his eyes was stricken as he shrank away from her.

Her words had been brutal, borne out of her own rage and self-reproach. But Belle refused to take them back. At least she had put an end to Phillipe's idiotic adoration of her. It was better for him this way.

Yet for the remainder of the journey, each time she saw his unhappy face, she wondered. Gazing at him was like looking into a mirror, watching her own youthful illusions shatter all over again.

Two

Rain drummed against the latticed panes of the window, the sky beyond a depressing shade of gray. Belle could not recall having seen the sun for the entire fortnight since she had landed in Portsmouth, and sat cooling her heels, waiting for some contact from Victor Merchant.

She felt grateful for the well-tended fire in the coffee room at Neptune's Trident. The flames hissed softly, casting a glow on the chamber's dark mahogany paneling and the gleaming row of copperware arranged on the chimney shelf. The blazing logs dispelled much of the damp chill that seemed to linger forever in the air of a seaside town. The brandy didn't hurt either.

Raising her crystal glass, Belle sipped at the golden liquid, then stretched, arching her spine like a restless cat. Gone were the black silks and heavy veil of the Widow Gordon. She had become Mrs. Varens again, in a fashionable muslin gown and close-fitting spencer of dark blue, her blond curls flowing down from a chignon at the crown of her head. A young waiter, the chamber's only other occupant, bustled about, quietly clearing away the remains of her luncheon, a boiled round of beef, pudding and parsnips, custard, tarts, jellies, and a bit of cheese.

She had come a long way from the Golden Sun. Then why did she keep thinking about the wretched place and what had happened there? Thirteen days ago she had parted from the Coterins at Portsmouth's quay. She never expected to cross paths with any of them again. Phillipe was young. Hopefully within the month he would meet some pretty English girl and forget his painful disillusionment with Belle.

As for herself ... Belle frowned, tapping her fingers against her glass. It might take her a little longer to forget. She kept seeing Phillips's shocked face, hearing him whisper, You killed that man. You shot him down and never looked back.

Maybe the reason she kept recalling those words was that the action had shocked her as well. She had seen too much of death during the Revolution, in its many violent guises. Had she become so calloused by it all that the taking of a life affected her so little? The thought frightened her. She took another gulp of the brandy, but felt no warmth from the fiery liquid.

"Is there anything else you could wish for, Mrs. Varens?"

Belle glanced up to find that the host of the inn himself had stepped into the coffee mom as the waiter exited, bearing off the tray of dishes.

A tall man of distinguished bearing, Mr. Shaw beamed at her over the rims of his spectacles.

"No, nothing except a bit of sun, perhaps?" Belle nodded toward the rain-glazed windows.

"I'll see what can be arranged," Shaw said. "The Neptune's Trident always strives to please its longtime patrons."

The slamming of a door echoed from the taproom beyond, announcing some new arrivals. Mr. Shaw consulted his pocket watch.

"Too early for the stage to have arrived," he said. "Perhaps it is someone traveling post, unless it turns out to be one of your, er—friends, Mrs. Varens. Please excuse me."

Giving her his smartest bow, Mr. Shaw hustled off to see. Belle permitted herself a wry smile. Behind those spectacles, the host's keen eyes missed little. Although he had never said anything, Belle had the feeling Mr. Shaw had long ago guessed what her occupation was, but the landlord was discreet and it made her comings and goings that much easier.

Lingering over her brandy, Belle watched with idle interest as Mr. Shaw returned with the latest guests—a formidable matron and another harassed-looking woman, obviously either a maid or a companion. Shivering, they divested themselves of dripping cloaks and prepared to draw near the coffee room fire. But as soon as the matron caught sight of Belle, her mouth pursed into a moue of disapproval.

Belle had no difficulty reading the woman's mind. How shocking! A woman dining alone in the public room of an inn. Obviously a creature of questionable morals. The haughty dame turned to Mr. Shaw, demanding to be shown immediately to a private parlor.

"Of course, madam," Shaw said. "Step this way, please." He waited until the woman's back was turned before he grimaced and cast an apologetic glance at Belle before escorting the two women from the room.

But Belle was accustomed to being snubbed by the so-called 'ladies' of this world. She did have a fellow agent who frequently acted as her maid, but Paulette was above stairs, applying a roast onion to her earache. Why should Belle have dined closeted in her room or have dragged the poor woman out of bed simply to feign respectability for some old harridan like that?

Snatching up her glass, she stalked over to the high backed bench by the fire and plunked down upon it. Heat warmed her cheeks, but she was honest enough to admit it was not caused by the fire. So she did still mind the snubs, even after all these years. What a fool she was!

Belle set her glass down upon the bench. She had no more sense than that eleven-year-old girl who had hovered outside her mother's dressing chamber at the Drury Lane Theatre, Staring deep into the leaping red-gold flames, Belle could almost envision the scrawny child she had been, peeking around the theater curtains at the galleries so far above her. How those tiers of boxes had dazzled her eyes with the ladies bedecked in an array of silks and gemstones, their gentlemen no less magnificent, so dashing, so attentive.

"I'm not going to be like you, Mama," she had vowed, "prancing down here on the stage to be gaped at and scorned. I'm going to be up there, one of them, a real lady."

What a foolish child's dream—to think that she could ever be a lady of quality, admired, respected and loved.

"But I did almost realize that dream, didn't I, Jean-Claude?" Belle murmured. These days the most she hoped for was to one day retire from this uncertain life, purchase a small cottage, perhaps in Derbyshire. There, with her past buried, she could at least end her days in the role of the respectable widow. Playacting, Belle thought wearily, forever playacting, just like Mama after all. She took another sip of the brandy. It tasted strangely bitter as poorly brewed beer.

Outside, the rain continued to beat a melancholy tattoo against the windows. Belle heard the flurry of another arrival in the taproom. More ladies, perhaps, to be horrified at finding a 'loose' woman frequenting Neptune's Trident?

Mr. Shaw had left the coffee room door ajar upon his last exit. Belle faced the opening, her chin thrust upward. But she relaxed her attitude of belligerence as she glimpsed a gentleman attempting to shake the rainwater from his greatcoat. When a waiter offered to help him out of the wet garment, he declined.

"I shan't be staying that long. When Mr. Carrington comes in from the stableyard, say that I await him in the coffee room."

Belle had no difficulty recognizing the reedy voice of Victor Merchant's messenger.

"Quentin Crawley," she said softly to herself. "It's more than time. You've only kept me waiting for two weeks!"

The wiry little man pushed open the coffee room door and bustled inside. He espied Belle by the fireside.

"Good afternoon, Mrs. Varens," he said, doffing his hat and mopping at some rain droplets which clung to his balding forehead. Tufts of sandy hair sticking out from behind his ears gave Crawley the appearance of being perpetually startled.

"Good afternoon, Mr. Crawley." Belle leaned back against the bench and saluted him with her brandy glass. "I was beginning to think you'd forgotten all about me."

"Unlikely, Mrs. Varens. Very unlikely." Crawley grimaced his version of a smile. He moved as though to warm his hands at the fire, but drew up short. His head shifted as he examined the coffee room and then frowned.

"This will never do for our meeting. We must have a private parlor."

Belle sighed. Quentin Crawley always treated the most perfunctory transactions between them as though they stood in danger of discovery from Bonaparte's agents lurking under every hearth rug.

"The private parlor is already engaged," Belle said. "We can manage well enough here."

"Entirely too public," Crawley fussed. "If we were seen together by someone I know, how would I ever explain the purpose of our rendezvous?"

Belle infused a sultry quality into her voice. "Why, Quentin, you could always say that I was soliciting your company for a night's entertainment."

Crawley colored to the roots of his hair. It was so easy to make him turn red, the temptation was irresistible. He eyed her sternly.

"Mrs. Varens! You have a sense of levity that is frequently unsuited to the serious nature of our work and furthermore—"

Belle had heard this lecture so often, she felt relieved when a sound from the taproom distracted Crawley. He whipped around. "Ah, that must be Mr. Carrington arriving."

"Who the devil is Mr. Carrington?"

But Crawley didn't answer her, having gone to thrust his head out the coffee room door and call, "In here, sir. In here."

Beyond Crawley's shoulder Belle saw a tall man garbed in a caped boxcoat and a high-crowned hat. She could discern nothing of his face as he bent over, struggling to close his umbrella.

French, perhaps? Belle wondered. Not likely with a surname like Carrington. And yet few Englishmen were practical enough to carry an article, however useful, that would earn them the contempt of their peers as being effeminate.

With a final spray of droplets, the man snapped the umbrella shut. He followed Mr. Crawley into the coffee room, presenting Belle with her first full view of the stranger's profile. She stared as the tall man whipped off his hat, raking his fingers through a mass of damp coal-dark hair.

He had a face no woman was apt to forget. Heavy black brows, his eyes hooded with a sensual languor, his granite jaw line softened by a small indention in the chin, his swarthy complexion—all conveyed an aura of dangerous attraction.

Absorbed in studying Mr. Carrington, Belle realized with a jolt that he was returning the favor. His gaze started at her face and continued in a lingering inspection of her curves. Belle sat down her glass on the arm of the bench and straightened self-consciously. Not that she was unaccustomed to being ogled by men, but mostly it took the form of bashful glances or sly leers. No one had ever regarded her with such open and frank appreciation.

The coffee room seemed suddenly warmer. Belle touched a hand to her face. Good lord, he had raised a blush to her cheeks, something no man had been able to accomplish since she was in her teens.

"This is Mr. Sinclair Carrington," Crawley said. "He is the newest member of our-ahem-little society,"

"Indeed?" Belle replied.

Dropping his umbrella and hat on one of the tables, Carrington strode across the room to stand before her.

"A pleasure to meet you," he said. She liked his voice. It was deep and resonant, his accent crisply English.

"How do you do, sir." Belatedly, she remembered to offer him her hand.

His fingers engulfed hers as he bent forward, raising her hand to his lips. He looked deep into her eyes, and she noticed that his own were a hunter's green, fringed with thick black lashes.

The warm texture of his mouth caressed her skin in a manner that made Belle's pulse quicken. She felt a spark of acute physical awareness pass between them, charging the atmosphere of the room.

As though from a great distance, Crawley's voice came, "Oh, yes. How stupid of me! Mr. Carrington, this is—"

"Isabelle Varens," Sinclair filled in smoothly. "The Avenging Angel."

The sound of that detested nickname snapped Belle back to her senses. She realized Mr. Carrington still held her hand and that she was permitting him to do so. She pulled free of him.

"I am simply Mrs. Varens."

"That does not suit you near as well." He smiled. He had a lazy, seductive kind of smile. "You don't look like a 'Mrs. Varens,' whereas you are the nearest thing to an angel I ever expect to see."

"When you have worked in our business long enough, Mr. Carrington, you will discover appearances can be deceiving." Her icy remark did not appear to daunt him. But whatever retort Sinclair meant to deliver next was interrupted by Crawley thrusting himself between them.

"Now that the introductions have been taken care of, perhaps we may get on with the purpose of our meeting."

"Certainly," Belle said. "If you like, I could summon Shaw to bring you gentlemen some refreshment. Or you are welcome to share the brandy with me."

"No, thank you." Quentin frowned at the glass she held.

"I forgot, Mr. Crawley. You disapprove of women drinking strong spirits." Belle looked at Sinclair. "And are you shocked, Mr. Carrington? Perhaps you also think I should be sipping tea."

"Not at all. The women I know who habitually drink tea seem to be the most insipid creatures."

A reluctant smile escaped Belle. "I have been called a good many things in my life, but at least insipid has never been one of them."

"Beautiful. You must have been called that often," Sinclair murmured, his gaze once more upon her face.

Belle felt as though his bold eyes caressed her, raising a fluttery sensation in the pit of her stomach. Annoyed with herself, she strove to hide her foolish reaction.

"You will find the decanter on the table over there," she told Sinclair. "I believe the waiter left another glass."

Sinclair retreated toward the table, stripping off his damp boxcoat as he went. So his broad shoulders had not been merely an illusion caused by the cape, Belle thought. The well-tailored frock coat straining across his back made it more than evident that he had no need to resort to padding. Her gaze strayed to the tight-fitting cashmere breeches that encased his tautly honed thighs. An embroidered waistcoat and military boots completed the outfit, that of a perfect gentleman. Or so it would have been if Sinclair's neckcloth had not been so carelessly arranged. But something made Belle doubt that Sinclair was ever a perfect gentleman. Likely it was the hint of roguishness in those disturbing green eyes of his.

As Sinclair helped himself to the brandy, Quentin bent over Belle and whispered, "Well, what do you think? What is your opinion of his attributes?"

Her gaze skated over Sinclair's muscular frame. She said in a low voice, "If you send him across the channel, I think there will be more than one Frenchwoman beckoning him toward her boudoir."

Mr. Crawley flushed. "I wasn't speaking of those attributes, Mrs. Varens. What I meant was, does he seem like a capable man to you?"

How on earth did Crawley expect her to answer that upon such short acquaintance? But her intuition told her that Sinclair would be very capable. His movements were characterized by a tigerlike grace, which made her think he might be good in a fight, as well as skilled in the bedchamber.

"What does it matter what I think?" she asked Crawley.

By this time their whispered conversation had caught Sinclair's attention. He regarded them with one dark brow upraised. Quentin straightened with a guilty smile.

"Ah, er—are you ready to proceed, Mr. Carrington?"

By way of reply, Sinclair picked up his glass and rejoined them by the fireside. Belle should have anticipated the man's next move, but she was too slow.

Sinclair lowered himself upon the bench beside her, sitting so close that his thigh brushed against hers.

"Sorry to crowd you," he said. "These settles are so narrow."

"There is a good six inches of space on the other side of you, Mt. Carrington."

"But there is a loose nail in that comer." His eyes twinkled. "You would not want me to tear a hole in the seat of my—um—coat."

Belle compressed her lips, but decided it would be best to ignore him, as much as one could ignore that much masculinity pressed against one's side. Giving all of her attention to Mr. Crawley, she fidgeted in her seat.

Crawley typically selected the most straight-backed uncomfortable chair he could find. He drew it over to the hearth and sat down, pulling a worn leather-bound ledger from beneath his greatcoat. The tide was inked in neat gold letters.

The Society for the Preservation of Ancient Relics.

Belle pulled a face. Crawley and his infernal mania for keeping up the appearance of being involved in legitimate business!

Mr. Crawley cleared his throat. "When you were fetching your brandy, Mr. Carrington, I was just on the point of informing Mrs. Varens that you are to be her partner in her next venture."

"What!" Belle sat bolt upright. She turned to look at Sinclair. Although his smile was bland, there was no mistaking the devilish gleam in his eyes.

"Out of the question!" she snapped.

When she saw Crawley start to bridle, she hastened to add, "Meaning no insult to Mr. Carrington, but I have always selected my own cohorts."

"Not this time," Crawley said. "It is Mr. Merchant's particular wish that you work with Mr. Carrington."

"Mr. Merchant must leave the choice to me as he has always done." Belle expected Sinclair to jump into the middle of this quarrel, but he appeared content to lean back, sipping his brandy. All the same she had the impression he was merely biding his time.

Crawley puffed up his thin chest, the prelude to delivering a lecture. "Mr. Merchant is not likely to tolerate much more of your insubordination, Mrs. Varens. You will find yourself without employment if you continue in this manner."

"Perhaps I would be glad. I never intended to follow this line of work forever."

"So you have told me many times, madam. But your retirement may come sooner than you desire if you anger Mr. Merchant. He was not at all pleased with what took place on your last assignment. You must not expect to be paid for the consignment you brought back from France."

The man's dry description of the unfortunate Coterin family only added to Belle's irritation. "I don't expect so much as a damned shilling."

"An attitude you can scarce afford," Crawley said. "You are a lady of expensive tastes—"

"If my bills worry you so, Quentin, I shall have my dressmaker send the reckoning to you next time."

"That should give him and Mrs. Crawley something interesting to talk about on a long winter's eve," Sinclair drawled.

Despite how annoyed she was, Sinclair's unexpected comment surprised a laugh from Belle. Crawley went scarlet.

"Mr. Carrington! I have enough difficulty with Mrs. Varens's unseemly humor as it is. She needs no encouragement from you."

"I beg your pardon," Sinclair said.

His intervention had helped Belle to check her rising temper. When she glanced at him, he winked back, and for a brief moment she felt a sense of kinship with him, as though they stood together in conspiracy against the officious Quentin Crawley.

"What's past is past," Belle said to Crawley in milder tones. "So what is this next assignment that Merchant believes I need Mr. Carrington's talents to accomplish?"

"That will be revealed to you by Mr. Merchant himself this evening."

"Victor Merchant is here in Portsmouth?" Belle asked. When Crawley nodded, she struggled to absorb this startling information. Merchant never came down from London. In the three years she had worked for the society, she had rarely met the Frenchman face to face. Always he had employed Quentin Crawley as his go-between. What was afoot that required the presence of Merchant himself?

"You and Mr. Carrington will meet with Mr. Merchant at the Maison Mal du Coeur. It is a mansion up the coast from—"

"I know where it is," Belle said.

"Good. Then I will expect you both to be there at midnight. Take the path up from the sea and enter by way of the garden door. A lantern will be left burning for you. Please be prompt." Crawley rose to his feet and began looking for his hat.

Sinclair stood up in more leisurely fashion, but Belle remained as she was. The Maison Mal du Coeur, she thought with a frown. It was a Georgian manor house owned by one Madame Dumont, a wealthy French émigré. The locals often gossiped about her. An elderly lady, believed to be crippled, she was scarcely ever seen. A meeting to be held in the home of this recluse, at midnight, Victor Merchant coming all the way from London ... These unusual developments left Belle feeling uneasy.

"At least give us some hint of what Merchant has in mind," she called as Crawley made for the door.

"You know I cannot do that, Mrs. Varens. You must wait until tonight."

Belle persisted with her demand for information, but Quentin Crawley shook his head. Bidding her and Sinclair farewell, he slipped out the coffee room door.

"Damn that man!" Belle's fingers tightened on her glass. "Why must he always be so mysterious? Forever playing at being a spy!"

"Don't be too hard upon Quentin," Sinclair said. "Only consider. Most of the time he works as a parish clerk, with a wife and eight little ones to support. His meetings with you are likely his only excitement."

"Good God! Does Quentin really have eight children?" Belle asked, momentarily diverted. To her, Crawley had been nothing more than the annoying little man who had scuttled in and out of her life for the past three years. Strange that Sinclair already knew so much more about Quentin.

With Mr. Crawley gone, Belle expected Sinclair also to take his leave. Yet although Sinclair had courteously risen to his feet to see Crawley off, he showed no sign of going anywhere. Belle was half-tempted to ask Sinclair what he thought about the forthcoming assignation with Merchant, but his mind appeared to be on other things. He was studying her again, and from the glint in his eyes, Belle didn't think he was assessing her competency as a fellow spy.

Well, she had dealt with overbold rakes before. As he walked toward her, Belle scooted over, spreading out her skins upon the bench, making it impossible for him to resume his place by her side.

"It seems there is nothing more to be done until tonight," she said pointedly. "You need not feel obliged to stay on my account."

Sinclair's lips quivered as though he suppressed an amused smile. "But I have not finished my brandy yet."

He retrieved his glass from where he had set it down by the bench, then straightened. Belle wondered if it was not worse having him tower over her in this fashion. The firelight brought out a bluish sheen in his dark hair and cast one side of his face into intriguing shadow. Belle had an absurd thought. If the devil had assumed the guise of mortal man for the purpose of seducing innocent maids, he would likely have taken on the form of Sinclair Carrington. But then—she was no longer an innocent.

"The rain seems to have almost ceased," she said. "You'd best finish your brandy and go before it starts to pour again."

"My dear Mrs. Varens." Sinclair feigned a wounded expression. "Anyone would think you were trying to be rid of me." He took a step back and rested one arm along the fireplace mantel. Somehow the nonchalant pose suited him.

"Shall I propose a toast?" he asked. "To our becoming much better acquainted?"

Belle regarded him in stony silence, making no effort to raise her glass.

"At least you will drink with me to the success of our assignment," he coaxed, "whatever it may be, and to the restoration of good King Louis."

Belle set down her glass with a sharp click. It seemed suddenly important that Sinclair Carrington should hold no illusions about her. "I could not care less about 'good' King Louis. Whatever I do, I do for the money."

Sinclair tossed down the rest of his brandy. He rested his empty glass atop the mantelpiece. "That's a practical enough reason. But what does Mr. Varens think of your dangerous occupation?"

His unfortunate question brought an image of Jean-Claude to her mind with painful clarity. She drove it back into the recesses of her memory.

"I no longer have to consider Mr. Varens's opinions," she said.

"I'm sorry." His voice gentled. Most people uttered that commonplace, but Sinclair sounded as though he really meant it. He regarded her with a compassion that brought a unexpected lump to her throat. Like everyone else, Sinclair obviously assumed that her husband had died, and Belle could not bring herself to correct him.

"Have you been widowed a long time?" he asked.

"Mr. Carrington! You'd best understand one thing. You were engaged to pry into Napoleon Bonaparte's affairs, not mine."

She pushed herself to her feet, but was startled to feel a tug on her gown. Gazing behind her in disbelief, she saw a fold of the soft muslin caught upon a nail. She tugged ruthlessly to free herself and the delicate fabric gave way, setting her off balance.

She staggered into Sinclair, and his arms folded about her, helping her regain her footing.

"I did warn you about that nail, Angel."

"I detest that nickname. I forbid you to use it. Now, let go of me."

If anything, his arms tightened, drawing her closer. "Forgive me." He continued to use that gentle tone which so unnerved her. "I didn't mean to distress you with my question. It was a clumsy attempt to discover if you were married."

"What has that got to say to anything?" she asked. She should have struggled to break away from him, not continue to bandy words within the circle of his embrace. But it had been a long time since any man had held her so tenderly. Sinclair's touch roused in her bittersweet desires which she had all but forgotten.

"Jealous husbands can be the very devil." A lopsided smile

curved his lips. There was a sensitivity about his mouth which had escaped her notice before. His head bent lower, the heavy lids hooding his eyes, but not enough to mask the fire in those brilliant green depths.

Belle braced her hands against his chest. She said rather breathlessly, "Mr. Carrington, I am becoming more convinced that any partnership between us would be most unwise."

"Unwise certainly, but it could be very pleasant."

"I don't look for pleasure."

"Maybe that is your problem, Angel."

"I told you I hate—"

She was silenced by the warmth of his lips grazing against hers. A quiver of response shot through her. Alarmed by her temptation to succumb to the kiss, Belle drew back her hand and struck Sinclair hard across the face.

Reeling back, Sinclair blinked and pressed a hand to the crimson imprint her fingers had left on his skin. Belle pushed past him, storming toward the door.

As her fingers closed over the brass handle, she drew in a composing breath before she trusted herself to speak. "I shall tell Mr. Merchant he must make other arrangements for this next mission.

"Good-bye, Mr. Carrington," she added, hoping he detected the note of finality in her voice Without looking back, Belle flung open the coffee room door and hurtled herself across the threshold. Slamming the heavy portal behind her, she did not hear Sinclair echo her parting words.

"Good-bye, Angel," he said with a rueful smile as he rubbed his stinging flesh. "At least until tonight."

Three

The rain had turned to a fine mist by the time Sinclair wended his way toward the house where he had rented lodgings—a two-story stucco building with black roof tiles glazed to withstand the buffets of winds blowing off the sea. He walked slowly, in no hurry to return to his empty rooms, especially when he saw the figure lurking beneath the narrow portico of the front door. It appeared to be a man of medium height, the collar of his coat pulled up to his ears, obscuring his face.

Sinclair hooked his umbrella over his arm and approached with deliberate casualness. Pausing a few yards down the street, he pretended to grope in the pocket of his boxcoat for his room key while he stole a glance at the bedraggled figure.

As he studied the blond curls plastered to ruddy cheeks, the wet cloak clinging to a familiar stocky frame, Sinclair swore, the tension between his shoulder blades relaxing. In civilian dress, soaked to the skin, the man looked not in the least like Lieutenant Charles Carr of the Ninth Cavalry, but very much like Chuff, Sinclair's nuisance of a younger brother, his junior by eight years.

Sinclair covered the distance between them in four great strides. "Chuff! What the devil are you doing here?"

"Waiting for you," Charles said in a disgruntled voice.

"At the age of three and twenty I'd think you would at least have the sense to get in out of the rain. Why are you here in Portsmouth? I told you not—" Sinclair broke off his tirade when Charles erupted into a fit of sneezing.

Sinclair gave vent to an exasperated sigh. "Well, don't continue to stand there. Get inside. If you caught your death on my doorstep, the entire family would be sure to blame me."

Sinclair opened the front door. Motioning Charles to follow, Sinclair led the way up a narrow stair to the second floor. Unlocking the first door at the head of the steps, he shoved it open and impatiently pulled the shivering Charles past him.

"Damnation!" Charles said, coming to a dead halt on the threshold. Sinclair pushed him the rest of the way inside, closing the door after them.

Charles's mouth hung open in dismay at the sight of the small floral-papered chamber that served as both sitting room and study to Sinclair. A battered oak desk was littered with papers spilling over onto the floor. Remains of last night's supper were stacked on a tray in front of the brick fireplace. One could scarce take a step without treading upon boots, stockings, and sundry other articles of clothing strewn over the carpet. A door stood ajar, revealing that the bedchamber beyond was in little better state.

Charles shook his head. "How can you live this way, Sinclair? If any of Merchant's people decided to ransack your rooms, you'd never know it."

"It is a little difficult to pose as a spy with a valet and chambermaid in tow." Impervious to his brother's horror, Sinclair added his cloak, hat, and umbrella to the heap upon the desk. "Besides, Merchant's people have no reason to search my room. They have all accepted me as one of them."

Or almost all, Sinclair amended to himself as he thought of golden silk-spun hair, a face so delicate, so fine-boned, it could have been sculpted from ivory, eyes that flashed blue fire. Isabelle Varens might detest her nickname, but if only she knew exactly how like an avenging angel she had appeared when she struck him. Wincing at the memory, Sinclair touched his cheek. It would not surprise him if he sported a bruise. For such a fragile-looking lady, she could land a man quite a facer.

Sinclair turned, forcing his attention back to his brother. "Take off that wet coat, Chuff," he said. "And I'll get the fire going again. I think you might find a bottle of indifferent port behind that stack of books in the corner."

"That's quite all right." Charles sniffed. "I am sure I would never be able to locate a clean glass as well."

Sinclair stepped past him to stir up the embers of the fire he had built that morning. Tossing on a few more logs and using the bellows, he soon had a blaze crackling. By that time Charles had peeled off his cloak and arranged it carefully over a wall peg whose existence Sinclair had never noticed before. Sinclair shoved his dressing gown and a copy of last week's London Times off a faded wing-backed chair and invited Charles to sit down.

"I'd offer you a change of clothes, but spies don't appear to eat as well as cavalry officers." Sinclair patted Charles's stomach straining beneath his waistcoat.

Charles self-consciously splayed his fingers across his slight paunch. "That will all disappear once I see some action again. Plague take this peace treaty. It won't hold for long, I tell you that. Not that our side will start anything, but old Boney will never rest quiet. Ambitious fellow, that Napoleon. Bound to stir up something."

"You need not try to convince me, Chuff. I am not arguing with you." Sinclair brushed the knees of his breeches clear of the dust that had clung when he had knelt to start the fire. "It would be more to the point, little brother, if you would tell me what you are doing here."

"Colonel Darlington sent a message for you."

Sinclair stiffened at the mention of the British officer highly placed in army intelligence.

"The courier chosen was Tobias Reed, an old friend of mine." Charles flushed guiltily, unable to meet Sinclair's stern gaze. "So I persuaded Toby to let me bring the message instead."

Sinclair scowled. "You could get both yourself and your friend in deep trouble. This was not the wisest course of action, Chuff."

"Wise be damned! II had to see you again before you disappear to parts unknown." He glanced up, coaxing, "Come now, Sinclair. You can't be angry with me."

With that pleading look on his face, Charles reminded Sinclair of nothing so much as a wistful puppy. Would his brother never mature?

"Hand over the message," Sinclair said wearily.

Charles brightened. Reaching inside his waistcoat, he drew forth a sealed, slightly damp square of parchment. "You're to burn it after you read it."

"No!" Sinclair arched his brows in mock astonishment. "I thought I was supposed to publish it in the Times."

Charles made a face and tossed the letter at him. "Sorry. I forgot you're not exactly a greenhorn at all of this."

Sinclair caught the letter and broke the wax seal. The message was in code, of course.

"Excuse me for a moment," he murmured to his brother. Sinclair strode over to the desk. Tumbling his coat, hat, and most of the papers aside, he finally located a quill, a half-dried pot of ink, and a blank sheet of vellum. Drawing up a chair, he began to decode the message. It was not a simple code, but Sinclair had worked with this particular one enough that he was able to accomplish his task with reasonable swiftness.

Darlington's letter began with a word of congratulations to Sinclair for having successfully insinuated himself into Merchant's group. Many French *èmigres* had fled to England during the Reign of Terror, most of them royalists dreaming and plotting to restore the French monarchy. But none of these French royalists were so well organized and so well funded as Merchant's Society for the Preservation of Ancient Relics. The British army, bearing no fondness for Napoleon, applauded Merchant's efforts to overturn the Corsican upstart's government.

At least, the army had done so until recently. Evidence from British spies operating in Paris revealed that one or more of Merchant's little band, possibly Merchant himself, was really working for Bonaparte.

Under the guise of being a royalist plotter, this counteragent was drawing maps of the English coastline and fortifications, passing the information back to Napoleon for use in a possible invasion. It was Sinclair's task to expose Bonaparte's spy and put a halt to these activities, an assignment which Sinclair understood well enough. There was no need for Darlington to elaborate further upon it. Consequently, the rest of the colonel's message was brief.

"Eliminate the name Feydeau from your list. Now beyond suspicion. The man died last week in a coaching accident.

Sinclair paused in his decoding to reach for his umbrella. He unscrewed the top and then slipped a scroll of paper from inside the hollowed-out bone handle. Unrolling the parchment, Sinclair read down the list of names and brief notes he had jotted about the agents known to work for Merchant. Laurent Coterin had already been scratched out. After dipping his quill into the ink, Sinclair put a line through the name of Simon Feydeau.

With two of the eight names thus eliminated, it made Sinclair's task that much easier. Thoughtfully stroking his chin, Sinclair studied the ones remaining. Baptiste Renois, Paulette Beauvais. Marcellus Crecy-Sinclair could form no conjectures about these people, for he had yet to meet any of them.

Victor Merchant—here, Sinclair had the advantage of one meeting and some sketchy background information. Merchant, once known as the Baron de Nerac, had fled France shortly after the execution of the late Louis XVI. He had arrived in England, possessing scarcely more than the shirt on his back, and yet in the intervening years, Merchant had somehow acquired seemingly limitless funds with which to finance the activities of his society.

Funds that could be coming from Bonaparte, Sinclair thought. Yet if Merchant was the counteragent, someone else had to be doing the actual spying for him, for Merchant rarely strayed far from his townhouse in London.

Reserving any further judgment on Merchant, Sinclair moved to the next name on the list: Quentin Crawley. Well, Quentin certainly traveled about enough to qualify. But a smile tugged at Sinclair's lips. He did not often trust merely his intuition, but he would be astonished if Crawley turned out to be the one he sought. As Mrs. Varens had pointed out, Quentin very much enjoyed 'playing spy,' but to involve himself in any real danger, the precarious position of being a counteragent-Sinclair doubted that Crawley possessed the steady nerves such a deception would require.

On the other hand, Sinclair thought, his gaze resting on the last name, there was Isabelle Varens herself, cool, sophisticated, obviously intelligent. Sinclair did not doubt that Isabelle had the courage to take such a risk. One didn't earn a sobriquet like Avenging Angel from one's peers for being a timid soul. And Isabelle traveled freely on both sides of the channel. She had balked at the notion of working with Sinclair, declaring her intention of telling Merchant he must make other arrangements. That, of course, Sinclair did not intend to let happen. Isabelle could have been genuinely angry about the kiss, or she could have a more sinister motive. It would not be easy for her to contact Napoleon with Sinclair tagging after her. Thus far, of all the names on the list, she seemed most likely to be Bonaparte's spy. Sinclair dipped his quill pen into the ink-pot and underscored her name with a thick line, only to frown and follow it up with a question mark.

He kept remembering how soft and enticing she had felt in his arms, how warm and sweet her lips. Yet he had had no business attempting to kiss her. He felt almost grateful that she had slapped him, bringing him to his senses. He knew some men might consider seduction a good method for gaining information, but Sinclair had his own code. He did not bed women in order to learn their secrets and then betray them.

In truth, he had not been thinking of information at all when he had held Isabelle, only the flaring of his own desire. That disturbed Sinclair more than anything else. He was no saint by any means. He had a keen appreciation for beautiful women, but he had always known how to check his passions until the appropriate place and time. What was it about Isabelle Varens that overrode his natural caution? Beautiful, she certainly was, but he had known many beautiful women before. Perhaps it was Isabelle's more elusive qualities. An aura of mystery seemed to cling to her, her fine sculpted features touched by a deep sadness even when she smiled.

When he had asked about her husband, he had seen the haunted expression in her eyes, as though some specter from her past had risen to torment her. Sinclair rarely felt protective impulses toward women, but he had had an astonishing urge to cradle Isabelle Varens against him, lay all her ghosts to rest.

A loud clatter from the region of the fireplace disrupted his wandering thoughts. Startled, he glanced up, having all but forgotten his brother's presence in the room. Charles, in the act of removing his boots, had accidently kicked up against the fire irons.

"Sorry," Charles muttered. "Are you nearly finished, Sinclair?"

"Another minute or two," Sinclair said with a grimace. Chuff never could sit still for more than five minutes at a time.

Sinclair set the list aside and dragged his attention back to Colonel Darlington's letter.

"This will be your last contact with headquarters. All further information will be provided to you by our agent in Paris. From this time on, I advise no further communication with your family, especially your father."

A wry chuckle escaped Sinclair.

Charles was warming his stockinged feet by the fire. But he paused to peer round the side of his chair at Sinclair. "I never knew old Darlington was given to cracking jests."

"An unintentional one," Sinclair said. "He tells me not to communicate with Father. Apparently he doesn't heed the gossip in the officers' mess or he would know that the general and I have not been communicating for years."

Charles looked unhappy and cleared his throat. "You know, Sinclair, that if there was any message you wished to send him, I have a few days' leave coming. I will be seeing Father ...." Charles's words trailed off and he seemed to be holding his breath, awaiting Sinclair's reply.

An unendearing image of General Daniel Carr rose to Sinclair's mind—a ramrod-stiff bearing, steel-gray hair, and cold green eyes. A handsome man despite his advancing years, Daniel Carr's features were so rigid, he might well have been an effigy carved from stone. Sometimes, when glancing into a mirror, Sinclair wondered if he would look like his father in thirty years' time. The thought scared all hell out of him.

"You can give the general a message for me," he said. "Tell him I've changed my name to Carrington, that he can stop worrying that I will drag the illustrious name of Carr into the gutters."

Charles heaved a disappointed sigh. "I suppose I cannot blame you for your attitude. Father was completely unfair. He despises intelligence work, yet he never hesitates to use the information spies provide when drawing up battle plans."

"Spying is a necessary evil," Sinclair said, imitating his father's gruff, stentorian tones. "But dirty work, not fit for a gentleman. Let someone else's son do it!" Sinclair concluded his impersonation by banging his fist upon the desk. Shrugging his shoulders, he forced a laugh. He had given over trying to please his father a long time ago. The old man had been outraged when he discovered Sinclair had traded his cavalry commission to become part of army intelligence. General Carr had used his considerable influence to get the appointment canceled. Sinclair had retaliated by resigning from the army altogether, thus becoming the first Carr male in five generations who would not go to his grave wearing regimentals. He continued to work for the army as a civilian spy and had not spoken to or seen his father since. That had been over five years ago.

Sinclair blocked his father out of his thoughts except for the times such as this, when Charles made a feeble attempt to effect a reconciliation.

"The general is not such a bad old fellow," Charles ventured. "He has always treated me quite decently."

Sinclair rocked back in his chair, regarding his guileless younger brother with an amused smile.

"That is because you always do exactly what he wants, Chuff."

Charles stiffened defensively. "But I like being in the cavalry."

"I am glad that you do." Sinclair spared his brother's feelings, although sorely tempted to point out that Charles would have liked whatever the old man told him to like. Sinclair was fond of his younger brother, but he knew that Charles was weak-willed, easily led just like Sinclair's mother and two sisters.

"I will admit the general can be a proper martinet when crossed," Charles continued. "But you've always defied him ever since I can remember. I often wondered how you dared."

"My philosophy has been the same with Father as it is with the rest of the world. You can do what everyone else thinks you should and be miserable. Or you can please yourself and let them all curse you. Then someday when you're an old man, at least you're not likely to have regrets about the way you've lived your life."

Charles looked troubled. "And don't you ever have any regrets, Sinclair?"

It was a strangely perceptive question to come from Chuff,

almost too perceptive. Sinclair got abruptly to his feet, dismissing the question with a laugh.

"I'm not an old man yet, even though I know I must seem like a graybeard to you. Ask me your question again twenty years hence."

He crossed the room, scooped up his brother's boots, and thrust them at Charles. "Get these back on. I assume you came here by stage. I want to make sure you are on the next one going out before Darlington finds out about this outrageous stunt you and your friend Tobias have pulled."

Reluctantly Charles took the boots and began to struggle into them. "Aye, I shouldn't like to land Toby in the suds. He's a good fellow."

But obviously not possessed of the secretive nature required for intelligence work, Sinclair thought.

"I expect Darlington will ask Toby if there was any return message," Charles said.

"Have Toby tell the colonel that when I have anything to report, I will send it through the usual channels." Sinclair laid pointed emphasis on the last words. "He can also say that I have met the Varens woman."

Something in Sinclair's tone of voice must have alerted Charles, for he glanced up sharply, red-faced from his exertion in donning the boots.

"Oho! A woman is it? Up to mischief again, I daresay."

"My dear Chuff." Sinclair regarded his brother with wearied patience. "Where do you come by this notion that I carry every female that I meet off to my bed?"

"Because you do. At least, all the pretty ones."

Sinclair grimaced. Charles would be astonished to learn that over half of the conquests attributed to Sinclair were the result of barracks-room gossip and Sinclair's own boastful attitude as a youth. Sinclair admitted to a certain amount of flirtation with the ladies, because he had discovered that flirting always kept affairs from drawing too near the heart. Becoming too serious about any relationship was one more set of shackles Sinclair had managed to avoid.

Choosing not to reply to his brother's comment, Sinclair fetched Charles's still damp coat from the peg.

Charles stood up slowly. "This has turned out to be a rather short visit," he said in forlorn accents.

"Bad timing, old fellow. In a few months, when this work is done, I'll look you up and we'll spend a night carousing and scouring the streets for wicked women."

Sinclair's words coaxed a faint smile from Charles, but as he helped Charles into his coat, the young man sighed. "I suppose you won't be slipping to Norfolk to see Mother anytime soon, either."

"Regrettably, no. You must give her and the girls my love." The girls? Sinclair rolled his eyes at his own choice of words. His sisters were older than himself, spinsters both of them because none of their suitors had ever measured up to the general's exacting standards. Eleanor and Louise had been pretty enough in their youth, soft and blond like Sinclair's mother, like Charles. It was rather ironic, Sinclair thought, that it was himself, the wayward son, who was the only Carr to bear a strong physical resemblance to the general.

Even after Charles pulled his cloak around him, he attempted to linger. Sinclair took his brother by the arm and guided him inexorably toward the door.

"Mother will be terribly disappointed to hear you can't come home for so long," Charles said.

"Can't be helped." Sinclair felt ashamed of himself for sounding so cheerful. Although he did occasionally slip home to see his mother when he knew the general would be gone, the visits were more penance than pleasure. His mother invariably began crying over his disreputable life, then his sisters would join in. Weeping females always made Sinclair uncomfortable. They generally could never find their own handkerchiefs and ended by snuffling against the shoulder of one's favorite frock coat.

As Sinclair maneuvered his brother to the door, for one moment he had the horrible fear that even Charles meant to burst into tears. But although Charles looked pale, he managed to smile as he held out his hand.

"I suppose this is good-bye then," Charles said. "Dammit, Sinclair. I hate seeing you go off on these things. It would be far easier to watch you charge a row of blazing cannons than this affair where you won't even know who your enemy is. I have a very bad feeling about this assignment of yours."

Charles caught Sinclair's fingers in a hard clasp. The gesture triggered a memory in Sinclair, his father barking at Chuff not to be a puling babe, that Charles didn't need a candle to find his way to the nursery. The general's orders bedamned—Sinclair had always let his brother clasp his hand, guiding Chuff up the dark stairs to his little bed.

Although much moved by Charles's concern, Sinclair tried to shrug it off. "Are you turning fortuneteller, Chuff?"

"It is nothing to make jests about. I keep having these horrible visions of you lying somewhere dead with a knife stuck in your back."

Sinclair had had the same premonition himself more than once —that he would end his life in just such a fashion, dying alone in some dismal set of lodgings like these. But he gave Charles's hand a reassuring squeeze before pulling away.

"I will watch my back," Sinclair promised. "And you take care of yourself, young scapegrace. After all, you're the only one of my relatives I can tolerate for more than ten minutes at a time."

He clapped Charles on the back, keeping their final farewell light. But as soon as he saw Charles out the door, the grin faded from Sinclair's lips. He found himself doing something he had never done before.

Striding to the window, he brushed back the lace curtain and peered through the dirty panes. He watched Charles trudge down the cobbled street until he lost sight of Chuff's stocky form in the rumble of carriages and other pedestrians scurrying along the walkway. It was almost as though he never expected to see Charles again.

Sinclair let the curtain fall, stepping back from the window. What was wrong with him? He was letting his brother's dark fears color his own mood.

"What an old woman you're getting to be, Carrington," Sinclair muttered. But he was forced to admit that he too carried an inexplicable apprehension about this latest assignment. Yet he had taken far greater risks in his life. What made this time so different?

Maybe it was the woman, Sinclair thought, his mind once more envisioning Isabelle Varens's gold hair and all too seductive curves. A woman like that could be a man's undoing. Sinclair had seen it happen to others of his sex many times, but he had always guarded his own heart too well. Maybe he was long overdue for a fall.

Four

The manor house known as Maison Mal du Coeur perched in solitary grandeur upon a hill overlooking the sea. Outlined against the starless midnight sky, the mansion appeared stark in the simplicity of its classical design, its only ornament the balustrade at the roofline, each corner surmounted by a stone urn.

No outbuildings nestled close by, no line of trees sheltered Mal du Coeur. The white stone walls seemed to hurl defiance at the breakers crashing upon the pebbled beach far below, daring Poseidon, great god of the sea, to do his worst—buffets of wind, maelstroms, tidal waves—Mal du Coeur would withstand them all.

Slipping along the path that led to the gardens at the rear of the house, Belle paused to gaze upward at the massive walls looming over her. The hood of her cloak fell back and the night wind tangled strands of her hair about her face. Belle brushed the tendrils aside, her eyes fixed upon the moon.

Partly obscured by a mist of clouds, the crescent hung in the sky like some ghostly scimitar suspended above Mal du Coeur.

Belle shivered, overcome by the same strange brooding sensation she had had when first glimpsing the mansion from the carriage. She had no idea what to expect from this meeting with Merchant tonight, but she had the feeling that in some way it would prove momentous, one of those events that would drastically alter the course of her life.

She would have dismissed such notions as nonsense, an irritation of the nerves, if she had not experienced such premonitions before, premonitions that had proved all too true. That long-ago evening in Paris, in the suite of rooms she and Jean-Claude had rented-had she not somehow sensed that something was terribly wrong? The intimate supper her maid had laid upon the table had long ago turned cold before Jean-Claude had burst into the room. He had never been late before ...

Lifting the hem of her gown, Belle continued along the path, hardly noticing the garden ahead of her with its low lying hedges and rosebushes set in a symmetrical line. The wind rustling the leaves, the distant roar of the sea all faded before the insistent clamor of voices from her past.

"You deceived me," she heard Jean-Claude accuse. "You have been doing so since the day we were wed, the hour we first met."

Then her own voice, pleading, "Please, Jean-Claude. I always meant to tell you the truth. I wanted to. Oh, how I wanted to, but I was afraid of losing you. I beg you to forgive me."

But her words were lost in the raw anguish of his cry. "You betrayed my trust, the one thing left in all this madness I had to believe in—our love, what we shared together. It has all been nothing but a lie."

"Before God, no! My past, who I am-yes, I did deceive you about that, but there is one part of it that was not a lie. I do love you, Jean-Claude. I always will."

Always will-the words echoed mockingly back to her upon the wind, the painful recollection swallowed up by the night.

Belle passed a hand across her brow. Why was she even

thinking about such things now, when she needed all her wits to deal with Merchant? Memories of Jean-Claude had a habit of creeping up on her at the worst times.

No more tonight, she vowed, moving forward into the garden. A lantern had been lit and left resting upon a stone bench just as Quentin Crawley had promised.

"Quentin?" Belle called softly. No one answered, and yet she sensed another presence in the garden, eyes watching her. The hair at the back of her neck prickled as she moved cautiously toward the lantern.

The folds of her cloak brushed against one of the rose bushes, the overblown blossoms as yet not fallen victim to the first frost. A cascade of pink petals littered the ground. The heady, almost too sweet fragrance wafted to Belle's nostrils, along with another familiar acrid scent. She sniffed the air. She had spent enough time in the company of gentlemen to recognize the smell of burning tobacco.

She caught a gleam just beyond the bench, the glowing tip of a cigar. A tall form with broad shoulders melted out of the shadows, a form that she instinctively recognized before the man stepped in the lantern's ring of light.

"'Evening, Angel," Sinclair Carrington said with his slow, easy smile. He dropped his cheroot to the gravel path and ground it out with the heel of his boot.

"Mr. Carrington." Belle pronounced his name with a wearied resignation.

"Well! You don't seem that startled to find me here."

"I'm not. Somehow I thought that you would not be that easily gotten rid of." Belle instantly regretted her sharp retort. She didn't want him to know she had been thinking about him at all, which she had, far more than she had wished. She had spent most of the afternoon rebuking herself for the little scene that had taken place in the coffee room. Slapping a man for stealing a kiss! Just as though she were some prim spinster! She was more accomplished in dealing with men than that. It irritated her no end that Sinclair had managed to overset her icy control, and make her behave like a fluttery schoolgirl. Even now she could not deny a small tingle of pleasure at seeing him again. But then, he was a sight to gladden most women's hearts—the night breeze ruffling his black hair, a scarlet-lined cape flung carelessly about his shoulders.

Realizing that she was staring at him, Belle wrenched her eyes away and demanded, "Has Mr. Crawley arrived yet?"

Sinclair stalked toward her. For such a large man he could move with incredible quietness. He stopped bare inches from where she stood by the roses, his shadowed features towering above her, his very nearness intimidating and enticing.

"No, we are all alone," he murmured, his voice husky, suggestive.

And she had regretted slapping him? Belle thought. She obviously should have hit him harder. She drew a sharp intake of breath, but before she could speak, Sinclair flung up one hand in a playful defensive gesture.

"No, I implore you, Mrs. Varens. There is no need to prepare yourself to take aim at my jaw again. I am glad that Mr. Crawley is not here, but only so I can apologize for my behavior this afternoon. The lapse of my gentlemanly instincts."

"I am not sure you possess any, Mr. Carrington."

"Occasionally I lay claim to a few noble scruples. I usually wait at least two hours after being introduced to a lady before I assault her."

Like a mask being stripped away, his devil-may-care expression vanished to be replaced by one of rare seriousness. "I truly am sorry for upsetting you. I could plead the excuse that your beauty overwhelmed me, but likely you've heard that one too many times. I can do no more than ask you to forgive me."

The directness of his request, the soft light shining from his green eyes, left her little room to doubt his sincerity. She knew how to handle his flirting, his teasing, but Sinclair in this gentle, chastened mood left her disconcerted.

She moved away from him. A few steps brought her to the edge of the garden terrace, where she could gaze down upon the surf pounding the beach below.

"Perhaps I owe you an apology as well, Mr. Carrington. I did not exactly claw my way out of your arms. My own behavior might have misled you, in which case it was not fair of me to have slapped your face."

She sensed rather than heard him come up to stand behind her. His voice rumbled warm and close by her ear. "Are you telling me that you were not entirely immune to my—er—charms?"

"Perhaps not," Belle admitted reluctantly.

His hands came up to rest on her shoulders. "That is rather dangerous information to hand over to the enemy, my dear."

"I never surrender any weapon, unless I am sure I have my armor well fixed in place." She turned and firmly thrust his hands away from her.

She risked a glance up at him. The moon skimmed from behind the clouds enough for her to make out the look of puzzlement furrowing his brow.

"I have never met any woman quite like you, Isabelle Valens," he said at last. "Most females think nothing of breathing hot, then cold upon a man. Few would ever trouble to explain their behavior or apologize for being unfair. Are you always this honest?"

Belle gave a tiny shrug. "I can be as devious as any of my sex. But at the moment I have no reason to practice my wiles upon you."

"I would be happy to give you a reason." He was standing too close again. Even the scent of him was thoroughly masculine, a combination of the salt sea breeze, tobacco, and musk. Belle was far too much of a woman not to feel a stirring of desire as he reached for her. A protest formed on her lips, but it was unnecessary. Sinclair stopped himself, although he lowered his aims with obvious reluctance. Belle was conscious of a feeling of disappointment.

"No," he said, "I told myself I would behave tonight. How else can I hope to convince you to change your mind about working with me? If I promised you, upon my honor, that I would act like a gentleman, that there would be no repetition of what happened at the inn—"

"Can I trust your promises, Mr. Carrington?"

"No, very likely you can't." He smiled.

Her own lips quivered in response. He was a complete rogue, but she liked him in spite of the fact, liked him perhaps too much for her peace of mind.

"You should reconsider anyway," he continued to urge. "We would make a perfect team. We have so much in common."

Belle shot him a look of incredulity.

"Obviously we both like to keep free of any entanglements. We both have chosen to thumb our noses at respectable society, to conduct ourselves as we please. We both like living just a little on the edge."

"No, Mr. Carrington. You may have chosen such a life. Mine was forced upon me. One day I still intend to—"

"Shh!"

Belle broke off as Sinclair held up one finger to his lips. "I thought I heard something."

Both of them lapsed into silence and stood tensed, listening. At first Belle detected nothing but the breeze rustling the rosebushes. Then she heard it, too, the sound of a twig crackling underfoot.

"On the path. Over there," Sinclair whispered. He pressed close to her side, and the two of them strained to peer through the darkness of the garden. The glimmer of moonlight was enough to outline a short figure all cloaked in black, stealthily making its way in an exaggerated zigzag pattern as though eluding some imaginary pursuer through the hedges.

When a rabbit flashed across the figure's path, a familiar voice let out a frightened croak. "Dear me!"

Belle sensed Sinclair relaxing even as she did so herself. "Quentin Crawley," they both murmured in the same breath. Their eyes met and they broke into simultaneous laughter.

"You see?" Sinclair said. "We have at least one thing in common. We both possess a most unseemly sense of humor." Sinclair so precisely imitated Quentin's peevish tones that Belle erupted into fresh laughter.

She felt Sinclair's gaze upon her face, warm, admiring. "Ah, that's much better. You should laugh more often. I shall make it a point to see that you do, Angel."

Belle checked her mirth at once. Now was the time to tell Sinclair firmly that he would not make a point of doing anything. They definitely would not be working together.

Instead she heard herself saying, "Mr. Carrington, if I give you leave to use my first name, will you please stop calling me by that detestable nickname?"

The moonlight glinted off his mischievous smile. "We have already established that my promises are most unreliable, Isabelle."

"Belle. I am usually called Belle."

"So you are," he said. Even through the night shadows, his eyes seemed to pierce her, the green lights becoming intent.

Belle's pulse raced. She felt relieved when Quentin Crawley slunk into the garden.

"Why, Quentin," she said. "I do believe you are two minutes late."

Crawley hushed her in a loud, stagy whisper. He would permit no greetings, frantically motioning them both to silence.

Sinclair bent down and murmured in Belle's ear, "Bonaparte is hiding in the shrubberies, don't you know?"

Belle muffled a laugh behind her hand. She didn't need the light spilling from the lantern to know that Crawley was glaring at both of them. Picking up the lantern, he gestured for Belle and Sinclair to follow him.

As they made their way toward the back of the house, Sinclair managed to link his arm through hers, somehow infusing even that courtly gesture with warmth.

Quentin led the way into the house through a pair of tall French doors. As they crossed the threshold, Belle pulled free of Sinclair, gazing about her. They were in some sort of parlor, as near as she could tell. Quentin was quick to draw the heavy velvet drapes and would only light one small candle.

"For heaven's sake, Mr. Crawley—" Belle started to complain.

"Keep your voice down, Mrs. Varens," Crawley said. "The servants here are all abed. Madame Dumont has been good enough to let us use her home for this meeting, but she expects no disturbances."

"Who exactly is this Madame Dumont who is so gracious with her hospitality?" Sinclair asked.

"That does not concern us, Mr. Carrington." Crawley made an elaborate show of arranging an armchair near the candle's glow. Belle recognized the piece of furniture at once as being valuable, a painted fauteuil with fragile carved legs, the upholstery done in a floral silk pattern.

When Crawley had done fussing with the chair, he said, "Make yourselves comfortable. Mr. Merchant will be here in a few minutes."

As soon as Crawley disappeared into the shadows beyond the salon door, Belle gave vent to an impatient oath. She snatched up the taper and proceeded to light a silver branched candelabrum she found on a tulipwood parquetry table. From there she stretched up to light the candles in all the wall sconces.

Sinclair said nothing, but watched her, his arms crossed over his chest, apparently as amused by her defiance as he had been by Quentin's furtiveness. Belle did not care. She was in no humor for any of Quentin's game playing.

The chamber now ablaze with light, Belle took full stock of her surroundings. This Madame Dumont had not fled France so much as brought it with her. The chamber appeared much like dozens of elegant salons she had visited as Jean-Claude's bride.

The high walls had been left tastefully plain to provide an unobtrusive background for the elaborate gilt furnishings, the patterned Savonnerie carpet. All but forgetting Sinclair's presence, Belle began to stroll about the room, examining each object with wonder—the pendulum clock with its face set in Roman numerals, the torchere holding a vase of fading roses, the painted ecran that screened the fireplace.

Above the mantel hung a three-quarter-length portrait of the late king, Louis XVI. He looked somehow ill at ease in his robes, but the artist had captured Louis's aura of gentle patience, the expression that Belle remembered so well from when the monarch had been trundled forth to meet his death upon the guillotine.

She averted her eyes, not wanting to explore that memory any further. To the left of the fireplace stood a console table, its polished surface laden with small treasures. Thanks to Jean-Claude's tutelage, Belle could identify most of them—a Sevres figurine of Cupid and Psyche; a snuff box, likely Vincennes, the enamel lid decorated with a scene from Italian comedy; a pastille burner of glazed white porcelain from the workshops of Saint-Cloud.

Belle touched this last with reverent fingers. She and Jean-Claude had had one nearly like it in their rooms in Paris. A wave of bittersweet nostalgia washed over her. Although scarce suited to Jean-Claude's station in life, Belle had loved that tiny cramped apartment. Of course, by the time Jean-Claude had come to Paris as a delegate to the revolutionary convention, they had no longer been the Comte and Comtesse de Egremont. Just plain Citizen and Citizeness Varens, having prudently dropped the de from their name. It had not been wise to flaunt aristocratic origins before the volatile Parisian mobs.

But Belle had preferred it that way. She had never been comfortable being the comtesse, tiptoeing through the vast cold rooms of Jean-Claude's château, the portraits of his dour ancestors seeming to glower at her with disapproval. She had always imagined that those noble forebears peering out of their gilt frames had guessed her secret long before Jean-Claude, that they knew she had no right to be within the halls of Egremont, polluting that hallowed ground with her commoner's blood, she, the illegitimate daughter of a second-rate actress from Drury Lane.

Lost in her memories, Belle did not notice that Sinclair had also begun to stroll about, examining the salon, but from a far different perspective. He had not her eyes for French antiques or *objets d'art*, but he recognized the trappings of wealth when he saw them. Apparently this Madame Dumont had fled France with her pockets better lined than most emigres. It was therefore possible, then, that she and not Napoleon could be the source of Victor Merchant's unexplained funds. A wealthy royalist patroness would certainly make Merchant a less likely candidate to be Bonaparte's spy.

But what of Isabelle Varens? Sinclair stole a glance at Belle, lingering by the console table, one finger tracing the pattern of the white porcelain. Her eyes almost luminous, she seemed to have retreated to some world of her own dreamings. A not entirely happy world, to judge from her expression. Her features were shadowed with grief, the set of her mouth soft and vulnerable.

Once more she roused in him that inexplicable urge to enfold her in his arms, pull her out of that dark, cold world with his embrace. He took a step toward her and then checked himself. He had vowed to himself on the way here tonight that he would maintain an objective attitude toward Isabelle, keep his desires under more rigid control. That vow had almost gone straight out the window with his first sight of her slipping into the garden. Sinclair was not often given to flights of fancy, but with a halo of moonlight rimming her fine gold hair, her pearly-hued skin almost translucent, she had indeed seemed like some angel sent to earth to dazzle the eyes of mortal man. Except that beneath her cloak, he had caught glimpses of the tantalizing swell of her breasts, the full curve of her hips, reminding him that she was very much a woman, vibrant and alive. It had been damned hard to apologize to the lady for kissing her when all he wanted to do was pull her into his arms and make a more thorough job of it. And for a brief moment he had thought she was equally as willing.

Ruefully Sinclair raked his hands through his hair. Such thoughts as these could scarcely be construed as objective. He tried again, this time stalking toward the long windows, deliberately putting the length of the room between himself and Isabelle. Lost in her own musings, she seemed oblivious to his movements, continuing to caress the china.

Fact one, Sinclair told himself, the lady apparently had a taste for the finer things, a very expensive taste. Fact two, she had told him herself this afternoon that she was only involved in all this for the money. With an attitude like that, she might not be particular where her funds came from, Victor Merchant or Bonaparte.

And yet- Sinclair frowned. That theory didn't agree with what Crawley had told him earlier. On the way to the inn Sinclair had had to listen to a long diatribe concerning how Isabelle Varens had abandoned her mission to rescue the penniless family of a fellow agent recently caught and executed. That didn't seem like the action of a mercenary woman.

There was only one way to learn the truth, and that was to continue to work with her, get to know her better. Remembering how skilled she was at closing herself off, it didn't promise to be an easy task. Yet it could be an all too pleasant one. In spite of himself, his thoughts focused once more on her lips, so soft and yielding, the way her gown clung—

Damn! He was doing it again. Sinclair swore at the familiar stirring in his loins. What he needed was a good blast of cool air to bring him to his senses. Moving toward the velvet draperies to undo the last of Crawley's careful arrangements, Sinclair stopped when he heard the door click open. He turned to face the threshold at the same time Belle snapped out of her reverie and also glanced in that direction.

A stocky middle-aged man garbed simply in drab breeches and frock coat strode into the salon and closed the door behind him. Victor Merchant's collar was fashioned of black velvet, a sign of perpetual mourning for his executed king.

Sinclair felt no more impressed by the man's appearance than he had been on the occasion of their previous meeting in London when Sinclair had been accepted as a member of Merchant's society. There was a coldness in Merchant's demeanor, a stiffness in his carriage that reminded Sinclair too much of his own father, although the Frenchman lacked the handsomeness that distinguished General Daniel Carr. Merchant was thick-necked, his complexion pasty white, and his right eye was fractionally higher than his left, giving him the impression of being dull-witted. Yet Sinclair had already surmised this was far from the case. Behind that unprepossessing exterior lurked a most calculating intelligence.

"Good evening, Monsieur Carrington. Madame Varens," Merchant said in his usual laconic tones.

"Good evening." Sinclair stepped forward offering his hand. Merchant ignored it, moving past him. Rather nonplussed, Sinclair lowered his arm, but Belle did not look in the least surprised by Merchant's rudeness. She must have expected it, for Sinclair noted she made no move to greet Merchant herself, but merely watched in wary silence as Victor selected his seat.

He chose that fancy painted affair that Crawley had fussed with earlier. Lowering himself into the fragile gilt armchair, Merchant sat ramrod stiff.

"Be seated," he commanded Sinclair and Belle, adding "please" as almost a reluctant afterthought.

Her head arched high, Belle arranged herself gracefully opposite Merchant upon a gilt-trimmed banquette. Although Sinclair settled in beside her, he could not have imagined anything more uncomfortable than this hard-cushioned bench without arms or back.

Silence settled over the room, unbroken except for the ticking of the pendulum clock. Sinclair sensed that Merchant maintained this rigid quiet on purpose, as though trying to make them nervous. His demeanor reminded Sinclair of the times he had been called in to face the headmaster at Eton after one of his pranks and had been kept waiting on tenterhooks to see if he would be sent down. Gradually, however, Sinclair realized Merchant's tactics were aimed at Belle rather than himself. It was she at whom Merchant stared. She seemed unperturbed by his scrutiny except for a certain belligerent tilt to her chin.

"It was good of you to wait upon me at this hour," Merchant said at last.

"You sent Crawley to tell us our presence was commanded here tonight," Belle said, a hint of mockery in her voice. "Don't I always make haste to carry out your orders?"

"Do you?" Merchant asked. "Then give me what I sent you to France to obtain. The listing of the number and type of boats being constructed at Boulogne."

He extended one hand, palm upward toward Belle. His fingers were white and puffy and put Sinclair in mind of the bloated flesh of a drowned man he'd once seen dragged from the Thames. He felt Belle tense beside him.

"You know full well I haven't got any list for you."

"Oh?" Merchant's fingers curled slowly as he withdrew his hand. "So devoted as you are to carrying out my orders, I wonder what important task caused you turn aside from your mission."

"I am sure by now you know that, too."

If possible, Merchant's expression grew colder. "So I do. But I admit that I am at a loss to account for your behavior. How do I write to His Majesty Louis XVIII where he awaits in exile and tell him that the cause for reclaiming his throne must perforce be delayed longer because one of my agents thought the lives of an insignificant widow and her brats of more value?"

Anger sparked inside of Sinclair, which he suppressed with difficulty. It would not help him achieve his own ends if he antagonized Merchant. Besides, there was no need for him to rise to Belle's defense. She managed quite ably on her own. Although she flushed, her voice remained level. "I am sure you will find some way to explain it all to His Majesty, Victor. But when you are writing, you might just drop Louis a hint that he does his cause no good by publishing threats of what he intends to do to the revolutionaries if he regains his power."

A trace of real emotion flickered in Merchant's dull eyes, an almost fanatical gleam. "His majesty does right to warn the vermin." Victor gestured to the portrait of Louis XVI above the mantel.

"Think you that the king will allow his brother's death to go unavenged or the countless numbers of our noble brethren who were butchered by the peasants?" Merchant's fist crashed down upon the delicate arm of his chair. "Non, I tell you there will be a new Reign of Terror in Paris one day. But this time it will be the blood of the canaille that will flow through the streets."

Belle shot to her feet. "If I thought you and your precious king had any chance of resurrecting that violence, I would not lift one finger to help you. I would walk out that door right now."

Sinclair had conceived a marked dislike of Merchant himself in the past few minutes. He would have been happy to offer Belle his escort from this place, but he had his own mission to think of. Standing up, he laid one hand soothingly upon Belle's arm.

To Merchant he said, "I didn't think you had gathered us here tonight to rake over the past or to speculate about the future. I was under the impression you have some important task for us to undertake."

Merchant's impassioned expression faded. "So I do. If

Madame. Varens could control her temper long enough to hear me out."

Sinclair shifted his attention to Belle. Her eyes were still stormy. He held her gaze until he felt her relaxing beneath his touch. She expelled her breath in a long sigh, then wrenched free of him, resuming her seat. Sinclair followed suit.

Another nerve-racking silence ensued, and then Merchant began again. "Before Madame Varens's unfortunate outburst, I had been about to assure her that I am willing to overlook her recent flouting of my orders and give her one more chance."

"How magnanimous of you, Victor."

Ignoring her sarcasm, Merchant went on, "But this time have a care, Madame Varens. The assignment I am about to give you is more dangerous, more difficult than any you have ever received If you should be seized by one of your whims again, you will put not only your own life at risk but Monsieur Carrington's as well."

"That's a comforting thought," Sinclair muttered.

Belle stirred restlessly. "Enough of these preliminaries. You are growing as tiresome as Quentin Crawley. Out with it, Victor. What do you want us to do, and how much do you intend to pay?"

Merchant leveled her a stony stare. He did not seem about to be hurried. He moved his head slightly, for the first time making an effort to include Sinclair in the discussion as well.

"I trust that both of you have heard of General Bonaparte?"

"His name has cropped up in conversation from time to time," Sinclair said. He was pleased to see that his dry remark nearly succeeded in coaxing a smile from the yet truculent Isabelle.

"Bonaparte assumed control of the French government in 1799," Merchant continued tonelessly. "For a time Napoleon held out the hope that he could be persuaded to use his power to restore King Louis to his throne. But we were misled. This summer Bonaparte had himself named consul for life, set himself up as the uncrowned king of France. This cannot be tolerated."

"We know all that," Belle broke in impatiently. "Exactly what you do want me and Mr. Carrington to do?"

"I thought I was making myself perfectly clear." Victor leaned back in his chair, lacing his fingers across his chest. His eyes glittered coldly.

"I want you to abduct Napoleon Bonaparte."

Five

Stunned silence settled over the salon, only to be broken by Sinclair's peal of incredulous laughter. But Belle was not even tempted to smile. Her earlier premonitions had proved quite correct. The meeting at Mal du Coeur had taken an extraordinary turn.

Sinclair's laughter abruptly died. "You must be jesting, Merchant, or else you are stark raving mad."

"I assure you, sir," Victor said coldly. "I am neither."

Sinclair regarded him with derision. "Why don't you simply ask us to abduct the Pope while we're about it or the tsar of Russia?"

"Neither the Pope nor the tsar interests me. They do not control the government of France." Merchant's gaze flicked to Belle. "You are strangely silent for once, Madame Varens. Are you also shocked by my request? Do you think the task as impossible as Monsieur. Carrington appears to do?"

"Not impossible," Belle said. "But extremely difficult."

"Difficult?" Sinclair snorted.

"Your reward, of course, would be generous," Merchant said, "commensurate with the risk." The fee that he named caused

Belle's eyes to widen. Such a sum could go a long way to securing her future—a respectable future far removed from the uncertainties of her present life. But when she considered what she must do to earn it, she slowly shook her head.

"It would mean returning to Paris." She could already feel the cold sensation of dread creeping into her veins. "I have not worked in the city for many years."

"Yet you still have contacts there. It is my understanding that you and Baptiste Renault once possessed a certain expertise for smuggling people out of the city."

"That was different. The people we smuggled were all willing to go. But abduction—" She broke off with a frown. She had never met Napoleon Bonaparte. There was no reason for her to be concerned about the man, but there was no reason to wish him harm, either.

"What would happen to General Bonaparte if we succeeded?" she asked.

"He would be kept here at Mal du Coeur in comfortable captivity. But with him gone, the government in Paris would be in a state of chaos and—"

"Hold! Just one moment if you please." Sinclair caught Belle by the arm and tugged her to face him. His brows drew together in a stern expression. "Isabelle! You are not seriously considering this outrageous proposal?"

"Perhaps," she said. "Is there any reason why I should not?"

"Yes, a good many reasons, the foremost one being, even granted that this crazed assignment could be brought off, it would be far too dangerous for a—"

Sinclair stopped short, apparently thinking better of what he had been about to say.

"Too dangerous for whom, Mr. Carrington?" Belle asked, her voice deceptively calm. "For a woman?"

Sinclair gave an uneasy smile. He relaxed his grip upon her shoulder and allowed his fingers to trail down her arm until he captured her hand. "No, I didn't mean that precisely. It is only that I doubt General Bonaparte will cheerfully acquiesce to Merchant's plans for him. Neither will the consular guard that attends him. More than likely there will be some fighting, bloodshed. You would be pitch-forked into all manner of situations unfit for ... for a lady."

Belle drew in a sharp breath. That was the sort of remark that might have come from the starry-eyed Philippe Coterin, and yes, of course from her beloved Jean-Claude. Why had she expected a little more perception from Sinclair Carrington? Belle was surprised to feel her throat constrict with disappointment.

"I am not a lady." She wrenched her hand free of Sinclair and then turned toward Victor. She had the fleeting impression that Merchant had been watching the exchange between herself and Sinclair with all the calculated patience of a cat at a mousehole. But Belle was feeling too annoyed with Sinclair to heed much of anything else. His attempted interference helped her to reach a decision.

"Obviously Mr. Carrington has not the stomach for your proposal, Victor," she said. "But I accept the assignment." She angled a defiant glance at Sinclair. "Tell your friend, Madame Dumont, to prepare some chambers for General Bonaparte. She will be acquiring a reluctant houseguest before Christmas."

Sinclair's hands came up in a frustrated gesture as though he wanted to shake her. He slapped his palms against his knees and swore, then thrust himself to his feet and stalked over to stand by the fireplace, turning his back on her.

Victor's lips parted in a thin smile. "Your decision pleases me, Madame Varens. But I expected no less from you. You never have been one to back down from a challenge."

Even this rare compliment from Victor did little to soothe Belle's agitation. Without looking at Sinclair, she could feel the full weight of his disapproval. Damn the man, anyway. What concern was it of his how she risked her neck? He could not possibly care what became of her, not on such short acquaintance.

"I am sorry that Monsieur Carrington cannot see his way clear to participate," Merchant continued. "I had hoped you both would accept the assignment."

"I don't need him," Belle said. "I can manage the arrangements on my own, as I have always done."

"Both of you march a damn sight too fast," Sinclair interrupted. "I never said I refused."

Victor and Belle both turned to look at him, Merchant's expression inscrutable, Belle, hostile, although a certain amount of confusion crept into her eyes.

Small wonder if she was a trifle bewildered, Sinclair thought. He was having difficulty understanding his own reaction to Belle's wanting to undertake this mission. Rubbing the back of his neck to ease the tension cording his muscles, Sinclair said, "I don't leap to these momentous decisions as quickly as Mrs. Varens. I need a little more time to think."

"Take what time you need, Monsieur Carrington," Merchant said. "If your decision is negative, I will understand. No one will question your courage, nor constrain you against your will. You will be under no further obligations to our society."

In other words, if he refused, he would be cast out on his ear. And after several months' work of carefully insinuating himself into Merchant's organization! Damn. Neither he nor the British army had ever anticipated anything like this. It was assumed he would be given some mission like intercepting diplomatic dispatches, or a bit of eavesdropping in government circles, nothing this dangerous.

But who was he trying to fool? It was not his own danger that concerned him, but hers. From the time Belle had showed any interest in the operation at all, he had been shot through with alarm. His chief concern had become to keep her out of it. He did not know where the devil this protective impulse had sprung from, never having been troubled by any Sir Galahad notions before. And with Belle of all women! He had sensed even before opening his mouth how she would receive his sudden burst of chivalry. She would be bound to resent it, as indeed she had.

His entire behavior was so blasted illogical. She obviously knew how to take care of herself. She would not have survived as a spy this long if she didn't. Instead of acting like such a fool, he should be glad she had taken this assignment, for it was surely a sign of her innocence. If she were Bonaparte's agent, she would hardly consent to kidnap the man.

And yet if Isabelle was the counteragent, would she not more likely go along with the plan, then take steps to thwart it after they arrived in Paris? If that was the case, any agent involved with her in the scheme would be heading for a trap. Sinclair's hand crept involuntarily to his throat as though he could feel a noose tightening, or more accurately the steely edge of a blade spattering his blood. The French weren't as tidy about such things as the English.

Sinclair paused in his pacing to stare at Isabelle. Her lovely profile might well have been carved of marble for all it told him. He could not help remembering how upset she had been when Victor had talked of the French king returning, the killing of the revolutionaries.

It could be she just despises violence, Sinclair argued with himself. She's a sensitive woman. She could merely be—he checked himself in mid-thought, suddenly realizing what he was doing— making excuses, finding reasons why Isabelle Varens could not be Bonaparte's spy.

It's because you don't want it to be her, his mind jeered at him. The woman has seduced you already and you've scarce laid a finger on her. Much as he wanted to deny it, he knew his emotions were already hopelessly entangled. If he had any good sense at all, he would walk away from this, let the army find some other way to ferret out the spy.

But as his gaze settled upon Belle, he exuded a long sigh. What had good sense ever profited a man anyway, except the right to live to a dreary old age?

"I'm in," Sinclair said brusquely. "Whether Mrs. Varens likes it or not, she has a partner."

Belle's head snapped up at his announcement. She looked at him and their eyes met. For long moments it seemed to Sinclair that he and Belle searched each other for a glimpse of the heart each knew how to hide so well. That glimpse, he thought, seemed to elude Belle for the present as well as himself. She was the first to look away.

Sinclair expected that she might choose now to make good on her previous threat, to tell Merchant that she flatly refused to work with Sinclair. Instead, she smoothed out her skirts, saying in a voice of acid sweetness, "Now that it has taken the cautious Mr. Carrington a full five minutes longer than me to make up his mind, perhaps we can get on with the rest of this meeting."

"Certainly," Merchant said. He appeared more relaxed than Sinclair had ever seen him, the expression on the Frenchman's face almost smug. Sinclair supposed it was natural that Victor would feel some satisfaction at their acceptance, but the man did have other agents besides himself and Belle. Why did Merchant seem so pleased that they would be the ones to attempt this dangerous assignment?

Merchant motioned for Sinclair to resume his seat, but Sinclair declined. He felt suddenly too restless to light anywhere, and from his vantage point by the fireplace, perhaps he could maintain a much more impartial study of Isabelle Varens.

Merchant said, "Nothing remains but to settle a few details. First, this mission is to be kept entirely between ourselves. No one, not even any of our own agents, is to be told of it, except for those necessary to carry out the plot. The fewer who know, the less likely any chance of betrayal."

Unless the wrong person already knows of it, Sinclair thought, his troubled gaze resting on Belle.

"All necessary funds will be placed at your disposal," Victor continued. "The actual details of the plot I leave to you. There will be no need for contact with myself until the abduction takes place. Then send a message to alert me of your expected arrival. Use old Feydeau as your courier."

Sinclair started at the sound of the name, banging up against the fire screen. Obviously Merchant had not yet received word about his own agent. Use old Feydeau? Not likely when the man was dead. Sinclair caught Belle staring at him and carefully composed his features so as not to betray a knowledge he would have difficulty explaining.

While Sinclair straightened the fire screen, Merchant went on. "I won't be returning to London. My headquarters will be at Mal du Coeur until the abduction is carried out. It is here where you will bring Monsieur Bonaparte.

"I have already sent word to Baptiste to expect our agents' arrival, telling him it would be most likely to you, Madame Varens. He will find lodgings in Paris for yourself and Monsieur Carrington." Victor droned on, offering his advice about obtaining passports, their travel arrangements, even the time of their departure.

Belle and I might well be a newly wedded pair about to embark on our bridal trip, Sinclair thought with a sardonic lift of one brow, as commonplace as Merchant made it all seem.

The clock chimed one just as Victor finished with his instructions. Sinclair stared in disbelief at the ticking pendulum. Had it really been only one hour since he had first entered this room, one hour in which arrangements had been made to abduct one of the most powerful men in Europe?

The whole affair bore an aura of unreality about it as though they were all merely actors in some farfetched play. Victor ended the meeting as abruptly as he had begun, clearly expecting Sinclair and Belle to take their leave.

As Sinclair moved forward to help Belle rearrange the cloak about her shoulders, he studied her face for any sign that she also was having doubts about what they had undertaken. Her eyes were beclouded, subdued. If she was Bonaparte's spy, Sinclair would have liked to have thought she harbored regrets at the prospect of betraying her new partner. More than that, he would like to think she was innocent. He had always told Chuff only a fool trusted a woman in any matter of real importance. But, God, how Sinclair wanted to trust this one.

Victor bestirred himself to rise. He unbent enough to offer Sinclair his hand in parting, but stayed the gesture at the sound of a sharp rapping against the salon door.

Merchant's eyes narrowed with annoyance. "Damn Crawley. I told him he was no longer needed tonight."

As the rapping came again, Victor strode over to the salon door and flung it open. But the tall lanky man hovering on the threshold was not Quentin Crawley. The shadows from the hallway made it difficult for Sinclair to see the stranger's entire face, but from what he glimpsed, he remarked a profile of almost perfect masculine beauty with a strongly sculpted jaw, an aquiline nose, and a broad forehead accented by silky hair swept back, hair so bleached by the sun, it was almost white.

That neither Belle nor Victor was glad to see the newcomer was obvious. But while Merchant merely appeared irritated, Belle had tensed, her features pinched white.

"Belle?" Sinclair whispered in her ear. "Who is it?"

"Lazare," she hissed back.

The name meant nothing to Sinclair. He watched as Merchant continued to bar the doorway, rebuking the man in a spate of low, urgent French that Sinclair could not quite catch. But Lazare pushed past Victor, stepping farther into the room.

As the candlelight fell full upon Lazare's face, Sinclair bit back a startled exclamation. The left side of that perfect countenance was a mass of thick red scar tissue as though someone had attempted to scorch a grotesque map on Lazare's flesh, the burn markings stretching back from his cheek to the stump where his left ear should have been. His hair was shagged in such a way as to flaunt the deformity.

Victor hastened after Lazare, looking agitated. "What are you doing here, Lazare? I told you there was no need for you to attend the meeting tonight."

"So you did. I thought you would be finished by now."

His gaze passed over Sinclair with as much indifference as though Sinclair did not exist. He stalked toward Belle, a strange passion firing beneath the pale lashes of his silvery eyes. The malice emanating from the man was as palpable as waves of heat pouring off a destructive flame. Sinclair had a strange urge to wrench Belle out of the man's path.

"The fair Isabelle," Lazare drawled. "It has been a long time since I've had the pleasure, *ma chére*."

"Not nearly long enough, Lazare." Belle drew her cloak more tightly about herself, as though any contact with the man would contaminate her. She turned toward Merchant, her eyes blazing with accusation. "What is he doing here, Victor?"

Merchant did not seem able to meet her gaze. He answered hesitantly. "Lazare. will also be accompanying you on your mission."

"Will he indeed! And when, pray tell, did you plan to inform me of that fact?" Belle asked.

Victor moistened his lips to answer, but he was given no opportunity.

"No!" Belle fairly shouted. "I won't have it. I told you after the last time that I would never work with Lazare again."

The last time? Sinclair wondered. His gaze flicked from Belle's pale face to Merchant's flushed features, then to Lazare's impassive expression. Lazare was obviously another agent in Merchant's employ, but he was not anyone whom Sinclair had been informed about. He made a mental note to add Lazare's name to his list of suspects.

"You forget yourself, Madame Varens," Merchant blustered,

trying to reassume a semblance of authority. "I will decide who goes on these missions. Only I."

But as Belle's lips thinned to a stubborn line, Victor apparently thought better of his words and adopted a more conciliatory manner. "You may have need of Lazare—"

"I would have more need of the devil," Belle snapped.

Merchant darkened with anger, but he controlled it. "There will be no trouble this time, I assure you. Lazare fully understands that you are in charge. He pledges to take his orders from you, is that not so, Lazare?"

Lazare acknowledged the words with a stiff bow. Belle's look of contempt showed clearly what she thought of such a promise.

"You must bury the past," Merchant continued, "and give Lazare a second chance."

"*Oui*," Lazare said. He fixed Belle with his compelling gaze. "You owe me that much, *ma chére*."

The low-spoken words had a curious effect on Belle. She turned away in almost guilty fashion.

"Very well. Lazare may come," she said at last, although the concession seemed wrung from her. "But the first time that Lazare seeks to challenge my authority ..." She left the threat unfinished, but Lazare appeared to understand her well enough.

Without another word to anyone, she pushed past Lazare and strode from the room, slipping through the French doors into the garden beyond. Sinclair hesitated for a moment, but neither Merchant nor Lazare looked likely to offer him any explanations for the scene that had just taken place. Sinclair knew Belle disliked questions, but this was one time he had to have some answers. Bidding a curt farewell to the two men, Sinclair went after her.

She was halfway down the path to the beach by the time Sinclair caught up with her, her expression as stormy as the sea-tossed wind tangling her hair. Her breath came rapidly, but whether from fury or fear, Sinclair could not tell. Maybe a combination of both.

"Would you mind telling me what that was all about?" he asked.

"We have acquired another accomplice, that is all," Belle flung back at him. She started to rush on when Sinclair caught her by the wrist, pulling her back.

"And why does this particular accomplice look at you as though he were the devil planning to drag you off to hell?"

Belle compressed her lips in that closed expression Sinclair was beginning to find so frustrating.

"Is he a rejected lover?" Sinclair persisted, trying to goad a response from her. "He has the look about him of a man scorned. Are you the lady who broke his heart?"

"No!" Belle wrenched herself free. She glared up at Sinclair.

"I am the woman who shot off his ear!"

LAZARE EXAMINED MADAME DUMONT'S COLLECTION OF china treasures displayed upon the salon's console table, hefting the pastille burner with his rough fingers and eyeing it with contempt.

Merchant snatched the china from him and carefully replaced it upon the table.

"There was no need for you to come here tonight, Lazare." I proposed to lead up to your part in this affair more gradually."

"Ah, but I did not quite trust your ability to persuade Isabelle into accepting me." Lazare strutted into the center of the room, his gaze continuing to rove over the chamber's aristocratic trappings. The elegance of Madame Dumont's salon inspired in him nothing more than a desire to see it all destroyed.

Dimly he became aware that Merchant was speaking to him, but the fool was addressing his deaf side. Lazare snapped his head around.

"You nearly ruined everything by arriving so unexpectedly," Victor was complaining. "You must take greater care. If Madame

Varens should guess the real part you are to play in her mission—"

"She won't," Lazare interrupted. "Until it is far too late." He lightly touched the thickened flesh of his scar. And then, by God, she'll wish that she had, he thought.

Aloud, he said, "And that silent dark-haired fellow. Is he going to be working with us?"

"Carrington. Yes, he is." Merchant scowled. "Only his name is not Carrington. He is a spy planted among us by the British army, the eldest son of General Daniel Carr."

"How did you ever manage to discover that?" Lazare made no effort to hide his scorn. He had a low opinion of Merchant's powers of deduction.

"Quite by accident," Victor said. "I recognized him. Sinclair bears a powerful resemblance to his father. I met the general once when he attended a ball at the house of Lord Elliot. He rebuked me for my manner of looking after his horse."

Dull red surged into Merchant's cheeks as he spoke of this old humiliation. Lazare suppressed an urge to laugh aloud. He had always enjoyed the tale of how Merchant, once the proud Chevalier de Nerac, had arrived in England so destitute, he had been forced to take a job as a groom for a while. It was probably the only honest toil the damned *aristo* had ever done in his life.

"When I noticed the resemblance," Victor continued, "I did some detailed checking on Carrington, found out that his tale of being a soldier of fortune was untrue. He was a soldier, all right, Captain Daniel Sinclair Carr with his own cavalry regiment. Although no longer in the army, he still works for British intelligence."

Victor's cold eyes locked with Lazare's "I very much dislike being spied upon, Lazare. Especially by an Englishman."

"So do I," Lazare agreed softly. In the pause that followed, they reached a silent understanding.

"And Isabelle?" Lazare asked.

"Madame Varens poses a different problem. She has never followed my orders to the letter, and has grown more insolent each time. And the exploits of the Avenging Angel are becoming too well known. I foresee a time when she will no longer be of much use to me."

"A very distant time?" Lazare's pulse throbbed with anticipation as he awaited Merchant's answer.

"No. What I am trying to tell you is that on this mission, both Carrington and Isabelle Varens are quite expendable."

Lazare's lips snaked back into a smile. "Thank you, monsieur. That is all that I have been waiting to hear."

Six

Dawn broke over the channel, the pearly-white light strewing the water with diamond-like sparkles. The waves lapped against the dockside, gently rocking the Good Lady Nell. Thick ropes creaked as the packet boat tugged against the moorings, as though the ship itself were eager for the journey to begin.

Even at this early hour the sailors had long been awake, scrambling about amongst the riggings, readying the single-masted ship to catch the tide. The mail for the continent had already been stowed on board as one lone passenger made his way up the gangplank. His face muffled in the depths of a woolen scarf, his flowing white-blond hair all but hidden beneath a red Phrygian cap, Etienne Lazare attracted little notice or comment from any of the busy seamen.

Sheltered from the stiff sea breeze, standing near a silk warehouse, Sinclair and Belle watched Lazare's progress to the ship.

Sinclair stuffed his hands into the pockets of his greatcoat. Brief as his acquaintance with Lazare was, the mere sight of the Frenchman inspired Sinclair to ball his hands into fists.

"Lazare appears to be taking no chances of being left behind," he grumbled.

"Perhaps if we are fortunate enough, he will fall overboard." Although Belle's voice was light, Sinclair did not miss a certain tightening of her mouth. Her face was shadowed beneath the brim of her straw bonnet as she studied the distant form of Lazare

"Why, Angel?" Sinclair demanded. "You clearly despise the man, so why did you agree to let him come?" It was a question he had been seeking an answer for ever since her initial outburst that night outside Mal du Coeur when she had blurted out that she had been the one to shoot off Lazare's ear and scar his face.

But Belle had refused to discuss the incident any further. For the past ten days they had seen little of each other, both too busy preparing for the journey to France for Sinclair to pursue the matter. But now that Lazare had crossed their path again, Sinclair felt he had to have some answers.

As always, Belle evaded the question. "Lazare has his uses," she said. "No one knows the streets of Paris better than he does, not even Baptiste."

Sinclair stepped in front of her, partly to shield her from the brisk wind that was causing her to belt her pelisse more snugly about her and partly to force her to look at him.

"That won't do," he said. "I think it is time you were a little more forthcoming with me about our friend Lazare."

"The quarrel between Lazare and me is personal. I told you before, it doesn't concern you, Mr. Carrington."

Belle tried to edge past him, but Sinclair closed in, all but backing her against the wall of the warehouse. He leaned one hand against the rough planking, using the length of his arm as a barrier to her escape.

"It concerns me a great deal, Angel." Sinclair watched Belle stiffen, the soft angles of her face turning hard. She was not the sort of woman to respond to demands or to being bullied. He infused a coaxing, almost playful note into his voice. "After all, I am rather attached to both of my ears. I wouldn't want to offend you in the same manner Lazare did, whatever that was." Sinclair allowed his eyes to rove suggestively over the outline of her lips down to the full curve of her breasts. A flickering of Belle's lashes told him that she was not unresponsive to the boldness of his gaze.

"If I was ever tempted to shoot at you, Mr. Carrington," she said tartly, "I would aim much lower than your ears."

As Sinclair chuckled, she thrust his arm aside, breaking past him. But she had taken only a few paces along the wharf when he caught hold of her arm.

"You might have a little pity on me, Isabelle. As a new member of your society, it is only natural I am curious about you and Lazare. Small wonder poor King Louis still languishes in exile if all you royalists persist in shooting each other instead of—"

"I told you I am no royalist. And as for Lazare—" Belle gave a derisive laugh. She spun about to face Sinclair, her hands on her hips. "He was once a sans-culotte, the more radical group of the revolutionaries. I daresay he cheered more loudly than any when Louis XVI was beheaded. According to Lazare, only the working class in Paris deserved to be left alive."

Sinclair frowned in confusion. "Then what the deuce is he doing working for Merchant?"

"Lazare claims to have seen the error of his ways, to now be a loyal monarchist. He likely thinks he has fooled Merchant, but I doubt if he has. Victor is far too shrewd for that. But they both hate Napoleon, the difference being Victor would replace the Corsican with a Bourbon king, Lazare with anarchy."

Belle added thoughtfully, "It will be interesting to see what happens when Victor and Lazare cease to be of use to each other."

Sinclair pinched the bridge of his nose as though the information she had given him was too much to assimilate. "It's enough to give one a headache," he complained. "This gets more confusing all the time, like reading a book with too many of the pages gone." He leveled a stare at her. "Some of which I think you hold."

So he was back to that again, probing into her own past concerning Lazare. Belle clamped her mouth shut. She hated questions regarding her own life. She had told Sinclair that at the outset. If Sinclair was going to be her partner, he would have to learn to tolerate her reticence, just as she was learning to put up with his infernal habit of calling her Angel.

Yet in this matter of Lazare, perhaps she was merely being stubborn. Belle exuded a weary sigh. Sinclair did have a right to know the whole tale, especially if he was going to be working with Lazare. He ought to be warned how dangerous Lazare could be.

As though he sensed her yielding, Sinclair remained patiently silent, stroking back the strands of night-dark hair the wind whipped across his eyes. Belle stared at a flock of sea gulls wheeling overhead, their strident cries breaking the quiet morning air, but she charted not so much their course as the course of a memory, a memory like too many others she possessed, painful, better forgotten.

"Two years ago Lazare and I were on a mission together," she began at last. "It was a simple enough assignment, to gain information on French troops, where they would be likely to strike next against the allied forces."

Belle shook her head dolefully, rubbing her arms. "But the expedition seemed ill-fated from the first. I took sick soon after we were set ashore in France. I became feverish, almost delirious. Lazare should have just left me, went on himself. But he insisted on nursing me back to health. I should have died but for his care."

"The man strikes me as being a most unlikely nurse." Sinclair only echoed what Belle had thought herself at the time. She struggled to account for Lazare's unexpectedly noble behavior.

"I seemed to hold a strange fascination for him. The streak of cruelty in him was not as strong as his vanity in those days. He was very conscious of his looks, and in me, I believe, he thought he had at last found a fitting mate."

"Him and you?" Sinclair growled. "It's enough to make my

flesh crawl just thinking about the possibility. So he took care of you until you recovered. Then what happened?"

"We went on with the mission. It went well enough until we were surprised by two soldiers and forced to take them captive. They were both so young." Belle closed her eyes briefly and could again envision the two lads, peasant farm boys in their ragged, ill-fitting uniforms, doubtlessly farther from home than they had ever been in their lives and so scared.

She opened her eyes and continued briskly, "We had them well trussed up, hidden in a ditch by the roadside. We would have been long gone before anyone found them. I saw no need to silence them permanently, but Lazare did not agree. He kept sharpening that damned knife and eyeing their throats. He used to be a knife grinder by profession. He would stroke that blade of his the way most men caress a woman."

Sinclair looked sickened. "Good God! The two soldiers. Lazare didn't—"

"No, he didn't, but only because I drew out my pistol and threatened him. Lazare tried to take the weapon away from me, and somehow it went off." Belle caught her breath. It was as though she could yet see Lazare clutching the side of his head, the blood gushing between his fingers, and she could still hear his screams, his horrible inhuman screams.

Belle became aware that Sinclair was grasping her hands. Her fingers felt cold even encased in kid gloves, but Sinclair's warm strength penetrated the thin leather, dispelling the chill that coursed through her. Lazare's screams faded to become nothing more than the cries of the gulls circling the pier.

"Somehow I got Lazare away from there," she concluded, "and found him a doctor. There was no possibility of saving his ear. Indeed it was a miracle he lived at all, considering the severity of his wound, the powder burns to his face." Wearily she shook her head. "I felt so guilty. I never meant to shoot him. I only wanted to stop him."

"The only thing you should be sorry for is not having had better aim. You should have killed that blackguard, Angel."

Belle glanced up at Sinclair, startled by the vehemence of his words.

"There is nothing more dangerous than a wounded jackal. When Lazare looks at you-." Sinclair's jaw tensed. "You should never have agreed to his presence on this mission."

"Perhaps not." Sinclair told her nothing that she had not repeated over and over to herself this past week. "But he did save my life once, and considering how badly he was injured by my hand, I fear Lazare is right. I do, at least, owe him another chance."

Sinclair did not look as though he agreed, but he vented a sigh of frustrated acceptance. "You just be careful around that man, Angel. Do you hear me?"

Sinclair's commanding tone should have irritated her, but strangely it did not. She gave a shaky laugh. "I am always careful, Mr. Carrington. But if Lazare wanted vengeance, believe me, he would have tried to take it long ago. He is not a subtle man."

"All the same, I would never turn my back on him for long, especially on board the packet. I don't want you anywhere near him on that open deck."

"No fear of that. I will spend the entire crossing below in one of the cabins." Although it hurt her pride to admit to what she considered a foolish weakness, Belle said, "I am frequently prey to seasickness."

Sinclair's grim expression softened. "So is Admiral Lord Nelson," he told her with a grin.

"Truly, is he?" Belle asked eagerly, then eyed him with suspicion. "Sinclair, you made that up."

"No, upon my honor, I did not."

Whether Sinclair had or hadn't, it didn't matter. Once again he had lightened her mood and charmed a smile from her. She became aware that he was yet grasping her hands. Rather reluctantly she disengaged herself.

They strolled some little ways along the dock together in companionable silence. Having resisted accepting Sinclair as a partner, it occurred to Belle that she had learned to be comfortable with him in a short space of time. He was so easy to talk to—

Too easy, she thought, frowning. What other man had ever induced her to reveal painful episodes of her past or to expose her weaknesses? Especially a man who was a virtual stranger to her. What did she truly know of Sinclair Carrington? Belle cast a sharp glance at him. He gazed out across the rough channel waters, making no effort to shield his already sun-bronzed features from the elements, seeming to take a keen enjoyment in the wind that tousled his hair and snapped the ends of his coat. His face indicated nothing to her except the countenance of a handsome rakehell, too damnably attractive from the lazy arrogance of his smile to the heat that radiated from his eyes when he looked at her.

Perhaps it was time she posed a few questions of her own. Belle halted so abruptly that Sinclair outstripped her by several steps, his boots ringing against the weather-beaten boards of the dock. When he realized she was no longer with him, he turned back, his thick brows arching an inquiry.

"Sinclair, I have been thinking—" she began.

"That sounds rather alarming, Angel."

She refused to be put off by his teasing. "You have learned some things about me these past ten days. Yet I still know next to nothing about you."

A certain wariness crept into his eyes. "What did you want to know?"

"To start with, you know my motive for working for Victor Merchant, but what about yours? And don't try to tell me you are a devoted royalist, because I don't think I will believe it."

"I wouldn't dream of trying to humbug you, Angel. Quite simply, I work for the money. I am a soldier of fortune, an adventurer, the same as you. Didn't I tell you at the outset that you and I have a great deal in common?"

His voice had dropped to an intimate pitch that she found as warm as a caress. Belle tried to ignore the way her pulse quickened in response.

"But despite how much money Merchant was offering," she said, "you seemed most reluctant to accept this assignment, traveling to France—"

"Speaking of traveling—" Sinclair reached inside the flap of his coat. "I have our passport right here."

Was he trying to distract her? It was not going to work. He would soon discover she could be as persistent with her questions as he. When Sinclair offered the traveling papers to her, Belle snatched them and subjected them to the most cursory inspection, intending to thrust them right back at him.

She hesitated as one line of the scrawled print leaped out at her. Issued to Mr. and Mrs. Sinclair Carrington, accompanied by one maidservant, Paulette Beauvais.

"Mrs. Carrington?" She subjected Sinclair to an icy glare. "I wasn't aware that you were bringing your mother along."

"You know full well that refers to you, Angel. I decided it would be best if you pretended to be my wife."

"You decided! It is my habit to select my own roles, Mr. Carrington." She slapped the passport back into his hand so hard that he winced. "And if you think for one moment I will—"

"Hold a moment, Belle, and reason it through clearly. If we hope to get near Napoleon, we will have to invade the upper reaches of French society. To do that we have to appear respectable."

"I could pretend to be your sister."

Sinclair's eyes drifted over her in one of those lingering appraisals that never failed to set her nerve endings a-tingle. "I would never be able to make anyone believe you were my sister. We look nothing alike. Besides, as a married woman, you will have greater freedom of movement."

She hated to admit it, but Sinclair's arguments made sense,

although she still distrusted his motives. Exactly how far would he try to take this pretense?

While Sinclair returned the offending document to his pocket, she grumbled, "Do you truly think you can carry it off? Frankly, you strike me as too much of a rake to convince anyone that you are a married man."

A mischievous glint appeared in Sinclair's eyes. "You can always give me the opportunity to practice."

Belle stiffened. That was exactly the sort of attitude upon Sinclair's part that she feared. Before she could prevent it, he had slipped both arms about her waist and was drawing her closer. Belle splayed her fingers defensively against his chest. Even through the layers of fabric, she could feel how tautly honed were the muscles beneath.

"This is not how respectable married people behave," she said, her heart beating erratically.

"No? This is how I would behave if you were my bride."

He was teasing her, as he was so fond of doing. Perhaps it would have ended there if their eyes had not chanced to meet. A spark of attraction coursed between them as undefinable as it was irresistible. Sinclair's easy smile vanished, his expression becoming more intent as he drew her closer. Her hands suddenly seemed too weak to hold him at bay.

As his mouth slowly descended to claim hers, a tremor shot through Belle. His lips tasted of the salt sea air. Her resistance melted, and her lips became soft and pliant, allowing his questing tongue to explore the sensitive recesses of her mouth in slow, fire-wrought circles. Desire flickered to life, stirring a sweet ache deep within her, a need that she had denied for far too long.

She retained enough sense to break free of Sinclair's all too seductive kiss and turn her head aside. "No," she said as his lips caressed her temple, the side of her cheek, his breath hot upon her skin. "We agreed that we should not- This is not wise— I—oh!"

Her protest ended in an exclamation of dismay. She found

herself staring deep into a pair of wide gray eyes that peered up at her from beneath the brim of a straw hat. Bare yards away, a small boy with wind-tossed sandy curls watched her and Sinclair with unblinking fascination.

"Sinclair!" Belle wrenched out of his arms. "We have an audience."

"Hmmm?" Sinclair's ardor appeared to wax too hot for him to make sense of her words. Then he saw the boy, too, and grimaced as though just doused with cold water. A blush surged into Belle's cheeks. If their passionate embrace had attracted ribald comments from one of the dockhands, that would somehow have been less embarrassing than the child's innocent regard. For once, even Sinclair seemed at a loss for words.

It was the boy who broke the tension. His snub nose crinkled like a rabbit's. He scratched it and broke into a grin whose charm was enhanced by a missing tooth.

"I like kissing pwitty girls, too," he announced.

After a moment of stunned silence, Sinclair flung back his head and gave a shout of laughter. Belle's lips curved into a reluctant smile.

"But I like sweets better," the boy added.

"Do you indeed? That will change when you grow a little older" Still chuckling, Sinclair slipped his hand inside his coat. He produced a small tin of peppermints, which he flicked open to share with the child.

Not in the least shy, the little boy dipped into the tin and crunched down upon one of the drops. "It's hawder to eat when your tooth gets knocked out by a wock," he confided, his mouth full.

Sinclair solemnly agreed, popping a peppermint into his own mouth and savoring it with the same boyish relish as the child did. When he noticed Belle's surprised stare, he said, "I have a sweet tooth, Angel—another of my vices."

"You appear to have so many of them, Mr. Carrington."

"At least this is one of my harmless ones." He cast her a wicked look, his gaze lingering on her lips, which yet felt tender from his kiss.

A kiss that would not happen again, Belle vowed. Deciding to ignore Sinclair, it seemed by far safer to concentrate upon the child, who was emptying Sinclair's tin. She stooped down so that she was at eye level with the boy's piquant features. She straightened his straw hat, which had been buffeted by the wind. The boy reminded her of an element there had never been any place for in her life—children. Once soon after her marriage, she had hoped, but a fall from a horse had taken care of that. A son like this with bright gray eyes and sandy curls was but one more thing that would forever be denied her.

Brushing aside a wave of self-pity, Belle asked, "What is your name, young sir?"

She had to wait several seconds until the boy chewed and swallowed, "John-Jack."

"And how old are you, John-Jack?"

The boy proudly held up all the fingers on one hand. Then as though smote by conscience, he looked a little sheepish and tucked under the thumb.

"Four years old," Belle said, feigning amazement. "I am sure that is quite grown up, but still a little young, I think, to be wandering these docks alone."

She made a closer inspection of the boy's attire. Although smudged with dirt, his trousers were woven of the softest fawn cashmere, his close-fitting jacket of crimson velvet studded with brass buttons, his collar of exquisite white lace. Obviously he did not belong to any of the rough dockhands or fisherwomen who sat mending their nets.

"Are you lost, child?" she asked.

John-Jack's small chest puffed out with indignation. "No such stuff. I give Nurse Gummwidge the slip."

This statement provoked another laugh from Sinclair. "The

young rascal appears to have a promising future ahead of him in intelligence work, wouldn't you agree, Angel?"

Belle glared up at him. "You should not encourage the child to think such behavior amusing. His poor mother will be quite distracted with worry when she discovers him gone."

"My mama's gone to heaven." The truculent set of John-Jack's chin was betrayed by a quiver. "And now Papa's going, too. On that boat." He pointed toward the Good Lady Nell. "He's going all the way to Fwance. That's fawther away than heaven, I think."

The catch in the child's voice tugged at Belle's heart. But what astonished her was Sinclair's response. His roguish eyes softened with tenderness as he scooped the child up in his arms.

"There now, Master John-Jack. France is not so far away as all that." He turned and directed the child's attention across the rippling green channel waters to the dark mass of land that appeared no more than a shadow on the horizon. "See? You can almost reach out and touch it. Your papa can come sailing home from there before you've even had a chance to miss him."

"Twuly?" Although John-Jack looked skeptical, he wrapped one arm about Sinclair's neck, and he leaned forward to squint. Sinclair soon had the little boy convinced that he very nearly had touched the coastline of France,

Belle could only stare. She knew few men who would have been perceptive enough to recognize the child's fear of losing his father, fewer still who would have troubled to do anything about it. Sinclair looked so natural, so at ease with the boy in his arms, he might well have been parent to a numerous brood of his own. Which he could be, for all she yet knew of Carrington.

Although his background remained a mystery to her, she was discovering more about Sinclair that she liked and desired. She supposed she should be angry with him for stealing the kiss, but how could she, knowing she had been a willing partner in the crime? She was no missish virgin to fool herself into thinking that women were not prey to the same passions as men. It had taken

Sinclair Carrington to remind her of that. If circumstances were different, if they were not facing such a dangerous mission ...

But they were, and in future she had best try harder to keep a clear head and him at arm's length. Both their lives might depend upon it. Even now it was high time one of them remembered the business at hand, that they should be boarding the packet before it sailed without them. Although loath to interrupt Sinclair as he charmed away the last of John-Jack's forlorn expression, she said, "We really must return that child to his family and—"

"*Jean-Jacques.*" A man's voice called in the distance behind her.

"And then-." Belle stumbled over what she had been about to say. The voice called again, its French inflection plucking at her heart like the haunting refrain of an old melody.

Hearing footsteps behind her, she turned slowly, the man's shadow falling across her. He halted at the sight of her, catching his breath, his familiar features becoming white and pinched.

Belle felt as though a hand of iron seized her heart and crushed it. A drumming sounded in her ears. Sinclair, the child, the bustling dockyard blurred, vanishing in a thick haze that left her alone with this man who stood so close she could have reached out and touched his hand.

The grains of Time appeared to have been magically pulled back into the top of the hourglass. She might once more have been standing upon the stone steps of Saint¬Saveur, the noble Comte de Egremont coming to claim his bride.

Except that Time was cruel, a malicious prankster. His waving hair, once so golden brown, was now shot through with silver. Deep furrows bit deep into his brow and alongside his mouth were lines far too harsh for such a gentle face.

"Jean-Claude," Belle whispered. Somehow she'd always known she was fated to see him again one day and had imagined what she would do and say. The time had come and her voice failed her. All she could do was scan his gaunt face for some sign that he had at last forgiven her.

He hadn't. His gray eyes no longer filled with dreams, only hurt and disillusionment. Neither Time nor the Revolution had done that to him. The guilt was all hers.

Belle lowered her gaze, no longer able to bear to look at him. When she and Jean-Claude stood silent as though struck from stone, Sinclair shifted restlessly behind her, the boy still in his arms.

Sinclair had watched Belle's eyes widen with recognition, the shock hard followed by the color draining from her cheeks as though she had taken to bleeding inwardly. Never had he thought to see the proud Isabelle look so stricken, so humbled, and the obvious cause of it was this pale stranger with his flinty, accusing eyes.

"Now, who the devil might this Jean-Claude be?" Sinclair did not realize he had muttered the words aloud until John-Jack answered him.

"That's no devil. That's my papa."

When the child squirmed to be free, Sinclair set him down. John-Jack ran over and flung his arms about the man's knees.

"Papa! Papa! This gent'mum's been teaching me how to touch Fwance."

The child's piping voice seemed to break the spell, at least for the stranger if not for Belle. The man she had called Jean-Claude slowly inclined his head toward the boy.

"Jean-Jacques. Where have you been? I have shouted myself hoarse calling you."

"Why, I was wight here all the time, Papa."

"The fault is mine," Sinclair said. "I was amusing the lad, and although I heard your call, I did not make the connection. The child told us his name was John-Jack."

Cold gray eyes shifted toward Sinclair as though recognizing his existence for the first time. "My son has difficulty with his native tongue. Your country seems to have made a proper Englishman of him."

What a world of bitterness lie concealed in those flat tones, Sinclair thought.

"I thank you for looking after Jean-Jacques," Jean-Claude continued. "I am sorry that he should have given you any trouble."

"It was no trouble."

The Frenchman took his son by the hand to lead him away without another word. The movement stirred some life back into Belle.

"Then the boy is yours, monsieur," she said in a small voice, as though she could not comprehend the fact. "You married again?"

"*Oui*, I did," was the curt reply. "But I am now a widower." As though dragged against his will, Jean-Claude turned back to Belle. Like thin ice cracking, some of his brittle shell seemed to melt.

"It has been a long time, Isabelle," he said softly. "You are still very beautiful."

The color rushed back into Belle's cheeks. "Thank you, Jean-Claude."

She sounded so damn grateful and looked so vulnerable, Sinclair felt a surge of irritation. The way she pronounced the man's name told him all he needed to know about how intimate she and this Jean-Claude once had been. Sinclair experienced a strange sensation, like a giant claw raking across his insides. He surprised himself by stepping closer to Belle and wrapping his arm possessively about her waist.

"It would seem that you and my wife are acquainted, monsieur."

He felt Belle stiffen at his words, a spark of anger firing her eyes. Jean-Claude flinched as though Sinclair had dealt him a blow to the face.

"Your—your wife?"

"No—" Belle started to say, trying to pull away from him.

"Just recently wed." Sinclair cut her off, tightening his grip. "Sinclair Carrington's the name. And you are?"

"The Comte de Egremont." Jean-Claude's lips tightened, but

he forced a smile. "My congratulations, monsieur, Isabelle." He regained his icy composure. "Pray excuse my rudeness. My son grows restless." He glanced down to where John-Jack wriggled, clearly impatient with all this mysterious adult conversation. "I must see him returned to his *bonne*."

"No, Jean-Claude. Wait." But Belle's protest came too weak and too late. Scarce giving John-Jack a chance to wave farewell, Jean-Claude tugged his son along the docks. Sinclair was astonished by the degree of vicious satisfaction he felt at the man's retreat, almost as though he had vanquished an enemy.

Belle wrenched herself away from Sinclair. He half expected her to go running after the Frenchman. She took a few hesitant steps and stopped, rounding on Sinclair. Her face was taut with fury.

"How dare you tell him that! How dare you refer to me as your wife!"

"I thought we had agreed on that, Angel."

"But you needn't have introduced me that way to—to—"

"To Jean-Claude?" Sinclair filled in. "Why? What difference does it make?"

Her lips parted to make a furious retort and then clamped shut. The fire in her eyes slowly died to be replaced by emptiness. "No difference, I suppose. None at all."

Wrapping her arms about herself, she walked to the end of the pier and stared unseeing at the channel. She looked weary, a woman defeated. Sinclair had an urge to go to her, pull her into his arms, but his mind reeled with confusion over his own feelings.

What the devil had gotten into him just now? He had been acting like a jealous lover. Which was absurd because he had never made love to Isabelle Varens. What had they shared? A kiss. Never mind that it had been a kiss unlike any other that he had ever known, that the ridiculous thought had flashed through his mind that in Belle he had found something he had been searching for all his life.

So this is what it felt like to make an idiot of oneself over a woman. Chuff, if only you could see your rakehell brother now, he thought with a groan.

Completely cool in his past relations with women, Sinclair was not sure how to cope with this new unsettling experience. Did one apologize for behaving like a jealous fool or simply let the matter drop? Belle seemed too lost in her own unhappy thoughts to take any interest in what he might have to say.

But he discovered he was wrong. She was aware of both him and his silence, for she remarked bitterly, "Well, Mr. Carrington? You are always so curious. I had expected by now to be barraged with questions about my relationship to the Comte de Egremont."

"I am not sure this time, Angel, that I want to know—"

"He was my husband."

For a moment Sinclair was too stunned to say anything. Then he blurted out, "Your husband! I thought he was dead."

"To me, he is, but it is a living death. In France they call it divorce."

Sinclair thought himself past the age of being shocked by anything, but he could not quite manage to conceal his dismay.

"Divorce?"

"Another of the Revolution's civilizing improvements, Mr. Carrington." She essayed a careless laugh, which stuck in her throat. "It does not require an act of Parliament to dissolve a marriage in Paris, only a few pen strokes on a piece of parchment, a mutual agreement to make an end."

How mutual had that agreement been in Belle's case? Sinclair wondered. One look at the misery brimming in her eyes answered his question. As he groped for his pocket handkerchief, he damned Jean-Claude Varens for a fool.

Usually adept at turning aside the flood of feminine tears he so disliked, for once Sinclair could not think of anything witty or consoling to say. He handed Belle the handkerchief in a gesture of silent sympathy.

She stared at the soft linen blankly at first, then her eyes widened with comprehension. "Oh, I see. You thought I was going to cry. No fear of that. I have forgotten how." She returned the handkerchief to him with a self-mocking smile. "A pity, isn't it? Weeping, when done prettily, can be such a useful accomplishment for a woman."

The way she sought to conceal her pain moved Sinclair far more than any tears would have done. He reached for her, but she shrank from his touch.

"If you do not object, Sinclair, I believe I will go on board now."

"Belle—"

"I always spend the crossing alone in the cabin, but I will join you when we disembark."

She backed away from him, so clearly rejecting his comfort. Sinclair allowed his arm to drop helplessly to his side. She spun on her heel and fled along the dock toward the gangplank.

Sinclair stared after her, crumpling the handkerchief in his fist, struck by the irony of the situation. All his life he had striven to avoid weeping females, yet he would have given much to cradle Belle in his arms and let her sob out her grief against his chest. But all he could do was stand there and let her go.

Never sure how she managed it, Belle hurried blindly aboard the Good Lady Nell. The ship's planking seemed to rock beneath her feet. When she located her cabin, she stumbled across the threshold. The chamber was narrow and dark but for the light filtering from one small lantern, giving her the queasy sensation of being swallowed whole into the maw of some mammoth sea beast.

But she welcomed even the creaking confines of the ship's cabin as a haven. She slammed the door behind her and leaned against it, closing her eyes as though that action could somehow also shut out the tormenting thoughts chasing through her mind.

Jean-Claude ... Had she only dreamed what had happened upon the pier, or after so many empty years had he actually walked back into her life again? No, she would have never imagined that sort of a meeting, that they would draw so close and never touch, strangers and yet not strangers, that he would appear to her and so swiftly vanish without a word of farewell. Not even her nightmares had ever been that cruel.

"Ah, *chérie*, there you are at last," Paulette Beauvais's cheery greeting jangled Belle's nerves.

Belle opened her eyes, her vision assaulted by the too-bright yellow of Paulette's low-cut gown, the garishness of the frock accented by the thin red ribbon she habitually wore tied about her neck and the blowsy disorder of her short brown curls.

Paulette stood over an open trunk, shaking out a somber gown of black wool. Her dark eyes twinkled. "I thought it time I changed into my guise of your oh so proper maidservant before—"

Paulette's stream of chatter halted as she peered at Belle. The scrutiny emphasized the elfin slant of the Frenchwoman's eyes.

"*Qu'est que c'est, chérie*? You look as though you have seen the ghost."

Paulette's remark hit so near the truth that Belle suppressed the urge to burst into hysterical laughter.

Paulette frowned, "Is it Lazare who has upset you? I saw him come aboard. The *varien!*. I will fling him into the sea if he—"

"No. It is nothing to do with Lazare." Belle moved away from the door. She sank down upon the cabin's hard cot. "It is only that-that you know how I feel about ships."

All solicitude, Paulette bustled to her side. "*Ma pauvre*. How stupid of me to forget." She pressed her thin hand to Belle's brow. "You anticipate the *mal de mer*. Never fret. Paulette will take care of you as soon as I change my frock."

Belle removed Paulette's hand from her forehead. Go away, Paulette, she thought wearily, wishing the vivacious Frenchwoman would sense her need to be alone.

Oblivious to Belle's mood, Paulette hummed a little tune and shrugged her short, wiry frame out of the yellow gown. Even to be rid of Paulette's unwanted presence, Belle could not bring herself to reveal any portion of the real cause of her distress. Despite having worked with Paulette for over a year, Belle had never been able to confide in her anything of importance. Useful enough for the role she played, Paulette seemed too flighty to ever be trusted in any great matters.

While Belle wished her elsewhere, Paulette slipped into the black dress, bubbling on about the amusement she had found amongst the handsome sailors in Portsmouth's Royal Navy Yard.

"All the same, I shall be glad to return to my Paris. That is the best place on earth to find love."

Or to lose it, Belle thought sadly. Her gaze roved toward the bare wooden beams of the ceiling as she strained to hear sounds coming from the deck above. The boy, Jean-Jacques, had said something about his father returning to France on this same ship. Could Jean-Claude even now be that close to her? Napoleon had granted amnesty to the émigrés from the Revolution. She had noticed that Jean-Claude had resumed the use of his title. Did he intend to resume his old life at Merevale as well?

Not that any of that was her concern. Belle lowered her head, pressing her fingertips to her throbbing temples. No matter what Jean-Claude's plans, there was no place in them for her. She thought she had learned to live with that fact years ago. Then why did seeing him again hit her so hard?

Perhaps it had been the look in his eyes, still so shattered and unforgiving of the deception she had practiced upon him long ago. Perhaps it was the knowledge that until he pardoned her, she would never be able to forgive herself.

"Here, *chérie*. Drink this."

Belle blinked, becoming aware that Paulette stood over her, offering her a glass half-filled with a muddy-colored liquid. Her curls secured beneath a mob cap, her lithe frame attired in sober black, Paulette had effected an amazing transformation into that of a proper, middle-aged lady's maid.

Belle eyed the glass with suspicion. "What is it?"

"Laudanam, *ma chére*. It will put you to sleep. Then you will not feel the ship's rockings."

Belle's lip curled with distaste. But with all those phantoms that lurked in the darker corners of her mind, waiting to be set free, Belle had found sleep more often a curse than a blessing.

Too weary to resist Paulette's insistence, Belle accepted the glass and set it down on top of a small shelf affixed to the wall. By pretending she would take the laudanum in a few minutes, she managed to be rid of Paulette at last, encouraging the woman to take the air on deck.

As the door closed behind Paulette, silence settled over the cabin, as heavy as the weight of memories pressing upon Belle's heart. She stretched out on the hard cot, flinging one arm across her eyes.

How strange it all was. After a lifetime of being haunted by thoughts of Jean-Claude, Fate should decree that their paths cross on this particular day, a day in which he had not once entered her mind, a day in which she had admitted to feeling desire for another man.

What must Sinclair be thinking of her now? Again she had told him more than she had ever intended. Even he had looked a little shocked when she informed him about the divorce. But there had been no censure in his eyes. He would have drawn her into his arms if she would have let him, and for a brief second the temptation had been great.

But what a mockery that would have been for both of them—to wail out her grief for her lost love against Sinclair's strong shoulder. For she did still grieve for Jean-Claude, perhaps more so than if he had died.

The feeling angered, frustrated and shamed her. Obviously, Jean-Claude had managed to rebuild his life and remarry. Doubtless his bride had been some winsome English lass of gentle birth, not the mongrel daughter of a second-rate actress from Drury Lane.

And now he was a widower, but with a sweet-faced little son to bring him consolation. A son that might have been hers if things had been different.

Groaning softly, Belle rolled onto her stomach. Her gaze fell upon the laudanum Paulette had left. With such agonizing thoughts to torment her, even sleep with all its attendant nightmares seemed not so bad. Against her will, Belle reached for the glass.

THE GOOD LADY NELL SHUDDERED, HER PROW SLUICING gracefully through the choppy channel waters. Overhead the sails snapped and billowed in the stiff breeze. The brisk wind had long since driven most of the passengers below except for the three men who ranged themselves along the deck and watched the outline of the distant shore emerge ever more sharp and clear.

Sinclair perched atop a barrel lashed to the deck, his easy pose belying the tension knotted between his shoulder blades. Through a haze of smoke from his cheroot, he divided his time between keeping an eye on Lazare and studying Jean-Claude Varens.

Varens stood alone by the deck rail, his fine-chiseled features suffused with an expression of melancholy. Despite the simplicity of his dark suit and high-crowned beaver hat, something in the comte's dignified carriage would ever mark him as an aristocrat, one of those noblemen who positively reeked of virtue, duty, and honor.

Sinclair tried to picture Belle as Jean-Claude's wife, tried and failed. She had too much strength, too much vitality to be wed to a dull dog like that. Yet it appeared to be Varens who had ended the marriage, and Belle the one who still grieved.

Sinclair wished that Belle had not bared so much of her heart to him that morning. She might come to hate him for that, making their relationship more awkward than it already was. And there was some of her private pain he did not wish to know. Bad enough that he desired the lady beyond all reason. He didn't need her stirring any deeper emotions inside him.

Yet it was his task to discover all that he could about her, to decide if she was the one passing information to Napoleon. But the assignment was beginning to leave a more bitter taste in his mouth than a stale cigar.

With a heavy sigh, Sinclair abandoned his lazy pose. Striding to the rail, he flung his cheroot into the churning waves. It was then that Lazare made his move. Out of the corner of his eye, Sinclair watched with some surprise as Lazare approached Varens.

Jean-Claude gave a start as though rudely awakened. Sinclair expected that the comte would snub any effort at conversation, sending Lazare on his way with a chilly dismissal. Instead, Jean-Claude made a stiff bow. Although he looked somewhat apprehensive, he listened courteously to what Lazare had to say.

A passing acknowledgment between travelers meeting by chance on the same vessel? Sinclair wondered. He wished he could inch close enough to hear what was being said without attracting attention, but that was impossible. It didn't matter anyway, for Lazare had finished his remarks. With a brisk nod, he moved on and Varens returned to staring over the side.

How strange, Sinclair thought, his eyes narrowing. Strange indeed now that he happened to think about it—that Belle's former husband should sail to France on the same ship as she.

Belle would doubtless dismiss Sinclair's concern with an impatient shrug. A bizarre coincidence, she would likely say.

"There's only one problem, Angel," Sinclair murmured. "I don't much believe in coincidence."

Relieved when Etienne Lazare stalked away from him, Jean-Claude directed his gaze toward the approaching shoreline. The sea spray misted against his cheeks, but some of the salt droplets originated from his own eyes. His beloved France. How he had ached for this day when he would once more gaze upon the only land he could ever call home. Yet the time had arrived and his vision blurred with tears. All he could see was her face. Isabelle, the woman he had once cherished as his wife.

The shock of seeing her again had been enough to kill him. Time had changed her so little, her face yet blessed with that radiance, that purity which had once captured his heart. It touched him even now when he knew the painful truth about her.

She was so beautiful. He had forgotten how much so. No, he lied. He had never forgotten. Isabelle's image had been ingrained upon his soul even when he had sought life anew in the arms of the gentle Lady Sarah Belvoir. God forgive him, even when he had laid his poor Sarah to rest in the churchyard, his thoughts had been of Isabelle, wondering if she yet lived.

And now he knew. Isabelle was very much alive and recently married to that darkly handsome man with the mocking eyes. Jean-Claude should at last be able to put her out of his heart, concentrate only on his return to France, the purpose that drew him back.

But he could not. The pain that she had caused him, the years of separation, even the knowledge that she now had another husband—one look at her and none of that seemed to matter. Jean-Claude buried his face in his hands. God help him, he still loved her.

What was that fool Varens doing? Lazare wondered as he studied the comte's trembling shoulders. Shivering with cold or weeping over his return to France?

"Bah!" Lazare snorted. "What a weakling!"

Why had he ever bothered to seek out Varens? The man would likely prove useless for the role Lazare had in mind. Lazare's gaze shifted to the companionway that led to the cabins. He knew which door Belle sheltered behind. Might it not be better even now to slip below and make an end? He fingered the hilt of the knife concealed beneath his cloak. Perspiration beaded his brow as he thought of pressing the sharp tip to Belle's slender white throat, the point breaking through the skin, slicing in a slow arc, the rivulets of her warm blood trickling over his fingers.

A shiver of ecstasy coursed through him, stirring an ache deep in his loins, but he forced his hand away from the knife. He had waited too long for his revenge to finish it that quickly, that easily for Belle. And that Carrington fellow was watching him again.

"Stare all you like, Englishman," Lazare muttered, self-consciously touching a hand to his scarred flesh. "In a month's time the maggots will have devoured your eyes."

And as for the Avenging Angel—Lazare sneered—she would count herself blessed if her own death came so swift as the one Lazare envisioned for Carrington. Because Lazare had far different plans for Belle, a vengeance more subtle and sweet. She herself had given him the key to it, that long ago night when her fever had raged. In her delirium she had cried out her terrors of being locked away in the Conciergerie, of mounting the steps to the guillotine, of her despairing love for Jean-Claude Varens.

"So rest while you may, *ma belle*." Lazare's mouth tightened with grim satisfaction. "I am about to make all of your worst nightmares come true."

PAULETTE'S LAUDANUM TOOK EFFECT. OBLIVIOUS TO the rocking of the ship and the three men who stalked the deck above her, Belle slept.

Seven

The drums pounded in Belle's head. Like marionettes, the soldiers' stiff arms rose and fell, beating out the steady rhythm. They kept step beside the rough wooden tumbril creeping through the streets, bearing the latest cache of victims to the guillotine's relentless blade.

Tossing on the cot, Belle moaned, trying to pull herself out of the dream. But the webbings of nightmare held her fast, as tight as the cords that seemed to bind her hands.

She was not a spectator. This time it was she who stood braced against the jolts of the cart, her arms bound behind her as she stared out over a sea of jeering faces that had lost all trace of humanity. Gaping mouths, burning eyes, their features were indistinguishable except for the man who stood a little apart, gentle and solemn, untouched by the hatred of the rabble surrounding him.

"Jean-Claude! Jean-Claude!" Her throat muscles ached with the effort of trying to call to him, but the drums sounded louder, drowning out her cries. The cart lurched to a stop, and rough hands seized her, dragging her to the ground. She strained toward her husband, but Jean-Claude had turned, about to vanish into the crowd.

"Jean—"

"Belle!"

This time her cry was cut off not by the drums, but by someone shouting her name.

"Belle! Wake up!" The hands gripping her shoulders gave her a brisk shake.

She felt herself slipping back into the midst of the mob, but the deep male voice, so familiar, so insistent, snapped the tenuous threads of the nightmare. With a gasp, Belle jerked to a sitting position. Forcing her eyes open, she struggled to focus on the person perched on the edge of the cot, bending over her.

Glossy black hair tumbled over a furrowed brow, anxiety mirrored in dark-fringed eyes of crystalline green. The mouth that should have been smiling with its customary lazy good humor was not.

"Sinclair?" she said thickly.

"Yes, I am right here, Angel."

The simple words had a strange effect on her. She flung her arms about his neck, burying her face against him, drawing comfort from the unyielding hardness of his shoulder. He felt so solid, so real after the phantom images of her nightmare.

His arms closed about her, strong and steadying. Tangling his fingers in her hair, he rested his chin against the top of her head, gently rocking her.

"It's all right, Angel," he murmured. "You are here, safe with me."

Belle released her breath in a tremulous sigh. Yes, but where was here? Her mind yet hazy with sleep, she turned her head enough to study the room through bleary eyes. She took in the swaying lantern, the trunks propped against the wall, the empty glass tumbled upon the floorboards of the cabin aboard the Good Lady Nell.

Memory flooded back to her, of waiting on the dock, finding the little boy, seeing Jean-Claude, telling Sinclair—

Sinclair! With a jolt, she realized how she clung to him like a frightened child. She struggled to break free. He attempted to soothe her, but she wrenched out of his arms. Her head swam so dizzyingly she was obliged to sink back flat on the cot.

With a low groan, she covered her face with her hands. It was the cursed laudanum. That was what was causing her to feel so weak and to behave so strangely. She'd be damned if she would ever touch the stuff again. The brief peace it had brought her was not worth the self-loathing she now felt.

She noticed Sinclair's weight shift from the cot and thought he had left her. But he returned to her side in a minute. Pulling her hands down, he dabbed a cool, damp cloth upon her brow.

"Don't!" she said, twisting away from him. "I am not ill. I was only having a nightmare."

"I know," he said softly. "Do you want to tell me about it?"

"No!"

She thought her blunt refusal brought a flicker of hurt to his eyes, but in the dim light it was hard to tell. He looked unconcerned enough as he straightened. "Well, perhaps some other time."

"How long have I been asleep?" she demanded.

"The entire crossing. We are anchored at Le Havre. When you did not come on deck, I grew concerned and came below to check on you."

And found her raving in her sleep like a madwoman. With another groan, Belle managed to sit up and roll her legs over the side of the cot. She made a futile attempt to smooth her hair, imagining how disheveled it must be, what dark hollows she must have beneath her eyes. She hated Sinclair seeing her this way. All her life she had made it a practice to conceal her hurts, her weaknesses from the scorn of the world. Yet in the last twenty-four hours, how much of her inner self had she paraded before Sinclair? She felt stripped naked in front of the man.

It only made matters worse when Sinclair noticed the empty

glass on the floor. He picked it up, sniffed it and tasted some of the dregs with one finger to his lips. Although he frowned, he said nothing.

Belle felt as though she could not face his contempt or his pity, but she had never learned to spare herself. Slowly she got to her feet and looked him full in the eyes, but found only understanding, an understanding that seemed to delve into the depths of her soul.

It alarmed her even more than the physical attraction she felt for Sinclair. She had spent too long building the wall about herself to have it so easily breached. Quickly she averted her gaze.

"Where is Paulette? I would have thought she would be the one to come down and wake me."

"She was ogling the sailors as they launched the longboat." Sinclair hesitated and then added, "All of the other passengers have already been set ashore."

Belle supposed that was Sinclair's kind way of telling her that Jean-Claude was already gone. Belle felt the familiar tug of loss, but suppressed it. What difference did it make? It was not as though she and Jean-Claude had anything more to say to each other, at least nothing that he would care to hear.

She drew herself up, groping for her dignity, that mantle of pride which had stood her in such good stead all these years.

"It is time we were going ourselves. Get Lazare down here to help with the trunks. As soon as we are ashore, we will want to see about hiring a carriage,"

"Belle." Sinclair stopped her as she moved toward the door, his hands resting on her shoulders. He turned her to face him.

"There is no need for such haste. We could linger a day or two at Le Havre, give you- give both of us some time to recover and lay our plans."

She refused to look up at him, but she saw his hand move and knew that he meant to caress her cheek. She felt so empty and aching inside. God, how she wanted Sinclair's touch—no, needed it.

For that very reason she shied away, refusing to let him come any closer. "No," she said. "Two days from now I intend to be in Paris."

Belle backed out of the cabin, slamming the door closed between them.

PARIS- THAT CITY OF BROKEN DREAMS AND SHATTERING nightmares. How many years ago had it been that Belle had crept through its gates, her meager possessions bundled in a shawl, her heart thudding when she thought of how narrowly she had escaped from the dank confines of the Conciergerie, that last stop on the journey to the guillotine. She had paused but once outside the walls surrounding Paris, vowing never to return and so risk her life again.

Yet here she was. Belle's lips curved into a self-mocking smile as she braced herself against the sway of the coach. Whoever said that wisdom was supposed to come with age? Well, she had survived seeing Jean-Claude again. She would survive the return to Paris as well. She had never yet heard tell of anyone being slain by a memory.

Paris seemed to press in about her, the eternal din of the city assaulting her ears, vendors crying their wares, newspaper hawkers bellowing out the headlines, workmen's hammers clanging, donkeys braying.

She stared out the window, every rut, every crack of the Rue St. Honoré as familiar to her as if she had ridden down it just yesterday. The street threaded through a narrow canyon of tall buildings, the smoke from the chimneys hanging in the air like a blue mist, the houses the same mad jumble of architecture, turrets, gables and neoclassic all crammed side by side. Little had changed except that she noted that No. 17 appeared unoccupied. The five-story dwelling had housed the flat she had shared with Jean-Claude those few happy days they had known together, before the Revolution had turned into a reign of terror, before he had discovered her secret.

But the timber frame structure now wore an air of dilapidation, the windows broken or boarded over. It was somehow appropriate. In that house all her dreams had died. Gazing upon it was like viewing an open grave, and she was quick to avert her eyes.

"Have we nearly arrived at this Baptiste's?" Sinclair's voice startled her. She had thought him asleep. Weary from the journey, he had hardly roused himself even when they had passed through the *barrière* in the thick wall that surrounded Paris. She turned from the window to find him sitting up on the seat opposite, wincing and rubbing his leg, cramped by the narrow confines of the coach.

"It is not much farther," she assured him.

"Good. I may never be able to straighten again." Flexing his arm muscles, he bestirred himself, leaning forward to peer out the same window as she did. In doing so, his shoulder brushed up against hers. She was quick to draw back. When she had slammed the cabin door between them, she had attempted to erect an invisible barrier as well, keeping Sinclair Carrington at arm's length, suppressing all response to his penetrating eyes and that seductively soothing voice.

If Sinclair noticed her reaction to his closeness, he made no comment upon it. Instead, he lowered the window glass to obtain a better look, and then grumbled, "These streets are crawling with French soldiers."

"Well, we are in France, Mr. Carrington," she reminded him. But she took another look for herself and saw that he was right. Caught up in her own memories of Paris, she had failed to notice one very obvious change.

The Parisians still crowded into the streets as though they owned them, heedless of being crushed beneath the wheels of any passing carriage. But few of the citizens any longer sported the red caps or the tricolor cockade of the Revolution. What she now saw in abundance were indigo blue uniforms.

Soldiers swaggered their way along the Rue St. Honoré, jostling civilians out of their way, cursing, laughing, some even singing at the top of their lungs.

"More signs of Bonaparte's influence," Belle said.

"It gives a fellow a damned uneasy feeling. The last time I saw that much blue it was facing me from the opposite end of the battlefield."

Despite her determination to keep her distance from Sinclair, his words intrigued her. So he had once been in the army, most likely the British.

Before she could pursue the matter further, the carriage drew to a halt before the faded brick building that housed Baptiste Renault's fan shop. Without waiting for the post-boy to come round, Sinclair opened the door himself and leaped to the ground. A disgruntled look crossed his face as his glossy Hessians sank up to the ankle in mud.

"Welcome to Paris, Mr. Carrington," she said dryly.

Grimacing, he turned to help her down. Instead of offering her his hand, he caught her about the waist and swung her clear of the coach, depositing her upon some planking that had been placed to bridge the distance from street to shop. Momentarily she was aware of the tensile strength in Sinclair's arms and other sensations caused by her breasts grazing against the hard wall of his chest, sensations she was quick to deny.

When their coachman whipped up the horses, moving off to seek out the stables, she glanced back the way they had come. "I don't see any sign of the other carriage with Paulette and Lazare."

"I am sure they will catch up with us. No fear of us managing to lose Lazare—" Sinclair broke off, giving vent to a startled oath.

Belle gasped as she saw it, too—the roan horse bearing down upon them in a blur of hard-pounding hooves and galloping legs. Paris boasted no such luxury as sidewalks. She and Sinclair had no choice but to dive to one side, slamming up hard against the brick wall of the shop.

The rider flashed past, missing them by inches, pelting them with spatters of mud churned from beneath the flying hooves.

"Damned idiot!" Sinclair straightened, staring in disgust at his sleeve, which now matched his boots. "Are you all right, Angel?"

Belle took a minute to catch her breath before nodding.

"Then let's get inside," Sinclair said, "before we are killed just trying to alight from our coach."

They had mounted the first step to the shop and Sinclair was reaching for the door when they heard the now distant rider's bellow. "Give way. Clear a path for the citoyen consul."

Belle arrested her movement in mid-step, her gaze flying up to meet Sinclair's. He looked as uncertain as she, caught between anticipation and disbelief. There was more than one man in France who held the title consul. It would be the most incredible piece of luck if she were about to obtain her first glimpse of—

"Bonaparte! Bonaparte!" The cry rose up from the crowded street behind her. Whirling about, Belle saw a troop of four mounted horsemen forging a path through the throng of carts, pedestrians, and donkeys. The first three—two wearing a profusion of gold braid on their military jackets, the third garbed in the more colorful attire of the Mamluke—acted as a vanguard for the fourth rider mounted atop a snow-white stallion.

It was this rider that the children ran alongside and cheered, while humble working women and ladies alike frantically waved their handkerchiefs, and the shouts of the men grew more frenzied.

"*Vive Napoleon! Vive la République.*"

Belle caught hold of the wrought-iron railing along the steps, bracing herself for her first view of the man she had come so far to abduct, that Monster from Corsica, as her countrymen termed First Consul Napoleon Bonaparte.

Her initial reaction was one of disappointment. Garbed in a

plain gray greatcoat, he seemed of insignificant stature with a poor seat as well. He rode his horse like a sack of grain, leaning slightly forward to maintain his balance. When he trotted farther up the Rue St. Honoré, only yards separated her from his prancing mount. Situated as she was, partway up the stairs, she obtained a clear but brief view of the profile set beneath the black beaver cockade. Pale as marble, Bonaparte's features held the fierce majesty of an eagle. When he turned slightly to acknowledge the greetings of the crowd, she saw that his eyes burned like live coals. As his mount surged past, she was left with an impression of boundless energy and an arrogant self-assurance.

No mean adversary would this Napoleon Bonaparte be, she surmised. But rather than being dismayed at the thought, it sent a tingle through her blood at the prospect of the dangerous challenge before her. She felt somehow stronger, more in control of herself than she had since experiencing the shock of Jean-Claude's intrusion back into her life.

Even after the cheering had died away, she still quivered with excitement as she turned to face Sinclair. She felt unreasonably delighted to sense he felt it, too. As Sinclair stared after Bonaparte's retreating figure, there was a spark in his green eyes, even though when he glanced down at Belle, he ruefully shook his head.

"We both have to be quite mad," he said in low tones. "The people in this city acclaim that man like a demigod. If we are caught trying to—"

"We won't be caught, Sinclair," she whispered back, clutching at his arm. "He can't always be parading in their midst, surrounded by his entourage."

Sinclair merely raised his brows before offering her a strangely wistful smile. "At least I can thank Monsieur Bonaparte for one thing. He appears to have jogged your memory. You finally have recalled my name. Ever since we left that blasted ship, you have Mr. Carringtoned me nigh to death."

His half-teasing, half-serious complaint doused some of her

excitement. She slowly withdrew her hand from his arm, remembering her vow to keep a wall between them. But at the moment she could not seem to lay her hands upon so much as a single brick. She experienced an uncomfortable vision of her recent behavior from Sinclair's point of view.

"Have I truly been that much of a shrew?" she asked.

"Not shrewish, merely distant, as though you had retreated to another world."

"I am sorry. I don't usually inflict my partners with such—such womanish moods." She had to swallow a large measure of pride before she could continue. "I fear I have always been something of a fool over Jean-Claude Varens, but I assure you I have recovered myself. You won't be treated to any more such scenes as took place in the cabin."

"Good God, Angel. You don't have to apologize to me for having bad dreams." His eyes held that expression of warm understanding, his smile soft. "I have never been one for the stiff-upper-lip attitude. When you are around me and something hurts you, feel free to go ahead and swear."

She felt herself returning his smile and half-reached out to take his hand.

"And you don't have to be afraid to touch me, either," he added.

"Yes, I do. Your touch seems to have an unaccountable effect on me."

"A bad one?"

"No, merely one I'm not prepared to deal with," she admitted frankly. "I am taking enough risks on this mission without hazarding anymore."

She tried to meet his gaze levelly, but looking into Sinclair's eyes could be as dangerous as touching him. She was quick to turn the subject.

"We should hardly stand here on the steps all day. They are accustomed to more curious sights here in Paris, but I fear eventually people will begin to stare. Come inside and meet Baptiste Renault, my one true friend in Paris."

Sinclair sketched an elaborate bow and opened the door for her, motioning her forward. As she passed beneath the portal, he gazed down at the top of her head, the soft blond curls haloing her perfect features. He felt as though he and Belle had at last reached some sort of an understanding, but the final line was the same. She had rejected him again.

He was not so conceited as to believe that every woman would fall at his feet. He had met with his share of rebuffs, but they had never mattered. He had simply moved on to find a more interested *partie*.

He could not possibly be yearning for a woman he had heard cry out in her sleep for another man, a woman who might be the very spy he had been sent to betray. He could not be that big of a fool, could he? Sinclair refused to answer that question, refused to examine his own feelings any further. Like Belle, there were some risks he was not prepared to take.

Realizing that while he had been consumed with such troubling thoughts Belle had already vanished into the shop, he followed her inside, closing the door behind him.

The interior would have been dark, the towering houses across the narrow street cutting off much of the sunlight, had it not been for the glow of dozens of candles. Looking about him, Sinclair realized he had stepped into a sort of workshop, the smell of glue and parchment heavy in the air. Four rough-hewn tables were covered with fans in varying stages of completion, some of the parchment newly stretched out on half circle hoops while others lay complete, spread out to dry.

Sinclair had never paid much heed to ladies' fripperies before. But he knew enough to recognize first-rate craftsmanship. Handles of wood, ivory, or mother-of-pearl were carved with an intricate delicacy. The classical scenes depicted upon the leaves of silk were miniature works of art.

The workroom was a hive of quiet activity. Several women were painting fans with fairylike strokes; a young man was busy with the stretching, while an older man deftly wielded a shaving iron upon a piece of tortoiseshell.

When Sinclair and Belle entered, the work abruptly ceased, curious eyes turning in their direction. Sinclair waited to take his cue from Belle, but she was silent, her attention focused on the older man.

This individual got slowly to his feet, and Sinclair was startled to see how short he was, a regular gnome, scarce coming up to Belle's shoulder. The craftsman's features even seemed elflike, the bulbous nose too large for his florid face, the chin pointed, the salt and pepper hair straggling over his forehead.

He regarded Belle calmly through eyes of chocolate brown possessing the twinkle of youth, although the pockets of lined flesh beneath them spoke more of the wisdom of age.

"*Bonjour*, madame, monsieur," he said. "And how may I serve you? I usually do not require beautiful ladies to come into my workshop. I would be happy to display my wares in the convenience of your home."

"No. I have not come about a fan." Belle's voice sounded odd to Sinclair, strangely suppressed. He noticed a gleam in her eye as she continued, "We are Monsieur and Madame Carrington. We have come about the apartment to let above stairs."

"But of course." The gnome bowed, rubbing his hands together. "Please to come this way." He motioned Belle and Sinclair toward a doorway at the side of the shop. Pausing only long enough to glance back at his workers and command, "Back to work, *mes amis. Vite, vite!*" He slipped through the door, moving with a light spring to his step.

Sinclair allowed Belle to precede him, concealing a slight frown. This was not precisely what he had been expecting, but Belle appeared unperturbed. Doubtless her friend Baptiste awaited them upstairs.

The little man led them into a small foyer, from which a narrow flight of stairs yawned upward, The gnome spoke in a loud voice, clearly meant to carry back to the workroom. "I am sure you will find the apartment most satisfactory, Madame Carrington. It belongs to a charming actress, Mademoiselle Fontaine, and her lover, but she likes to have the lodgings sublet when she is touring in the provinces."

His voice died away. As soon as the connecting door to the workshop was closed, the man underwent a startling change. He no longer faced Belle with that obsequious deference. His face broke into a crooked smile which infused his ugly countenance with an unexpected charm.

"So, *mon ange*," he said, stretching out his hands to Belle. "You have come back to Paris at last!"

"Baptiste." Her voice was filled with warmth as she stepped forward, flinging her arms about the gnome's neck. Watching the two of them embrace, Sinclair blinked, trying to assimilate the fact that this droll little man was the agent Baptiste Renault, whose aid he and Belle had come to seek.

Mentally he reviewed all the information he had managed to glean about Renault thus far. He and Belle had apparently worked together during the Revolution, smuggling dozens of people proscribed out of Paris. Although he had been arrested once, somehow Baptiste had managed to be one of those few who had survived all the twists and turns, the changes in government that marked the Revolution.

And Sinclair knew one thing more. This was the man Belle had described as her one true friend in Paris. Watching her as she returned Baptiste's fierce hug, Sinclair thought he had never seen Belle relax her guard so much, for one moment looking radiant, unreservedly happy. He felt a twinge of envy that this Baptiste could inspire such an expression upon Belle's face. But Sinclair immediately brought himself up short. He was indeed in a bad way if he was starting to feel jealous even of this older odd-looking man.

When their enthusiastic greeting showed no sign of abatement, Sinclair coughed discreetly to remind them of his presence.

Belle swung around to face him, her eyes still glowing, Baptiste's arm entwined about her waist. "Sinclair, allow me to present to you, Baptiste Renault, the most skilled fan maker in all of Paris."

"The world, *mon ange*," Baptiste interrupted.

"And the most modest. Baptiste, this is Sinclair Carrington, Victor's recent recruit" Smiling at Sinclair in slightly mocking fashion, she added, "And for the moment my husband."

"Ah, a role for which I envy him." Baptiste sighed. "Having adored you these many years."

"Bah, you smooth-tongued rogue. You never adored aught but your precious fans and your horrid Paris."

Baptiste grinned. At last disengaging himself from Belle, he stepped forward. "Forgive me, monsieur. I forget myself. You must blame it on my excitement at seeing Isabelle again." He offered Sinclair his hand, his skin as dry and thin as the fan parchment, but his grip surprisingly strong.

"A pleasure to meet you at last, Monsieur Renault." Sinclair addressed the Frenchman in his native tongue.

Baptiste studied him, and Sinclair had the uncomfortable sensation of being sized up at a glance. He could not tell what the man's verdict was, but he nodded toward Belle, saying, "He speaks passable French for an Englishman."

"*Merci du compliment*, monsieur," Sinclair said wryly. He returned Baptiste's stare, attempting to do a little sizing of his own. The genial little Frenchman looked neither ruthless nor daring enough to be any sort of spy, let alone one playing a dangerous game of double dealing. Yet Sinclair would not have dismissed Baptiste as a suspect by his appearance alone. The chief thing that seemed to disqualify Renault was that according to Belle, the fan maker rarely ever strayed far from Paris. If he were passing information about the English coastline to Napoleon, he would have to have an accomplice.

Sinclair's gaze strayed to Belle, her apparent closeness to Renault giving rise to all manner of unpleasant thoughts. He was glad to relinquish them for the time being as Baptiste clapped his hands together briskly and said, "*Bien,* so it appears the three of us will have much to discuss, but not here, not now. You are tired from the journey, yes? I will show you upstairs. Come along, then."

The steps were narrow, poorly lit, and of such an alpine steepness that Belle and Sinclair moved cautiously for fear of a misstep. They were quickly outstripped by Baptiste, apparently well accustomed to the climb. His stream of chatter floated back down to them.

"I still live in the rooms behind the fan shop. Madame Fontaine's place, the apartment you will have, takes up the second and third floor. These stairs can be reached through the fan shop or the outer door, which has a porter on duty. He is a good fellow and will run errands for you."

Baptiste paused before an oak door on the first landing, fumbling through a ring of heavy keys attached to the belt beneath his apron. The steps twisted at a sharp angle, continuing upward to the next floor.

"Is anyone living in the apartments above us?" Belle asked.

"A retired shoemaker and his wife." Baptiste clucked his tongue in disgust as he tried first one key, then another. "But you need not worry about them. They keep to themselves. They will take no heed of your comings and goings."

"And the garrets?"

"At the moment empty. When Merchant wrote to say that he was also sending along Lazare—" Baptiste fairly spat the name. "I assumed that you would not wish him sharing your quarters, I thought that the garret would do well enough for the likes of him."

"I can see that you are a gentleman of great discernment, Monsieur Renault," Sinclair said.

Baptiste flashed him a grin, then grunted with satisfaction as he found the right key at last. Turning the knob, he shoved the door open, bowing Belle and Sinclair past him with a sweeping gesture.

As soon as Belle stepped across the threshold, she was beset by a cold draft and that musty smell of rooms left too long closed. She wrapped her arms about herself and shivered—not so much from the chill in the air, but a shiver of reminiscence as she studied her surroundings. The actress Mademoiselle Fontaine's apartment held all the garish glitter of a stage set with its high ceilings and neo-Greek cornices. The crystal chandelier would have appeared too ostentatious for a king's palace, let alone an apartment. The outer room was a combination antechamber and dining room, the walls hung with Indian cloth, the scattered chairs covered in crimson corded silk of Tours.

As Belle moved farther into the room, her footsteps seemed to strike out a lonely echo upon the black and white tiled floor, and she could almost feel herself dwindling into a child of ten again. The place reminded her depressingly of the sort of chambers and furnishings her actress mother had chosen those fortunate times when Mama had acquired herself a rich benefactor. Jolie Gordon never had known the difference between the lavish outlay of money and real elegance. She would have fancied herself quite the grand lady with such an establishment. But even at such a tender age Belle had known better and so had the tradesmen who had waited upon Mama, outwardly so polite as they vied for her custom. Only Belle had noticed their thinly veiled sneers and blushed with shame.

She had vowed then she would never live in the midst of such tawdry glamour. But like so many of her vows, it was worth about as much as the dust now coating the surface of a heavily ornate mahogany dining table. Belle trailed her gloved finger along it, leaving a glossy streak.

Baptiste bustled forward, apologizing. "Ah, I meant to get up here, have the place cleaned and aired, but I had no notion when you would arrive. I will get a fire going at once."

He flung open a set of double doors leading into a cream and gilt drawing room furnished with a stiff-backed settee supported by clawed griffin feet and cases of books whose pristine spines suggested that the volumes did little more than adorn the shelves. As Baptiste bent to his task by the hearth, Belle felt Sinclair touch upon her shoulder. She glanced up to meet his eyes and saw a frown creasing his brow.

"You don't like this place, do you?" he asked.

She started, but she did not know why. She ought to be accustomed by now to how easily Sinclair seemed to discern her thoughts.

"What's not to like?" she quipped. "It has all the charm and elegance of a high-priced brothel."

"We don't have to stay here. I am sure I could find us someplace else."

"Don't be ridiculous. We have a job to do and this place will serve our needs as well as any. You seem to keep forgetting that you are not an eager husband striving to please a new bride."

"So I do. What a fortunate thing that I have you to keep reminding me."

As Sinclair stalked away to explore another door, taking the stairs that led to the next floor of the apartment, Belle nearly called him back to apologize for her ungracious manner of rejecting his concern. But the next thing she knew, she might find herself explaining her reaction, telling him all about her mother, telling him far too much. If she had annoyed him, it was far better to leave it that way.

She followed Baptiste into the drawing room, stripping off her cloak and gloves, glad to have a moment alone with her old friend.

She had seen little of him these past years, since she never went into Paris and he never traveled far from that city. All that they had shared had been hurried meetings in Rouvray Forest, and those had always been too fraught with the urgency of varied missions to allow much time for idle chat.

Baptiste knelt before the hearth, applying the bellows to a tiny flame he had coaxed amongst the kindling. His ruddy cheeks and leather apron were smudged with ash, the fire's light dancing in his large brown eyes. He reminded Belle of an illustration she had once seen in a book of legends, the dwarf-king at work upon his forge, conjuring treasures from the dark secret places beneath the earth.

But then Baptiste had always given Belle the impression of not being quite of this world. Some of the smuggling feats they had pulled off together during the Revolution had been nothing short of wizard's work. She smiled softly at the remembrance, watching as his nimble fingers stacked more wood upon the fire.

"And how have you been, my old friend?" she asked.

"Well enough," he replied without looking up. "Not getting any younger."

"That is what you have been telling me ever since the day we first met."

"And it is as true now as it was then." Baptiste stood up, dusting off his knees. He paused, a chuckle erupting from deep in his chest. At Belle's inquiring gaze, he said, "I was thinking of that first day, *mon ange*. What a mad lady you were, all draped in your fake mourning, attempting to transport that coffin with the petite Duc de Ferriers hidden inside past the very noses of the soldiers sent out to look for him."

"I was doing well enough until the poor child happened to sneeze Then you popped out of nowhere, covering for me with your little snuff box, spilling so much of the stuff, you had half the street sneezing until no one could tell where the first sounds had come from."

"Ah, I recall it well! How ridiculous those great hulking soldiers looked, wheezing until the tears ran down their cheeks. Having thus come to your rescue, I would have been far wiser if I had gone about my own business."

"But think how much duller your life would have been. Besides, my 'funerals' proceeded much more smoothly after you had become partner to them."

"*C'est vrai.*" Baptiste scratched his chin, his thoughtful manner belied by the twinkle in his eye. "How many elderly aunts and uncles did you have perish in that one year alone?"

"Oh, a dozen at least. I was once part of a very large family."

Baptiste's smile faded and Belle could have bitten out her tongue. Her jest came too near the truth for Baptiste. Once the eldest of five siblings, he was now the last of the brothers Renault.

He turned away from her, picking up the poker and taking sharp jabs at the logs. "Why is it so easy to burn down the house," he said gruffly, "but wood never catches when you want it to?"

Belle realized he was signaling her that he wished the subject turned, and she regretted that it had ever been broached in the first place. Even the lighter recollections of their days during the Revolution invariably led to other ones more tragic. All memories were better left untouched.

While Baptiste struggled with the fire, Belle moved toward the chamber's high narrow windows, their latticed panes overhung with double curtains of gold-fringed silk. Belle parted them to allow more light into the room.

The Rue St. Honoré in all its bustle lay sprawled below her, and she pressed her face against the glass, the pane cool against her cheek. She had spent much of her time in that other Paris apartment at No. 17, too much perhaps, staring down into the street.

From such a lofty height she had once watched a king pass by in the frosty morning hours of a winter's day to keep his appointment with death, and a host of other folk as well, more humble perhaps but bearing the same regal dignity as they were trundled forth to meet the guillotine's embrace. Would she be able to behave with such courage if faced with the prospect of such a terrifying death? Belle had often wondered.

"You should not have come back, *mon ange.*"

Belle turned, surprised to discover Baptiste standing at her elbow, even more surprised by his remark.

"And I thought you were so glad to see me again," she mocked.

"I am—but it is a most selfish joy." His mouth turned down at the corners, and Belle sensed for the first time a subtle change in her friend. Despite what blows life had dealt him, Baptiste had ever remained Baptiste, a man with a fierce, unquenchable joy in life. Such a somber mood was most unlike him.

"I wish Merchant had sent someone else," he continued. "My Paris has never been good for you."

"Perhaps this time will be different. Who knows? If we succeed in removing Napoleon, restoring the king, perhaps you will finally be able to show me that glorious Paris of the old days which you have always told me about, the city that you so adore."

Baptiste merely shook his head, his dour expression calling forth to Belle once more the image of the brooding dwarf king.

"Eh *bien*, in any event you are here. There is naught to be done about it now." He sighed. Detaching the apartment key from his belt, he pressed it into her hand. "So! And what else would you have me be doing besides procuring you an apartment?"

His abrupt question caught her off guard. She had focussed so much of her energies into the task of simply getting to Paris, surviving the floodtide of memories, she had given little thought to the next step. As she ran her hand distractedly through her hair, her mind worked quickly.

"Give me the rest of the day to settle in, then tomorrow afternoon I want a meeting to lay out our strategy, you, myself, Sinclair, and Lazare. I also want you to get word to Marcellus Crecy and old Feydeau."

"That might prove difficult. Old Feydeau has been summoned by an angel with higher authority than yours."

Belle frowned at him in confusion.

"The Angel Gabriel." Baptiste rolled his eyes heavenward. "Feydeau is dead, *mon ami*."

Feydeau dead? Belle thought she should have been accustomed by now to the uncertainty of life, but Baptiste's words sent a shock through her all the same. Had it not been only a month ago that she had stood in the innyard of the Golden Sun, listening to Feydeau swear at her for having no outriders?

"When did he die? How?"

"A coaching accident, not long after your little adventure with the Coterins. Feydeau was believed to have been drunk."

"Feydeau had his faults," Belle protested, "but he loved his horses. I never saw him take the reins into his hands when he was anything less that stone-cold sober."

"There is always a first time, *mon ange*. Regrettably for Feydeau, it was also the last."

Belle frowned. It still made no sense to her, but she supposed the important fact was not how Feydeau had died, but that she had lost a reliable fellow agent.

"We shall need to find someone else to drive coach for us," she said.

"Leave that to me. I will see to it."

And Belle knew that Baptiste would. She had always been able to depend upon him. She caught his hand and squeezed it. "Despite the fact you were so unkind as to be wishing me gone, I am very glad you are here, my old friend. I would not have thought of accepting such a dangerous undertaking for one moment without your support."

The little Frenchman had never been in the least shy about accepting any sort of compliment. It therefore surprised Belle when he tugged free of her, his cheeks mottling with red.

"Bah! You've little use for an old stick like me, not with a strapping specimen like your Mr. Carrington about."

"He is not my Mr. Carrington," Belle said. "What is your opinion of Sinclair?"

She tried to make the question sound casual, but knew she had not succeeded when Baptiste eyed her shrewdly. "How eagerly she asks that. Like a shy little maid, bringing her latest swain home to meet Papa."

Belle tried to laugh at his raillery, but felt the color seep into her cheeks. "That doesn't answer my question."

"Eh *bien*, I think Monsieur Carrington is tall, young, handsome, everything that I am not. I also think you should take care, *mon ange*." Baptiste abruptly averted his gaze. "You should not place too much trust in any man.

"And now, I have more important things to consider than abducting the first consul of France. Mademoiselle Pierrepont will have my head if I don't have her fan finished by five of the clock."

Baptiste stood on tiptoe to plant a brusque kiss upon Belle's cheek before skittering out of the apartment. Belle stared at the door long after it had closed behind him, his words echoing through her mind. "You should not place too much trust in any man."

It was not like Baptiste to offer such platitudes or needless advice. Perhaps what disturbed her the most was that his words had not really seemed so much like advice. They had carried more the ring of a warning.

But a warning against whom? Sinclair? What could Baptiste have possibly detected about Sinclair upon such short acquaintance? This was absurd, Belle thought, rubbing her hand across her eyes. She was reading far too much into one casual remark. Likely she was tired. It had been a long day, a long journey. She would feel much better after a good night's rest.

But that notion brought a bitter smile to her lips. When had she ever enjoyed a restful night in Paris? Her gaze strayed back to the window. Her earlier excitement and her joy in seeing Baptiste again had fled. With a feeling of dread, she marked the sun's downward course, shedding a final burst of golden glory above the rooftops, the street shadows lengthening.

In a few hours it would be night, and eventually she would have to try to sleep. She might assure herself that she had survived the return to Paris in full light of day, but the dark would release all those phantoms she had subdued. The moment she closed her eyes, the nightmares would crowd forward: of Jean-Claude, of the Revolution, the massacres, the guillotine and the heavy, dank walls of the Conciergerie

No one has ever been slain by a memory, she told herself again. Then why could she already feel herself dying a little inside?

Eight

His first night in Paris was not the worst Sinclair had ever spent, but he could not rank it among the best, either. The next morning he awoke to the sound of rain drumming against the window and a dull ache behind his eyes.

He had slept poorly, and insomnia was not an affliction he was accustomed to endure. It was partly the fault of this damned bed, he thought as he rolled over with a groan. He stared with disgust at the golden canopy suspended tent-like above him, the corners caught in the grasp of fat, grinning cherubs. The mattress and pillows were too soft. His weight seemed to sink beneath a billowing cloud of silk, silk moreover that reeked of eau de heliotrope. The cloying scent clung to him, making him feel like he had spent the night with a Covent Garden doxy.

But the bed, he had to admit, had only been part of the problem. Most of his sleeplessness was owing to the sounds that had emanated from the bedchamber adjoining his, the creak of the floorboards, the footfalls which told him that Belle had stayed awake well past midnight.

Glancing toward the sheer bed-curtains drawn together to keep the draft from his naked flesh, Sinclair could just make out the gray light of morning and wondered if Belle had paced until nearly dawn. More terrifying dreams? Or was her restlessness owing to those memories that frequently brought that look of hopelessness to her eyes?

Sinclair's urge to go to her had been strong, but he knew from bitter experience she would spurn his comfort. Belle seemed to have learned a long time ago to endure her pain alone. Who had helped her to con that lesson, the Comte de Egremont, Jean-Claude Varens? Astonishing, Sinclair thought, that one could begin to harbor an intense loathing for such a noble gentleman, one that he scarcely knew.

All things considered, it was for the best that he had curbed his desire to slip into Belle's room. He was no saint, and Belle had been honest enough to admit she was not impervious to his touch. What might have begun as comfort could have ended far differently. He had known casual encounters in bed before and so, he suspected, had Belle, but he feared that the emotion that pulsed between them was too intense for that. She might finish by hating him, and he didn't want that. But it was a prospect he had to face all the same, for it had occurred to him there might be one other reason to account for her sleeplessness.

She could be suffering from a guilty conscience. An ugly thought that—and he had lain awake a great deal of the night, attempting to convince himself beyond all doubt that it could not be so, that it could not possibly be Belle who was the traitor he had been sent to capture. His every instinct told him that she was not, but could instinct be trusted when clouded by an image of hair of spun gold; eyes, the color of an azure sky; a face so rife with hidden strength and delicate beauty it could haunt a man to the end of his days? How he prayed the counteragent would prove to be Lazare. If it was, he could derive great pleasure from putting an end to Lazare's activities in passing information to the enemy.

Slowly Sinclair raised to a sitting position, wincing at his stiff muscles. However the affair turned out, he needed to stop thinking and start acting. He was in Paris now. Time to cease the speculations and set about finding out the truth.

He started to fling the coverlet aside when he heard the door to his chamber swing open. Astonished, he froze in position, observing a shadowy figure rustling about beyond the bedcurtains. Who in thunder would enter his room that boldly? He had been careless in not locking his door, in not keeping a weapon close to hand, especially with a madman like Lazare, overly fond of his knife, living just two floors above in the garret.

Cautiously Sinclair parted his bedcurtains just enough to peer out. He relaxed somewhat. It was only that woman Paulette, Belle's erstwhile maid, her brown curls peeking out from beneath a frilled cap. She had deposited a white pitcher upon the dressing table and now stooped to pick Sinclair's shirt off the floor. In one day he had already managed to reduce his room to a state of comfortable clutter. Paulette would have appeared the image of the perfect maid tidying up, garbed in her somber gown, except for the thin red ribbon forming a bright slash about her throat and an indefinable something in her manner that rendered Sinclair uneasy.

As he watched her bend to retrieve his breeches, all but caressing the fabric, he felt his flesh crawl. Thrusting the bedcurtain back, he gripped the sheet about himself and boomed out, "What the devil do you think you are doing in here?"

She straightened with a tiny gasp, clasping her hands to her ample bosom. "Monsieur Carrington! How you startled me. I thought you still asleep."

"That doesn't answer my question."

"I brought you up some hot water for shaving and started to tidy some of your things. Since you have no valet—"

"I manage quite well without one. You might have seen fit to knock, mademoiselle."

"But I did, monsieur. You must not have heard me." She lowered her lashes demurely but not before Sinclair sensed her hot

gaze rake over him. He felt at a distinct disadvantage. It was difficult to appear indignant reclining on a bed, garbed only in a sheet.
With a low curse he stretched down to scoop up his dressing robe.
Retreating behind the bed-curtains, he struggled into the garment,
tying the sash with a hard tug.

When he emerged, he discovered Mistress Beauvais had
nonchalantly gone on with her task of cleaning up, moving toward
his cloak draped over a chair and his umbrella. Sinclair leaped out
of bed and started toward her, his bare feet padding across the
thick rosette-patterned carpet. He reached her side in time to
snatch the umbrella from her grasp and toss it upon a gilt-edged
dressing table. It was unlikely that anyone could detect the secret
compartment in the handle that housed his papers, but he wasn't
taking any chances.

"*Merci bien*, mademoiselle," he said. "If I require anything
else, I will ring."

She used the opportunity of his nearness to sidle up against
him. "I could help you with your shaving," she purred. "I have
helped many gentlemen before."

"I would never trust any woman with a razor."

She flung back her head, giving a throaty laugh. "Monsieur is
so droll." Making no attempt to hide the hunger in her gaze, she
brushed her hips against his. "Monsieur wears no nightshirt? Even
in October our nights in Paris can be cold. You will catch your
death."

"I'll be sure to build a large fire," he said.

She ran her hand up the folds of his wine-colored robe, her
fingertips grazing the exposed vee of his chest. "I am very good at
starting fires."

"I'll wager you are." He arrested the movement of her hand,
thrusting it back at her. "But you won't be starting any here."

Her eyes narrowed to slits, her full lips pursing into a pout.
Sinclair took her by the elbow, preparing to steer her out the door

if necessary, when he halted, dismayed to hear Belle's voice calling from the adjoining chamber.

"Paulette! Where have you got to? Paulette?"

Though not guilty of anything, Sinclair could not explain the impulse that caused him to frown at Paulette and indicate with a jerk of his head that she should take her leave as silently as possible.

Her teeth parted in a malicious smile. "*Oui, ma chère ami*!" she shouted. "I am in here."

Sinclair bit back an urge to curse her. The door between his chamber and Belle's swung open.

"Paulette? What on earth are you doing in—" Belle broke off. Clad only in her nightgown and dressing robe, her blond hair spilling about her shoulders, she drew up short on the threshold. She stared first at Paulette, her gaze then traveling questioningly toward Sinclair.

To his annoyance, he felt the red creep up his neck, and he tugged self-consciously at his robe, adjusting it more tightly over the bared expanse of his chest.

As Belle's initial shock faded, she arched one brow. "I beg your pardon, Mr. Carrington. I would not have barged in upon you, but hearing Paulette in here, I assumed you must have already gone below. I did not realize you had er—pressed her into your service."

"I was just telling Miss Beauvais that her services were not required," Sinclair snapped.

Unperturbed by the embarrassment she had caused, Paulette sauntered to the door. She cast a wicked look back over her shoulder. "Another time, perhaps, monsieur."

Sinclair glared at her, but the woman had already slipped past Belle into the other room. Belle also made a movement to vanish, but Sinclair shot forward, catching the side of the door to prevent her doing so.

"Belle, I know how that must have looked, but—"

"You don't have to explain anything to me, Mr. Carrington."

Her voice was maddeningly cool. "1 am not your wife. Remember?"

"All the same, I don't want you having the impression that I was trying to seduce that French strumpet."

Belle's lip quivered. She tried to look away, but she could no longer hide the gleam of amusement in her eyes. "Alas, I know my Paulette very well. Though I always thought her tastes ran more to English sailors, I could tell when I entered that she was, shall we say —rendering you somewhat uncomfortable."

Sinclair folded his arms across his chest. "To put it mildly. I am not accustomed to having my virtue assaulted."

A trill of laughter escaped Belle. The sound coming from her was so rare, so delightful, Sinclair forgot his annoyance. He stared down at her. After a night spent in a bedchamber as heavily perfumed as a Turkish seraglio, Belle was like a breath of sweet English country air. A fresh womanly scent emanated from her.

Her face was a trifle pale, but he had imagined that she would look pale upon rising, her complexion almost translucent. His gaze traced the slender column of her throat, the neckline of her night-gown just visible beneath the robe she wore. That, too, was as he would have imagined, so totally like what she would choose, of fine linen with no lacy frills. Likely it would cling to her skin, revealing just a hint of the blushing hue of her curves beneath.

The sight of her never failed to stir his senses, and he shifted uncomfortably, trying to check his errant thoughts.

"So how did you ever become connected with a doxy like that Beauvais woman?" he asked. She does not seem like the sort of effi-cient companion you would choose."

"Paulette does well enough when set to simple tasks. I never tax her with any great matters. She can play the role of lady's maid to perfection. Even you must admit she looks the part."

"Except for that damned ribbon she always has tied about her neck. Why does she wear that thing?"

Belle's smile faded. "Paulette wears it as a form of memorial. Her parents both died upon the guillotine."

"Don't you find that a little macabre?"

"We all have our own ways of remembering and forgetting." Her voice sounded wistful, a little sad.

Before he could stop himself, Sinclair reached up one finger and traced one of the delicate blue shadows beneath her eyes. "And what were you trying so hard to forget last night, Angel?"

She shied away from his touch."I never sleep too well in Paris." I am sorry if I disturbed you."

"You didn't disturb me. I only wish you had ..." He let the thought trail away unspoken, sensing her withdrawal even before she took a step back.

"I think we both had better get dressed," she said. "The others will be here for the meeting soon."

She slipped back into her own bedchamber and closed the door upon him. Again. But this time he made no movement to stop her.

"You only wished she had what, Carrington?" He mocked himself. Come to him last night, let him hold her in his arms while she poured out all the secrets of her heart? Everything is all right, Angel. You can tell me anything. Trust me.

Sinclair's mouth twisted into a frown of self-disgust. Well, his father had always told him that being a spy was a profession only for a blackguard. For the first time in his life he was beginning to fear the old man was right.

Several hours later, after a light breakfast, Sinclair stood in the drawing room. Hands on hips, his dove-colored frock coat shoved back, he watched the rain wash past the tall latticed windows. It gushed from gutters above, sending a stream of water cascading upon the hapless pedestrians in the street below. Huddled beneath cloaks and umbrellas, they scurried along like soaked rats through the river of chocolate-colored mud which the Rue St. Honoré had become. With a warm fire crackling on the hearth behind him, Sinclair felt grateful to be up here, rather than out there.

Isabelle Varens in many respects made his job seem well nigh impossible, but in this one instance she had rendered his task easier for him. By calling this meeting she had gathered all his chief suspects under one roof, giving him a chance to assess each of them.

Turning from the window, he faced the other three men who occupied the drawing room. Lazare slouched on a wing-backed chair before the fire, his muddy boots perched on a delicate table. Although divested of his greatcoat, he had not troubled to remove his red Phrygian cap, the ends of his white-blond hair damp from the rain. It was abundantly clear that he was tired of waiting for Belle. He kept twisting a length of rope with his large hands, the firelight casting his hideous scar into shadow and accenting the sullen set of his aquiline profile.

The fallen angel Lucifer, Sinclair thought wryly, toasting his buttocks in hell. Lazare remained his favorite candidate for the counteragent, but he could not afford to indulge in wishful thinking.

His gaze moved on to the man seated on the settee opposite from Lazare. Marcellus Crecy, Sinclair's most recent acquaintance, the last of the names on his list. The fragile piece of furniture groaned under the man's bulk. Despite his size, Crecy was a handsome man, his silvery hair swept back from a leonine brow. He exuded a manner of suave charm, his waistcoat exquisitely tailored to fit his portly girth. At the moment he appeared to have nothing weightier upon his mind than nibbling pastries from a china plate balanced upon his knee.

Sinclair mentally reviewed what information he had been provided about the man, Crecy was descended from a prominent noble family, the grandson of a marquis, but at present Crecy was the proprietor of a most discreet and successful gaming house. He might in truth be a devoted member of Merchant's society, longing for the return of the monarchy, or he might well be content with his life just as it was. Only time would tell,

Dismissing Crecy for the moment, Sinclair shifted his attention to the last of the three. Baptiste Renault was not as easy to mount a covert study of. The little man never kept still, leaping up to jab the poker at the fire, to straighten some books upon the shelf, or to peer out the door for Belle. His restlessness reminded Sinclair of his brother Chuff's fidgets, but with a marked difference. Renault's movements appeared to stem more from a man not accustomed to idleness or a man whose mind was not quite at ease.

These then were his choices. Despite a professed loyalty to Merchant's cause, one of these three had likely been selling maps of the English coastline and encampments to Napoleon Bonaparte. These, all his chief suspects but for one ...

Belle's light step was heard approaching in the antechamber. She paused a moment, framed in the drawing room's double doorway, Garbed in forest green jaconet, she wore matching spencer, the close fitting jacket trimmed with military frogging. Her golden hair was swept up in a chignon, the rather severe style emphasizing her high cheekbones.

Sinclair mentally applauded her choice. She was a woman entering a roomful of men over whom she needed to establish dominance, be acknowledged as their leader. To do that she needed to suppress all hint of softness. Yet Sinclair suspected she knew how to make full use of her femininity, her beauty when occasion demanded.

She was either the most complex woman he had ever known or the most accomplished actress. She insisted she worked only for the money, yet she had forfeited her pay to rescue the Coterin family. Sinclair had seen her look strong, almost ruthless, as she did now, and he had held her in his arms, vulnerable, trembling like a child from a bad dream. He had watched how tenderly she could caress a small boy's curls, but he knew those same delicate-veined hands were equally capable of shooting a man.

Isabelle Gordon ... Isabelle Varens? What other names might she have?

"Who are you really, Angel?" Sinclair murmured to himself. He needed to know as much for himself as any other reason.

Stepping into the room, her glance angled toward him as though she perceived how strongly his thoughts centered upon her. Sinclair was quick to erase the troubled frown from his face, and her gaze moved on to encompass the other men in turn.

"Gentlemen." She acknowledged them all in her cool, clear voice. Baptiste beamed at her while Crecy stopped eating long enough to scramble to his feet with a polished bow. Only Lazare remained seated, twisting his head to stare at her.

"Our intrepid leader at last," he drawled.

Belle ignored him as though he had not even spoken. "I am glad that all of you could be so prompt. Pray do not stand on formality. Please be seated."

Baptiste and Crecy settled themselves upon the settee. Sinclair drew up a stiff-backed chair, but remained near the windows, deliberately keeping outside of the circle, the better to observe. As Belle closed the double doors behind her, Lazare called out, "So where's the dark-haired slut?"

"If you mean Paulette," Belle said, "I saw no need for her to join us today. She is usefully engaged in taking care of more practical matters such as the marketing."

"Indeed." Crecy paused from licking his fingers to chortle. "Even spies must eat."

"Some more so than others." Lazare shot him a contemptuous look, before turning back to Belle. "You kept us cooling our heels long enough. We are all breathless to hear your instructions."

With a fixed smile, Belle approached Lazare."To begin with, you can remember you are under my roof, not in a tavern." She swept Lazare's feet off the table, knocking them to the floor. Then she snatched the cap off his head, tossing it into his lap.

Lazare caught it reflexively. He stiffened, his eyes flashing dangerously. Sinclair tensed, coming half off his chair. If Lazare made one move-

But with great visible effort Lazare controlled his temper. He stuffed the cap down on the seat beside him and settled back. Sinclair sat back down, yet felt far from easy. Lazare, his mouth set in a sullen line, resumed snapping the ends of the rope between his fingers.

You are going to have more than your share of trouble with that one, Angel, Sinclair mused grimly. If Belle thought so, too, no sign of it appeared in her cool demeanor, but Crecy mopped nervously at his brow with a handkerchief.

"It would seem to already be a trifle warm in here," Crecy muttered.

"I will open the window a crack." The restless Baptiste was ready to leap up at once to do so, but Belle stayed him.

"You are forgetting the rain."

"And the infernal noise from the street," Lazare growled.

"That is the music of Paris." Although Baptiste subsided back in his seat, he raised his face eagerly to Belle. "Did you happen to notice yester eve, *mon ange*-the bells of Notre Dame? They ring again."

Belle relaxed her rigid manner enough to smile at him. "I noticed, my friend."

"That at least is one good that Monsieur Bonaparte has brought, the restoration of our faith."

Lazare snorted. "The restoration of superstition, old man. The way of the wealthy to control the minds of the peasants."

A glint of mischief twinkled in Baptiste's eyes. "As one of the latter, Lazare, I expect you would know."

Before Lazare could retort, Belle stepped smoothly in between them. "We already wander from the purpose of this meeting, gentlemen. I don't think I need to remind you what this is. We had best begin by pooling what information we already possess on Napoleon Bonaparte."

"Damned little—" Lazare began, but Belle cut him off.

"You who have been in Paris for the past few years possess an advantage over me and Sinclair. Thus far we have only obtained a glimpse of the first consul. Does he often parade thus through the streets?"

"Frequently," Crecy said. "He believes such a display gives the citizens a feeling of security in their government."

"It works quite well," Baptiste added in jovial tones. "I know every time I see our brave young general, I sleep a little more snugly in my bed."

Lazare leaned forward impatiently. "This is the plan, then? To snatch Bonaparte off the streets in full view of the populace of Paris? Wonderfully clever. How brilliant."

Sinclair shifted on his chair. It was his plan to observe in silence, to have his presence overlooked as much as possible, but he was beginning to have a bellyful of Lazare's sarcastic remarks.

"Maybe if you could hold your tongue, Lazare," he said, his pleasant tone not quite disguising his irritation, "Belle might have a chance to explain what she has in mind."

Lazare's attention snapped to Sinclair. Giving him a hard stare, his hands jerked a knot in the rope with which he toyed. "And maybe, Englishman, if you want to keep your tongue—"

"Gentlemen, please. We are not here to quarrel amongst ourselves." Pacing before the fireplace, Belle heaved a wearied sigh. She turned back, appearing to gather the ends of her patience. "Of course I don't intend to assault Bonaparte in the streets, Lazare. Part of our course of action will be to determine less public places where he might be found."

"Perhaps I should get quill and ink and keep some notes," Crecy offered.

"No," Belie said. "I don't like anything to be put in writing which could wind up as evidence in the wrong hands. Besides it is unnecessary. I have an excellent memory."

Crecy returned to regarding the crumbs on his empty plate. Did he seem unduly disappointed? Sinclair wondered. Perhaps Marcellus did not have such a keen memory. A damned inconvenience if one were eager to pass the details of this meeting along to Bonaparte.

"Now," Belle continued. "What other places in Paris does Bonaparte frequent? Where does he go to take his relaxation?"

"Certainly not to my gaming establishment," Crecy said with a sigh, "or to anyone else's for that matter."

"The consul must be given that much credit," Baptiste added. "He has very few vices."

"It seems to me you give Bonaparte a little too much credit," Lazare snapped. "I begin to think you secretly admire the man."

"Oh, I positively dote upon him. After all, he is the only man in Paris not much taller than I." Baptiste flashed a wide grin. He was clearly baiting the humorless Lazare and enjoying every moment of it. An angry flush crept up Lazare's neck.

Sinclair suppressed a smile. He might have enjoyed it, too, if only he could be certain that underneath the jocular manner the little Frenchman was not in earnest with his praises of Napoleon.

With a quelling frown for both Lazare and Baptiste, Belle dragged them ruthlessly back to the topic at hand. "All right. So Monsieur Bonaparte does not care for cards or dice. What does he like?"

Mostly from the observances of Baptiste and Crecy, a sketchy portrait of Napoleon emerged. When Sinclair thought of Bonaparte at all, it was always as a brilliant general whose bold tactics had made him the scourge of most of the other armies in Europe. As he listened, he learned of another side to the man, the hardworking first consul, so absorbed in the business of government, he spared little time for anything else. Except for an occasional visit to the theater, Napoleon made few social outings all but

eschewing the fashionable salons and soirees. Most of his enter-
taining was done at receptions held at the Tuileries. Even at supper
parties, he barely permitted himself more than twenty minutes to
dine.

After a half hour of such discussion, Belle heaved a sigh, apparently finding the information far from encouraging. Massaging the
bridge of her nose as though to rub the weariness from her eyes,
she said, "However we decide to proceed, we will still need certain
things. A light coach that can travel swiftly, very plain and
nondescript."

"I can supply that," Crecy volunteered.

"Alas," Baptiste said. "I have not as yet thought of someone to
replace Feydeau as your driver. If it comes down to it, I suppose I
can always take on the task myself."

Lazure broke his unusual stretch of silence to glance mockingly toward Sinclair. "Perhaps Monsieur Carrington knows how
to drive a coach. It would give him something more useful to do
than sit in a corner and stare at all of us."

"I am a fair hand with the reins," Sinclair said, returning
Lazare's stare. "Enough to avoid an accident like the one
Feydeau—"

Sinclair halted. It didn't take Belle's sudden intake of breath
for him to realize he had just made a serious mistake.

"How did you know about Feydeau's accident?" she asked.
"Baptiste only informed me of it yesterday afternoon."

The attention of the entire room was suddenly focused on
Sinclair. Although he did not betray his consternation by so much
as a flicker of an eyelash, he felt his mouth go dry. Belle's eyes
clouded with trouble and not a little suspicion. Baptiste and Crecy
merely looked curious, but Lazure's gaze sparked with malice, an
almost predatory gleam.

Sinclair thought quickly, deciding to take a grave risk. "Sorry. I
must have forgotten to mention it. Shortly before I met you on the
docks at Portsmouth, I received word from Merchant via Quentin

Crawley, about the old man's death, that we needed to look out for a new coachman."

"It would have been convenient if you had passed the information on to me," Belle said.

"Between one thing and another, it simply slipped my mind."

A derisive snort came from Lazare. Belle did not look quite satisfied, but after a lengthy pause, she said, "I suppose it is not that important."

She turned back to discussing Bonaparte, and the tense moment passed. But Sinclair did not relax. He was going to have to be much more careful. The attention of the others was centered on Belle. Except for Lazare. He continued to regard Sinclair with a smirk and a lift of his brows.

Almost as if he knows, Sinclair thought, then dismissed the notion as ridiculous. There was no reason why Lazare should. Sinclair had been extremely careful to conceal his identity. His recent gaff was simply making him edgy.

With some difficulty he forced his thoughts away from Lazare, trying to concentrate on what Belle was now saying.

"I need to get closer to Bonaparte, observe him for myself. Baptiste, is there any chance that a certain Monsieur and Madame Carrington might be able to attend one of those receptions you mentioned earlier?"

"I anticipated you might ask that, *mon ange*." Baptiste's smile was a trifle smug. "It so happens one of my customers is Madame Josephine Bonaparte. The lady is a husband's nightmare, a tradesman's dream. She spends with great liberality. I delivered five new fans to her at the Tuileries only last week."

What a convenient way that would be of passing along information, Sinclair thought, and without rousing a shade of suspicion.

"Would Madame Bonaparte invite an unknown couple to the palace at her fan maker's recommendation?" Crecy objected.

"Of course not, imbecile," Baptiste said. "But visiting the

palace gives me access to many other people, people who handle the invitations, people who understand an honest bribe."

"And how soon could you secure us such an invitation?" Belle asked.

"Would tonight be too soon?" Baptiste produced a square of gilt-edged vellum from his pocket. He handed it to Belle. She slit the seal with her fingernail. Even Lazare craned his neck with curiosity as she examined the paper's contents. Her lips parted in a brilliant smile.

"You are as much a wizard as ever, Baptiste."

Belle crossed the room to Sinclair. "Well, Mr. Carrington, I trust you brought along your finest evening attire. It would appear we are going to the palace."

With a forced smile, Sinclair accepted the invitation she handed to him. He could not get over the ease with which such a thing had been obtained. A little too easy perhaps? He was beset by a feeling that from this moment on, he had best walk with great care. Like traversing a field set with hidden snares, one misstep could bring him to disaster.

Still musing over the invitation, Sinclair did not notice the meeting was breaking up until the other men rose to take their leave.

"But stay one moment more, gentlemen," Baptiste said. He bustled out of the drawing room only to return bearing a tray laden with a flagon of wine and glasses. "Tonight we take the first step in our perilous venture. I think it only right we drink a toast to its success."

Crecy smacked his lips in approval of the suggestion as Baptiste poured out the wine. Belle regarded him with amused indulgence. Only Lazare appeared inclined to refuse, but he finally accepted a glass with his customary bad grace.

"Monsieur Carrington?" Baptiste beckoned Sinclair to join them.

The five of them stood before the hearth in a solemn circle, raising their glasses. The wine sparkled blood-red in the firelight's glow.

"To our success, gentlemen," Belle said.

"May we all come through unscathed," Crecy added, "safe from the embrace of Madame Guillotine."

"If we fail, we need not worry about that, my friend," the irrepressible Baptiste called out. "The people of Paris would tear us to pieces long ere we reached the scaffolding."

On this grim note they clinked glasses and drank. As Sinclair sipped his wine, he studied the others—one of whom he was certain was not sincere. One who had toasted, smiled, and drank was secretly planning to betray them all.

The toast finished, they all returned their glasses to the tray. It disturbed Sinclair to note that Belle's glass alone remained nearly full. She had barely tasted the wine.

She stood by Sinclair's side as the other men gathered up their hats and cloaks. Crecy was the last to exit, bowing himself out, expressing his thanks for their gracious hospitality.

Sinclair had to suppress an urge to erupt into laughter. Crecy's words spun the most ludicrous illusion as though he and Belle were indeed an ordinary married couple, on an ordinary afternoon, bidding their callers farewell.

Yet one glance at the chair vacated by Lazare abruptly ended any illusion and equally any desire to laugh. Lazare had left his rope behind. It was fashioned into a perfect noose.

Nine

With the others gone, a silence settled over the drawing room, the rain beating out a monotonous rhythm against the window. Belle glanced out at the slate-colored sky. Not a hint of the sun. The rain was likely to continue all day—typical Paris weather as she remembered it, the city forever washed in gray.

Watching the rivulets trickle down the panes of glass, she reviewed the morning's events. The meeting had gone well enough, she judged. She had maintained a reasonable amount of control over Lazare, as much as anyone could. But she was glad he had no share in what was to take place tonight.

At last she would meet Bonaparte face to face—the plot would begin to take form. From this night on, there could be no turning back from the course she would set into motion. A shiver—part fear, part anticipation—coursed through her.

But first there was the interminable dreariness of the afternoon to be gotten through. She was not the sort of woman to spend an entire day preparing herself for an evening's event. Time enough to worry about her appearance whenever Paulette returned.

Her chief concern for now was what to do in the hours

stretching until then, hours to be spent in the apartment, alone with Sinclair.

Although she had her back to him, she remained conscious of his presence. She knew he sprawled in the chair where Lazare had sat. As soon as the men had gone, Sinclair had made himself comfortable, stripping off his frock coat and cravat. Even without looking at him, Belle retained a clear picture, Sinclair's image imprinted upon her mind, the way his dark head rested against the back of the chair, the cast of his rakehell features for once solemn and thoughtful.

He was so quiet. Too quiet for Sinclair. What was he thinking? She had no idea. Sometimes she wondered if she ever truly knew what went on in his head. It occurred to her more forcibly than ever how little she knew of her partner.

Belle frowned as her thoughts shifted back to Sinclair's disturbing remark about Feydeau. Sinclair's explanation had been plausible enough, and yet it had startled her, his betraying knowledge that she found unaccountable.

Over the years, Belle had acquired an instinct for detecting when a man was being less than honest. When she had asked Sinclair about Feydeau, she could have sworn Sinclair was lying to her. And all those questions about Paulette this morning. Sometimes Sinclair seemed far more bent upon seeking information about the society than about Napoleon. But why?

Vague suspicions drifted through Belle's mind as intangible as wisps of smoke. She shook her head as though to clear it. Perhaps once more she was building a case upon trifles. That was the difficulty sometimes. Being suspicious, not trusting, had become second nature to her. It had saved her life upon more than one occasion. But life on the edge as Sinclair described it could be a wearisome affair.

Hearing Sinclair stirring at last, she turned to face him. He had shifted to the edge of his chair, removed his pocket watch from its fob to examine it, shook it first, then held it to his ear.

As though feeling her gaze upon him, he glanced up and smiled. When he smiled at her like that, she felt that she knew him very well, his eyes reaching out to encompass her in their warmth, something in his glance establishing a conspiracy between them, a conspiracy of hearts which shut out the rest of the world.

An absurd thought. Yet she found herself returning his smile, slowly pacing toward the side of the room where he sat. She stood over him, watching as he deftly wielded a tiny gold key, winding his watch. The timepiece bore a look of spartan plainness, the face set with bold black Roman numerals, no scene engraved upon the gold case, yet somehow more elegant for its simplicity.

"That's a most handsome timepiece," she remarked.

"A gift from my father," Sinclair said, without looking up from his task. "One of those rare occasions I ever merited his approval."

It was the first time Belle could ever recall Sinclair mentioning anything about family. Drawing up a stool from in front of the hearth, she settled herself upon it, so close that she could lean upon the arm of Sinclair's chair.

"You and your father," she asked, "you do not get on well?"

"Well enough—as long as neither of us speaks to the other."

He spoke in his usual light fashion, but Belle detected an undercurrent, a hint of regret that perhaps only she could have caught, harboring so many regrets herself.

As she observed him give the key one final turn, she said, "I never had the opportunity to quarrel with my father. I never even knew who he was."

Why had she told Sinclair that? she wondered. Perhaps there was something about sitting before a crackling fire on a wet gray day that invited confidences. Perhaps for some odd reason she could not define, she felt it was time Sinclair knew the truth about her.

"I am illegitimate, the daughter of a Drury Lane actress." She pretended to gaze into the orange-gold glow of the flames, all the while covertly studying him, awaiting his reaction.

"Well, Angel," he drawled as he reattached the watch to its fob. "I have frequently been called a bastard myself."

His response provoked a laugh from her, the words so irreverent, so improper, so totally Sinclair. She had just told him her greatest source of shame, the secret that had devastated Jean-Claude Varens, and Sinclair had not raised so much as an eyebrow. Instead he had managed to make her laugh over something that had always caused her pain.

In that instant she knew what it was about Sinclair that disarmed her. He never judged. He gave her complete freedom to be exactly who she was, nothing more, nothing less. A rather overwhelming gift and a little frightening. She was not sure she was ready to accept it as yet.

She felt relieved when he turned the subject, although she suspected he might have been doing so to avoid any more discussion about his own past. Picking up the rope that Lazare had been toying with earlier, he said, "I suppose you noticed our friend Lazare's handiwork."

"The noose? Yes, I observed him fashioning it during the meeting. I expect he thought to unnerve me."

"Angel—"

"I know." She cut him off, recognizing Sinclair's warning growl. "You want to tell me again to be careful. I shall. I do assure you that I shall keep Lazare's role in this affair to a minimum."

Sinclair did not appear satisfied, but he swallowed what he had been about to say. He fiddled with the rope, and the knots Lazare had made easily came undone. Sinclair gave a snort of contempt. "The man appears to be handier with his knife than a rope. Whatever part he plays, I hope if there is any trussing up to be done, you don't entrust it to him."

Belle smiled. "If anything in that line becomes necessary, I could do it myself. I tie a very wicked knot."

Sinclair said nothing, casting a skeptical glance at her hands. She could tell he was assessing the softness and whiteness of her fingers, then drawing his own doubtful conclusions. This hint of male arrogance sent a prickle of annoyance through her.

"Believe me, Mr. Carrington," she said. "If I ever tied your hands together, you would not get them undone very quickly."

"Care to wager on that?" A wicked sparkle appeared in his eyes.

"No," she retorted, "for I fear any wagers made with you would not involve money."

"But what have you to fear?" He favored her with the most maddeningly superior grin. "If milady is so sure of herself."

He dropped the rope in her lap. She should have laughed off his remarks and let it go at that. But she had never, from the time she was a little girl, borne sense enough to back down from a dare.

Sinclair clasped his hands together in front of him and docilely held them out to her. Slowly Belle picked up the rope.

"Oh, no," she said. "I would never make it that easy for someone I had captured. Stand up, turn around, and put your hands behind you."

He did as he was told, but with such a smirk on his face, Belle resisted the urge to give the rope an extra hard tug as she began knotting it about his wrists. Frequently she had found one could judge the strength of a man by his hands. Sinclair's tanned fingers were long and well formed, the tips slightly calloused. She could feel the tautness of the muscle coming down from his forearm and took great care to make the knots tight, well secured.

"There." She stood back, admiring her handiwork. "I would likely bind your ankles as well, but since I don't have another rope, this will do for demonstration purposes."

He cast a patronizing look over his shoulder. "If you wish, I will pretend to have my ankles tied." Stiffening his legs together, he took a slight hop forward.

"Step back and give me a little room. After capturing me, I would assume you went on your way, pursuing your nefarious schemes."

"Consider me gone." Belle dipped into a mocking curtsy. She moved back to the doorway, hands propped on her hips, waiting to see what he would do next.

Sinclair dropped to his knees and rolled to one side. Belle watched him flex his shoulders back, straining to move his arms past the hard curve of his buttocks, then down over his legs in an effort to draw his hands up in front, It was rather an incredible maneuver, considering Sinclair's muscular build and the tightness of the shirt and waistcoat restraining him. He appeared to be quite limber, but from the beads of perspiration dotting his brow and the set of his lips, Belle could tell the movement was not performed without some pain.

She had never intended the foolish game to go that far. "Sinclair—"

"Quiet," he said through clenched teeth. "I need to concentrate."

Taking a deep breath, he exhaled and with a final strain that seemed likely to dislocate his shoulders, he succeeded in getting his arms behind his knees. With one fluid motion, he eased his bound hands around his feet, then drew them up in front of himself, struggling to a sitting position, a triumphant expression on his flushed features.

"Very good," Belle said grudgingly. "But now what? I wouldn't have been stupid enough to leave a knife behind or any sort of a candle for you to burn through the rope."

"Then I shall just have to do it the hard way." Raising his hands, he began tugging at the knots with his teeth. Belle folded her arms over her chest, watching him in confident silence. There was no way he was ever going to undo her knots in that fashion. None whatsoever.

It took him less than ten minutes. He leapt to his feet with a self-satisfied flex of his back muscles and dangled the undone length of rope before her eyes. The chagrin must have shown upon her face for he laughed and said, "There was nothing wrong with your knots, only your choice of rope, Angel. It wouldn't seem so, but this thick hemp is far easier to undo than say a silken cord from a robe. Never let your captive dictate his own bindings."

"I shall strive to remember that."

With a mischievous glint in his eyes, he fingered the rope and advanced upon her. "Now it's my turn."

"Oh, no." She shook her head firmly. But he continued to stalk toward her. Belle backed away. Slowly, but relentlessly, he pursued her around the chair. Belle suppressed a ripple of laughter.

"Behave yourself, Mr. Carrington," she said in as stern a tone as she was capable of. "I would never permit my enemy to tie me up."

"What would you do to stop me?" he asked in tones of silken menace. He had her nearly backed up against the bookcase, twin devils dancing in his eyes. Well, Belle thought, if he insisted upon pursuing this game of pretense, she was going to make up a few of her own rules.

She startled him by snatching an object from the shelf behind her. It was only the end of an unlit candle, but she brandished it at him.

"I would draw forth my concealed pistol." With her thumb she feigned cocking the 'weapon'. "Now you must stop or I will blow a hole in your chest."

She was not certain if Sinclair would acknowledge the imaginary pistol. His lips twitched with amusement. Still clutching the rope, he raised his hands, such an expression of deceptive meekness upon his face, she did laugh.

It was all so absurd. She did not know why she was enjoying it so much. Maybe because so many times she had enacted this scene in deadly earnest. There had never been any place in her life for frolic or lightsome behavior. And maybe it had something to do with the undercurrent of challenge that had existed between her and Sinclair from the very beginning. She became suddenly aware of how her heart thudded, of a stirring in her blood.

That was her mistake, forgetting one of her own basic rules and allowing her attention to wander when training a weapon upon someone. Sinclair was quick to sense how she wavered and took full advantage. With a lightning-quick movement he tossed the rope toward her face. In the second she took to blink, he pounced, deflecting the hand that held the make-believe weapon. If it had been a pistol, it would have discharged harmlessly in the air.

Seizing her wrist, Sinclair forced her arm down and the candle end dropped to the floor. He pinned her against the bookcase, his face only inches away, his eyes glittering.

"Checked again, milady."

Did he truly think so? Belle tilted her face upward, her lips curved in a deceiving smile, Then she trod down hard on his instep.

Sinclair's smirk vanished, his eyes widening with pained surprise. "You little vixen—" He had loosened his grip enough for her to hook her foot about his ankle, setting him off balance. But the maneuver backfired. As Sinclair went down, he pulled her with him. As they tumbled to the carpet, he still maintained his grasp. They wrestled for a moment, banging into the chair, until Belle felt her carefully secured hairpins coming free, her tresses falling about her shoulders. She shook her hair back, clear of her eyes, just as Sinclair pinned her flat on her back beneath his weight, both of them slightly breathless with laughter.

"So you want to play rough?" he asked with a low seductive growl. Her struggles to pull free of his viselike grip on both wrists were futile. She could not match him for sheer strength. Pausing, she panted for breath, staring up at him.

As their eyes locked, the laughter shared between them stilled. Belle became all too conscious of the intimacy of their position, the hard length of his masculine body trapping her against the floor, just as she sensed Sinclair's awareness of it, too. His eyes hazed a smoky shade of green, his dark hair tumbled over his brow, his pulse beating at the base of his throat.

"Surrender, Angel." His light taunt came out somewhat unsteady.

"Never," she said. "You gloat too soon, Mr. Carrington."

She allowed herself to go limp beneath him and cast him her most sultry look from beneath the thickness of her lashes, then slowly undulated her body against his.

He regarded her with astonishment that soon became a flash of some more heated emotion. When he released her wrists, she insinuated her hands between them, caressing his shoulders. Undoing the top button of his shirt, she slipped her fingers inside the linen, the crisp fabric in marked contrast to the warm pulsing flesh of his chest beneath.

"You don't fight fair, Angel," he said.

"Alas, sir," she whispered. "I am but a poor weak woman. I haven't a gentleman's notions of honor."

"The problem is, neither have I."

His arms closed roughly about her, his mouth seeking hers, claiming her with a searing kiss. He shifted onto his back, pulling her on top of him, but Belle felt no rush of triumph, for she was no longer in any more control of the situation than he.

Like a reckless child, she had played amongst the embers, and fire is what she had found. She tasted of it on Sinclair's lips, felt it in the heat of his body beneath her. As her lips parted, inviting the probing sweetness of Sinclair's tongue, those same flames flickered to life inside of her.

She should stop him, but how she had needed this. Last night had been so endless, she still felt the chill of it in her soul. Sinclair was all that was warmth, all that was life, stirring in her desires she had too long ignored.

He made an effort to put her from him, although she could tell from the tremor coursing through his arms what effort it cost him. "Angel, I am sorry—"

"No!" Recklessly she pressed herself atop him. "Don't stop. Please. I have been alone for so long."

Her plea dissolved whatever resistance he had mustered. With a low groan, he reclaimed her lips. She buried her fingers in his hair, clutching him to her, prolonging the heady sensation of the kiss, for once casting caution to the winds. Her whole life had been a gamble, so why was she so afraid to take one more risk—that perhaps with Sinclair, this time might be different.

The apartment fell silent except for the crackle of the fire, the more raging inferno Belle felt building inside her. Sinclair was just beginning to undo the braided loops of her spencer when they heard the click of the latch on the outer door. The sound, soft as it was, seemed to crack through the apartment with the force of a pistol shot.

She and Sinclair exchanged a startled glance. The clatter of footsteps on the marble floor of the antechamber beyond terminated their mounting passion as effectively as if the casement had been flung open, dousing them with chilling rain.

Sinclair was the first to react. Cursing under his breath, he scrambled to his feet. Grasping Belle by the wrist, he hauled her up after him. She had time to do no more than draw in a composing breath and attempt to smooth back her hair before Paulette peeked into the drawing room, rainwater yet beading upon the covered basket in her hand.

Paulette's lips rounded in momentary surprise, then her insolent gaze swept from Belle's disheveled hair to the undone buttons of Sinclair's shirt. Belle was annoyed to feel a wave of heat course into her cheeks.

"I hurried to finish the marketing, *chérie*, for fear you might need me for something else," Paulette said, "but I see that my return is most out of time."

Sinclair glared at her, but Belle straightened, gathering up the ends of her dignity.

"Not at all. It is fortunate you are back so soon. I will be going out tonight and need you to help me with, my hair and gown."

"*Certainment.*" There was mockery in the curtsy Paulette made. She raked Sinclair with a hungry gaze. "My congratulations, chérie. You have the *bon chance.* Do not allow me to disturb you. I will be in the kitchen."

Smirking, Paulette backed out of the room, leaving an awkward silence behind her. Belle turned to face Sinclair, but there was no question of resuming her place in his embrace. Paulette's return had effectively shattered whatever longings had pulsed between them. They regarded each other for a moment, both feeling somewhat foolish.

"Good fortune, indeed!" Sinclair said, echoing Paulette's remark. "The pert trollop! Though perhaps we ought to thank her for the intrusion. We appear to have gotten somewhat carried away with our role-playing."

"So it would seem, Mr. Carrington." Belle managed to force a smile.

"I am sorry, Angel. I usually have a little more finesse than to attempt to make love upon the drawing room carpet. I don't know what the devil got into me."

His apology was all that was gallant, but Belle would have none of it. She had ever borne responsibility for her own actions.

"I was the devil," she said. "I deliberately provoked you."

"But I am sure you never meant matters to go that far—"

"Don't try to tell me what I meant. It is not my way to arouse a man and then play the part of outraged virtue."

"And it is not my way to compromise a lady's reputation, either."

"Compromise? Good God, Sinclair." Belle essayed a bitter laugh. "You talk as though I were some sort of an innocent—which you well know I am not."

"What you are"—he cupped her chin with his fingers, forcing her to meet his gaze—"is a woman with a most vulnerable heart."

His words, the tender look that accompanied them, pierced her with a feeling so poignant it was nearly akin to a physical pain. Belle thought it would be far easier to stand naked before him than have him peer into the most hidden recesses of her soul.

Gently, but firmly, she pushed his hand away from her. She said as brightly as she could, "I am a woman who must look a positive fright. I best make some effort to bring myself to order, or there will be no need to abduct Bonaparte. I will scare him to death."

Kneeling down, she allowed her hair to veil her face as she made a great show of searching for her hairpins. She feared Sinclair would bend down to help her, but after heaving a deep sigh, he said, "I think it might be best if I went out for a bit. I could use a breath of air."

She nodded, making no effort to dissuade him, only saying, "Take care not to get lost. The streets of Paris are like a maze."

He promised to be careful, and then he was gone. Belle could hear him in the antechamber beyond, gathering up his cloak and umbrella. She rubbed her arms, still so conscious of his touch, fighting an urge to fling open the drawing room door and summon him back.

How ridiculous, she thought. It was not as though she would never see Sinclair again. If she truly wished it; she knew there would be other opportunities to find herself in Sinclair's embrace, uninterrupted by Paulette.

She was glad of Paulette's untimely return. It had saved her from rushing headlong into something she might have cause to regret, gave her more time to think.

Over the years she had learned life could be far less painful that way, trusting more to reason than feeling. There was only one problem with such an approach. One frequently ended with a clear head, but an empty heart.

From the room beyond, Belle heard the outer door slam and knew that Sinclair had left the apartment. Staring into the blazing fire, she wondered how the logs could crackle so, but still leave her feeling cold. And once more she was conscious of the rain.

Sinclair emerged into the street, his steps aimless, with no other purpose in mind than to escape from the apartment, the overwhelming desire to go back and pull Belle into his arms. He didn't bother opening his umbrella, grateful for the cold rain that pelted his face and dripped off his hair in rivulets, cooling his overheated senses.

He must have made a curious sight, he though wryly, except the other pedestrians appeared too busy in their efforts to keep themselves dry to worry overmuch about a madman who would thus expose himself to the elements. A driver of an ancient fiacre pulled by two raw-boned horses did slow to a halt, urging Sinclair to hire his vehicle. When Sinclair ignored him, the cabman cursed and drove on.

Slouching back against a patisserie's shop front, out of the way of the traffic, Sinclair replayed over in his mind the recent scene between himself and Belle. He wanted to curse Paulette Beauvais, but he was forced to admit that her return truly had not mattered. Even if she had not interrupted them, Sinclair would have found the strength to thrust Belle out of his arms.

That would have been a first. He nearly laughed aloud. The rakehell Sinclair Carrington refusing the seduction of a beautiful woman. But how could he have done otherwise, knowing he had been sent to spy upon her, even knowing he might have to betray her one day?

"So now you're developing a conscience, Carrington," he muttered to himself. At that moment he realized his loitering in front of the shop was attracting suspicious glances from the owner. Prudently Sinclair moved along, the rainwater pelting his face.

He expelled a breath and patted his empty breast pocket. He would have given anything for a quiet corner, the pleasure of one of his cheroots. He always seemed to think better with a cloud of smoke curling about his head, helping him to get his roiling emotions under control. But he had forgotten his cigars, and he was not about to go back to the apartment until he could put what had happened into some perspective.

He had nearly made love to Isabelle Varens. That was not surprising, considering that his desire for the lady had been building all along. But what had driven him over the edge—that was the surprising factor. Not the scent of her hair, or the feel of her soft skin, or her lips so sweet and pliant. It had been that wistful look in her eyes, the whispered plea, "I have been alone for so long."

"Damn it, Angel," he said, drawing up his coat collar tighter against the rain. "So have I." It had taken him until that moment to realize it. He was not a mooncalf like his brother Charles. He cherished no notions about romantic love or experiencing the *grande* passion. No, only an inkling that at last he had found the woman who was more right for him than any of the others.

A woman who might also be his deadliest enemy.

But it didn't matter if she was. That was the hell of it. Even if Belle was Napoleon's spy, Sinclair was no longer sure he would be able to do his duty and hand her over to the British authorities.

No, it could not be Belle, he told himself, raking one hand back through his rain-soaked hair. "She cannot be the one. I would stake my life upon it."

That is exactly what you are doing, a voice inside him jeered. It was the most damnable coil, and he didn't see any way out of it— no way but one, to trust his instincts about Belle and lay all his suspicions to rest. To do that he must find the real spy as soon as possible, a purpose he was not going to accomplish by wandering through Paris and soaking his head in the rain.

Sinclair reversed his steps. He had no difficulty finding his way back to the apartment, for he had not wandered that far along the Rue St. Honoré. He was within a stone's throw of the fan shop when he saw a familiar figure emerge upon the steps. Etienne

Lazare paused long enough to pull his red cap down lower upon his head.

"Well," Sinclair breathed. "Look what crawled down from the garrets." Some instinct caused him to dodge within the shadows of the entranceway of a nearby shop.

Thrusting his hands deep in the pocket of his greatcoat, Lazare cast a seemingly casual glance both up and down the Rue St. Honoré. He did not appear to have noticed Sinclair, for he set off to cross the street, expertly avoiding a passing carriage and all the deeper mud holes.

"Only a raving lunatic would be out in this weather without some good reason," Sinclair told himself, a self-mocking smile curling his lips. It might do no harm to attempt to trail his good friend Lazare, see what the man was up to. After all—Sinclair winced, feeling the rainwater trickle down the back of his neck. He was already soaked to the skin.

He waited until he judged Lazare to have gotten a safe distance away but still within view before Sinclair left the shelter of his doorway. He put up his umbrella, using it to shield his face, and plunged across the street himself, the mud dragging at his boots and spattering his breeches.

He had nearly gained the other side when he was all but knocked down by an *auvergnot* dragging his water butts mounted on heavy wheels.

"Some drinking water, monsieur?" this bedraggled individual inquired. "Fresh from purified fountains. I could deliver it to your lodgings within the hour."

More likely fresh from the Seine, according to what Sinclair had heard Belle say about these carriers.

"No, thank you," he told the man curtly, shoving past him. He glanced anxiously down the street and cursed, fearing he had lost Lazare.

But he spotted the familiar red cap not more than a dozen yards away. Lazare walked at an easy pace behind several elderly gentlemen huddled beneath the brims of their beaver hats. Lazare appeared in no great hurry, but Sinclair still found following him no easy task in the crowded street. Apparently the Parisians were accustomed to the rain. The inclement weather seemed to have kept few of them from shopping or otherwise going about their appointed business.

Sinclair kept doggedly after Lazare, only hesitating when the Frenchman turned off the Rue St. Honoré and vanished down one of the side streets. Sinclair remembered Belle's warning about becoming lost and tried to read the street marker on the cornerstone, but the letters were worn too smooth. Looking about him for some sort of landmark, he settled upon the little peasant trader who had ensconced himself on that corner to sell kindling wood.

The side street down which Sinclair forged was narrow, scarce wide enough to permit two carriages to pass each other. Sinclair remarked with dismay that there were fewer pedestrians here, making his chances of being spotted by Lazare far greater.

But Lazare appeared to entertain no apprehensions of being followed. Although his pace took on a new urgency, he never once glanced back. He moved forward with the confidence of a man who knew exactly where he was going.

"Which is a great deal more than I do," Sinclair mumbled, picking up his own pace as he trailed Lazare down yet another street, then through a series of alleyways and murky lanes, the buildings about him growing increasingly more dingy, the high walls of plaster cracked and flaking. Picking his way past piles of refuse, Sinclair struggled to avoid the torrents of rainwater pouring down from open gutter spouts.

He judged he had been skulking after Lazare for more than half an hour when the Frenchman finally slowed his steps on one of the less frequented streets of the city. Many of the houses on the narrow roadway sported broken or boarded-over windows. Only one shop appeared to be in operation, a confectioner's, whose sign creaked on its pole, the letters barely legible. Lazare paused on the doorstep of this establishment.

"Wouldn't that be a glorious end to your career, Carrington?" Sinclair thought. "Dying of pneumonia from trailing a man with nothing more sinister on his mind than a craving for chocolates."

Still he watched from the opposite side of the street. Lazare made no move to enter the shop, merely drawing back into the shelter of the doorway as though he were waiting for something. To appear less conspicuous, Sinclair adjusted his umbrella lower over his face and pretended he was making a purchase from one of the street hawkers—an elderly peasant selling kindling wood, Sinclair noted with grim humor. These little men seemed to be found on nearly every street corner in Paris. So much for his landmark.

The minutes ticked by and Lazare continued to slouch in the doorway. Sinclair began to feel as though he'd come on a fool's errand. He would have to move along in a moment or run the risk of attracting Lazare's attention. And how he would ever find his way back to the Rue St. Honoré, Sinclair did not know.

But all such concerns were swept aside as Lazare stiffened to attention. A cabriolet drew to a halt in front of the shop, pausing only long enough to deposit a gentleman garbed in black before the vehicle trundled on its way.

Sinclair abandoned caution as he strained to have a better look at the slender man approaching Lazare. He could not remark the man's face, the stranger's hat was pulled too low, the collar of his cape too high, but something about the fellow struck Sinclair as being elusively familiar.

Lazare stepped forward. The two men greeted each other, although no move was made to clasp hands. Lazare appeared his usual insolent self, but it was obvious the stranger was nervous, all his movements furtive He started to gesture toward something, but to Sinclair's frustration, a slow-moving diligence lumbered up the street, cutting the two men off from his view.

The outside passengers clung to the top of the stage, looking as miserable as Sinclair felt. He waited impatiently for the heavy vehicle to rattle on past.

Lazare and the stranger had vanished. Sinclair, however, did not feel unduly concerned. There was only one place they could have disappeared to that quickly—within the confectioner's shop.

Hesitating for only a moment, Sinclair slogged his way across the street and cautiously approached the shop. Sheltering deep beneath his umbrella, he risked a glance through the dirty latticed pane. Except for a slatternly woman behind the counter, the shop was empty.

But that was impossible. The stage had blocked Lazare from his view for but a moment. There was nowhere else the two men could have gone but inside.

Tired, chilled to the bone and tormented by the feeling that he was close to discovering something, Sinclair decided to take a grave risk. Closing his umbrella, he turned the knob and boldly entered the confectioner's shop himself.

The shop bell tinkled dismally. The silence of the narrow wooden room seemed thickened by dust. The establishment appeared as though it had been untroubled by customers for months, let alone being used for a rendezvous by a Napoleonic spy. Even the proprietress bore a most laconic expression.

She roused herself enough to wipe her hands on her grimy apron and say, "Good day, monsieur. And how may I serve you on such a cold, damp afternoon?"

"It is that, indeed," Sinclair said, rubbing his hands briskly and flashing his most charming smile. The woman was as impervious to it as if she had been blind. She clearly waited for him to make his selection and leave her in peace.

Feigning an interest in the shop's wares, Sinclair studied the rows of marzipan, chocolates, mushrooms of sugar, and multicolored sugar almonds. Even with his sweet tooth, none of the confections displayed in the midst of such filth tempted him, but he took his time selecting some marzipan, giving himself an excuse to linger. His gaze tracked toward a curtained door at the rear of the shop.

"This foul weather appears to be keeping your customers away," he remarked to the woman.

"That's right," she said as she wrapped up his purchase. "Haven't seen nary another soul all day."

"How strange. I thought I saw two gentlemen precede me into the shop." Sinclair studied the woman's dull eyes carefully.

She did not flick so much as an eyelash as she replied, "Alas, I wish it were so, monsieur. I shall be a pauper at this rate."

With a taut smile she accepted Sinclair's money and handed him his purchase. Sinclair accepted it and nodded graciously. Perhaps he had made a mistake. But if Lazare had not ducked in here, it was obvious Sinclair had lost him. There was nothing for him to do but try to retrace his steps.

In the corridor behind the curtained door, Lazare heard the bell's chime as Sinclair left the shop. After a pause the proprietress thrust her head past the curtain to announce, "He's gone, monsieur."

"So I heard, madame."

"Another of your creditors, Monsieur Lazare?"

"Just so, madame."

"Well, I didn't let on you'd come in."

"For which I am most grateful, madame." Lazare forced an ingratiating smile.

The proprietress shrugged. "As long as you pay me the rent for the rooms upstairs, your other debts are nothing to me." With that she lowered the curtain, retreating back into the shop. Lazare turned toward the flight of rickety stairs leading to the floor above, his smile fading into a savage frown.

Of course the old bitch would get her rent money, as long as it suited him. Even though he was ostensibly living in the garrets above Baptiste's fan shop, he had need of these rooms here, far from Isabelle's observant eye, a convenient place to receive a certain visitor she must know nothing about for the present.

As for Sinclair Carrington, the Englishman was becoming a damned nuisance. If Lazare had not happened to spot him across the street, Carrington might have discovered far too much about Lazare's secret dealings.

For his vengeance to be complete, Lazare needed Belle alive until the end of this affair. But Carrington was another matter. The next time the English dog was so unwise as to go traipsing alone through the city streets, it might be well that he meet with an accident. Paris could prove to be a very dangerous city.

With this pleasing thought, some of the tension in Lazare's shoulders relaxed. He started up the stairs, but before he could reach his room, a slender figure melted out of the shadows, regarding Lazare through worried eyes.

"Is anything wrong, monsieur?"

Lazare raked a contemptuous glance over the nervous figure of his guest.

"No, not at all." Lazare's teeth flashed in a wolfish grin. "Nothing that I cannot take care of, Monsieur Varens."

Ten

The iron gates stood guarded by the towering statuary, the famed winged horses of Coysevax, each ridden by a figure of Mercury. Tonight the myth-born sentinels seemed almost benign, the gates flung back to admit the stream of elegant equipages inching their way past the tree-lined square toward the Tuileries.

But Belle shifted away from the coach window that framed the brilliance of the distant palace beyond the iron bars. Drawn against her will, she peered out the opposite side of the carriage toward the shadowy darkness of the square. The stark branches of the trees bent gently with the wind, the stone pavilions appearing silvery in the moonlight. Lush fountains sprayed wreaths of water with a peaceful hush.

The Place de la Concorde, Baptiste had told her the square was now called. To those who knew no better, the name would seem apt. But in Belle's mind it would always be the Place de la Revolution.

The guillotine was gone now. Even the scaffolding had been torn down. So many lives lost, so many innocents swept from the face of the earth, and nothing marked the place other than a handful of brittle autumn leaves being swirled by the night breeze.

Belle had only attended the executions once. What a fool she had been! She had thought to find some way of rescuing victims from the very steps of the scaffolding. Donning a tricolored cockade, she had mingled with the crowd at the Place de la Revolution. But she had seen almost at once such a scheme was hopeless. The press of spectators was too great, the guards leading the tumbrils too many.

She had tried to retreat then, but it had been too late. Caught up in the eager crowd, she had been pushed and shoved, until she found herself at the base of the scaffolding. She had had no choice then but to remain. With her eyes fixed firmly on the ground, she had uttered a silent prayer for each unfortunate as he mounted the steps. She had never looked up, but she never had to. There was no escaping the sounds; the dull thud of the board being fixed into place, the deadly hiss of the blade and the merciless cheers of the crowd. And the blood that had spattered the hem of her gown.

"Angel?"

She dragged her gaze from the carriage window to meet Sinclair's concerned eyes.

"Is something wrong?" he asked. He had leaned forward from the seat opposite, his hand reaching out to cover hers. For the first time she realized how rigid she held herself.

"No." She drew in a steadying breath, relaxing her muscles."I was woolgathering, that's all."

She could not tell whether he accepted this explanation or not. But he withdrew his hand, leaning back. His touch had called her back to the present. She did not look out the window again, but focused her concentration upon Sinclair and the night ahead of them.

He looked magnificent in his black evening clothes and white silk waistcoat, his dark hair swept back, his cravat tied with his customary careless grace. The only ornament he wore was a heavy ruby ring, which flashed against his tanned fingers. He could have been a gentleman bent on a night of carousing at some discreetly fashionable gaming hall or a courtesan's salons, equally as well as prepared to attend this sort of government reception. He could take his place anywhere by right of a kind of arrogance, that cheerful 'take me as I am or be damned' aura that Belle envied him.

She wondered again where he had spent the afternoon. He had been gone a long time, or had it only seemed that way to her, ever alert for his return? She had been bathing when she heard him stirring about in the room next to hers, but she had not seen him until she stood in the antechamber ready to leave and be handed into the carriage.

She had expected a certain awkwardness between them. After all, the man had nearly made love to her on the drawing room floor, but any constraint was dispelled by Sinclair's remarking that since his afternoon's jaunt, he was now thoroughly familiar with all the sorts of mud to be found in Paris. She had laughed, and once more they were at ease with each other. Indeed, Belle was finding it difficult to imagine ever being estranged from Sinclair for long.

He appeared completely relaxed as their coach finally crept past the gates, drawing closer to the palace itself. The Tuileries was ablaze with light. Time appeared to have been turned back to the days of the glorious Sun King, Louis XIV, for whom the palace had been built. Moonlight skimmed over the palace's massive seven stories, revealing to Belle that the scars to the woodwork and the broken windows had all been repaired as though the angry mob had never dared storm this majestic dwelling.

As the carriage drew to a halt in front of the palace, the coach door was opened by a footman, but Sinclair leapt down to hand her out himself. As she placed her gloved hand within his, their eyes met, and although the smile Sinclair gave her was casual, his gaze was not. She knew then that she had been fooling herself to think that either of them could forget what had happened in the drawing room. The awareness of something begun and not finished crackled between them.

Although the contact of his hand upon hers was fleeting, it was enough to quicken her blood, adding to the excitement she already felt at the prospect of meeting Napoleon. Anticipation mingled with a sense of danger as she entered the palace.

Within the antechamber to the reception hall, other arrivals were already removing their cloaks, handing them off to servants garbed in blue and gold livery. Belle and Sinclair found it difficult to move forward for a party of chattering young ladies. Despite the autumn chill, the demoiselles were attired in gowns of thin muslin cut in the Grecian style, the sheer fabric clinging to nubile young bodies, making it obvious they wore nothing underneath but pink tights.

Sinclair paused in the act of helping Belle off with her cloak, too much the male not to avail himself of an interested stare.

"The latest fashion in Paris, Mr. Carrington. Do you approve?"

"That all depends." Sinclair shifted his gaze back to Belle, a mischievous glint in his eye. "Do you intend to adopt it?"

"Alas, no, I am supposed to be a proper English lady on this journey, remember?"

"More's the pity." Sinclair sighed. But his teasing expression vanished as he slipped the cloak the rest of the way from Belle's shoulders.

He had seen Belle's beauty in many guises, but tonight she appeared an ethereal vision, a queen stepped from the pages of legend, a Helen of Troy. Her womanly curves were accented by a high-waisted gown of white silk, gleaming beneath an overtunic of silvery gauze, with a long train sweeping behind. Gloves drawn up to the elbow emphasized the slenderness of her arms. Her hair was pulled into a chignon, the soft curls wisped about her cheeks and forehead, a netting of tiny pearls winding mistlike through the golden strands.

"On second thought," Sinclair murmured in her ear, "forget the Paris fashions. I will settle for the proper English lady."

"You are too kind, sir." Although she acknowledged his compliment with a mocking smile, the color heightened in her cheeks. Gracefully gathering the train of her gown over one arm, she linked her other arm through Sinclair's, resting her hand lightly on his coat sleeve.

As they joined the line moving into the reception room, Sinclair glanced down at her with a swelling of pride. Absurd, he thought. He behaved as though she belonged to him. But in a sense tonight she did. To the world about him she was Mrs. Sinclair Carrington, his wife. He could see the curious, half-envious stares of the other women, the open admiration of the men.

Did Belle realize the sensation she caused? There was no way of telling from the proud, unconcerned lift of her chin. On one level Sinclair believed that she did, not out of vanity, but with an almost cynical acceptance, regarding the men who ogled her as foolish. But he doubted that Belle would ever really appreciate what havoc her beauty could wreak upon a man's heart.

As they stepped inside the reception room, Belle felt tempted to reach for her fan. The press of people, the fire banked high in the great marble fireplace, the glow of candles shining off the bright yellow cast of the walls gave her the feeling of having walked into a blaze of sunshine. Obviously neither the first consul nor his lady had yet made their appearance through the huge double doors at the opposite end of the room. The guests milled about talking, giving Belle the leisure to observe a crowd no less brilliant than the glittering candelabra.

The ladies appeared in a profusion of diamonds, feathers, and silks, their cheeks rouged with the Parisians' unashamed regard for cosmetics, which made Belle feel pale as a ghost by comparison. As for the gentlemen, dashing uniforms weighted with medals mingled side by side with crisp evening coats and the more fantastic wasp-waists of those French dandies known as the Incroyables.

Perhaps it was not the same august assemblage that had once graced the halls of a king. Here and there Belle caught snatches of vulgar language, the odor of doubtful linen, a glimpse of muddy shoes, which never would have been tolerated at Versailles, but this was still the respectable world of Paris.

The world that she had once sought to belong to as Jean-Claude's wife. But she had never been quite at ease, ever aware of being the actress's daughter from Drury Lane, always waiting to be found out. So many years had passed since then, but so little had changed. She crept into their midst, still the imposter.

Belle snapped out of her musings as she realized she and Sinclair were being approached by the English ambassador. He introduced himself and as they were supposedly there according to his auspices, Belle favored him with a gracious smile. His lordship must have been quite accustomed to his staff selling invitations to unknown English travelers. His interest in them was polite, but distant.

As the ambassador moved on, Sinclair whispered in her ear, "You look ravishing tonight, Angel. But I fear that gentleman's stares over there are a little excessive. Do you know him?"

Following Sinclair's nudge, Belle casually fixed her attention upon a lean man standing in the shadow of one of the chamber's massive pillars. The fellow studied her from beneath an unprepossessing shock of yellow hair, his wan skin appearing stretched too tautly over sharp features.

"Fouché!" Belle tightened her grip on Sinclair's arm. At his enquiring gaze, she explained in low tones, "He was Napoleon's minister of police up until a few months ago. He is believed to have been dismissed because Bonaparte feels secure enough to deem Fouché's services no longer necessary. The *on dit* is that Fouché would give a great deal to prove Monsieur Bonaparte wrong."

"Marvelous," Sinclair said through gritted teeth. "The former minister of police. And now he is coming this way."

"So he is." Belle fluttered her fan before her eyes. "Keep smiling, my dear husband."

She would have wagered that no other man in the room looked more relaxed or gracious than Sinclair, only she herself aware of the tension that stiffened his arm, perhaps because she felt that same tension knotting in her stomach as Joseph Fouché edged toward them through the press of people.

Fouché pulled up short, snapping into an ingratiating bow, but Belle noted his eyes never wavered from her face. Ferret-like eyes, she thought, repressing a shudder. She had never liked the cast of them.

"Forgive my impertinence, madame, monsieur," Fouché said. "May I make so bold as to present myself—Joseph Fouché."

"Sinclair Carrington," Sinclair replied easily, "and my wife, Isabelle."

"Isabelle. A beautiful name for a beautiful lady." Fouché compliment seemd as insincere as his smile."I must confess that it was the sight of you, madame, that rendered me so bold. As foolish as it may sound, I have the feeling we have met before."

Belle's heart thudded, but she met Fouché's speculative stare. "I do not believe so, monsieur."

There was finality in her tone, but Fouché was not so easily dismissed. "But such beauty one does not forget." He stroked his chin, his eyes narrowing. "In Paris, I believe, during the Revolution—"

"No one with any wisdom lived in Paris during the Revolution, monsieur."

"I did." Fouché's manner of strained geniality vanished for a moment. "You look so extraordinarily like an unfortunate lady I saw summoned to face charges of treason before the Revolutionary Tribunal."

"Ridiculous, monsieur," Sinclair growled. "This is the first time my wife has ever been to Paris."

Belle affected to lay a soothing hand on Sinclair's arm. "Please, my dear. I am sure Monsieur Fouché intends no offense. It would not be unusual if I did resemble at least one of those wretched people. It is my understanding that half of Paris was called to trial before that court."

"Not quite so many as that, madame, but most who were did not survive to talk about it."

"And some," Belle retorted before she could stop herself, "possessed the uncanny ability to survive no matter what the cost."

Fouché's pale skin washed a shade of dull red, his lips giving an angry twitch. "Well, it would seem I was quite mistaken. Your pardon for having disturbed you, madame."

He bowed stiffly and stalked away. Sinclair vented his breath in a manner that was part curse, part a sigh of relief. Belle discovered that her hand was shaking, but more from anger than alarm.

"Disgusting viper," she said. "He dares talk to me of surviving when he made his own way through the Revolution along a path paved in blood. He was one of those who found the guillotine too slow, and organized a plan to have the condemned lined up in front of cannons."

"Disgusting he might be, Angel, but vipers can also be dangerous. Did Fouché see you on trial?"

"He might have, but I doubt it. He had had a falling out with Robespierre at that time and was running for his own miserable life."

"But if he should remember you," Sinclair persisted, "as the woman tried for being the Avenging Angel and rescuing aristocrats—"

"No one could possibly remember me from those days," Belle said. "Do you have any notion what I looked like after weeks in prison? The rats that scurried along the floor of the Conciergerie were more attractive."

Sinclair said nothing more, but his doubts remained. Belle possessed a beauty that no prison pallor could have disguised. Her eyes alone would have been enough to haunt a man's dreams.

All concerns about Fouché had to be set aside for the moment. The double doors at the end of the room were flung open. A hush fell over the room as the assembled company divided into two respectful lines, leaving a path between them.

Josephine Bonaparte made her entrance on the arm of that wily old statesman, Talleyrand. The Creole beauty's braided hair was fixed into place with a shell comb, her graceful form garbed in a silk robe with short sleeves. Her regal bearing attracted so much attention that the man who slipped into the reception room behind her went unnoticed and unheralded.

But Belle's attention riveted upon Napoleon Bonaparte. Attired in a simple uniform, a blue coat with white cashmere breeches, he wore a tricolored sash of silk tied round his waist, his hat tucked under his arm. He appeared far less dashing in contrast to the other military men with their embroidered coats overloaded with ribbons and jewels. And yet his very simplicity made Bonaparte seem so much more the soldier.

Still, it was hard to credit that this unassuming person could be the man whose ambitions set most of Europe atremble, the brilliant general who had spilled his share of English blood. He bore no resemblance to the formidable villain depicted in the British press.

As Bonaparte moved down the line of guests, Belle was struck once more by his sense of restrained energy. She had a clearer view of his face than when he had passed her by on horseback. His skin was of a marble whiteness, his brow wide and high, his smile surprisingly gracious. She could discern none of his remarks until he stood but two persons away from her. Disconcertingly blunt, he put more than one lady to the blush. Pausing before one of the young demoiselles Belle and Sinclair had noticed earlier, Bonaparte remarked to his equerry, "See to it that the fires are banked higher in here. I fear for the ladies' health, as some of them are nearly naked."

A choke of laughter escaped Belle at the pert misses' disconcerted expressions. The sound drew Bonaparte's attention. As he turned in her direction, Belle felt the full force of his eyes, large and bluish-gray. The first consul studied her, appearing not to miss a single detail. It would have been Belle's manner to meet his challenge boldly as she always did Sinclair's raking gaze. But Sinclair enjoyed their silent battles of will. Somehow Belle sensed that such a thing would not serve with Bonaparte, who reportedly liked his women all soft femininity.

As Napoleon approached, she sank into a low curtsy, her eyes cast demurely down.

"And this is?" he asked.

Belle heard the English ambassador's bored voice intone, "Mr. and Mrs. Sinclair Carrington, newly arrived in Paris, Your Excellency."

Sinclair bowed and murmured his greeting. Stealing a glance upward, Belle noted how the two men measured each other.

Bonaparte commented at last, "You are tall, Monsieur Carrington. You have the build of a cavalry officer."

Sinclair started perceptibly at his words, but he said smoothly, "The build, sir, but not the ability. I have no taste for the soldiering life."

"That is as well." Bonaparte offered him a taut smile. "You would be fighting in the wrong army." He turned abruptly to Belle. "You are possessed of a most beautiful wife. She should provide you with many handsome children."

It was all Belle could do to stifle a small gasp. She was accustomed to dealing with compliments, but none so roughly delivered.

"How many babes have you?" Bonaparte demanded.

"None so far." Sinclair struggled to hide his amusement. "We are but newly married."

"See that you get some soon."

Bonaparte's words touched Belle on the raw, an unexpected thrust at her own private grief.

"I would be only too pleased to follow Your Excellency's command, if in my case the doctors did not deem it impossible." The quiet rebuke in her voice was obvious.

Appearing disconcerted by his blunder, the first consul nodded and moved on. As she watched him retreat, Belle could have slapped herself. What an opportunity she had lost. The admiring light in Bonaparte's eyes had vanished. She had obviously made him feel like a boorish idiot.

What the devil was wrong with her? She knew far more adept ways of turning aside his blunt remarks. Instead she had let herself be betrayed into being brutally honest. Once she had been far better at concealing her feelings.

Flushing with chagrin, she scarce dared look at Sinclair. He had good cause to be aggravated with her clumsiness, but his eyes reflected only concern.

"What a wonderful beginning," she muttered. "I shall have to go after him and apologize."

"The man should apologize to you, Angel. He was damned impertinent."

Yes, but she was the one hoping to ingratiate herself with Bonaparte with a view to arranging his abduction, not the other way around. Belle refrained from reminding Sinclair of that fact, lapsing into a dour silence.

Her spirits did not improve as the evening wore on. Bonaparte, making his rounds of the guests, took great care not to come near her again. Although it was far from being the end of her plans, Belle could not help reflecting how much easier her task might have been, if only she had managed to exert a little charm.

"Why don't you join Madame Bonaparte's circle?" she suggested to Sinclair at last. "Perhaps you can glean some information from her that might be useful. I have not proved to be much help."

"Belle." Sinclair's tone was warm, admonishing.

"Away with you," she said. "There is nothing more ridiculous than a husband hanging upon his wife's sleeve. You will have all the men of Paris saying I have you under the cat's paw."

He gave her a wry grin. With some reluctance he moved off to obey her command. Belle unfurled her fan before her face and continued to brood over her error. What had happened to her customary sangfroid? Ever since her return to Paris, her emotions seemed far too near the surface. It was as though the carefully constructed barriers around her heart were beginning to crumple.

She began to find the reception room unbearable. The heat, the crush of people, the endless chatter started the beginnings of a headache behind her eyes. When she noticed Fouché about to close in on her again, she felt unequal to dealing with him. Seeking escape, she slipped out the main door. If nothing else, she might at least glean some notion of the layout of the palace.

But she soon dismissed any idea of attempting the abduction from the Tuileries as absurd. Although she was permitted to wander the corridors, the members of the consular guard appeared everywhere, discreetly following her movements with their eyes.

She did not find herself alone until she reached a dimly lit hall ornamented with busts set upon pedestals. Most of them depicted classical figures: Brutus, Cicero, Hannibal, Alexander, but a few represented more modern statesmen, Frederick the Great, Washington and Mirabeau.

She paused before the last statue, absently returning the figure's vacant stare of stone. A low voice came from behind, startling her.

"That is Julius Caesar, possibly the greatest general who ever lived, in my opinion."

Belle spun about to find Napoleon Bonaparte watching her, barely a yard away. Was he now further annoyed to find her wandering in a part of the palace where she did not belong? His grave expression told her nothing.

"I beg your pardon, sir," she said. "I daresay I should not have wandered in here."

When he did not reply, she made a stiff curtsy and attempted to slip past him.

"Stay," he said, then softened the command with an added, "Please. It is I who must ask your pardon for the distress I caused you earlier. Madame, can you forgive a soldier's blunt manners?"

Belle expelled a long, slow breath, her thoughts racing. Could it be that she was being offered another chance? This time she must weigh her remarks far more carefully.

"The fault was mine, sir," she said, "for being so foolish. I am not usually oversensitive, but some things I have not found easy to bear. I should not blame you if you held me in contempt. Being such a bold soldier yourself, you must—"

"Madame, there is as much courage in bearing with a sorrow of the heart as in facing a battery of guns."

His solemn answer surprised her, a surprise that she could not quite conceal.

"Do I astonish you, madame?"

"Yes, you are quite different from what I had been led to expect."

"No doubt by your British papers. I forbid their circulation here in France. The lies they spread. They make me out a gorgon with two heads, do they not? Come, tell me."

With a slight smile Belle said, "Well, I have heard mothers warning their children, 'Baby, baby, he's a giant. Tall and black as Raven steeple. And he dines and sups, rely on't, every day on naughty people.' "

Bonaparte looked nonplussed, and for moment Belle feared she had gone too far. Then to her relief, the first consul flung back his head and laughed.

"And what about you? Are you a naughty person, Madame Carrington?"

Touching her fan to her cheek, a wicked arch of her brows was the only answer Belle gave.

Napoleon's mouth widened into a smile, warmth firing his stern gaze as he stepped closer. "I confess that I have not a high regard for your country, madame. I thought naught came from London but pestilence, all the great evils of the world. But 1 might be persuaded to change my mind."

SINCLAIR LINGERED ON THE FRINGES OF THE LAUGHING crowd surrounding Madame Bonaparte. Although the Creole had smiled upon him, and he was given enough encouragement to wend his way to her side, Sinclair's heart was not in the task.

He had been aware of the moment when Belle had slipped out of the room, and his gaze had followed her anxiously, knowing how distressed she was, although she sought to conceal it. He had also observed Bonaparte going after her, realizing the implications as did half the room, judging from the smirking faces.

Sinclair found himself prey to a ridiculous range of emotions, jealousy and suspicion as to her motives warring with fear for her safety. With sly glances cast toward him, the role of complacent husband became difficult to play. Despite the fact he would likely make an idiot of himself, the urge to charge after her was strong and only increased as the minutes ticked by and she did not return.

Taking a restless step, Sinclair backed into a young man dogging his heels. Sinclair curtly begged his pardon and started to brush past him.

The man coughed diffidently. "Mr. Carrington?"

"That's correct." Although he smiled politely, Sinclair made another attempt to evade the man.

"Warburton's the name. I am under secretary to the ambassador."

He looked like one, Sinclair thought. Modestly dressed, with nondescript features, Warburton was the sort of fellow one would forget five minutes after meeting him.

"It was I who arranged for your invitation to the reception," Warburton said, modestly lowering his eyes.

So this then was the agreeable person Baptiste had bribed. Sinclair swallowed the urge to retort that he hoped Warburton had put the money to good use.

"Most kind of you," he said, making another effort to slip past the man. But for one so timid-looking, Warburton was persistent.

"I particularly wanted to meet you, Mr. Carrington. You see, we have a mutual friend. Colonel Darlington."

Sinclair halted, glancing sharply at Warburton. Of a sudden the man appeared not so meek, his eyes knowing.

"Indeed?" Sinclair said in cautious tones. "Myself, I have not heard from the colonel in some time."

"I have. Quite recently. The colonel is most concerned over the sad state of English coastlines, erosion, that sort of thing, the changing shoreline." The under secretary flashed a bland smile. "Still, with accurate maps, I suppose one might gain a good idea of the damage to be inflicted."

"Yes, if such maps were available," Sinclair said, never taking his eyes from Warburton's face.

"They seem to be everywhere these days. Some have even turned up here in Paris." He met Sinclair's stare without flinching, and in the pause that ensued, Sinclair realized that they understood each other clearly.

"It is very stuffy in here," Warburton said, still smiling. "Perhaps we could step out through those windows into the garden for a breath of air."

Sinclair nodded. "I could do with a smoke."

Nothing more was said until they emerged through the window, the chili of the autumn night striking Sinclair. He welcomed it after the heat of the reception room, even more so for the fact that the brisk temperature kept all the other guests inside. The garden was a mass of rustling shadows except for the dim lighting provided by a suspended Argand lamp. Sinclair moved the glass lantern aside long enough to light his cheroot from the glowing wick. He offered a cigar to Warburton, who refused.

Sinclair inhaled deeply, then said, "Perhaps now you will explain yourself more clearly, Mr. Warburton."

"I, too, have been commissioned into service by Colonel Darlington."

"I gathered that or we wouldn't be talking now. The colonel told me I could expect to find an ally here in Paris."

"More than one, sir. Another of our agents is also present on these grounds. He works here as a gardener. It was he who discovered that a very accurate accounting of the warships in Portsmouth naval yard has been passed to the enemy, along with some maps drawn of coastline around that area."

"And this was a recent acquisition?"

"Passed this very afternoon. At a meeting held in the guardhouse."

"Did this gardener agent see the spy who brought the information?" Sinclair felt his stomach knot. He almost dreaded Warburton's answer.

"No, the informant was cloaked and hooded, the meeting brief, broken off when the guard was summoned by a courier demanding admittance at the gates. Our man could not draw near enough to hear clearly, nor could he follow the informant without rousing suspicion. We didn't even know what was passed, except that later our agent had the opportunity to overhear when the material was passed along to the first consul's secretary."

"What time did the meeting with this hooded figure take place? Do you have any idea?"

"I know precisely. Quarter past one."

"Quarter past one! Are you certain?" Sinclair could not conceal the excitement in his voice.

"Yes, I am. Is the time important?"

Not to you, Mr. Warburton, Sinclair thought, or the British army. But to Sinclair Carrington it was as though the world had been lifted off his shoulders. At quarter past one Belle had been in the apartment with him, staring out at the rain.

Sinclair wanted to fling back his head and shout his relief aloud. He had the urge to laugh and astonish the solemn Mr. Warburton with a hearty slap on the back. He could have embraced the fellow except there was someone else he would far rather embrace instead.

Sinclair contented himself with a broad grin. "Well, you gentlemen seem to be doing an excellent job of settling this affair. I scarce see what you need me for."

Warburton shot him a reproachful glance. "There is the small matter that this counteragent supplying the information has still not been identified. We had rather hoped you would start doing something from your end."

"I have a notion who your man might be, but I have no proof as yet." Sinclair thought of how Lazare's whereabouts at the crucial time were unaccounted for, to say nothing of Lazare's furtive behavior later in the afternoon. Some of Sinclair's relief at discovering Belle's innocence evaporated as a grim fact occurred to him. As long as the real counteragent remained unchecked, she, as the leader of this plot to abduct Napoleon, stood in more danger than anyone. The thought sobered Sinclair at once.

"Was any other information passed?" he asked Warburton.

The under secretary looked puzzled by Sinclair's abrupt demand.

"The group I have infiltrated is plotting to abduct Bonaparte," Sinclair explained. "Was there any hint of that in the message passed today?"

Warburton frowned. "Not as near as we could tell."

Sinclair found the man's answer far from satisfactory and not a little strange. If Lazare was the counteragent, what was he waiting for? Perhaps for Belle to finalize the details so that the information he passed would be specific?

"It would be a good thing if this counterspy could be stopped before he does decide to lay information about the plot," Warburton said.

Sinclair heartily concurred.

"I say, Carrington. Do you think there is any chance Merchant's group could succeed in their endeavor?"

Sinclair shrugged. Between trying to detect the counteragent and worrying it might prove to be Belle, he had not given the objective to capture Napoleon much serious consideration.

"If the counteragent could be stopped," Warburton said, "and you could still bring about the abduction of Bonaparte, I do not think either the army or the diplomatic corps would raise any objections about your participation in such a maneuver."

"How very generous of them, I'm sure," Sinclair said wryly. He dropped his cheroot and ground it out beneath his heel. "I trust you will find a way to keep me posted of any further developments here at the palace."

"Of course," Warburton said.

Judging that they had been in each other's company long enough, Sinclair suggested they return to the salon. Any longer an absence might draw unwanted attention.

As the two men reentered the reception area, they drifted apart, Sinclair's thoughts already no longer with Warburton. The under secretary's remarks had raised a new problem for him. If he did expose Lazare in time, should he permit Belle to go ahead with Merchant's mad scheme? Could she succeed in abducting the most important man in France—perhaps in all of Europe?

He glanced about the crowded reception chamber. Both Belle and the first consul were conspicuous by their absence. He experienced a growing sense of unease as he consulted his watch.

He would give her five more minutes. If she was not back, the abduction plot, the British army, and Bonaparte could all be damned. He didn't care if all of Paris sneered at him for a jealous husband. He was going after her.

"AND OVER THERE."—BONAPARTE TAPPED HIS FINGER against the window's night-darkened pane—"is the house where I once watched the mobs break through the fence to get at the king." He indicated the outline of a distant building beyond the iron fence surrounding the Tuileries Gardens. "It was a very hot summer's day."

Belle remembered it well herself. August tenth. She had not been there to witness the event, but the word had spread fast about the mob descending upon the king's palace, the king and his family forced to flee for protection to where the assembly sat. But Belle's concern had not been for the fate of the gentle King Louis. She had been terrified that the unreasoning mob might also attack the assembly, of which Jean-Claude had been a member.

"The king was too soft. He should have ordered his Swiss guard to fire. He could have scattered that rabble." Bonaparte mused. "It is not enough to inhabit the Tuileries. One must remain here."

The consul's eyes darkened with ferocity. "But just let the mob ever try to come here again—"

He left the threat uncompleted, but a chill coursed through Belle. From the hour's conversation they had shared, she sensed that for all his unexpected charm, this Bonaparte knew how to be ruthless to his enemies. If her plan failed, despite his seeming admiration for her beauty, she knew she could expect little mercy.

His fierce expression faded as quickly as it had come. "I fear I have absented myself from the reception too long. These affairs are a boring nuisance, but necessary. One who governs should not be aloof. In any case, I fear I have wearied you with my discourse."

Belle assured him this was not the case. He was a fascinating talker, extremely gregarious. It had not been difficult to draw him out, elicit his most decided opinions on art, history, and literature. He had not much use for novels, declaring them fit reading only for chambermaids, but he was fond of music, and most especially the theater.

In fact, he was willing to talk to her of anything, as long as it concerned matters of no real importance. Belle detected a certain hint of male patronage in that he would never burden a woman's mind with anything beyond her comprehension such as military or political matters.

Still, he had behaved in a gentlemanly fashion, and Belle could not deny that she had enjoyed the hour spent in his company. But she felt no further along with finding a way to accomplish her purpose in coming to Paris.

She had no choice now but to allow him to conduct her back to the reception salon. Before they crossed the threshold, he surprised her by stopping suddenly, placing his hand on her arm. She noted the whiteness of his fingers not much larger than her own.

"I should like to see you again, madame," he said in his usual direct fashion. "Would you sup with me some evening?"

Before she could reply, he added, "Alone."

Belle did not pretend to be coy or to misunderstand his meaning. She had to lower her lashes to conceal her elation. A supper alone with him, presumably without his guards in attendance. Her heart pounded so violently she feared he would hear it.

"I should like that," she said. "My husband frequently goes out to enjoy the gaming houses in the Palais¬Royal, but I have no taste for such."

"Nor have I." He raised her hand to his lips and saluted it with a brusque kiss. "I shall send my valet Constant to you to settle the date."

Belle hoped he mistook the excited flush mounting into her cheeks as gratification at this mark of his favor. But she saw she need not have worried. His attention had already been claimed from her by the reception salon. He surveyed the crowded chamber with satisfaction.

"The Due de Nanterre has finally put in his appearance," Bonaparte said, nodding toward an elderly gentleman. "Many of those stiff-necked emigres have been accepting my invitation to return. They finally see that France can be better rebuilt through me than a doddering Bourbon king. When the Comte de Egremont arrives, I shall count this evening a complete success."

Bonaparte's last remark brought an abrupt end to Belle's mood of elation, driving the blood from her cheeks. "The Comte," she faltered.

"Egremont. Jean-Claude Varens."

"You expect him here tonight?" How Belle kept her voice steady, she did not know.

Bonaparte angled a curious glance at her. "You know him?"

Belle concealed her dismay behind her fan. "I met him in London once."

"He emigrated to England. I am glad a man of such ancient family now chooses to resume his life in France." Despite his expressed pleasure, the consul's brow was marred by a frown. "Except that he is a divorced man. Did you know that?"

"I—I—no, I didn't."

"Apparently he separated from his wife during the Revolution, as so many men did. I suppose divorce was bound to come under our legislation, but I think it a great misfortune that it should become a national habit. What becomes of husbands and wives who suddenly become strangers, yet unable to forget one another?"

Belle shook her head, glad to see that he did not expect an answer to his impassioned speech. Her throat had become so constricted she doubted she could have given him one. She felt grateful to see Sinclair approaching, although he was not looking quite calm himself.

"Ah, Mr. Carrington," Bonaparte said. "I have enjoyed the

company of your lovely lady. As you see, I have brought her back to you."

"Excessively gracious of Your Excellency." Sinclair's voice carried a hard edge to it. For one playacting the jealous, suspicious husband, Belle feared he was doing too good of a job.

But Bonaparte looked more amused than annoyed by Sinclair's scowl. He extended an invitation to both of them to attend his upcoming military review and then moved off and was soon seen to be deep in conversation with Talleyrand.

Sinclair glowered after the first consul before shifting his gaze to Belle. "What the devil has Bonaparte been saying to you? You look pale as a sheet."

"Nothing," Belle lied. "It all went splendidly. I am to have supper with him. It is only I have developed the most dreadful headache. I would appreciate leaving now."

Sinclair favored her with a hard stare, but he asked no further questions, much to Belle's relief. She wished for nothing but to retrieve her cloak and be gone as quickly as possible. She felt herself to be a coward, but knew she could not endure the prospect of encountering Jean-Claude again, not here.

Leaning upon Sinclair's arm for support, she permitted him to guide her through the press of people, but once more her luck was out. A familiar slender figure blocked the doorway, his somber black attire and melancholy air seeming out of place amidst all the gay chatter.

Belle felt her heart sicken within her. Sinclair halted with a sharp intake of breath. "Varens. What the devil—" His gaze shifted to Belle. "You knew, didn't you? You knew he was due to arrive."

Belle abandoned any further attempt at pretense. "Yes, Bonaparte mentioned it to me just a moment ago."

"What in blazes is Varens doing here? I assumed he had retired to his estates in the country."

"So did I." Belle's mind reeled in disbelief as she watched

Bonaparte approach Jean-Claude. The comte greeted the first consul with obvious reluctance.

"Belle, there is something I need to ask you," Sinclair said, his voice low, urgent. "Does Jean-Claude know Lazare?"

Belle dragged her eyes from Jean-Claude long enough to frown at Sinclair, astonished by his peculiar question. "Of course not. Lazare came into my life long after Jean-Claude and I were divorced."

"But is it possible that Jean-Claude met Lazare somewhere on his own? I never mentioned the matter before, but there was a moment aboard the packet boat when I had the impression they knew each other."

"Lazare is not the sort of man Jean-Claude would know." Belle scarce knew why her reply came so sharp. Sinclair's suggestion sounded harmless enough on the surface. Why then did she feel as though he had slandered Jean¬Claude's honor? She passed her hand wearily over her brow. "I would truly appreciate it if you would summon our carriage. I just want to get out of here."

Sinclair appeared as though there was much more he would like to have said, but he nodded, giving her shoulder a compassionate squeeze. As he hastened off to fulfill her request, Belle had a strong urge to lose herself in the crowd.

Her pride rebelled, and in the end she placed herself so that inevitably, she must fall under Jean-Claude's gaze. He had just finished speaking to Napoleon and was stepping farther into the room.

He blanched at the sight of her, the shock obviously greater to him. She at least had been forewarned. But Jean-Claude was quick to recover. Looking right through her, he prepared to turn in the opposite direction.

Anger flashed through Belle. Did he think she was going to keep letting it be that easy for him? She had allowed him to brush her off in Portsmouth. Napoleon's words echoed through Belle's mind-husbands and wives who suddenly become strangers to each other. But she and Jean-Claude were not strangers. She had to acknowledge that fact; so should he.

With a quick movement she placed herself in his way. "Monsieur le Comte," she said, sweeping him a brittle curtsy.

He started, the muscles in his face working, making a great effort at keeping his features impassive. "Madame Carrington."

"How astonished I am to see you here in Paris. I thought you had gone back to Merevale." She had not meant her remark to be an accusation, but somehow it came out that way.

"Egremont is no longer mine, madame," Jean-Claude said "Although the first consul has been gracious enough to pardon emigres, lands were only returned if they had not been sold off. Unfortunately for me, that was not the case." He could not disguise his bitterness or his pain.

"Jean-Claude, I am so sorry. I didn't know." She touched his hand, but he flinched from her.

"Still so unforgiving?" she cried. "How long, Jean-Claude? I know I once did you a great injury, but how long will you continue to curse me for it?"

"I believed we had settled that issue years ago, madame." The coldness in his voice struck deep into her heart.

"Nothing was ever settled," she said. "You refused to listen to me."

His gaze skated past her to the door. "Your husband awaits you, madame. You'd best be going."

Belle gritted her teeth, beset by a desire to lash out, to hurt him as he was hurting her. "Sinclair is not my husband. I only live with him."

Jean-Claude's eyes widened with shock.

"You should not be so surprised," she taunted. "What more would one expect from the lowborn bastard of an actress?"

He flinched, and Belle knew that she had drawn blood at last, but she took no satisfaction in it. Blindly she turned, seeking the door and the support of Sinclair's strong arm.

White-lipped, Jean-Claude watched her go. He saw Carrington wrap Isabelle's cloak about her, noted with agony the tenderness conveyed in the simple gesture. Carrington, her lover. The knife Belle's words had plunged in Jean-Claude twisted. Despite all the bitter recriminations he spoke against her in his heart, he did not want to believe that she was capable of playing the harlot in any man's bed.

Whore? It was not a word he could bring himself to apply to Isabelle. In spite of her background, her deceits, he knew that some part of her remained innocent, untouched.

There had been such longing, such genuine sorrow in her lovely face when she had reached out to him a moment ago. He rubbed his hand where she had caressed him, her touch so butterfly soft. He thought he would have given anything not to have pulled away.

It would have been better had he never seen her again. Better still if he had not returned to France at all, trembling once more on the brink of events that portended to sweep beyond his control.

And yet he had a debt to repay, to his ancient family name, to his son's heritage, to the gentle king whom Jean-Claude had failed. In a future so fraught with danger and uncertainty, he had no business to be thinking of Isabelle at all.

But her image persisted, her words echoing through his mind. "Sinclair is not my husband." Isabelle had not married again. No matter what else she had said in the heat of her anger, one fact remained. She had bound herself to no other man. Despite the bleakness that was his life, for the first time in years, Jean-Claude Varens felt a thread of hope.

Eleven

The ride back from the Tuileries was accomplished in silence. Belle retreated deep within her hood, still deeper within the confines of herself.

When they reached the apartment, Sinclair saw that she meant to bid him good night in the antechamber and turn to go upstairs without another word.

He gently caught her arm. "Belle, please stay a moment. I'd like to—"

"I know. We have much to discuss. I want tell you all about what happened with Bonaparte. But I am so tired. We can talk about everything in the morning."

Sinclair frowned. From her shuttered expression, he knew that 'everything' was not likely to include Jean-Claude Varens. He found something strange about the Comte's sudden reappearance and was still disturbed by the possibility of a link between Varens and Lazare.

But one glimpse of Belle's pale face and Sinclair couldn't bring himself to mention the man's name again tonight. Her shoulders sagged with fatigue, her eyes beset by a kind of defeated weariness that appeared to run soul deep.

He stepped aside and permitted her to retreat up the stairs. As he watched her solitary figure trudge toward the shadows of the landing above, Sinclair was reminded curiously of Chuff, how he had held his younger brother's hand to help him brave the hobgoblins waiting in the dark. Sinclair wished he could do the same for that proud, lonely woman as she vanished up the stairs to battle with her own demons.

He cursed, consigning Jean-Claude Varens to the bottom of the Seine. Astonishing what havoc that stiff-necked nobleman could wreak upon Belle. When Sinclair had returned to the reception salon with her cloak, he had seen her speaking to Varens.

It had been obvious that they quarreled. Belle had been angry, but the anger had been quickly replaced with devastation. Sinclair could not understand it. Bold enough to flirt with a dangerous man like Bonaparte, capable of snapping out commands to a half-mad dog like Lazare, and yet Belle could be crushed by one unkind word from Varens. What hold did that somber man possess over her?

Sinclair could think of only one—love, the once and forever kind. For all her cool exterior, Belle was an intensely passionate woman. When she chose to love, it would be for always, and Jean-Claude just happened to be the man who had stirred those feelings inside of her.

"I came into your life years too late, Angel," Sinclair murmured sadly.

Belle had told Paulette not to wait up, but the woman hadn't listened. She bustled about the bedchamber full of questions about the reception. Had Belle met Napoleon? What had happened? Did Belle have any more idea of what her plans were?

Belle was of no humor to answer questions or to listen to Paulette's bright chatter. As soon as the woman helped Belle out of her gown, Belle dismissed her to her own bed. Paulette's eyes narrowed with annoyance, then her mouth twisted into a smirk.

"But of course, *chérie*. If there are any other services you want performed, you can always summon Monsieur Carrington."

Belle did not reply to this pert comment, all but shutting the door in Paulette's face. She leaned up against the barrier listening to Paulette retreat down the hall. Then she exuded a wearied sigh. Her mind felt numb from the bewildering whirl of events that had taken place that evening. She could not allow herself to think about any of it.

Belle pushed away from the door and, with motions that were instinctive, gathered up her gown. She smoothed out the folds, then put it away and returned her slippers and chemise to the wardrobe drawer before donning her nightgown. After removing the pearl netting, she brushed out her hair with rhythmic strokes, then rearranged the things on her dressing table until they lay with their customary mathematical precision.

It was as though by restoring order to the room, she hoped she could restore order to her mind as well, but it was not working. A montage of scenes from the reception whirled through her brain: the heat of Sinclair's gaze as he had handed her from the carriage, the uneasiness of being questioned by Fouché, the brief interlude with Napoleon, her sense of triumph which had faded with the sight of Jean-Claude, the grim confrontation that had followed, Sinclair's tormenting question, "What the devil is he doing here in Paris?"

How she longed to be able to answer that, even if only for herself. That reception at the Tuileries was the last place she would have expected to encounter Jean-Claude. Had he come to plead for the return of his estates, or to seek his fortune with the new government? Neither action sounded like the proud Comte de Egremont. Jean-Claude had ever been a man of principle. Although he supported some goals of the Revolution, he had remained fiercely loyal to the Bourbon kings. To think that he might at last be capable of sacrificing his notions of honor brought Belle real pain. The Revolution had robbed him of so many of his dreams, and she had helped. She had always been able to console herself that at least Jean-Claude had been spared his pride.

A shiver coursed through her, and she noticed that the fire on the grate was dying, a chill settling over the room. She must abandon these miserable thoughts and seek out her bed. Time to face what she most dreaded, the extinguishing of the candles.

The elaborate bed looked empty and uninviting. Over large, it might have been a state bed for a queen, the gauzy white curtains stirring eerily in the draft, a fit place to be laid out to die.

Belle tried to close her mind against the grim thought. This night would be no better than last. She faced another lonely vigil in hell. She was already so cold.

The sound of someone stirring in the next room carried to her ears, Sinclair, preparing for bed. She must take care not to disturb him tonight with her pacing. Belle ran her fingers over her chilled flesh. She could not help remembering how warm, how strong Sinclair's arms could be, what fire his kisses had spread through her body.

Her eyes tracked to the door connecting their chambers, the thought rising unbidden that she need not be alone tonight. Sinclair's voice echoed through her mind, "If anything is troubling you, Angel, feel free ..."

Only a few steps, a door separated them. What would Sinclair do if she came to him? She had read enough of want in his eyes. She did not think he would send her away.

She glided forward like a sleepwalker, only staying herself when her hand encountered the hard reality of the doorknob. No, how could she? She had tried passion a time or two before as an opiate to her pain. It could be as effective as laudanum, but the aftereffects of making love without love were more bitter. And she had nothing but passion to give. Hazarding one's life was one thing, but her heart- she could never do that again.

But the thought persisted that with Sinclair, this time would be different. There would be no regrets. Yet when she tried to turn the knob, her hand fell away, her courage deserting her.

But to face the prospect of that lonely bed, the nightmares, was equally impossible. She fetched her shawl instead and swirled it about her shoulders. She knew of a bottle of brandy that had been left below stairs in the kitchen When all else fails, seek out Mama's tried and true remedy for heartache, she told herself bitterly. She would sit by the window and get quietly drunk.

The clock had just chimed quarter after two when Sinclair thought he heard a noise downstairs. He went to investigate, still clad in his shirtsleeves and breeches. He had been unable to sleep in any case. Attempts to read a book had proved futile. The silence from Belle's room had seemed to roar in his ears.

How he sensed that she also was not asleep he could not have said. Nor even why he stalked so fearlessly downstairs, not in the least apprehensive of whom the intruder might be. Somehow he already knew.

The antechamber was dark, but light emanated from the drawing room. Through the half-open door, Sinclair could see a fire crackling upon the hearth, a candle left lit upon the mantel. But when he peered inside the chamber, he discovered Belle ensconced on the side of the room that remained cold and uninviting, where the wind rattled the glass of the tall, latticed windows. She huddled upon a wing-backed chair, an Indian shawl flung over her nightgown as she sat staring past the draperies. Silhouetted by the moonlight, her golden hair appeared spun from its beams, her eyes hollowed by shadows as foreboding as the night itself.

Although she started at Sinclair's entrance, she did not acknowledge his presence. Her breath stilled as though she waited to see if he would go quietly away and leave her prey to her night terrors, to fight on alone as she must have done so many times.

"Not this time, Angel," Sinclair murmured to himself. "Curse me, hate me, try to shut me out. But I cannot leave you alone tonight."

He crossed the room silently. She did not look toward him even when his shadow fell across her.

When she spoke, her voice was calm. "Good evening, Mr. Carrington."

"Perhaps you should say good morrow. It must be nearly half past two."

"Is it?" She leaned closer to the window pane, tipping her head back. "It looks nothing like morning to me. But then, the sky always seems to me much darker over Paris. There have been times I would have sworn dawn would never break here again."

Sinclair frowned at the sight of a tripod table propped near her elbow, bearing a half-empty glass of golden-colored liquid. He wondered if she was drunk. But as he examined the bottle of brandy, he saw that it had hardly been touched.

She stretched back in her chair, curling her bare feet beneath her. "I would invite you to join me, Sinclair," she said with a weary smile, "but I fear there is not enough. I intend to make myself quite drunk. I have never tried it before. But isn't that what you gentlemen do to make it through a rough night?"

"From one who has tried that remedy upon occasion, I would advise against it," he said. "Far from making the morning come quicker, your head will make you regret that it ever came at all."

She gave a soft laugh. He had never known that laughter could sound so sad. She pushed her glass away and turned back to staring out the window. Although she did not ask him to stay, she did not demand that he leave her, either, Pushing the velvet drapery back farther, Sinclair stood beside her, joining her in her vigil.

The night was dark, the stars like splinters of ice. In the street below, an occasional carriage clattered by even at this late hour. Some drunken stragglers slogged past, their voices raised in bawdy song. Otherwise the Rue St. Honoré remained quiet, the feeble glow from the Argand lanterns not enough to dispel the murky shadows. To Sinclair, it was nothing but an empty street, yet he would have wagered that was not what Belle saw. He glanced down at her.

Completely still she sat. Beneath the soft sweep of her lashes, he fancied he could glimpse the shadings of her past, all the misery of the world seeming centered in those luminescent blue eyes. But he waited patiently, refraining from questions. If Belle wanted, needed to talk, she would.

Just when he began to think her silence would stretch on until dawn, she stirred, saying, "Monsieur Bonaparte was full of plans tonight for improving Paris. He intends to start with the streets. God knows the Rue St. Honoré could use a little improving, at least some paving. It hasn't changed all that much since—"

"Since the Revolution?"

She nodded. "I used to spend a lot of my time then just staring out the window. It was safer, you see, to stay indoors, mind one's own business. Jean-Claude and I had an apartment not far from here, just up the street. I used to be able to watch the tumbrils go by on the way to the guillotine." Her voice dropped lower. "Sometimes the carts were crammed full of people, whole families, even the children."

"It must have been pure hell."

"No, that was the frightening thing. After a while we all grew accustomed to the horrors and simply went on with our lives."

Did she truly believe that? Maybe the others did, Sinclair thought, but not you, Angel. The torment of those days was yet reflected on her face. The tumbrils might still have been passing below for all the peace there was to be found in Belle's eyes.

"So you just went on with your everyday life," Sinclair said, "smuggling people out of Paris."

She acknowledged his ironic tone with a wry smile. "Yes, Baptiste and I. We got to be quite good at it, but for every one we helped to escape, there were a hundred more we couldn't save."

Sinclair knew he should not ask, but the question exploded

from him before he could help himself. "And where the hell was Varens when you were risking your life in such a fashion?"

"He had emigrated. We were divorced by then."

"I see. He took himself off to England and left you in the middle of a revolution."

"He didn't leave me anywhere. I chose to stay. He had given me money, provided for me. It was far more than I deserved, considering what I had done."

Sinclair clenched his jaw, surprised by the depth of contempt he was learning to feel for the most honorable Comte de Egremont, his anger only strengthened by Belle's steadfast defense of Varens. Sinclair knew that no matter what Belle had done, he would have made sure she was safely out of Paris. Then again, Sinclair was fast realizing, if she had been his wife, he would never have left her in the first place.

"If you don't mind my asking," he said, "what terrible crime did you commit to precipitate the divorce? Were you unfaithful to him?"

"You should be able to guess. I have already told you that I am the bastard daughter of an actress. I concealed my low birth from Jean-Claude when I married him."

"And that was his reason for divorcing you! Then he is a bigger fool than I took him for."

"It was an excellent reason," Belle said. "Jean-Claude is a gentleman from an ancient and honorable family. Discovering the truth about me was a harsh blow to his pride at a time when he he had already suffered—"

Sinclair realized some of his skepticism must have showed, for she broke off and cried, "You understand nothing about Jean-Claude. Nothing! So don't dare to stand there condemning him."

He was making her angry, but at least it brought a flush of color into her cheeks, the spark back into her eyes.

"I am trying to understand," he said. "If you would care to enlighten me."

Belle compressed her lips, retreating deeper beneath her shawl. She had been so glad of Sinclair's presence when he had first entered the drawing room. It had been such relief to talk to someone at last about her nightmarish memories of the Revolution. Why did he have to speak of Jean-Claude? Sinclair was not even her lover. There was no reason in the world she had to account for her past to him. None.

She glared up to where he stood, poised by the window curtain, his dark hair and compelling eyes making him seem at one with the night, but night as she had never known it, a warm, protective mantle, a night in which one could whisper all one's sins and heartbreak and never fear to see one's weakness exposed in the garish light of day.

She did not know what impelled her to do so, perhaps it was that empathetic link she had ever felt with Sinclair. Belle only knew that once she had started to speak, she couldn't seem to stop.

"I was sixteen that summer I met Jean-Claude," she said, leaning wearily back in her chair. The candle upon the mantel flickered and went out. In the wisp of smoke the years seemed to disappear.

Sixteen and traveling abroad for the first time. Belle could still remember her excitement. It had been one of those rare times of good fortune in that mad up-again, down-again life she had known as the daughter of Jolie Gordon.

That summer Jolie had been lucky enough to take as a lover the foolish but amiable Count Firenza, a wealthy Italian nobleman. No more being sent by Mama to fend off the bailiffs while Mama hid in the wardrobe, no more being abandoned with disgruntled relatives while Mama disappeared for weeks on end

The count's generosity had extended to including Isabelle in his entourage, the kindly man taking a bluff paternal interest in her. He had swept both Jolie and Belle off to the south of France. They had done Marseilles in grand style, Mama feigning to be a countess, Belle, the nobleman's pampered step-daughter. Firenza had looked on with indulgence, seeing it all as the most marvelous jest ever played upon the snobbish French aristocrats. Certainly, Belle had never intended to take in Jean-Claude with her masquerade. She had never intended anything by him at all. He was handsome enough, but too solemn, too serious. She had far more witty admirers than the gray-eyed young man who propped up the wall at soirees, following her every movement with his wistful gaze.

The intentions had come afterward. With her usual flightiness, Jolie had run off with a Prussian officer. But the good-natured count had not held Belle to blame for her mother's defection. He had permitted her to keep the frocks, the jewels, even giving her a small sum to see her back to England before setting sail himself for Italy.

Only Belle had gone nowhere. Sick to death of her uncertain life, she had finally perceived a way out in the admiration of the young Comte de Egremont. It had been so easy to convince the guileless Jean-Claude she had been left in the care of a governess for the sake of her health. Easier still to appear frail and helpless, entrapping the adoring man into marriage.

Here Belle paused in her recital, wrenched back to the present, wondering what Sinclair thought of her scheming.

She risked a glance at him. He leaned against the window, his arms folded, but his still features passed no judgment as he merely waited for her to go on with the tale.

Sighing, she continued, "I never counted on the fact that I would fall in love with him. As I grew to know him better, he seemed so different from any man I had ever met, so gentle. But more than anything else, he had dreams." A wistful note infused itself into Belle's voice. "Not dreams like my selfish ones for a place in society, material possessions, but such visions for a better world."

Her eyes misted as she recalled those long-ago evenings by the fireside, the glow on Jean-Claude's face as he talked of the brotherhood of mankind, a world where inequalities would be destroyed, injustice forever banished, a society where one's birth would not be so important as the value of a man's soul.

From such talk Belle had been encouraged to hope Jean-Claude would not mind so much when she told him the truth. But she could never work up the courage, always terrified of losing his love.

"He thought me perfect," she said. "It was very hard to live up to his image of me. I feared what he would think if he knew how I had lied. Tomorrow, I always assured myself, tomorrow would be a better day. I would tell him then."

But her secret had paled before the greater events sweeping through the country. The Bastille had fallen the day after their wedding, the repercussions of that event slowly spreading throughout France.

Yet for a long time the village of Merevale had remained untouched. The people on the Egremont estate were devoted to Jean-Claude, suspicious of any wild idea coming from such a 'foreign' place as Paris. It had been Jean-Claude himself who had let the Revolution within the chateau walls. Enthusiastically embracing its principles of equality and freedom, he had voluntarily resigned his title and talked joyously of a liberated France governed by a constitutional monarchy. His happiness had known no bounds when he had been elected to the second national assembly.

"And so we came to Paris," Belle said. "I had just passed my eighteenth birthday, but I already had seen far more of the ugly face of men than Jean-Claude. From the first day we rode through the streets, I sensed something seriously amiss. Most of the noble speeches only served to disguise the ambition of hard and ruthless men."

But for Jean-Claude's sake she tried to quell her doubts and uneasiness, a task that became harder and harder as the weeks sped by and the violence of the Revolution grew. Frenetic mobs invaded prisons massacring priests and aristocrats. The Tuileries was attacked, the king and queen arrested. More and more the moderate voices in the assembly such as Jean-Claude's were being drowned out by the roars of the fanatics.

"Each day," Belle said, "I looked into Jean-Claude's eyes and saw his belief in the goodness of men, dying a little more. And there was no way for me to recapture those dreams for him, hold them fast, although I would have given my life to have done so."

You did, Angel, far too much of it, Sinclair longed to assure her, but he knew she would not want to hear that.

Overcome by her recollections, she doubled her hand into a fist, pressing it against her eyes. With her words, she had painted a picture for Sinclair, but not the one she wanted him to see. Her tale roused not a particle of sympathy in him for Jean-Claude.

Someone should have smacked his noble lordship awake, Sinclair thought savagely. He doubted that Jean-Claude could have suffered overmuch, passing through the Revolution in a rose-tinted dream. But Belle, ever the realist, facing all the horrors with her eyes wide open—how many scars she yet carried, how many pain-filled memories were seared into her soul.

Hunkering down, Sinclair closed his hand over hers. Her skin felt so cold. He tried to chafe some warmth back into her.

After a moment she lowered her fist from her eyes. Once more in control, she resumed her story. "Jean-Claude managed to continue his work in the assembly until the trial and condemnation of the king. Even to the very last, Jean-Claude did not believe the people of Paris would let the execution happen."

Using Sinclair's hand for support, Belle levered herself to her feet. Sweeping the curtain aside, she beckoned him to join her at the window, pointing toward the distant street corner. "Down there on the morning the sentence was to be carried out, Jean-Claude mounted one final plea to the crowds to attempt a last-minute rescue as the coach went by.

"I was terrified that the mob would turn on him, and I tried to make him stop. It scarce mattered. The cheers, the drums beating were so loud when the king's carriage passed that no one even heard what Jean-Claude was saying.

"The rest of that day I held him as he wept in my arms. It was shortly after that Jean-Claude discovered the truth about me. I suppose it was bound to happen one day. An Englishman traveling in Paris had once visited Mama backstage at the theater and he remembered seeing me. When he told Jean-Claude the truth, it nearly killed him."

Her voice faded to silence. For a long time Sinclair said nothing, but she was aware of how close he stood to her, drawing comfort from his nearness.

"How long did you stay in Paris after Jean-Claude had gone?" he asked.

"Until the summer of ninety-eight. The Terror was at its worst then, so many innocent people proscribed. Baptiste and I got a little reckless trying to help and were caught. I was imprisoned in the Conciergerie, an experience I never care to repeat. That I would be found guilty was a foregone conclusion.

"I would have taken that long ride down the Rue St. Honoré myself except that Robespierre was so obliging as to make himself unpopular. Shortly after he was executed, those he had had arrested were set free. I didn't wait for anyone to change their minds. I left Paris the same day and have never been back until now."

She rested her head against the cool pane of the glass. "I returned to England and lived the best I could until I met up with Merchant. I decided it was better to become a royalist spy than turn whore. So there you have it, the whole dismal story of my life. Not very impressive, is it? I sometimes feel as if it would have made no difference to anyone if I had not been born at all."

Sinclair stepped behind her, resting his hands on her shoulders. He began to knead the tension from her muscles. "I doubt if those whom you helped save from the guillotine would say that."

"Perhaps not," she murmured, soothed in spite of herself by

Sinclair's touch. "But I so wish the good memories would outlive the bad. At least that would be something to hold on to on a long dark night."

Sinclair turned her to face him. "You could hold on to me, Angel."

He made no move to force her, only beckoning her with his eyes. Belle responded to that unspoken call, winding her arms about his neck. How good it felt to be held by him, his fingers stroking her hair.

Belle sensed that he would have restrained himself to just that, offering her comfort alone. It was she who sought more. Raising her face, she invited his kiss.

He brushed his lips against her brow, her temples, her cheek. Belle closed her eyes, savoring the warm contact, dreading that he might stop, draw away as he had done earlier today after being interrupted by Paulette.

"Sinclair," she whispered. "Help me, please. Help me make it through this night."

Never in her life had she begged, never had she asked such a thing of any man before. But she felt no shame, no wish to call back the plea that had escaped her. She knew that Sinclair would understand.

He pressed his mouth to hers in a gentle kiss, then swooped her up in his arms to carry her upstairs.

From the beginning Belle had refused to allow herself to imagine what it would be like to make love with Sinclair. If she dared any thought at all, she supposed that because the physical attraction between them coursed so strong, they would come together in a feverish rush.

She was bemused when Sinclair's first action upon entering her bedchamber was to tuck her into bed, pulling a coverlet snugly about her shivering form.

While she watched from the bed, he gathered logs and rekindled the fire upon the hearth until the flames crackled, sending out waves of heat to ward off the chill of the room.

A smile, part amusement, part gratitude tugged at Belle's lips. What an eminently practical man Sinclair was. When he had the fire going, he went about the room, lighting lamps and candles, until the chamber glowed, the shadows dispelled. It was almost as if he knew-

The flickering firelight illuminated the strong line of his jaw, the dark sweep of his lashes and the intensity of his eyes. Mesmerized, Belle studied his every movement as he piled on more logs, the way the muscles of his back rippled beneath his linen shirt, the striking contrast the white fabric made against his bronzed skin.

He spread out a downy coverlet and piled pillows before the hearth before returning to her side to offer her his hand.

"Milady?" he said, his teasing drawl coming out hoarse.

Belle slipped her hand in his and followed him as though she walked in a dream. They stood facing each other before the fire. Although he did no more than trace the contours of her cheek with his fingers, Belle felt the beginnings of desire flicker to life inside of her, a desire that seemed to run far deeper than the wants of her flesh. She had a strange feeling that she had been waiting a long time for this moment.

Sinclair brushed back her hair, allowing the strands to cascade over his fingers as though reveling in the feel of it.

"Belle," he said, his face more solemn than she ever remembered. "I don't want to take advantage of—" He drew in a deep breath. "What I am trying to say is, you don't have to offer yourself to me to make me stay with you. I could simply hold you in my arms until morning."

"Could you?" she challenged softly. She ran her fingers slowly up the hard plane of his chest, feeling the thud of his heart beneath the crisp linen of his shirt.

His lips crooked into a reluctant smile. "No, likely not, but it was a most noble impulse."

"I don't want you to be noble, Sinclair." She wound her arms about his neck, pressing close to him. "Not tonight."

He caught her hard against him, his mouth descending over hers. He coaxed her lips apart, invading her with the fiery sweetness of his tongue, swirling in slow tormenting circles. The heat of his body seared her even through her nightgown.

As of one accord, they sank down to the coverlet. Sinclair tumbled her back against the pillows. Bending over her, he explored her face and the column of her neck with feathery kisses that sent lashings of fire through her veins.

She began to undo the buttons of his shirt one by one. The material parted, falling away to reveal the crisp dark hairs matting his chest. Belle slipped the shirt down his arms, letting it drop to the floor.

She ran her hands over his hard muscled flesh and felt a quiver course through him. He undid the ribbons of her nightgown, slipping it off her shoulders until she lay naked beside him.

Then he stood to remove his breeches, easing the cloth down over the taut line of his hips, past the lean hardness of his thighs. He towered naked above her in the full glory of his manhood, leaving her in no doubt as to the extent of his arousal.

He paused a moment to stare down at her. "You are beautiful, Belle," he said hoarsely. For once the compliment did not ring hollow in her ears.

She remained quite still, making no self-conscious effort to cover herself, permitting Sinclair to devour her with his eyes. For perhaps the first time in her life, she experienced a genuine gratitude for the perfections of her form, grateful because of Sinclair's response.

He sank back down beside her and hungrily pulled her into his arms with a kiss that was long and deep. The fire that blazed upon the hearth behind them seemed as nothing beside the flames Sinclair stirred inside her.

He sought her lips again and again, the softness of her hips and breast molding to the hard length of him. His fingers whispered over her flesh, exploring her most intimate curves, rousing her wherever he touched.

Who would have thought, she marveled, that he could be so tender—Sinclair Carrington, that arrogant rogue, that teasing rakehell.

Jean-Claude had ever been a gentle lover, approaching her like a pilgrim to a holy shrine. Belle had once teasingly accused him of making love to her as if she were the Virgin Mary. He had been deeply shocked by her blasphemy.

But for all his gentleness, there remained no doubt that Sinclair came to her as a man to a woman. When he lowered his mouth to her breast, teasing the pink crest with the roughness of his tongue, she was pierced with longing so fierce, she nearly wept. How she did need this man's loving, perhaps too much.

Yet for all his expertise, Sinclair felt more awkward than he ever had in his life. Never had his partner's pleasure meant so much to him. Curbing his own raging desires, he deliberately prolonged the love play until it became the most delicious torment to them both.

"Now," Belle cried, her nails raking his back. "Please, Sinclair, take me now."

She opened herself to him, and he could no longer resist the invitation. He eased himself inside her, his own pleasure heightened by the sight of her flushed features, so beautiful.

He began to move slowly at first. Moaning, Belle rose to meet his thrusts, urging him on to a faster, more frenzied tempo. Fighting against his own climax, he sought to bring her to the peak of her desire. He knew when she had reached it, for she flung back her head, emitting a soft cry of ecstasy.

Only then did he give way to his own passion, which had mounted to the point of pain. The release was shattering and sweet. He collapsed, spilling his seed deep within her.

For long moments after, he held her, burying his face against the softness of her throat, her heart thundering in rhythm with his own.

Have no regrets, Belle, he prayed silently, for I have none. He knew not how long they lay there, lost in each other's embrace. When he felt Belle stir, he raised his head to seek out her reaction now that all passion was spent.

She smiled tremulously and stroked his hair back across his brow behind his ear. "Thank you," she whispered.

Her simple expression of gratitude tugged at his heart. He cupped her hand in his and pressed a kiss against the upturned palm.

"For what?" He chuckled. "I was not exactly a disinterested party. I had a few selfish desires of my own, you know."

She shared his laughter, but sobered immediately. "I fear it is I who has been the selfish one. I want you to know that I have not just been using you because I felt lonely and afraid. Tonight has meant more to me than you could ever know. I only wish—" She paused ruefully. "I only wish I could say more to you than that."

"Hush, Angel." He silenced her with a quick kiss. "I don't expect you to pledge your undying devotion simply because I made love to you."

"The only man I have ever made such promises to was—"

"Yes, I know," he said when she was not able to finish. A dull ache throbbed near the region of his heart, but he managed to shrug it off. He cradled her closer. "You keep your memories of Jean-Claude. I don't mind, for it's my arms you are in right now."

Crooking his fingers beneath her chin, he tipped up her face. "We are practical people, you and I, Belle. Neither of us believe in forever, but we both know what has happened between us tonight is very rare indeed. Let's not spoil it by trying to offer apologies and explanations."

She gazed back at him, her eyes wide and searching. Then she nodded slowly, moving closer to accept his kiss. Locked once more in each other's embrace, it did not take long for the passion to build again.

This time Sinclair scooped Belle up and carried her back to the bed. As he began to caress her, she stopped him, gently forcing him onto his back.

"No, Mr. Carrington," she murmured, smiling down at him, "This time it's my turn to drive you to the brink of madness."

PROPPED UP AGAINST THE PILLOWS, THEY WATCHED THE dawn break over the windowsill, the rosy-gold light creeping across the carpet to where they nestled beneath the coverlets. Cradled against the lee of Sinclair's shoulder, his strong arms locked about her, Belle sighed deeply. Never had she expected to view the arrival of morning as an intrusion.

With the cold light of day, now will come the regrets, she thought, the confusion, the embarrassment. She waited but she felt none of those dreaded emotions, nothing but this wondrous sensation of contentment. Day or night, to be lying here in Sinclair's arms seemed the most natural thing in the world.

She felt the warmth of his breath against her curls, so even and deep, she wondered if he had fallen asleep. Before she could raise her head to glance up at him, he stirred, depositing a kiss upon the top of her head.

"I should be stealing back to my own room," he said. But he only held her tighter, making no move to do so.

"Why?" she murmured teasingly. "Are you yet trying to protect my reputation?"

"No, simply to let you get some sleep. You look exhausted. You did not get any rest at all last night."

She laughed. "But for once it was because of the right reason."

She felt his smile as he buried his face against her hair. Shifting slightly, she met his questing lips with a kiss that was chaste, but rife with warm memories of all they had shared the night before.

Drawing back, she caressed the stubble of beard that roughened his cheek and the stubborn line of his jaw. She liked the stark contrast he made to the silken femininity of her bed, his dark hair tumbled against the pillow, the hard musculature of his frame, the swarthy cast of his skin. But she also noted the deep hollows beneath his eyes.

"I suppose I should let you go," she said reluctantly, "and catch what sleep you still can. We have a busy day ahead of us."

"Do we?" His eyes fixed tenderly upon her face. "Strange, but as tired as I am, I feel as though I could abduct a dozen Bonapartes."

"One will do," she said. But she knew what he meant. She too had the curiously elated feeling she could accomplish anything, overcome any obstacle. "I never told you all that happened at the reception when I was alone with Bonaparte."

Easing herself out of his arms, she plumped up her pillow and lay down upon it. Settled more snugly beneath the covers, she gave a tiny yawn and began to relate the conversation she had had with the first consul.

But Sinclair barely heard a word she said. Propping himself up on one elbow, he played with one of the strands of her hair, twining it about his finger. How soft Belle was in the morning, like a lovely pastel, all hazy rose, cream, and gold. He studied the tranquility that had settled over her features.

For one night she had not cried out in her sleep for Jean-Claude Varens. At least he had gifted her with that much, Sinclair thought with great satisfaction, a night of pleasure, a night of comfort. That had been all that he had set out to do. Why, then, did he feel he wanted to give her so much more, speak tender words she would not want to hear, words that would cause her to shrink from him?

With great difficulty he thrust such foolish thoughts aside and attempted to focus on what she was saying.

"And so I agreed to have supper with him, an intimate supper.

The abduction promises to be much easier than I thought, and yet —" She frowned.

Sinclair traced the furrows pinching her brow, attempting to smooth them away. "And yet?" he prompted.

"I never expected to somewhat admire Bonaparte, to almost like him," she admitted sheepishly. "What did you think of him?"

"I suppose he can exercise a certain sort of fascination," Sinclair conceded. To him, as a loyal Englishman, Bonaparte would ever be simply his country's enemy. But if Belle was beginning to have second thoughts about the abduction, Sinclair was ready to encourage her, fearing as he did that the plot might be betrayed by the traitor in Merchant's organization.

"Are you saying that you might not be disappointed if for some reason the abduction had to be called off?" he asked.

"I don't know. Yes, I think that I would. After all, Merchant has offered us a considerable reward.-

"Is the money that important to you, Angel?" Sinclair stroked the hair back gently from her brow. "What would you do with such a sum?"

"Invest it wisely." She suppressed another yawn, burrowing deeper into her pillow. "I told you I don't intend to be a spy forever. Someday I mean to leave my past behind me and buy a cottage in some quiet little village."

When Sinclair smiled, she peered up at him beneath eyelids becoming increasingly heavier with the need for sleep.

"Why are you smirking at me like that?" she demanded.

"Because I can't imagine you sitting about stitching samplers and having the vicar and local tabbies in for tea."

"You don't think I could act the role of a respectable lady?"

"Oh, I think you could act the part all right, but whether you would be happy doing so is another matter," Sinclair did not believe that Belle would be content in her little village. Any more than if she had managed to remain married to the dull, but virtuous Jean-Claude. But Sinclair knew he would only anger her by raising such speculations.

"Such a tame life would not suit me," was all he said.

"Then you must spend your share of the money some other way." Despite her efforts to stay awake, her lashes drifted downward. "Though you may be right about one aspect of it," she mumbled. "The pretense, hiding my past, would grow tiresome after a while."

She forced her eyes open long enough to give him a drowsy smile. "You know that is the one thing I truly adore about you, Sinclair."

"What's that, Angel?" he asked.

"That there is never any pretense between us. No deception. Yours is probably the first honest relationship I have ever had."

Sinclair's answering smile froze. He was glad when she closed her eyes again so that she would not see how she had disconcerted him.

That is your cue, Carrington, a voice inside him nagged. Time to tell her the truth about who you are, what you are really doing in Paris. But how could he, after what she had just said, especially after what had taken place between them? He could just hear himself trying to explain. "I work for the British army, Belle. I was sent here to spy upon you and your companions, to discover which of you is a traitor."

Might she not misconstrue the compassion that had led him to encourage her to talk out her sorrows last night, even misunderstand his motives for making love to her?

And yet, he had to tell her the truth, let her know what danger she risked by going ahead with a plot that might at any moment be betrayed. How would she react? Would she help him uncover the counterspy?

Sinclair studied Belle's serene profile, the golden lashes fanning her cheeks. He had learned enough of Belle to know that her loyalties were to people above nations. If Lazare were the one, Sinclair did not doubt that she would aid him gladly. But Englishwoman or no, if the traitor should prove to be Baptiste or even if Jean-Claude were somehow involved, then Sinclair did not know how far he could trust to Belle's support.

He ground his fingers against his weary eyes. Everything had seemed simplified when he had discovered Belle could not be the counterspy. But he now saw clearly that matters were more complicated than ever. He still could not risk telling Belle the truth.

In any case, the present opportunity for confession had passed. While he had debated the matter, Belle had fallen soundly asleep. Slipping quietly from the bed, he donned his breeches. By the time he retrieved his shirt, he had reached a decision. He would not tell her, not until he had proof certain the traitor was Lazare. In the meantime, he must keep a vigilant watch over Belle and make sure she remained safe.

He tiptoed over to the bed and adjusted the coverlets more snugly about her. But as he bent to kiss her smooth untroubled brow, he could not rid himself of the nagging sensation that by keeping silent he was making a grave mistake.

A mistake he might heartily come to regret one day.

Twelve

When Belle awoke hours later, she bore vague memories of Sinclair tucking her in, the feel of his warm lips grazing her forehead. The recollection was marred by the impression of a tension in the hands that had so tenderly pulled the coverlet up to her chin, a glimpse of an anxious frown.

Though why that should be, she could not say. She tried to recall the conversation they had been having when she had drifted off to sleep, but her memories of it were hazy. In the end she dismissed her misgivings as imagination, more pressing matters crowding forward to occupy her mind.

The promised invitation from Bonaparte arrived that afternoon, setting the date of their supper for a week hence, to be held at his private apartments in the palace of Saint-Cloud, some twelve miles outside of Paris.

One week, Belle reflected as she smoothed her hand over the crisp sheet of vellum. That did not give her much time.

The ensuing days passed in a flurry of activity. To avoid any hint of suspicion, she and Sinclair continued to play their role as the typical English couple touring abroad, accepting invitations to some of the salons, being seen walking along the Petite Coblentz at the fashionable hour, exploring the Louvre like the other foreign visitors to gawk at the masterpieces Napoleon had plundered from the nations he had conquered.

Contrasting to these public appearances were the clandestine meetings with Baptiste, Crecy, and Lazare to finalize the plans for the abduction. These sessions proved long, the arguments many. Lazare favored waylaying the first consul's coach en route, The road to St. Cloud contained quarries where a contingent of armed men might easily be hidden.

But as Belle pointed out, Bonaparte was no fool. She had gleaned the information that these quarries were always checked before Napoleon set out for St. Cloud. She favored a more subtle approach. Their own men disguised as members of the consular guard would have a greater chance of drawing near to the coach, overpowering the escort before the deception was discovered,

While the merits of this suggestion were debated at length, Belle frequently found her attention wandering, her gaze tracking toward Sinclair. It was most strange, she thought. Part of her reluctance to succumb to Sinclair's charm had been her fear of the distracting effect it would have on their work. Yet at most, when their eyes met, the warmth of a knowing glance would pass between them. An accidental brushing of his hand upon hers would send a tingle rushing through her veins. But she doubted that any could have guessed from the cool sophistication of their manner that their relationship was anything other than professional.

By day Monsieur and Madame Carrington presented the image of the well-bred married couple, courteous and dispassionate. Ah, but by night, in Sinclair's arms, in the dark of her bedchamber, that was entirely another matter.

By the morning of the military review, five days had passed since the reception, and Belle felt able to relax somewhat. Her plan had been adopted in the teeth of Lazare's objections; most of the details had been settled. Work on the light coach to which Bonaparte would be transferred was complete, some reliable men for added force recruited from Crecy's servants, the stitching on the duplicate guard uniforms nearly finished.

Belle had naught to do but wait and continue to enact her part as the alluring Mrs. Carrington. As she prepared to dress to attend the review, she paused long enough to force open the window casement in her bedchamber.

The weather had turned unseasonably warm these past few days, the breeze whispering past the curtains seeming more borne of May than October. Belle selected her lightest gown, a high-waisted walking dress of pearl-colored jaconet, the hem bordered with narrow tucks, then summoned Paulette to help her with her hair.

But the Frenchwoman was nowhere to be found. Belle pulled a wry face. Paulette had been more flighty than usual of late, unreliable. She supposed it might be the weather or the woman's excitement at being back in Paris again. It would not have surprised Belle if Paulette had found herself a lover somewhere.

Shrugging off her annoyance, Belle scooped up the hairbrush from the dressing table. She had indeed allowed herself to become a pampered dolt if she did not still know how to do her own hair.

Brushing the strands into an arrangement of soft curls, Belle donned a gypsy hat of straw, bending it into bonnet shape by use of a sky-blue ribbon. Fetching her silk-fringed parasol and a lace shawl, she headed briskly downstairs.

It did not surprise her to find both antechamber and drawing room empty. Punctuality, at least for social functions, she was rapidly discovering, was not amongst Sinclair's list of virtues. But this particular time, for the military review, she did not intend that they should be late.

Marching back up to his room, she delivered a thundering summons against his door, but was disconcerted to discover that Sinclair was not in the apartment at all. He surely would have had no place to go at such an early hour. She could not imagine where he might be unless ...

She had noted that Sinclair found time each day to stop below to pass a few minutes with Baptiste in his lodgings or the fan shop, a fact that pleased Belle. Once accustomed to being surrounded by a large family, she knew that Baptiste was often lonely, the gregarious little Frenchman always glad of any company, ever proud to display his crafts. Despite Baptiste's initial wariness of Sinclair, she sensed that a liking had developed between the two men.

Likely that was where Sinclair was now. If she hurried down, she could visit with Baptiste herself for a moment, and they would still have time to attend the review.

Hastening below, she again met with disappointment. A placard bearing the word closed had been placed in the shop's front window. That was as odd as Sinclair's unexplained absence, Belle thought. Today was the *decadi*, a proclaimed holiday. But Baptiste had ever ignored the Revolutionary calendar, the decree that every tenth day should be treated as a day of rest.

Frowning in puzzlement, she went round to the back of the building where Baptiste had his lodgings behind the shop. She half-feared again to meet with no answer, but the door swung open at once with her first knock.

"Oh! Baptiste, you are here. Is Sinclair with—" She broke off in surprise as she obtained a better look at her old friend. This was Baptiste as she had never seen him before. Gone were the much-darned brown clothes and the leather apron. Dressed in an old-fashioned, but immaculate green frock coat, he had knotted a modest white cravat and black tie about his throat. In one work-worn hand he carried a gray felt hat trimmed with silk cord, his straggly salt and pepper hair smoothed back in neat waves.

"Why, Baptiste! You look *trés beau*."

He blushed at her compliment, the red spreading from the tip of his nose across his leathery cheeks. He shrugged. "It is nothing, only the *habillement* I wear to mass."

"But it is not Sunday. What is the occasion?"

"Did not Monsieur Carrington inform you?" Baptiste regarded her in rather anxious fashion. "You see, I was telling him but yesterday afternoon that I had never taken the time to attend any of Bonaparte's reviews. They are acclaimed as quite the spectacle. And if our plan succeeds, this could well be the last, so ..." He trailed off, staring humbly down at the brim of his hat.

"So Monsieur Carrington suggested you accompany us?" Belle asked with a smile.

"If you have no objections, *mon ange*."

"Of course I do not object. But where is Sinclair? Have you not seen him this morning?"

When Baptiste answered in the negative, she frowned, the first stirrings of unease beginning to niggle at her.

"Are you sure he is not yet upstairs?" Baptiste asked. "Perhaps he lingers in the bath."

Belle shook her head. "No, he has definitely gone out. Both his cloak and umbrella are missing." She had noted some time ago, that rain or shine, Sinclair rarely stirred without his umbrella, an unusual affectation for an Englishman. She could only suppose that he carried it for protection, likely having a swordstick concealed in the handle as many gentlemen were wont to do.

"Do not look so worried, *mon ange*," Baptiste said. "I am sure he will return in good time. I wish to check the shop once more to make certain the doors are secured, then I will meet you out front to search for him if you wish."

Belle agreed absently. Moving away, she had already decided to check the apartment herself one more time in the event that Sinclair had returned while she talked with Baptiste.

As she started up the outer stairs, she was relieved to hear a footfall on the landing above her that seemed to pause just outside the apartment door.

"Sinclair?" she called out eagerly.

"I fear not," a silky French voice drawled.

She heard the scrape of a boot as a tall masculine form emerged from the shadows above.

"Oh. Larare," Belle said in flat tones of disappointment. She froze in mid-step. He continued to saunter down the stairs, taking each one with a slow deliberation, those cool blue eyes of his fixing her like ice picks.

Belle experienced a strong urge to retreat, although she could not have said why. These past days Lazare had kept to his pledge of not giving her any trouble. Aside from his usual brand of insolence, he seemed to acknowledge her position as leader, carrying out whatever commands she gave in his own grudging fashion.

Yet she still did not relish the prospect of a *tete-a-tete* with him, something she had managed to avoid thus far.

His lips thinned to a sneer. "What, *ma chére* Isabelle? Never tell me you have misplaced the estimable Monsieur Carrington?"

"No," she said coldly, not about to display any of her anxiety before Lazare's sarcastic gaze. "Sinclair has simply gone out. When I heard you on the stair, I hoped it was him returning. We do have the review to attend this morning."

"Ah, yes, one of Bonaparte's infamous military displays. It would be a thousand pities if Monsieur Carrington did not return in time."

Belle did not like the smile that accompanied Lazare's words. He seemed to be taking a kind of sly amusement from the situation.

In no humor to be baited by the Frenchman's blunt wit, she said nothing more, but turned and made a dignified exit, to stand outside, observing the morning bustle of pedestrians and carriages thronging the Rue St. Honoré, peering anxiously for some sign of Sinclair.

To her annoyance, Lazare followed her. He lounged in the open doorway, paring the dirt from beneath his nails with his knife. The sunlight accented the angel-white tint of his hair and flushed his scar a shade of dull angry red.

"Monsieur Carrington, he has a habit of wandering off, does he not?" Lazare asked as though making idle conversation.

"I am sure I don't know what you mean," Belle said.

"It is just that I have noticed each day he has an errand that takes him somewhere, *n'est pas*?"

Belle had not given the matter much consideration. At other times she had been much too occupied herself to keep track of the length of Sinclair's brief absences. But now that she thought about it, she supposed that Lazare was right.

"Now, where do you imagine he goes?" Lazare purred.

"Out for a walk, to make a purchase, I don't know," Belle said. "Since I am not in truth his wife, I don't keep him on that tight of a leash."

A hint of irritation crept into Belle's voice, although she determined to ignore Lazare and whatever he was attempting to insinuate about Sinclair. The Frenchman had a penchant for making mischief. It seemed as necessary to him as breathing.

"Very much the man of mystery, our Monsieur Carrington," Lazare continued to muse, rubbing the tips of his fingers beneath his chin. "Have you ever found that strange, Isabelle? I have. After all, we all know a little something of one another, yet we know next to nothing about him."

Although Belle kept her features impassive, she tensed. How like Lazare to hit upon the one fact that did yet disturb her about Sinclair. As intimate as she and Sinclair had become, his background did remain closed to her. When he took her in his arms, touched her heart with that look of soul-deep understanding, she could tell herself she knew Sinclair well enough. That his reluctance to discuss his own past did not matter and yet ...

"Merchant considered Sinclair suitable enough to employ him," Belle snapped at Lazare. "That is sufficient for me,"

"Is it? For *moi*, I am afraid not. I have never placed that much faith in Merchant's judgment. Now, this Carrington—" Lazare wagged the tip of his knife at her. "He never seems to show that much enthusiasm for the little project that has brought us all to Paris."

"I don't ask for enthusiasm, just efficiency."

Once more she had to admit to herself that Lazare spoke true. At all their meetings Sinclair remained silent, never putting forth any suggestions, though Belle was certain his mind equaled her own when it came to weaving plots. Sinclair had been reluctant from the first, yet he had undertaken the mission. His lack of enthusiasm signified nothing. All the same, Belle wished that Lazare would take himself off. His voice was beginning to affect her like the rasp of a file on an iron bar.

She glanced once more up the street, annoyed to feel her foot begin to tap out a rhythm of nervous impatience.

"Maybe Carrington has lost his nerve," Lazare said softly. "Maybe he has simply gone off and does not intend to come back."

"I hardly think so." She spun about to glare at Lazare. "Do you have nothing better to do than stand here jawing at me?"

Lazare ignored her tirade. His teeth glinted as he continued inexorably, "Maybe you will find yourself a widow again. Maybe I will have to take over Carrington's role

"That will not be necessary, Lazare."

The sound of that familiar resonant voice flooded Belle with a welcome sense of relief. She caught a glimpse of Lazare's stunned expression before she turned to face Sinclair.

"Sinclair, where have you ..." Her words trailed off in dismay as she took in Sinclair's appearance, his hair wildly disheveled, dirt smudging his cheek, the capes of his garrick torn and smattered with mud, the curly-brimmed beaver hat he gripped in his fist smashed beyond recognition.

"What happened to you?" she asked.

"I went out to find a tobacconist," Sinclair said, "when I was nearly run down by two soldiers on horseback."

While Belle exclaimed, taking Sinclair's arm to assure herself he had not been hurt, she thought she heard Lazare mutter a low curse. But when she glanced his way, his head was ducked down as he slid his knife back into its sheath.

"You should be more careful where you walk, Carrington," Lazare grunted.

"I was being careful enough. Those two had to have been blind not to see me."

Lazare shrugged. "Ah, well, you know these soldiers. They think they own the streets of Paris. A pity they ruined your pretty coat, but it could have been your head."

So saying, Lazare turned and lurched back into the building. Sinclair stared hard after him. "Now, why do I get the feeling that our good friend Lazare is disappointed it was not my head?"

"Never mind him," Belle said, making a brisk attempt to brush some of the dirt from Sinclair's sleeve. Although relieved to have him returned unharmed, her mind was already racing ahead. "I am glad to see you back safe."

"Are you, Angel?" Sinclair glanced down at her, his look becoming warm.

"Certainly. Have you entirely forgotten about the review?"

"Ah, yes, Bonaparte. And to think I imagined your joy to see me was entirely for my own sake."

Although Sinclair spoke in his usual jesting fashion, she thought she detected a flash of hurt in his eyes. She would have liked to reassure him in a most intimate manner, but Baptiste joined them just then and she had no choice but to urge Sinclair upstairs to quickly change his coat.

THE SUNLIGHT FLOODED THE PLACE DU CARROUSEL, glinting off the bayonets as the troops marched into place for the review, their colorful regimental flags snapping in the breeze.

Flanked on either side by Sinclair and Baptiste, Belle unfurled her parasol to shield her face. Baptiste's height placed him at a disadvantage when some taller gentlemen moved in front of him, but he craned his neck, leaning to one side straining eagerly for a view as the soldiers maneuvered into position. Belle noted with some amusement that his enthusiasm was little different from the small boys who stood at the vanguard of the crowd gathered outside the gates, pressing their faces against the bars.

Sinclair, however, observed the entire proceedings with folded arms, a half-frowning expression upon his face. Belle supposed that one could not expect an Englishman to be much diverted by a display of French military might.

"You do not seem to be much impressed, Mr. Carrington," she murmured to him in a low voice.

"This is not the way I would choose to spend such a fine morning, watching a parcel of saber rattling."

She arched one brow. "We are a little surly today, are we not?"

"What do you expect, recollecting that the entire purpose of this expedition is to escort my wife here to flirt with another man. I am acting out the part of the jealous husband."

"And you do it so well, sir," she teased, "though I doubt you have much to fear from Monsieur Bonaparte this morning. He will be fully occupied."

Sinclair smiled, but said nothing. He made greater effort to appear more himself, but the truth was, he was worried. He had accomplished little these past five days, for all his subtle questioning, attempting to delve deeper into the backgrounds of Baptiste and Crecy, trying to keep a close watch upon Lazare.

Sinclair felt that Lazare almost mocked him with the correctness of his behavior. On the surface Lazare appeared to be working as industriously to achieve the abduction as any of them, and yet something in the Frenchman's manner left Sinclair continually uneasy. His mistrust of Lazare had grown to the point of superstition, where he had all but fancied the miscreant had had something to do with his own near accident this morning.

That, Sinclair reluctantly conceded, had to be absurd. If there was anyone Lazare wished to harm, it was not himself. It was Belle whom Sinclair frequently caught the fellow watching like an adder about to devour its prey, waiting, always patiently waiting. But for what? That was the question that tormented Sinclair.

"Mr. Carrington?"

Lost in his own thoughts, Sinclair scarce heard the voice speaking his name above the blare of the military band. "Good morrow, Mr. Carrington."

Sinclair felt a nudge against his arm. Glancing around, he discovered that George Warburton had edged his way through the crowd and now stood at Sinclair's side.

The man bore his usual phlegmatic expression as he studied the distant figures of the soldiers lining up in columns. Never averting his gaze, he continued to address Sinclair. "Such a fine spectacle, don't you agree, Mr. Carrington? But I find the noise a little excessive."

With one of his bland smiles Warburton beckoned slightly with his head for Sinclair to follow him. Sinclair stole a glance at Belle, but she appeared too absorbed by the spectacle to notice his defection.

Edging cautiously away, Sinclair trailed Warburton at a distance. But he thought the ground could have opened to swallow him and no one in the crowd would have paid any heed. At that moment Bonaparte had arrived upon the scene, and all eyes were trained upon him.

The first consul rode down the ranks astride a white horse, wearing a black beaver hat and gray greatcoat, surrounded by the more dazzling uniforms of his staff. The throng of spectators appeared mesmerized.

Sinclair and Warburton drew back further into the gardens of the Tuileries. Standing beneath the stark, sprawling branches of a poplar tree, they feigned an avid interest in the troop inspection taking place.

"So, Mr. Carrington," Warburton said, "how goes your tour of Paris? Rewarding, I trust?"

"Not so much as I would have hoped, Mr. Warburton."

"That is most disappointing."

"I am all but convinced I know the identity of the—er, gentleman we both seek. But proving it! He is quite a slippery devil."

"I suppose I don't have to remind you, Carrington. You are running out of time. According to the message you sent me the other day, Merchant's society plans to make its move in—in what?"

"Two days' time," Sinclair said through gritted teeth. "And you are sure that no word of the plot has reached the Tuileries?"

"As sure as I can be. Oh, we did think our informant had returned to the guardhouse yesterday, but it turned out to be only a wench, come for a lover's tryst. Besides"—one of his rare smiles touched Warburton's lips—"if the plot were discovered, I imagine you and your group would know of it before I did."

"That is what I am afraid of," Sinclair said grimly.

There seemed no more to discuss, and he was prepared to move on, but Warburton asked almost desperately, "And you have learned nothing more, Mr. Carrington? Nothing whatsoever?"

Sinclair hesitated. The one new bit of information he had uncovered appeared to him so vague as to be not worth mentioning. However, when Warburton persisted, he said, "Well, I have questioned the porter at our lodgings. Someone has been seen leaving our building and returning late at night. It was too dark for the porter to remark who the person was beneath the hood of the cloak, but the fellow was familiar with the driver of the cabriolet. I tracked him down just yesterday, but all the cabman could do was give me the address he had delivered his passenger to, somewhere in the vicinity of the Palais¬Royal."

"Then that is something surely," Warburton said eagerly. "Have you checked this address?"

"No, not yet."

Sinclair stiffened defensively at Warburton's incredulous look.

"I am supposed to have nothing on my mind, Warburton, other than participating in a certain plot. It is a little difficult for me to get off by myself during the day."

"What about your nights, man? What are you up to then?"

Sinclair compressed his lips. He did not feel that the answer to that concerned either Warburton or the British army. Yet perhaps it did. Perhaps it concerned them greatly that one of their agents was allowing himself to be dangerously distracted.

The truth was Sinclair did not know if he could have absented himself from Belle's side at night even if he tried. He made love to her each time as though it might be the last, for which all he knew it could be. He could not delude himself that this affair was like countless others, that the passion would burn itself out.

It was different with Belle, had been from the first. He had always known that, though even yet he feared to acknowledge how deep his feelings for her ran.

And as for her? What did she feel? He had asked himself that question so many times, asked it now as his gaze tracked toward the crowd of onlookers, toward where she sheltered beneath her parasol, her face shaded from his view, even as her heart continued to be.

He would like to believe she was learning to experience some deeper emotion other than gratitude and desire when he took her in his arms. But, Sinclair thought sadly, he could not delude himself on that score, either.

He realized with some chagrin that while their lovemaking might have distracted him somewhat from his task, Belle remained absorbed with her work, nothing seeming to sway her from her purpose.

Even now, her gaze focused intently upon Bonaparte, only shifting when she bent to exchange some comment with Baptiste about the review.

Bonaparte had dismounted and was barking out maneuvers to

the troops in a clear resonant voice, which they executed with precision.

The first consul was more in his element doing this, Belle thought, than he had been mingling with the guests at the reception.

Deeply engrossed in the orderly demonstration, Baptiste murmured, "It is a great deal different than in the old days, eh, *mon ange*? I can remember the time when the gathering of a crowd such as this would have raised a knot in my stomach."

Belle remembered all too well. A crowd could so easily turn into a mob bent upon violent and vengeful purposes. Yet as she gazed about her, she too felt the difference Baptiste spoke of. Even the throng that clustered against the gates seemed remote from that unruly crowd who had once overrun the Tuileries. Everywhere there was a new sense of order, which seemed to emanate from the short man in gray with his booming voice.

Bonaparte might not be an impressive figure on horseback, but rapping out commands to his troops was another matter. Belle turned to gauge Sinclair's impressions and was surprised to find him gone.

Searching about for him, she saw him some little distance away, in earnest conversation with a quiet-looking man Belle did not recognize.

Belle frowned. Something in Sinclair's manner made her feel as if the man was an acquaintance, but Sinclair had said he had never been to Paris before, that he knew no one. Was this a friend from England perhaps?

When Sinclair finally rejoined her, she asked casually, "Did you chance upon an old crony of yours?"

Sinclair replied easily enough. "No, that was only a fellow I met at the reception the other night, a secretary or clerk or some such to the ambassador. Boring chap, but it seemed rude to cut him."

"Oh, I see," Belle said, but she didn't. Why did she once more have that uneasy feeling that Sinclair was not telling her quite the entire truth? Perhaps it was the way his eyes, ever bold, skated away from making contact with hers. And yet what reason would he have to lie? She felt guilty herself for being so suspicious. She was worse than a jealous wife thinking her husband had acquired a mistress. It was only that she had made herself so vulnerable, given so much of herself to Sinclair, if she should once more be proven a fool ...

Suppressing such thoughts as best she could, she realized that the review had come to its end, the troops filing off. If Bonaparte had remarked her attendance or even recalled inviting her, he gave no sign of it. He mounted his horse and rapidly rode away.

But as the crowds began to disperse, Belle was approached by a dapper little man. In a low voice he introduced himself as Napoleon's valet, Constant. With a low bow he slipped her a note with the Napoleonic seal holding it closed before turning and vanishing back through the gardens as quickly as he had appeared.

Sinclair glanced at the paper with a jaundiced eye. "Another billet-doux, I suppose?"

"We will know soon enough when we return to the apartment." She gave him an arch smile and proceeded to outline her plans for the rest of the afternoon. "I think we should go over the details of the plan one more—"

But she was interrupted by a heartfelt groan that issued from both Baptiste and Sinclair at once.

"Have mercy, *mon ange*," Baptiste pleaded. "This plan—we could recite it in our sleep. Such a beautiful day to spend in the stuffy apartment. Surely you could spare an hour. It is so rare that I take a holiday. I thought to treat you and Monsieur Carrington to a petite repast at a small café that I know."

"What an excellent notion," Sinclair was quick to agree.

"Out of the question—" Belle began, but Sinclair and Baptiste exchanged a glance past her. She found herself firmly seized by one man on either side and propelled forward.

"I think I am the victim of a conspiracy," she grumbled, but her resistance was only token. To say truth, she felt in something of a holiday mood herself. Perhaps it had something to do with the stirring notes of the brass band, the warmth of the sun on her face, or even more the warmth in a certain wicked pair of green eyes. In any case, she gave over all resistance, allowing herself to be whisked away by Sinclair and Baptiste.

The Café D'Egalité was a modest establishment, not far from the river, its rough-hewn walls giving the impression that it had stood nearly as long as the Seine flowed. The aroma of spirits and fresh-brewed coffee hung in the air so strong it might have been steeped into the woodwork of the tables. A placard hung on the wall, slightly askew, proclaimed, "Here we still honor one another with the title of Citoyen."

Even this obviously half-forgotten reminder of revolutionary days was enough to curtail Belle's pleasure in the café's quaintness. As though sensing her stiffen, Baptiste suggested they occupy one of the tables in the small garden. The day was certainly warm enough.

While Belle ordered *bavorosie* and Baptiste his wine, Sinclair opted for some "genuine English beer."

"I thought you did not like beer," Belle said as she stripped off her gloves.

"I don't." Sinclair sighed. "But the waiter appeared so proud to be able to offer it, how could I disappoint the poor fellow?"

Offering him a half-amused smile, Belle glanced about the garden which boasted no more than five tables, all of the others being vacant. The only others present were two elderly gentlemen playing at *jeu des bagues* at the opposite end of the garden. She decided she might just risk a glance at the note from Bonaparte.

Breaking the seal, she scanned the contents. The opening amused her somewhat.

"Since the night of the reception, your beauty fills my memory. My thoughts have been only of you."

This was yet another side to the blunt Corsican soldier. Who would imagine he could be such a romantic. It was the sort of infatuated nonsense she might have expected to have received from a boy like Phillipe Coterin, But as she scanned farther down the page, her smile faded,

"Damn!" she said.

Sinclair paused in the act of raising the flagon to his lips. "What's amiss?"

By way of answer she simply handed the note to him.

"The white curves of your soft, sweet—" Sinclair began to read aloud.

"Not that," she interrupted sharply. "Read the closing paragraph."

Belle could tell when Sinclair had found the crucial part, for one of his eyebrows jutted upward.

"Well, what is it?" Baptiste cried. "Or do you both mean to slay me with this suspense?"

"Bonaparte has canceled his supper with Belle," Sinclair said. "He leaves Paris within the week for an extended tour of the provinces."

"*Nom de Dieu!*" Baptiste exclaimed. He shook his head. "*Quelle catastrophe*! Why, once he is out of Paris on a ceremonial tour, there will be no getting near the man. He will constantly be surrounded by his entourage and adoring crowds."

Belle bit ruefully down upon her lip. "I know."

"And so the note is his farewell?" Baptiste asked. "He makes no further mention of seeing you again, *mon ange*?"

"Not at an intimate supper. But by way of consolation, he offers a discreet meeting in one of the boxes at the Theatre Odeon to attend the current performance."

"Ah, but of course." Baptiste nodded. "The general is most fond of drama. He often attends incognito."

"It doesn't matters if he comes disguised as a Turk," Sinclair said. "I would defy anyone to arrange the abduction of a man from so public a place as a theater."

He tossed the note down upon the table. "So that's the end of that."

An unexpected modicum of relief had been mingling with Belle's disappointment. But Sinclair's almost cheerful acceptance of their failure acted strangely upon her.

"What do you mean—the end?" she demanded.

"I mean that you cannot go any further with this scheme, which was absurd from the start."

Although she acknowledged the situation as hopeless herself, Sinclair's complacent dismissal of the mission, all the work and planning she had poured into it, irritated her. Of course, he had never been very enthusiastic about the assignment, she recalled. She was not the only one to remark the fact. Lazare had said something very similar only this morning.

Of a sudden some of Lazare's other comments came back to her, seeming to whisper in her ear, seep through her like subtle poison. *He has a habit of disappearing, our Monsieur Carrington. Where does he go each day?*

Belle turned over in her mind things about Sinclair that had always disturbed her: his knowledge about Feydeau, his conversation with the strange man at the review, most of all his evasion of any questions regarding his past. Could it be that- No, Belle refused to consider the possibility that the man who loved her so tenderly each night could be plotting against her.

Sinclair must have other less sinister reasons for rejoicing that the plot must be abandoned. He had oft teased her about her ambition to use the money from this mission to retire from the business to Derbyshire. Perhaps some of his teasing had been in earnest, fathered by a secret wish to keep her working with him. Perhaps he was glad that she would not now be paid. Or his relief could be stemming from some arrogant male notion of protecting her, a lack of faith in her ability to see the abduction to a successful conclusion.

Whatever the reason for his resistance, it stirred her stubborn pride to life.

"The assignment has become more difficult," she said, "but I still do not find it impossible."

Sinclair cast her a look, part indulgence, part impatience. "Belle, give it up. You have done your best, doing all that Merchant could require. I would be the first to tell him so."

"I am not worried about Merchant," she snapped. "But when I am hired to do a job, I finish it."

"Just as you did in the affair with Coterin?" he reminded her with a skeptical smile.

Belle bristled. "That was different." In that instance she had chosen to deviate from her task, but she would be damned if she would be forced to give up by simply a lack of daring and resolve.

"You were reluctant from the start," she accused Sinclair. "If you didn't wish to take any risks, I don't know why—"

"Risk," Sinclair snorted. "This would be suicide."

"All I have to say is that if you are going to change your mind, it would be better if you had not accepted in the first place."

"I beg you, *mes enfants*, no quarrels," Baptiste said. "You are throwing those poor gentlemen off their game."

Belle was startled to realize that she and Sinclair had been raising their voices loudly enough to attract attention.

One of the elderly men at the other end of the garden paused in the act of tossing his ring to frown at her.

Sinclair subsided, but Belle could not let the matter rest. She said in low but forceful tones, "I trust you will remember, Mr. Carrington, I am the one in charge. I will say when the mission is called off."

"If you can develop a sensible plan, I will follow you anywhere, Angel." Sinclair drank the rest of his beer, looking so smugly confident that she couldn't, Belle had a strong desire to break her coffee cup over his head.

As though to prevent further argument, he got up and deliberately strolled across the garden to watch the old men at their game. It did not take long before he was invited to join in, the elderly Parisians showing him how to toss the wooden rings, laughing indulgently at his efforts.

Belle could tell from the flash of Sinclair's smile that he was not merely staying away from the table to be spiteful, but genuinely enjoying himself with the same gusto with which he smoked those horrid cigars and ate his peppermints.

"He has the *joie de vivre*, that one," Baptiste commented. "He could well have been a Frenchman."

It was an enormous compliment coming from Baptiste. But Belle recognized that her friend was right. Sinclair did have that vitality, that zest for life she felt lacking in herself. It was one of the things that made him so undeniably attractive.

"He is also a man of good sense," Baptiste added.

Belle glanced sharply at her old friend. "Does that mean you agree with him that the mission must be abandoned?"

Baptiste frowned into his empty glass. "*Oui*, at the risk of also angering you, I fear that I must. Monsieur Carrington takes the logical view—"

"Logic has nothing to do with it," Belle said scornfully. "I believe Sinclair is merely having one of his misplaced gallant urges, the feeling that he somehow needs to protect me. Well, I have been doing rather nicely without him for a good many years. I think I can decide what chances I should take."

"Except that you would not be the only one taking the risk." This gentle reminder and the grave look that accompanied it brought a flush to Belle's cheeks.

"You are right. Forgive me, Baptiste. I did not think. Indeed, I would not blame you for wanting no more to do with this scheme."

"It was not myself so much I speak for as the others." Baptiste shrugged. "What have I left to lose—my life? I have never been much afraid to die as long as I can be laid to rest here in my Paris. I am no longer such a young man."

He became suddenly pensive. "As the oldest in my family, I always imagined I would be the first to go, my bier borne aloft on the shoulders of my strong brothers with love and all honor. I never thought that I should be the one to survive."

The light that shone from those ageless brown eyes dimmed as he continued to muse, "Artur, he died by the guillotine for being too free with his opinions, Francois, murdered, his only sin deciding to be a priest instead of a fan maker, Odeon fell before the cannonfire with the army in the Alps, and Gervaise perished of the fever on General Bonaparte's glorious Egyptian campaign."

He groped for his handkerchief and dabbed unashamedly at his eyes. "All I want now is peace."

Belle reached out to cover his hand with her own. "And you shall have it, my friend, perhaps if Sinclair and I did go away now and leave Bonaparte alone. I cannot help but notice some of the sense of order, of well-being the man has brought back to Paris."

"That he has. The schools and churches are open again. We have a new code of laws. But peace?" Baptiste shook his head. "This Bonaparte, he is to France like the false spring of this day, a warm flooding of light you know cannot last for long. You saw him with his army today. He is not a man to be content with just playing soldier. Napoleon Bonaparte may bring France many gifts, but peace will never be one of them."

Brushing the last of the moisture from his eyes, Baptiste blew his nose loudly. "*Non*, I am still with you, *mon ange*. Perhaps we must surrender our plans for now. But there will come another day."

Shoving back his chair, he said, "For now, I have been away from my fans for too long."

Belle tried to protest, "For shame. And to think you were scolding me earlier for wanting to work upon such a fine day."

"Ah, but it is different for you and your Monsieur Carrington. You are still young. And Paris, she was once the best place in the world to be young. She still is. Maybe Monsieur Carrington can teach you how to enjoy yourself for an hour." The old man fixed her with a shrewd gaze. "He has already brought a sparkle to your eye that I am glad to see."

Belle could not help but blush under Baptiste's knowing gaze.

"Now, why do you blush so? Bah, you prim English. It is more than time you took a lover. This Sinclair, he has helped you at last to bury the past, *hein*?"

"I don't think anyone could ever do that," Belle said. A soft smile escaped her. "But, yes, Sinclair does make the past so much easier to bear."

"Then let him also help you learn to cherish the present. It does have a way of slipping away from one."

With that the old man deposited a kiss upon her cheek. He sauntered off down the street, leaving Belle to mull over his words.

A few moments later, when Sinclair returned to the table, he discovered Belle lost in thought. He approached her cautiously, as though he half-expected to find her still angry.

"Where is Baptiste?" he asked.

"Gone back to work."

Sinclair sighed. "And I expect you will say we should do the same. Look, Angel, I don't want to quarrel with you anymore. I know you have suffered a keen disappointment, how much the money from this mission meant to you, your little rose-covered cottage in Dorsetshire—"

"Derbyshire," Belle interrupted with a smile. "Forget about it, Sinclair. It so happens I don't want to think about the assignment anymore this afternoon, either."

She rose briskly to her feet, drawing on her gloves. "Let's play truant. We could go for a stroll down by the river."

She almost laughed aloud at Sinclair's look of astonishment. He regarded her as though he could not believe what she was saying. Indeed, she could scarce believe it herself.

"After all," she said. "We are only young once. And who knows how many such afternoons will be left for us?"

She knew from the glance he cast her that he understood she was talking about more than the unseasonably sunny weather.

"Yes, who knows?" he echoed sadly. He raised her hand to press a kiss against her fingertips before tucking her arm within the crook of his own.

However their mission ended, their time together in Paris was drawing to a close. Belle had never deluded herself that their relationship was a permanent one. They would be bound to go their separate ways. She was surprised to discover how empty that thought made her feel, and she was quick to dismiss it.

Arm in arm, they went walking along the quay by the Seine, the familiar wet-reed smell drifting to Belle's nostrils. The greenish-brown water had not yet risen to its winter height, leaving some of the quayside exposed. The river lapped gently against the rocks, casting a breeze upon the land, which made Belle glad of her shawl.

She and Sinclair wended their way among the *bouquinistes*, those booksellers who had ever displayed their wares along the stone embankment, many of the manuscripts quite ancient, threatening to crumple apart at a touch.

Over this section of river the Pont Neuf stretched out its stone arches, the ancient bridge reaching across to the Ile de la Cite, the oldest part of Paris. The bridge was crammed with many others enjoying the day, the hawkers, the artists, the flower girls, the lovers slipping beneath the shoreward arches to steal an intimate moment.

Even as the Seine waters sparkled in the sunlight, so did the city seem to do so today, sparkling with life as much as the man who strode by Belle's side. Her chief enjoyment came from observing Sinclair, how much he reveled in the bustle and activity about him.

He made her laugh as they wandered through the open air market, teasing her with the prospect that he meant to buy a plump, squawking chicken. He bandied words with the *racoleurs*, who were ever alert to recruit with a drink any healthy male into joining the army. He applauded a group of street tumblers, tossing them coin, paused to chat with some fishermen angling their lines over the end of the quay, tipped his hat to a saucy group of laundresses in their boats anchored just offshore.

Belle found herself seeing Paris through Sinclair's eyes as for the first time, experiencing the charm, the zest for life, the gaiety that had ever escaped her before. She began to have some inkling of why Baptiste so loved the place.

Lingering beneath a chestnut tree, its leaves a burst of golden glory, Belle and Sinclair stooped down to feed some bread to a flock of wild ducks gliding on the river.

Belle chuckled to herself. "I can hardly believe I am doing this."

"What? You mean you never took time before to invite these fine fellows to dine?"

"No. Do you realize that one November during the wheat shortage, I slept overnight on a baker's doorstep simply to be able to buy a loaf of bread?"

Yet somehow standing here beside Sinclair in the bright sunlight, the grim memory faded to become exactly what it was—a memory and no more than that.

"From some of the things you tell me, Angel," he said, "you make me glad I could not come to Paris before this."

As she watched Sinclair squinting past the Pont Neuf to the not far distant shore, she remarked, "Yet it seems so strange to me than an adventurer such as yourself never did so."

He shrugged, tossing the last of his bread down to the ducks. "My father was not exactly the sort of man to spend money on a grand tour."

"No, doubtless he was not," she agreed. Sinclair had never said, but Belle retained the comforting feeling that Sinclair's background was not so different from her own. Like herself, he was an adventurer who had never known wealth, rank, or respectability. There was not that social gap between them that had existed between herself and Jean-Claude. It was what made their relationship so much more comfortable.

Sinclair pointed to a distant spire across the river. "Is that Notre Dame?"

"It is." But when she saw the eager look cross his features, she said, "Oh, no. I have no intention of trudging all the way across the Pont Neuf to tour Notre Dame. You would be quite disappointed anyway. The cathedral was damaged during the Revolution, and I understand the repairs have not been completed."

"Don't distress yourself, Angel." He favored her with a lazy grin. "Touring churches is not exactly my style, either. I am content to admire the *grande* Dame from a distance. But what are those ugly towers there in the foreground?"

Belle squinted toward four conical-shaped towers, grim and forbiddingly cast in stone.

"The Conciergerie," she said softly, looking quickly away.

Sinclair frowned. Gripping her by the elbow, he began to lead her in the opposite direction.

"The sight of it doesn't upset me that much," she assured him. "There is no need to run away."

"No, we have more a need to act casual," Sinclair said, slowing the pace. "I think we are being followed."

Belle suppressed a startled exclamation, the immediate desire to whip around and look. "Who?"

"The man in the gray. Just over there by that last bookseller's stall. He—" Sinclair broke off. He had been in the act of taking a cautious look behind him when he froze.

Belle also stole a peek. The man in gray was making no attempt to hide the fact that he was coming after them. As he drew closer, he called her name. "Isabelle."

Jean-Claude. Although her eyes widened with incredulity, her heart didn't do its usual patter at the sight of him. She felt the tension cording her muscles. Scarce knowing what to expect, she waited while he caught up to them.

"Monsieur le Comte," Sinclair said, a hard edge in his voice. "We meet yet again. They tell me Paris is one of the largest cities in the world, but I am beginning to doubt it. The place has begun to seem too infernally small."

His face rigid with dignity, Jean-Claude looked through Sinclair. He fixed his attention upon Belle.

"I have been following you ever since you left the military review," Jean-Claude admitted. "I have been waiting, hoping for a chance. Isabelle, I must speak to you."

"Of—of course," Belle stammered, taken completely aback. After Jean-Claude's behavior at the reception, that he would seek her out again was the last thing she would have expected.

"Speak to you alone," he added pointedly. He glanced hesitantly toward Sinclair as though seeking his permission and despising himself for doing so.

"That would be entirely up to Belle," Sinclair said coldly.

Belle found herself in the awkward position of being stared at by two pairs of masculine eyes, both of them questioning, both of them hostile. But even if other ages-old feelings were not stirred in her by Jean-Claude, curiosity alone would have won out.

She placed her hand upon Sinclair's arm. "Sinclair, if you truly would not mind—"

"I can manage to amuse myself." But he took the sting from his harsh answer with an intent look. "You know where I'll be if you need me."

She understood what he was trying to convey and flashed him a grateful smile. As Sinclair stalked away, Belle turned expectantly toward Jean-Claude.

"Perhaps we could walk out on the bridge," he said. "Sit on one of the benches."

She nodded in agreement, further astounded when he offered her his arm. After a moment's hesitation she took it.

Sinclair watched their retreat from his vantage point by one of the bookseller's stalls. He noted the stiffness of Jean-Claude's gesture, but it was a gesture toward Belle all the same.

Sinclair felt the beginnings of that familiar hollow ache. He had once told Belle he did not mind her memories of Jean-Claude. He could live with them.

"It seems that I lied, Angel," he murmured. "I do mind. I mind like hell."

When he had said that, he had not yet known he was in love with Isabelle Varens. Yes, in love, he admitted at last. But it was the devil of a time to realize that as Belle vanished on the arm of Jean-Claude.

Sinclair glanced about him, his pleasure in the day, the city life teeming about him, suddenly gone. He wondered if the time would come when he would never want to come back to Paris, loathing it with the same bitter memories as Belle.

Thirteen

Belle walked alongside Jean-Claude, her silence as rigid as his, two stiff figures jostled by the gay crowd that flocked over the bridge. Hawkers displayed their wares to pretty ladies shaded beneath parasols. Artists dabbled with oils upon their canvases. Street singers warbled their tunes, offering for sale the new sheet music.

It was strange, Belle thought. Only a moment ago with Sinclair, she had felt so much a part of all this color, this gaiety. Now once more she had the sensation of being removed, as though in the carnival of faces pressing past her, life itself were passing her by.

She glanced at Jean-Claude, wondering if he could feel that, too, but the stony set of his profile told her nothing, only the deep-set misery of his eyes. Why? She wanted to shout at him. He had made it clear at the reception he could never forgive her, that he could scarce bear the sight of her. Then why did he choose to seek her out again, subject them both to an interview that would only cause them fresh pain?

They had not even passed by the second arch of the bridge

when she halted. "I think we have come far enough, Jean-Claude," she said. "What did you wish—"

"No, not here. Please, Isabelle. The noise." He nodded upward toward La Samarataine, the huge hydraulic pump rising three stories above the bridge, its facade adorned with gilded figures of Christ receiving water from the Good Samaritan. The pump shuddered with activity as it sped a water supply to the Louvre and the Tuileries.

"Let us go just a little farther," he pleaded.

Belle found the clatter of the pump somehow more bearable as a backdrop than the happy chatter and laughter of the Pont Neuf's other occupants, but she fell into step beside Jean-Claude once more.

They continued on until they reached the next half moon embrasure, one of the bridge's many stone bays which jutted out over the Seine. The semicircular seat was unoccupied. Belle settled herself upon it, and Jean-Claude sank down beside her, taking great care to keep a decorous distance between them.

Still, he seemed unable to break the silence, his gloved hands fidgeting nervously with the silver-tipped handle of his walking cane. Once even for all his coldness, his rigid anger, Belle would have given much to have him seated thus by her side. Now she was surprised to discover she felt nothing but impatience. Certainly she had no desire to make this any easier for him, or to offer him any encouragement.

She stared out across the sluggish waters of the Seine watching the ferry boats and the flat-bottomed barges laden with their cargoes.

Jean-Claude cleared his throat. "There seems to be more river traffic than I recall."

"Is that why you have been following me all this time?" Belle asked. "To discuss the number of barges on the Seine?"

"*Non.*" She heard him draw in a tremulous breath. After a long moment of hesitation, his hand reached out and tentatively covered hers where it rested upon the balustrade of the bay.

Startled by the gesture, her gaze flew up to meet his. He said, "I sought you out to tell you that I am sorry for my behavior at the reception the other night."

Belle blinked, almost unable to assimilate the meaning of his words. Apologizing? He was actually apologizing to her for his hurtful remarks, for attempting to ignore her.

"My manners were atrocious, my words certainly not those of a gentleman."

"Not at all, sir." Belle slid her hand from beneath his. "You were ever the gentleman." Even when Jean-Claude had been demanding the divorce, he had been so unbearably civil, so damnably polite.

"Truly, Isabelle," he continued, sounding more earnest. "I am sorry. I didn't want to offend you or wound you. It is just that it was so hard for me seeing you again."

"It was not precisely easy for me, either."

But he stared at her with that wistful look in his eyes. She had never been proof against it.

"Let us simply forget the quarrel," she said with a weary sigh. "I am not so easily wounded these days. I survived the incident." She reflected that this was true. In these last few days she had given little thought to the ugly scene with Jean-Claude. Sinclair had had a great deal to do with that.

"I am glad," Jean-Claude said. "It is a great relief to know you are not angry with me."

"And you?" she asked. "Does this mean you have forgiven me at last?"

"I am trying very hard. I wish more than anything that we could both simply forget the past."

"Forget the past? Do you truly believe that's possible?"

"Perhaps not. But maybe we could learn to recall only the good. There were some good times, were there not, Isabelle?"

She had always thought so, but she had believed his own memory of them erased the day he had learned the secret of her birth.

A soft light came into his gray eyes. "We often used to stroll upon this bridge together that first summer in Paris. Do you recall?"

"I remember," she said. A reluctant smite escaped her. "Mostly you walked along daydreaming with me attempting to steer you through the crowds and see that you didn't fall off the bridge."

"I don't do much of that anymore—daydreaming." An expression of melancholy washed over him. The brief spark that had appeared in his eyes vanished, and he fell into a brooding silence.

Belle's urge to comfort him was strong, but instead she studied the man whom for so many years she had regarded as the entire possessor of her heart. His face was pale, but then it always had been. The strands of silver were new, but not unbecoming to his gaunt face. His countenance had never been an animated one, not like Sinclair's— She broke off the thought, refusing to compare the two men. Impossible. They were so unalike.

Jean-Claude's attractiveness had come from the dreamy, otherworldly expression in his eyes. Without that he was an empty shell of a man, broken and defeated. Looking upon him like this was enough to break her heart, wrenching feelings deep inside of her, but was that feeling love?

It shocked and frightened her that she should question something that she had believed in for so long. Unable to bear to examine her own emotions too closely at this moment, she sought to draw him out of his unhappy reflections.

"So what are you doing here in Paris?" she asked. "Have any of your old friends returned as well?"

"I don't know. I have not troubled myself to find out. I have little use for the company of *philosophes* these days. I prefer men of action."

"Such as Napoleon Bonaparte?" Even at the risk of offending

him, she was burning to know what Jean-Claude had been doing attending the reception at the Tuileries.

The vehemence of his answer startled her. "*Non*, not Bonaparte! I despise him. It sickens my soul to breathe the same air as he."

Belle regarded him with astonishment, not a little discomfited. She had never seen such a fierce light in Jean-Claude's eyes, never heard him express such hatred of any living being.

She laid her hand soothingly on Jean-Claude's arm. "I understand what you must feel, being deprived of your estates, your home, but—"

"That has nothing to do with it." Jean-Claude glared down at her. "It is Bonaparte, himself. What he is. Do you not see it? He is the dark side of the Revolution."

When she looked at him with incomprehension, Jean-Claude flung his hands wide in an impassioned gesture. "He is the embodiment of all the violence, all the greed, the power hunger that destroyed the fine ideals, the noble purpose and the quest for freedom that the Revolution should have been."

"I will grant you that General Bonaparte is something of a freebooter, an opportunist, perhaps, who took advantage of the circumstances—"

"He is evil incarnate."

Belle tried to reason with him, but saw it was of no avail. Jean-Claude, who had ever thrived on debate, attempting to see all viewpoints, was totally beyond reason. It was as though he had taken all the anger and the bitterness of the Revolution he had never been adequately able to express and had found an outlet for it by settling his hatred on the person of one man. Foreboding coursed through her.

"If you hate the man so," she asked, "why were you at his reception?"

"Because at last I have learned the advantage of playing my enemy's games, disguising my feelings, watching, waiting—" The glazed look in Jean-Claude's eyes made her acutely uneasy. "There is the future of France to consider and my son."

"Yes, Jean-Jacques." Belle seized eagerly upon the boy's name, hoping to snap Jean-Claude out of this strange mood. "Jean-Jacques is the most charming child. Do you intend to bring him over to France to live with you?"

"Not until things are different."

"How different?" Belle asked sharply, now thoroughly alarmed. She knew that the members of her group were not the only plotters to be found in Paris. There had always been other wild dreamers, some of them even highly placed in the French army, hoping to generate another coup, sweep Napoleon from power. A ridiculous fantasy, considering Bonaparte's military skill and his popularity with the people. Surely Jean-Claude could not have fallen prey to any of those fanatics.

"Jean-Claude," 'she demanded. "Exactly what have you gotten yourself involved in?"

"Nothing." He forced a smile. "Nothing that I would wish you to be concerned about. All I can tell you now is that these past few months I have been like a man slowly coming awake from a dream, beginning to know myself for the first time. I am a fool."

"No, Jean-Claude. You—"

He shook his head, gently pressing her hands to silence her protest. "Even worse than a fool, I was a villain of the worst sort. I did France more harm than any of those murderous scoundrels who marched in the streets. "I discovered too late that the careless tossing around of ideas is more dangerous than the blaze of cannonfire. All I did was muse and dream of Utopia, and while I did so, I let them murder my king."

Jean-Claude raised one trembling hand to cup her cheek. "I failed you as well, didn't I, my Isabelle? I let my pride murder our love."

"You could not help it," she assured him. "After all you had been through—"

"After all I had been through, I foolishly flung away the one precious possession I had left. My Isabelle."

For a moment she thought he meant to catch her up in his arms. How often had she prayed for such a thing. She was surprised at the relief she felt when he didn't. It was just that she was so confused. Her head was reeling.

"You do still care for me, don't you, Isabelle? A little?"

"Yes, of course, I do," she stammered. "A great deal"

Pressing her fingertips fervently against his lips, he said, "Dare I hope that perhaps—" He checked himself with great difficulty. "No, at the moment all I can ask is that you be my friend until after ..."

"After what?"

"After my prospects improve." He stood up abruptly. "I think it best if we walk back now before I am betrayed into saying something most unwise."

Now thoroughly in control of himself, she could sense him trying to put some distance between them, except for a certain warmth in his eyes.

He had all but declared he had forgiven her, even intimated that his love for her might once more be revived. There had been a time when she would have been contented with much less from him. And here he stood, promising so much more, yet she could feel nothing but alarm.

Jean-Claude had no more notion of how to conduct himself in an intrigue than a babe. He was bound to end in disaster.

But he's not exactly your responsibility anymore, is he? a surprisingly irritable voice inside her demanded. Haven't you got enough to contend with? Yes, but she would never forgive herself if she let anything happen to him.

Still, there seemed nothing she could do but fall into step beside him as they wended their way back across the bridge

"Sinclair will be wondering what has become of me," she remarked.

At the mention of Sinclair a shadow crossed Jean-Claude's face. "Sinclair," he repeated, as though the very way she had pronounced his name had dealt Jean-Claude a blow. "The other night at the reception you told me—"

He stopped himself, stiffening his jaw resolutely. "No, I won't ask you any more about him. We will pretend he does not exist. He does not matter."

Belle nearly protested she could pretend no such thing, that indeed Sinclair did matter. But she kept silent, not wishing to shatter the tentative peace between them.

She permitted him to escort her back across the bridge, but back on the quay she saw no sign of Sinclair. Jean-Claude refused to take his leave of her.

"I could scarce leave you here unescorted with no male protector."

Belle heaved an impatient sigh. Sinclair would have sensed at once her need to be alone, that she was capable of shifting for herself. It seemed to have never occurred to Jean-Claude to inquire after her manner of life during these intervening years. He simply assumed she had continued to live like a lady. He might no longer be a day-dreamer, but he was still as impractical.

The critical thought startled her. She suppressed it and after much firm insistence persuaded him to go. As Jean-Claude took his leave of her, she could not forbear making one last attempt to draw him out.

"You worry me. I fear you are in some sort of trouble. I don't think it was wise for you to return to Paris."

"If it eases your mind," he said, "I plan to leave very soon, in a few days' time."

"That would be for the best," she urged. "You should go back home."

"If only I knew where that was." He gave her a sad smile and looked deep into her eyes one last time. Then he brushed a hard kiss against her brow. Turning abruptly, he vanished into the crowd thronging the quay.

"Damn!" Belle muttered as she stood staring after him. It was as though the solid ground she had forged for herself all these years had been swept from beneath her feet. She had never had any doubts that she would know what to do if Jean-Claude came back into her life and opened his arms to her.

And now she stood cursing him. It was not that she did not still care for him. Indeed she did, too much. Cared for him and ached for him as well. He needed her now more than ever, although he might not know it himself.

But in the interval there had been Sinclair, a man who at last had broken through the barriers she had constructed around her heart, who had taught her how to live again. She could not delude herself that Sinclair only fulfilled a need of her flesh. Their relationship went much deeper than that. There had been a bond, an understanding between them from the very beginning.

But was that love? It was very different from the feeling she had cherished for Jean-Claude for so long. She rubbed a hand over her throbbing temples.

Only one reality remained crystal clear to her. Jean-Claude was deeply unhappy, more tormented than she had ever seen him. If only there was something she could do to help him now, something that would at last truly make up for that ancient hurt she had inflicted upon him.

He belonged back at Egremont, with his treasured books, watching his little son romp in those quiet gardens, sheltered once more behind the high walls of the chateau of his ancestors. She could not turn back time for Jean-Claude, but if only she could restore him to his own.

Perhaps she might have accomplished that if she had succeeded with her plot to abduct Napoleon. With the monarchy returned to France, all the dispossessed nobles would likely have their estates returned.

But these were all absurd speculations. With her own carefully laid plans in ruins, she might as well leave Paris herself. She scarce saw much reason to keep her rendezvous with Bonaparte unless perhaps to lay the groundwork for a future plot.

Why did the damned man have to change the site of their engagement to the theater? Belle all but tossed her head with contempt. As if she had ever had much use for French theater. The stage had been so heavily censored since the days of the Revolution, the sentimental and preachy tripe that remained was scarce worth the bother. And she doubted if conditions had improved much under Bonaparte's strict regime.

The playbill plastered over there on the wall of the quay was a prime example. The Dutiful Wife—likely an overdone drama about a virtuous and doubtless patriotic French lady wrongly suspected by her husband. After he ends by killing her, he would discover the truth and be so remorseful. And the playbill promised the lead role would be enacted by none other than the renowned Monsieur Georges Carribout.

And, God help the theater owner, Belle thought with scorn, if for any reason the said Monsieur Georges failed to appear. She knew these emotionally charged Frenchmen. Their fury that day at the Bastille would be as nothing if denied their favorite actor. Likely there would be a riot and the theater would be thrown into a state of utter confusion—

Belle broke off, catching her breath. A state of utter confusion. The words triggered something in her mind, an idea, a daring idea that seemed to burst inside her head like the shattering of a skyrocket.

Lost in her thoughts, she didn't notice Sinclair coming up behind her until he touched her lightly on the shoulder. With a startled gasp, she spun around.

"Belle?" He frowned, staring down at her. "I didn't mean to frighten you." He peered at her more closely. "Are you all right?"

Well might he ask that. Belle knew that she was trembling, but with excitement.

"Yes, I am," she breathed. "You see, I know how we can abduct Bonaparte."

BEYOND THE GAUZY CURTAIN OF BELLE'S BEDCHAMBER window, the sun set over Paris, stippling the sky with rose, mauve, and gold, the colors bleeding together like an artist's canvas left in the rain.

Yet as he stood moodily near the window, Sinclair remained impervious to the sun's glorious display, only aware of the shadows lengthening between him and Belle.

She sat at her dressing table, rearranging the bottles of lotion, hair ornaments, and other toiletry articles as though she could find no pattern of order that suited her.

Both of them had lapsed into a discontented silence. They had been arguing for the better part of the afternoon over Belle's newest plot for the abduction. Yet Sinclair sensed that it was not in truth Bonaparte who fueled this quarrel, but rather another solemn gentleman whose name each of them was reluctant to mention.

"Your plan will never work, Belle," Sinclair muttered for about the tenth time.

"How can you be so all-fired certain?" She snatched up a brush from her dresser, venting her frustration upon the soft tangle of her curls. "It is no more risky than the old plan, and you appeared willing enough to go along with that."

"That one had some chance of success. This one is pure madness."

Belle slammed the brush down. She drew in a steadying breath before she spoke in a voice almost too taut with control. "I will present my plan to the others, see what they think, but I am sure they will agree with me. If you are still so strongly opposed after hearing what they have to say, why, then, you are free to go. I don't need you."

"I am fully aware of that," Sinclair said in flat tones, yet still not able to disguise some of the pain her words dealt him.

She glanced around at him quickly, some of her anger appearing to dissolve. Heaving a deep sigh, she pushed herself away from the table. "I am sorry, Sinclair. I did not mean that."

She crossed the room to his side. After a moment's hesitation she placed her palms lightly against the flat of his chest. A smile crooked her lips. "It is only that you can be so damnably stubborn, Mr. Carrington."

"So can you, Mrs. Carrington." Although he half-returned her smile, he forced himself to remain unyielding beneath her touch. "I thought you had agreed to abandon this impossible task. I wish I knew what really happened to make you almost desperate to go through with it again."

"I told you. I saw that playbill. It gave me the idea to—"

"I wonder." Sinclair regarded her through narrowed eyes. "Or did it have more to do with something he said to you today?"

He could feel the sudden tension in the soft hands that rested against his chest.

"I suppose," he said bitterly, "you will tell me it is none of my concern what Varens wanted of you."

Her hands fell away from him. She took a step back. "He wanted nothing. Only to apologize for his behavior at the reception—that is all."

"Was it? I feared that perhaps the noble idiot finally realized what he had thrown away when he let you go."

Her indignant glance should have stopped him, but he had gone through far too many agonies of jealousy and suspicion while waiting for Belle's return. He feared if he did not release some of it, he would explode.

"Perhaps Varens is the reason for your sudden eagerness to make your plan work at all costs. You are no longer thinking of a little cottage in Dorsetshire, are you, Belle? Maybe it has occurred to you that with Bonaparte gone, Varens might get his estates back and you could be his countess again. And you expect me to risk my neck to help you."

Her throat constricted. "I don't expect anything from you—ever again." Whipping away from him, she strode to the door that connected their bedchambers and yanked it open. "I think you had better go."

"Right." He marched toward the door, but when he reached the threshold, he hesitated. He glanced down at Belle, her face so pale, the set of her jaw so obdurate, yet the misery roiling in her eyes matched the turmoil he felt in his own soul.

Ever cool in his relations with women, he was not accustomed to these gnawing feelings of anger, the suspicion that he was behaving like an ass.

"Oh, hell." He expelled his breath in an explosive sigh. Prying her fingers from the knob, he eased the door closed. He gave her a rueful smile. "We have really gotten our parts down well, Angel. We are even starting to sound married."

His remark choked a reluctant laugh from her. When he held out his arms, she cast herself into them. He strained close, burying his face against her hair.

"I told you once that I did not mind about Varens, but he is not just a memory anymore, is he? And I am very much afraid—" Sinclair drew in a deep breath and then took the plunge. "I have fallen in love with you."

"Oh, Sinclair." She gazed up at him, earnestly scanning face. "I wish that I could tell you how I feel, but I am so confused. Nothing is clear to me anymore."

Her arms tightened about his neck, and she rested her head wearily against his shoulder.

"It's all right, Angel. You don't have to try to say anything. We agreed from the beginning, no promises, no forevers. But no matter how things turn out between us—" Sinclair felt his jaw tighten as he pleaded, "Don't go back to Varens. He's bad for you, Belle. You don't belong in his artificial world of dreams. You are too strong, too real for that."

"I am not planning to go off with anyone," she said. "He has not even asked me. But there was some truth to what you said earlier. I would like to see him regain his estates, at least some part of what he has lost. But that is not my only reason for wanting to go ahead with the plan against Bonaparte."

"Forget Bonaparte. Forget Varens," Sinclair groaned. He forced her face up to his. "For this one last night, just be mine."

He crushed her mouth beneath his in a kiss that was hard and long, only breaking off to continue the feverish caress along the soft white column of her throat. He felt Belle stiffen with surprise, resistance at first of this fierce onslaught, only to give way with a burst of passion that matched his own.

They clung, kissed, tumbled to the bed, and embraced in a manner that was little short of desperate. The tenderness, the playful skill that had always graced their previous couplings was gone. Sinclair bore but one determination. If he could drive Jean-Claude from Belle's heart with the ferocity of his loving, he would do it. And she responded eagerly, her own desire as savage as though equally determined to forget.

Yet when they at last lay spent in each other's arms, they experienced none of the usual glow of satisfaction. Belle drew away from him, and they rested side by side, without touching. And when their eyes met, it was clear that Jean-Claude was yet very much with them. Nothing had been resolved.

Fourteen

B y day the Palais-Royal appeared nearly the same as it had
for the generations when it had been owned by the D'Or-
leans family. The gardens were a place of great charm with
rows of lime trees and broad expanses of lawn. The quadrangle
structure itself stretched upward in a series of galleries, connected
on the ground floor by a colonnade done in the neoclassic style.
But the palace that had once sheltered the household of a duke
with claim to royal blood was now broken into a series of small
businesses and apartments.

In the bright sunshine it was a whirl of activity, one of the
favorite shopping spots of Paris with its collection of restaurateurs,
confectioners, florists, milliners, hair-dressers, watchmakers.

But by night the gardens rustled with shadows, the shops were
all shuttered, and the denizens of the upper floors stirred to life,
the Palais becoming a hive of the most respectable vice to be found
in Paris. The galleries boasted a seemingly endless array of
gambling salons, to say nothing of the discreet apartments of those
women known as the *femmes du monde*, their daring low-cut
gowns replacing those demure muslin of the ladies who had
strolled about shopping in the afternoon. These bold creatures lay

claim to the gardens, lingering in the shadows of the colonnades along with the cutpurses and scores of other rogues.

One such pert dame, what youthful attractions she possessed buried beneath a layer of rouge, eyed with speculation two strapping soldiers lounging near one of the colonnades.

The older of the two, a fellow with a pointed chin, appeared more interested in swilling from a bottle of gin. But the younger, crudely handsome with a fine set of bristling mustaches, offered the wench every sign of encouragement.

When she tried to approach, the weasel-faced one glared at her. "Off with you, slut. Go peddle your wares elsewhere."

"Ah, you are hard and cruel, m'sieur," she started to whine, but when he menaced her with upraised fist, she cursed him, melting back into the night.

"You didn't have to drive her off, Giles," the youth protested. "I could have used a bit of diversion."

"We are here for business, Auguste, not diversion." Giles took another gulp from his bottle. "Lazare is already wroth with us."

Auguste snorted. "You may fear the displeasure of Monsieur Scar Face, but I promise you that I— oof!" He broke off with a grunt when his older brother poked his stomach in warning fashion.

A figure stalked toward them, draped in a black cowl and cape like some sinister monk of the Inquisition, a man seeming spawned of the night shadows. Moonlight rendered the wisps of Lazare's hair ghost-white, his handsome scarred face like some grotesque mask depicting good and evil.

For all his bravado, young Auguste went pale, and Giles's hand, yet clutching his bottle, was seen to tremble. Lazare's mouth thinned to a smile. They feared him, both the brothers Marboeuf, despite their bluster to the contrary. Their courage was about as real as the false uniforms they wore upon their backs, a clever device they had long ago adopted to avoid being pressed into the army. If any officer ever questioned them or examined their regimentals too closely, the Marboeufs were quick to take to their heels.

But against an unarmed opponent in the dark, Lazare thought cynically, the two bore courage enough. After ascertaining they were sufficiently cowed by his stare, Lazare said, "You are on time for once, citizens. You show great wisdom."

"Been waiting for nigh half an hour," Giles ventured to grumble. "Damned chilly tonight." He lifted his bottle to his lips for another swallow.

Lazare's hand shot out, knocking the bottle from Giles's grasp. The glass shattered against the colonnade. But in a night already disrupted by raucous laughter, the shameless squeals of the light-skirts pursuing their trade, the splintering sound went unremarked.

Giles glowered at Lazare, but he dared not comment, merely rubbing the back of his hand across his lips.

"I want you sober," Lazare hissed. "There will be no mistakes such as you made yesterday morn."

"We done our best," Giles whined. "Who'd of thought the Englishman could move so fast? I never did see the likes of how he fair dived from beneath the hooves of my horse."

"We could scarce take another pass at him, either," Auguste added. "Not in broad daylight."

"Well, it is dark enough now," Lazare said.

"Oui." Auguste fingered the ends of his mustache and slapped his sword in a swaggering manner. "This time we will see how well Monsieur Carrington can dodge a blade."

"I care not how you do it." Lazare eyed him coldly. "But sunrise tomorrow must find Carrington quite dead."

MARCELLUS CRECY'S GAMING DEN WAS LOCATED UPON the second-floor arcade of the Palais-Royal. The discreet looking door opened onto a vast chamber glittering with light. Large gilt mirrors reflected back the fashionable men and women of Paris gathered about tables, lost in the pursuit of roulette, vingt-et-un, and other card games.

Sinclair blinked, taking a moment to adjust his eyes after the darkness outside. By the time he moved to help Belle off with her cloak, a servant had intercepted him in the task. The fellow's powdered wig and maroon-colored livery with gold buttons would have done justice to a ducal household.

Crecy, who ambled forward to greet them, might well have been the duke, his girth elegantly garbed in a silk coat and knee breeches, his leonine mass of silvery hair swept back from his broad forehead.

"Ah, Madame and Monsieur Carrington." Marcellus's round face creased into a bland smile. "So good of you to grace my establishment."

While Belle offered her hand to be kissed, Sinclair could only manage a curt nod. He had not much more capacity for keeping up this pretense. Today had already proved enough of a strain. His hope that the others in the society would dissuade Belle from pursuing her reckless plan had proved unavailing. To a man, they had all approved her idea. The day had been spent in another frenetic round of preparation. Tonight would see the confirmation of the plot's final details.

Crecy leaned forward conspiratorially. "You could not have chosen a better night. The most discreet game of euchre is being played in a private room in the back. Perhaps it would be more to your taste than this crowd."

Belle's low reply gave nothing away. "Thank you, monsieur. You are the perfect host."

With a graceful bow, Marcellus led the way.

I've got to put a stop to this thing soon, Sinclair thought desperately, as he had more than once these past hours. Yet how he was to do so without revealing to all of them his true identity and purpose, Sinclair did not know.

For the moment all he could do was to keep step with Belle, trailing after Crecy. Marcellus appeared very much the master of his establishment, pausing here and there to greet some of his clientele, to deliver a sharp rebuke to a footman not leaping swiftly enough to attend the guests' wants, thereby allowing them to wander too far from the tables with money still in their pockets. Fortunes seemed to disappear in the blink of an eye, swept away beneath the croupier's nimble rakes.

Despite the seriousness of their purpose in coming there tonight, Marcellus was not too preoccupied to display to Sinclair the amenities of his house.

When they passed by a curtained alcove, he gestured proudly toward it. "In there I have what I call the refuge of the wounded, Monsieur Carrington. Those gentlemen who ruin themselves at the tables have access to a private balcony, a selection of pistols, also ink and paper for any farewell message."

"How excessively civil of you," Sinclair said dryly. Crecy did not seem at all perturbed by this hint of his disapproval.

"Ah, well, we French have always been more sophisticated about such things than you English."

"God preserve me from such sophistication," Sinclair muttered. He stole a glance at Belle to see what she made of Crecy's accommodation, but she had paid little heed. He did not know where her thoughts were, but he judged from her distant expression that she was miles away.

With Jean-Claude, he wondered, then forced the painful supposition aside. He and Belle had made a pact after rising from her bed last night. They would discuss neither the Comte de Egremont or the future until their mission was resolved. Nor would they seek to touch or embrace.

Sinclair found both agreements hard to keep, and he wondered if Belle was feeling the same. She continually avoided meeting his eyes.

Sinclair's attention was drawn back to Crecy as he held open another door, indicating they should precede him into his private study. The dark paneled room was as solemn and businesslike as the gaming salon was full of light and frivolity.

Lazare and Baptiste were already there waiting. A dour silence pervaded the chamber and was little dispelled even when Crecy rang for extra candles. A waiter appeared bearing a silver tray laden with tempting morsels, oysters, cold tongue, grilled partridges, cream cheese a la rose. But the delicacies went untouched, even Crecy bearing little appetite.

This meeting tonight differed from any thus far, Sinclair thought as they gathered about Crecy's mahogany-topped desk. No repartee, no squabbling, only their faces taut with purpose as they all focused their attention on Belle. She unfolded a diagram of the theater that Crecy had sketched that very afternoon.

Her plan was familiar to all of them by this time, but she took them through the details of it one last time as though determined to dispose of any last-minute objections.

"To begin with," she said, "Marcellus will see to it that Monsieur Georges does not reach the theater tomorrow night."

Crecy nodded. "That will not be difficult. Many of the actors frequent my establishment. Georges is heavily in my debt. He will not like it, but I can coerce him into taking ill so that my unknown nephew from the provinces can make his debut."

"And that unknown nephew will be one of Crecy's footmen," Belle added.

"Will he be able to learn his lines that fast?" Baptiste asked.

"If I know the people of Paris," Belle said, "the poor man will never have to open his mouth. Once they see he is not their favorite leading actor, they will begin pelting him and hissing him off the stage."

Sinclair could not help giving voice to his chief concern. "You are counting a great deal on the audience's adverse reaction, Belle."

"Their reaction will be helped along by Lazare." Belle pointed to a spot on the diagram. "He will be sitting here in the pit."

"Lazare bears a great talent for rousing a crowd to a state of violence, Monsieur Carrington," Baptiste explained quietly.

"And my talents have grown considerably, old man." Lazare's lips split in a sneering smile, but his gaze seemed more centered on Belle. "You would be surprised at some of the places, some of the people over whom I have influence."

A strange sort of boast, Sinclair thought. What was Lazare hinting at? Belle chose to ignore the remark, continuing on. "In any case, Baptiste will place himself here." She indicated the rear section of the pit. "He will do what he can to aid Lazare. Once the riot has begun, it will be my turn. I shall be up here, with Monsieur Bonaparte in one of the first tier boxes, closest to the stage. It has been a long time since I simulated a swoon, but I think I can still manage.

"Bonaparte will have his hands quite full by the time Crecy's men burst into the back of the box, garbed in the uniform of the consular guard."

"And Bonaparte's own guards?" Sinclair demanded.

"He is likely to have one or two at the most," Crecy said. "When he attends the theater in this discreet fashion, the first consul usually is not closely attended."

"These guards will be dealt with if necessary," Belle said. "It only remains for Crecy's men to tell Bonaparte they were alerted as to his possible attendance at the theater and have come to escort him from the riot scene in safety. Once outside we must rely upon the dark and the hysterics I will have to keep the general from noticing it is not his own carriage he is being bundled into."

"Sinclair—" Belle dared a brief glance at him—"will be waiting with the coach, to help me subdue Bonaparte if necessary. After he has been bound, we will hide him beneath the false seating of the carriage and be off. Forged papers, a bribe if necessary, will get us out the city gates before it is even known Bonaparte is gone."

With a final sweep of her hand across the map, she concluded, "I will already have sent Paulette out of Paris with our luggage. We will meet at the rendezvous point in Rouvray Forest for a change to swifter horses. As we make all speed for the coast, Lazare will hasten ahead to make sure the fishing ketch is waiting."

Belle made it sound so simple. Indeed, perhaps her plan was not so farfetched after all. Sinclair tried to be objective. Extremely daring the plot was, but Sinclair's past experience told him that often the more outrageous schemes were the ones that did work, being so unexpected. Under other circumstances, the challenge of it all might have intrigued him—but for the traitor in their midst. Sinclair's gaze tracked to Lazare. Every so often the Frenchman's lips thinned in a narrow smile, a smile that iced Sinclair's blood.

Tonight was his last chance, Sinclair thought. The address he had uncovered in this district, his only clue, as yet remained not investigated. It was tonight or never. Sinclair could only hope the luck would be with him.

If the address turned out to be but one more blind alley, he would have to admit defeat. He had let matters proceed too far by not taking Belle into his confidence sooner. Now he would have to confess the truth to all these people, even at the risk of losing forever his chance to uncover the spy he sought. And what Belle's reaction would be, Sinclair scarce dared to think.

When Belle began to go over their escape route to the coast, where they would change horses, Sinclair forced a yawn and took a chance of excusing himself.

"I am sure I can leave all that in your capable hands, Angel," he said. "I will gain nothing by going through it all again. Since this is likely my last night in Paris, would you mind if I tried my luck at one of Crecy's tables?"

Crecy looked mildly surprised, Baptiste thunderstruck with disapproval.

"Somehow I never set you down for a gamester." Belle shrugged. "Suit yourself, Mr. Carrington."

She was obviously annoyed, probably seeing this as more of his disinterest in her plan. But the situation was growing far too serious for him to worry about quarreling with Belle. He could smooth things over later.

Outside in the salon Sinclair summoned a servant to produce his cloak. The thought occurred to him that he had neglected to provide himself with a weapon. He did not know exactly what awaited him behind the door of No. 32, but some sort of protection might be a wise precaution.

He wandered toward the alcove that concealed Crecy's refuge of the wounded. The little room was empty except for a small desk with the writing materials Crecy had described previously, but along one wall was a shelf containing pistol cases. Sinclair examined several of them before selecting a small lightweight pistol, finding ball and powder conveniently at hand. What a cool devil that Crecy was! After loading the pistol Sinclair slipped it carefully inside his cloak pocket.

After peeking behind the curtain, making sure he was not observed, Sinclair slipped back into the main salon, heading casualty for the main doors. He paused only long enough to inquire of the doorman the exact location of the address he sought, then he stepped out into the cool night air.

Lazare paced the study, immune to the charms of the crackling hearth, the fine wine Crecy had provided. The others—Belle, Baptiste, and Marcellus—were going through the entire plan one more time, checking it for any glaring flaws. Lazare's lip curled with contempt. He did not possess Belle's fastidious attention to detail, nor her need to drill a plan over and over again until it was letter perfect.

Besides, he already knew that tomorrow evening's events were going to proceed in far different fashion from Belle's carefully laid designs. At the moment Lazare felt far more interested in discovering what Carrington was doing.

Clearing his throat, he bluntly excused himself from the room on the grounds of answering the call of nature.

Crecy sniffed, looking disgusted, but Belle merely waved him away with a distracted gesture of her hand. For a second Lazare's eyes narrowed, unable to disguise the ugly thoughts churning through his brain. She dismissed him so easily, looking right through him, all memory of that day by the ditch erased from her mind. But he hadn't forgotten. How could he when he bore the imprint of it seared upon his flesh. And after tomorrow night Isabelle Varens would bear the memory of Etienne Lazare and his vengeance for the rest of her life ... whatever remained of it.

His hatred of her flared up inside of him so strong that he quit the study more rapidly than he intended, lest he at last reveal to her some of his purpose. Bursting out into the hum of noise that was the gaming salon, Lazare drew several calming breaths before he looked around for Carrington.

There appeared to be no sign of the blasted fellow. Lazare pushed through the midst of the wealthy, glittering throng, their heads adorned with diamond aigrettes, pomaded locks, beribboned ringlets, heads that would have looked better stacked in the basket at the foot of the guillotine. But no Carrington.

Lazare located Giles and Auguste Marboeuf at one of the roulette tables. They appeared very much out of place in Crecy's exclusive establishment, placing their modest bets beneath the croupier's supercilious stare. Obviously being admitted to such a place had gone to their heads.

With a snarl, Lazare strode over and dragged them both aside. "Where's Carrington?"

"Isn't he yet in the back room?" Giles asked.

Lazare swore. "You fools."

He had set the pair of them to keep an eye out, watch for a chance to get Carrington alone if possible, otherwise waylay him en route to the carriage later. Now Carrington had presented them with the perfect opportunity, and they had lost it.

There might yet be a chance. Carrington could not risk being gone from the meeting for too long, so he could not have gone far.

"Come on," he growled at Giles and Auguste. Lazare had

taken great pains not to arouse suspicion in Belle by sharing a part in Carrington's demise. But now he could see he must take a hand in the affair himself.

His umbrella hooked over his arm, Sinclair moved at a hurried pace, accustoming his eyes to the darkness beneath the Palais's first-floor colonnade. The lamps from the gardens cast but dim illumination here, the darkened shop windows only serving to add to the sense of isolation.

Other shadows moved about beneath the colonnades, a pair of lovers entwined in a hot embrace, a beady-eyed fellow who studied Sinclair as though to gauge the location of his purse. But something in Sinclair's stance made him think better of it, and he slunk away.

Sinclair located No. 32, the last door at the far end of the Palais, the placard in the curtained window proclaiming it as a seamstress's establishment. His shoulders took on a disheartened slump as he feared he had but come on a fool's chase.

Still a light glowed beyond the filmy curtains along with the chatter of voices. Strange that such a shop should still be open this time of night.

When Sinclair knocked at the door, a feminine voice bade him enter. He stepped cautiously inside. He had not much experience of seamstresses' shops, but he wagered that most did not look like this. The sitting room wore an aura of tawdry luxury, all crimson velvet and gilt, the cloying scent of perfume heavy in the air. Gold curtains framed an arch which led to some other mysterious area beyond.

Draped upon a settee were two ladies of dubious virtue, a redhead and a blonde. If they did possess any talent for sewing, Sinclair doubted they were expending much of it upon their own scanty attire.

An elderly woman bustled forward to greet Sinclair, her

rouged cheek puffed out with a smile. "Good evening, m'sieur. How may we serve you?"

Sinclair swept off his hat. "*Bonsoir*, madame. I—er- am looking to have some alterations done."

His words sent the young women upon the settee off into a fit of giggles. One called out, "On your breeches perchance, m'sieur?"

The elderly dame silenced them with a dignified glare.

"M'sieur must understand. We do not serve any gentleman who walks in off the streets. All our callers come here by recommendation."

Sinclair decided to take a great chance, watching the woman carefully for her reaction. "Lazare sent me."

Her puzzlement appeared genuine. "Lazare? I have never heard of this Lazare." She glanced toward the two girls as though soliciting their help.

The blonde one cooed, "I am sure it is all right, madame. I think I have heard Paulette talk of a Lazare."

"Paulette?" The name sent a jolt through Sinclair.

"*Oui*." The girl nodded to a point behind Sinclair."There she is. Ask her yourself."

Sinclair spun about to face the woman who entered the room beneath the velvet-draped arch. Although the saffron gown was not her usual attire, the red ribbon about her neck, the soft brown curls were all too familiar to Sinclair.

"Madame, I need you to—" Paulette Beauvais choked off in midsentence. As her eyes locked with Sinclair's, the shock of recognition for her appeared as great as his own.

"M-monsieur Carrington." Her dismay paled into a look of fear. She turned and vanished beneath the arch. Sinclair bolted after her.

"Stop, m'sieur!" the elderly woman cried. "You cannot thus barge in upon us." She followed after Sinclair, squawking like a frenzied chicken.

Sinclair pursued Paulette down a corridor of doors. She

whipped inside the last of these, but not quickly enough to slam the door behind her. Sinclair put his shoulder to the flimsy pine barrier as Paulette struggled to keep him out.

"I will send for the police," the old woman behind Sinclair was still blustering.

But Paulette seemed to realize the futility of the struggle. As her initial panic subsided, she released the door, allowing Sinclair to enter. "Bien, Margot. Calm yourself," she said to the old woman. "I do seem to know this gentleman after all."

Although the madame looked far from satisfied, she was persuaded to retreat. She did so, casting dire warnings at Sinclair to behave himself. "We tolerate no roughness here, m'sieur."

When she had gone, Sinclair closed the door behind him, facing Paulette across the small bedchamber, the glow of an oil lamp giving the walls a rose-colored cast. The chief feature of the room was its bed, the canopy caught above it giving the impression of some exotic Egyptian tent. Paulette hovered near it, twisting the fringe. Obviously nervous, she strove to hide the fact behind a brazen smile.

"So, Monsieur Carrington, have you tired of *ma chère* Isabelle's charms? What brings you to a place like this?"

Sinclair folded his arms, leaning up against the door. "I was planning to ask you the same thing."

"Madame Margot is an old friend of mine. I have known her since the first days of the Revolution. She still allows me to visit her upon occasion, make myself at home." Recovering some of her bravado, Paulette tipped up her chin. "And you need not look down your long English nose like that. Madame was good to me after my parents sneezed into the sack."

"I beg your pardon?"

"After they had been guillotined," she explained impatiently, then added with a hint of ferocity, "You have no notion what it took for a girl to survive during those dark days."

"Or in our present time?" Sinclair asked with a cynical cast of one brow. All the while to himself, he thought. Paulette Beauvais. How could he have been so blind? Maybe if he had not been so determined to prove Lazare the spy, he might have seen.

"I do sometimes still entertain for Madame to earn a little more money," Paulette admitted. She abandoned some of her defensive posture, infusing a hint of appeal into her tones. "None of this affects the role I play for Isabelle. Surely there is no need to tell her you found me here? You keep my secret and I will keep yours."

"Belle would likely be more understanding about all this than I," Sinclair said, flicking a contemptuous glance about the chamber's trappings. "But you have been doing other things she will find less forgivable."

Although Paulette's face was filled with defiance, Sinclair could sense the beginnings of alarm in her, an alarm that only deepened when he moved forward and picked up a black cloak she had left draped over a chair.

"For example, Belle might be more interested to know why you pay frequent visits to the guardhouse at the Tuileries."

"I never—" Paulette started to bluster and then she shrugged. "I have a lover there."

"Indeed? Yes, I have remarked your penchant for soldiers and sailors. They taught you quite a bit about the royal dockyards at Portsmouth. Perhaps one of the fools even helped you make a map of the coastline!'

"I don't know what you are talking—" But Paulette flinched away from Sinclair's steel-eyed gaze. She seemed to realize that denial would not serve. She sidled closer to him, moistening her dry lips.

"Perhaps I have sold a few maps to Bonaparte. Where is the harm in that?" She tried to angle a provocative glance up at Sinclair, fingering the brass buttons of his coat. "England and France are at peace. There is no chance that any information I provided will be used, but if the first consul is silly enough to pay, why not?"

Sinclair thrust her hands away. "I don't know if Isabelle and your other friends in the society will see your betrayal in the same light,"

Paulette crossed herself. "Upon the graves of my mother and father," she whined, "I have done nothing to betray the society. I never gave Bonaparte any names, never told anything that would hurt *ma chére* Isabelle."

"Truly? Then you won't mind if I have a look at this." When Sinclair had moved the cloak, a folded document had fallen to the floor. He bent to retrieve it, but Paulette dived for it with a shriek.

"That is nothing to do with you. It is but a letter from my lover."

Sinclair pried her fingers from the vellum, nearly tearing the note in the process. He thrust Paulette ruthlessly away. She sagged back against the bed, watching helplessly as he perused the document.

Sinclair could see clearly now how Paulette had adopted the perfect guise to be the counterspy: her entire pose as a flighty maid-servant, a man-hungry female who liked to flirt with the English sailors, whose marketing left her coming and going from the house unquestioned. Paulette had never been in Belle's confidence, but she was in an easy position to overhear much that would be to Bonaparte's advantage. It also explained why no information had been laid about the abduction plot sooner. Never included in their meetings, Paulette had had difficulty in obtaining accurate knowledge of what was going on. Even in this report her information was sketchy, alerting Bonaparte only that an abduction attempt would take place from the theater with none of the details. But the names were all there, Isabelle's, Baptiste's, Crecy's, Lazare's, his own.

"You would never hurt your *chére* Isabelle, eh?" Sinclair said, casting a fulminating glance at Paulette. "You bitch!" He savagely rented the paper and tossed in into the fire.

Paulette shrank back from his anger. "Ah, please, monsieur. You will not hurt me. I have not told anything yet. I was even changing my mind about that note."

Beneath Sinclair's stony stare, she wrung her hands and wailed. "It was just the temptation. You cannot imagine how much they would have paid me for information like that. I—"

The rest of her plea was lost as the door to the chamber crashed open. Sinclair started and Paulette shrieked in fright, cowering back against the bed.

Framed in the opening were two burly soldiers. One squinted at Sinclair through narrowed eyes like a ferret seeking its prey. The other sneered beneath his mustache. From the reek of gin they were obviously drunk.

"Wrong room, gentlemen," he said. He tried to close the door, but the mustached one blocked it.

"I don't think so, do you, Giles?" The younger soldier grinned at his companion.

"*Non*, Auguste, it looks like the right place to me." The ferret-faced one pushed his way forward into the room.

The two men were not as drunk as Sinclair had supposed. A sense of real danger coursed through him as his gaze flicked from one crude face to the other, the dawning of suspicion.

"Have I not met you somewhere before?" he asked.

He never received an answer, for at that moment Paulette saw her chance to flee. Grabbing up her cloak, she made a dash for the door. Neither of the soldiers tried to stop her, but Sinclair lunged to do so, catching hold of her sleeve.

The movement threw him off guard, left him unprepared for the sudden savage blow the man named Giles dealt his stomach. As pain spiked through him, Sinclair doubled over. Paulette wrenched herself free, making good her escape.

Panting and forcing himself upright, Sinclair's one thought was to go after her, but the other man, Auguste, was attempting to circle around behind.

Narrowly avoiding the stranglehold of his arms, Sinclair cracked his fist against Auguste's jaw. But he was not quick enough to deflect another blow from Giles. This one sent Sinclair crashing across the bed. Before he could regain his footing, Giles hefted him up, preparing to pummel him again. Somehow Sinclair's hand closed round the shaft of his umbrella, and he cracked it across the bridge of the man's nose. Giles staggered back with a howl as the blood flowed, giving Sinclair time to maneuver.

He had no idea who had set these two against him, but he had no time to find out. He had to go after Paulette. Quickly Sinclair jammed his hand into his cloak pocket and pulled the pistol free.

Before he could fire, Auguste jumped him. The weapon discharged into the air, sending the plaster of the ceiling showering down upon them.

Sinclair was dimly aware of the shrieks in the hallway outside. Madame would be sending for the authorities soon, only adding to the desperation of his situation. He glanced toward the door, but that way out was blocked by his assailants. It was impossible that he could fight his way out of here in time.

He fended off Auguste with another hard blow to the man's ribs, but Giles was struggling to pull out his sword. Backed near to the wall Sinclair sought another avenue of escape.

The window! But he needed to buy himself a few seconds of precious time. Seizing up the oil lamp, Sinclair dashed it down in front of the advancing Giles, who leaped back roaring as the carpet caught fire.

Sinclair yanked at the casement, but it was jammed. He grimaced, recognizing the inevitable. Smoke from the flames was already beginning to sting his eyes. With no more time to think Sinclair snatched up his umbrella, smashing the glass.

The sudden rush of cool air made the flames lick higher, forcing the two soldiers back to the door. Shielding his head as best he could from the remaining shards, Sinclair dived out the window amidst another hail of shattering glass.

. . .

LAZARE LINGERED IN THE PARLOR OF NO. 32, HIS presence unremarked amidst the hysteria of the brothel's workers and patrons. From sounds emanating from the back of the house, for once it appeared as if the Marboeuf brothers were earning their hire. Perhaps he should go to make sure, but he had done enough by titling Sinclair to this place. When seeking Carrington, he had overheard enough of the conversation in the bedchamber for Lazare to know he had a far greater problem- Paulette Beauvais.

Lazare glimpsed her at last, pulling on her cloak, slipping out the brothel's front door. Following quickly, he intercepted her before she had taken five steps. When his hand closed over her shoulder, she fairly collapsed from fright.

"Good evening, Paulette."

She spun about, taking a step sideways as though tempted to dart upon her way, pretending that she did not know him. But then she drew up short, shifting back her hood enough to reveal a nervous smile.

"Why, Lazare. How fortunate that I have run into you. I have quite lost my way and I was trying to find Monsieur Crecy's establishment—"

"I don't think so, *chérie*," Lazare said silkily. "I don't think you are in the least interested in going there." He indicated the door to No. 32 from which she had just emerged. "But perhaps that place over there holds more fascination for you."

"I don't know what you mean," Paulette said, backing away. Lazare could see she was on the verge of panic, and if he wished this handled subtly, he must proceed in careful fashion.

He leaned forward, whispering, "Do not be alarmed. I have but come to help you. Carrington is a British spy. He would see you arrested."

"I—I know. He was—" Paulette broke off, turning deathly

pale as she realized how she had just betrayed herself. She stared at Lazare with a mixture of suspicion and terror.

"But, how did you know?" She bit down upon her knuckle. "Dear God. What am I going to do? I must get away."

Lazare slipped his arm about her waist, preventing her retreat. "Be calm, chérie. I understand everything. I would never see one of my own countrywomen handed over to the damned English.

"Come with me now. I have a place to hide you." Lazare's teeth flashed in a feral smile. "A place where you will be quite safe."

Fifteen

Crecy's sketch of the theater lay unheeded beneath Belle's hand. She could scarce remember when she had stopped speaking, when the study had fallen quiet with her, Baptiste, and Marcellus simply staring into the fire upon the hearth.

The wine Crecy had poured out went untasted, no one of a humor to propose a toast tonight, all three of them, she sensed, sobered by the realization of what they would undertake tomorrow night.

She knew that Marcellus had prepared a little packet, some money, a farewell message to be sent to his married daughter in Marseilles should the worst happen. And Baptiste ... Earlier Belle had watched him close up his fan shop, lovingly fingering each tool, looking rather wistfully at a design he had yet to finish.

He had handed her a folded fan then. "Just a little trinket for you to carry with you tomorrow, mon ange," he had said. "For luck." Slipping the fan inside her cloak, Belle had been tempted to tell Baptiste he need proceed no further. They could manage the enterprise without him.

But he was as determined to go forward with the new plan as

she Out of the four men she at least knew she had the full support of Crecy and Baptiste, And it was not because of the money this time—not for any of them.

They all pursued some more intangible reward. Crecy, perhaps because he had grown weary of playing lord to a gaming house and wanted his birthright returned; Baptiste, because he sought peace for himself, for his beloved Paris.

As for Lazare? Who ever knew what went on in the dark corners of his mind? Likely his reasons were just the opposite of Baptiste's—the hope that Bonaparte's removal would bring back the return of violence and turmoil.

And her own motives? Belle wondered as she slowly refolded the diagrams and the map. She hardly understood her own determination. Perhaps Sinclair was partly right when he had accused her of doing it for Jean-Claude, upending the world to turn back time for one man.

But how far did she wish for Jean-Claude's future to concern herself—of that she was no longer certain. Time was not so easily turned back for her. In the interval there had been Sinclair.

Belle harbored no doubt of Sinclair's reluctance to go ahead with this scheme, his opinions of their chance of success. Why, then, was he going through with it? Did it have anything to do with the words he had whispered to her yesterday? *I have fallen in love with you.*

What joy such words were supposed to bring to a woman, not the almost bittersweet ache they had brought to her, a mingling of fear and guilt. It might well have been different, if she had never known Jean-Claude, if she had ever learned to know her own heart. A most strange realization, she mused, to be having at this time of her life.

She was jolted from her thoughts by the sound of the clock upon the mantel chiming out the hour.

"Midnight already?" Crecy said, also bestirring himself. "I wonder what has become of Monsieur Carrington and Lazare?

They certainly are nonchalant about this business. I wish I possessed such sangfroid."

"I was beginning to wonder about them myself," Belle said. She did not wish Sinclair to think she was trailing after him, controlling his every movement as though she were indeed a possessive wife. But the meeting did seem to have broken up.

Sinclair had been in a strange humor all day, moody, most unlike himself. She knew that he did not want to go ahead with the abduction, but she was beginning to feel that his reluctance was owing to something more than misplaced gallantry, his concern for her. Yet what other motive could he possibly have?

She shoved herself up abruptly from the desk. Excusing herself, she went to find Sinclair. After the quiet of the study it took her senses a moment to adjust to the glitter and noise of the gaming salon.

It seemed strange. While they had been behind that oak door, planning such a dramatic event, one that could change the entire course of France—perhaps the world—Crecy's establishment had gone on heedlessly. Belle wondered if that was true with most earth-shattering moments in history. The bulk of mankind simply went on with their lives. To those here tonight, nothing seemed more important than the numbers on the dice or the flick of the next card. But this world appeared to have gone on without Sinclair. He was nowhere to be seen.

Belle summoned the servant who had taken their cloaks. She found him lingering in conversation with the doorman, behavior that would have earned them both a sharp rebuke from Crecy. She asked, "Have you seen a tall, dark, good-looking gentleman? The one I came in with?"

"Monsieur Carrington? *Oui*, madame," the servant relied. "He left some time ago."

Left? The information startled her. Sinclair had said nothing about venturing off the premises.

"Did he happen to mention where he was going?"

The servant exchanged an embarrassed glance with the door-man. The doorman cleared his throat. "I am sure madame's husband will return soon. If you wish to leave, I can summon you a cabriolet, or I am sure that Monsieur Crecy will have his own carriage fetched round for you."

Belle fixed the man with a cool stare. "Where has my husband gone?"

He tried to bluster his way out of it, but he quailed before her haughty gaze. "Well, he did ask the directions to Number 32."

Belle frowned. The address meant nothing to her. Where in blazes had Sinclair slipped off to which would cause these two men to squirm so? A suspicion occurred to her when she thought of one of the chief businesses of the Palais-Royal besides gaming.

"What sort of establishment is at Number 32?" she asked.

Their continued reluctance to answer confirmed Belle's suspicion. "It's a brothel, is it not?"

"Ah, madame!" The doorman reddened with acute discomfort.

Belle heaved an impatient sigh with all this male subterfuge. She commanded a servant to bring her cloak.

The doorman mopped his brow with relief. "And I will see to obtaining a coach for madame."

"I don't need a coach," Belle said, swirling a cloak about her shoulders. "Just the directions to Number 32."

"It is at the end of the lower arcade-but, madame!" The doorman looked aghast. "You cannot think of going there."

"I am not just thinking of it." Belle gave him a taut smile. "I fully intend to do so."

Over his protests she stalked out into the night air. The cool breeze did nothing to ease the hot flood of anger and confusion coursing into her cheeks. She could think of no reason Sinclair should have wandered off to a brothel—none but the most obvious.

Her judgment rejected this solution almost immediately. For

all his pose of being a rake, such behavior seemed most unlike the Sinclair she knew, the Sinclair who had held her in his arms, told her he loved her.

Yet what do you know of him? A voice inside her jeered, a voice that sounded remarkably like Lazare's. *He has a habit of disappearing, our Mr. Carrington. Where do you suppose he goes?*

Trying to suppress the memory of Lazare's mocking questions, Belle quickened her steps. There was only one way to gain answers and that was to find Sinclair.

Belle had no difficulty locating the correct place. Even without the doorman's reluctant directions, No. 32 was the only apartment on the lower level erupting with such commotion. Scantily clad women stood about shrieking in the street while an old lady bellowed for the police, a brassy-haired girl weeping against her shoulder.

When Belle saw the two uniformed guards coming, she ducked into the shadows. This was no time to risk being caught up in a raid, or whatever it was, and find herself getting arrested. But what about Sinclair? Was he still inside?

Belle crept round to the back of the place, trying to figure out what was happening. She had just decided there was a fight in progress within, when she was startled. A dark object came crashing through the window, rolled, and came to a halt almost at her feet.

It was a man. The moonlight rimming down past the trees enabled her to make out the dazed features.

"Sinclair?" she gasped.

Stunned, he stared up at her for a moment. "Angel," he said in a bemused voice. He shook his head as though to clear it, fragments of glass tinkling to the ground. Leaning upon his umbrella, he attempted to rise. Belle put one hand beneath his elbow to assist him.

"Have you seen Paulette?" he asked.

"What!" The question made no sense to her. Sinclair's forehead was bleeding. She wondered if a blow to his head was making him disoriented. But at the moment she could think of nothing else but getting him away from here.

As he struggled to his feet, his vision seemed to clear somewhat, but Belle found his next remark equally as confusing. He gave a soft grunt, managing a painful smile through his split lip. "The devil seems to be after me. Or at least two of his henchmen."

Belle heard the sash of another window being thrown up in the building behind them. A mustached soldier was silhouetted in the opening, brandishing a sword.

"There he goes, Giles. The English pig!" the man shouted, beginning to clamber out the window.

"Two new friends of mine," Sinclair murmured, reeling slightly on his feet. "Giles and Gus."

"I don't think you are in any condition to continue the acquaintance!" Belle exclaimed. "Let's get out of here."

Tugging on his hand, she started to pull him away from the Palais-Royal. Behind the glittering palace the streets were dark as pitch, only the moon to guide the way, a fact not much in the their favor, despite the concealing blackness. It was too easy to trip and fall over the refuse tossed beside the buildings or lose one's way in the narrow mazelike passages. Belle saw that she had made a mistake by heading away from the lights and the other people of the Palais¬Royal, except that the police might prove as great a threat as the two heavy-footed soldiers charging behind them.

Belle could easily have outdistanced them, but in Sinclair's battered condition, he soon drew up, panting, clutching his side. "Go on, Angel. Get out of here. I can hold them off."

But Belle wanted none of his heroics. "This way," she said, yanking him beneath the arch into an inner court.

Too late she realized she had drawn them into a trap. Ahead of them loomed a high stone wall surrounding someone's private garden. The heavy iron gate was barred from the other side, a pair of-black mastiffs snarling at them through the bars. The Argand lamp affixed atop one of the posts only served to light their presence as though they had been caught in a flood of sun.

Belle snatched Sinclair's umbrella from his grasp and tugged frantically at the handle.

"What are you doing?" he asked.

"Trying to get out your swordstick."

Sinclair looked at her blankly. "What swordstick?"

"Why, I always assumed ..." Belle's voice trailed off in the sickened realization that she indeed held in her hands nothing but a common umbrella.

Sweat and blood trickled down Sinclair's face. He dashed it aside with the back of his hand. "Do it my way, this time, Angel." He shoved her farther into the shadows of the wall. "It's me they are after. When you see your chance, get the devil out of here."

She had no opportunity to argue. One of the soldiers loomed at the entrance of the court, moonlight revealing the murderous snarl on his weasel-like features. Sinclair didn't wait for him to take the offensive. He charged forward, tackling the man and dragging him to the ground.

The entrance to the court was cleared, but the possibility of flight never entered Belle's mind. Tossing Sinclair's umbrella. aside, Belle slipped her hand beneath her cloak and tugged at the jeweled ornament affixed to her bodice, drawing forth a sharp stiletto from the sheath sewn into the gown.

As Sinclair and the soldier locked in a death struggle, the Frenchman screamed, "*A moi, Auguste!*"

It took the second soldier but a moment to come running to his comrade's aid. Auguste raced forward, his sword arcing as he prepared to run Sinclair through the back. Belle rushed at the soldier. He heard her approach in time to turn, but not to deflect her blow.

She drove the knife deep into his shoulder. He emitted a shriek of pain, then staggered back, dropping his sword. The other large man now had Sinclair pinned beneath him, his hands going for

Sinclair's throat. Belle snatched up the fallen sword and crept toward the battle, but Auguste with a furious grunt had ripped the knife out of his flesh. He stepped in between her and the struggling men, wrenching the sword from his companion's scabbard. Auguste approached her with an ugly scowl.

Belle was forced back from Sinclair's desperate struggle. She tensed as the soldier closed in. He lunged wildly, but she deftly parried the blow, the scrape of steel ringing out into the night.

Auguste's thrusts were savage, hard, but with little skill behind them. Belle parried easily, but knew if she did not make an end to this soon, he would wear her down. Panting, she circled, looking for her opening, aware that Sinclair was not able to come to her aid, terrified that he was being choked to death.

The man made a wild slash, coming perilously near to cutting open her face. It took him a moment to recover his balance. In that unguarded instant Belle drove her own weapon home, piercing Auguste's sword hand. With a cry, he dropped his weapon, clutching at his bloodied hand.

As Belle pressed the tip of her sword in menacing fashion against the paunch of his stomach, Auguste stumbled back from her in wide-eyed terror. Sparing not so much as another glance for Giles, he whirled about and fled the court.

Belle's own gaze flicked to Sinclair. He appeared to have gone slack beneath the large soldier's hands, with their brutal crushing grip upon his neck.

Gripping the sword in her sweat-slickened hand, Belle staggered to his aid, but at that moment Sinclair's hand closed about a rock and dealt a hard blow to his assailant's temple.

His grip broken, Giles tumbled to one side. Sinclair rallied enough to deliver one more punch. With a low groan Giles sagged back, subsiding into unconsciousness.

Belle's relief was short-lived as she watched Sinclair also sink down, clutching his throat. Belle bent over him, pushing his hand aside, ripping away his disheveled cravat, loosening his shirt buttons.

"Sinclair?" she whispered, studying his pale, bruised features, the bloody cut on his forehead, one eye all but swollen shut.

Behind them in the house beyond the gate, at last a light appeared, and the sounds of the occupants stirring awake were heard.

"Sinclair!" she called more frantically.

He forced his good eye open to regard her. He could hardly get his breath, but he still managed to give her his roguish grin.

"And you would trade all this for a cottage in Dorsetshire?" he rasped.

"You fool!" she said with a choked sound that was part laugh, part sob. Drawing her arm beneath his shoulders, she struggled to help him to his feet. "Let me get you home, or we may yet end this night in gaol."

SINCLAIR SAGGED BACK AGAINST THE PILLOWS OF Belle's bed. He emitted a low groan as she dabbed a cool cloth at the cut upon his brow. He winced as her fingers accidently brushed against the huge swelling below one eye.

"I suppose it could have been worse," Belle muttered, surveying the damage.

"Much worse. You saved my life tonight, Angel. Where did you ever learn to wield a sword like that?"

"From Jean-Claude's old sword master. Jean-Claude had not much employment for the man, so I persuaded him to give me lessons to pass the time—" Belle broke off, annoyed with herself for nearly admitting she had oft found life at Egremont a little boring.

"Now, stop talking and hold still," she snapped. Now that the danger was past, a cold anger took possession of her. Sinclair had jeopardized everything, getting involved in a fight in a brothel like some drunken sailor on shore leave. Why, she wanted to know? What had it all been about?

"As soon as I have attended to this wound, we have a great deal to discuss, Mr. Carrington."

"Yes, I fear we do." He sighed, closing his eyes.

Belle drew back, regarding his cut and the bloodied cloth in her hand with some frustration. "I cannot seem to get the blasted thing to stop bleeding."

"There is some sticking plaster in my room," Sinclair said. "In the wardrobe."

"I will go fetch it. You just lie still and don't move." She left the room, striding into Sinclair's adjoining chamber. She pulled a face. As always, it was a mess, perhaps now even worse than usual. When he had returned from the fight, the first thing Sinclair had done was strip off his bloodied cloak and waistcoat, adding them to the heap.

After a lengthy search she found the sticking plaster. But hastening toward the door, she tripped over something and nearly sprawled headlong. As it was, she banged her elbow on Sinclair's bedpost.

Straightening, she cursed and moved to kick the object that had caused her fall out of the way. Sinclair's blasted umbrella! Her lips curved into a wry smile as she conjured up a mental image of herself, how ridiculous she must have looked earlier, seeking a swordstick where there was none.

Bending down, she retrieved the umbrella, intending to toss it upon the table with Sinclair's shaving gear, where it could do no further harm. She noticed the bone handle had been cracked in the fight. When touched, it came off in her hand. Strange, but the interior appeared almost hollow, like a place of concealment. When she tipped it up to examine it, a piece of paper dropped to the floor.

Belle felt a surge of annoyance with Sinclair. She had made it clear that she wanted nothing written down, no matter how clever the place of concealment. What sort of damaging evidence had he felt the need to commit to paper?

She scanned the paper briefly, but frowned. It had nothing to do with their mission. Rather it was some brief notes, a list of all the names of those who worked for Victor Merchant.

A prickling of uneasiness coursed through her. Why would Sinclair have something like this hidden away?

She studied the list more closely. Lazare's name was scrawled at the end, like a hurried addition. More interesting still, Laurent Coterin and old Feydeau's names had been crossed off. None of the others bore any special notations except for her own, which had been underlined with a question mark placed beside it.

Her heart gave an uneasy thud. The men's names who were crossed off were dead, had both met their ends in a fairly violent manner. The lines through the names only added to the sensation that it was as if as if they had been eliminated. Belle ran a hand over her brow. What could it all mean? A daunting suspicion occurred to her. She tried to shut it out, but couldn't quite manage it. A montage of scenes whirled through her brain: Sinclair's ever-present reluctance about this mission, his joining the society out of nowhere, his reticence about his past, his inexplicable knowledge about Feydeau's death. Then there was the mysterious man who had approached Sinclair at Bonaparte's review.

Belle sagged down on Sinclair's bed, wanting to fight off such disturbing thoughts. They all pointed to one thing, a most clever enemy who had infiltrated their organization with a view to destroying it from within, possibly an agent of Bonaparte himself. But why would any Englishman want to help Napoleon?

The reason most adventurers embarked upon their schemes—money. Sinclair had ever assured her he was an adventurer, no gentleman. And did that mean that Sinclair plotted her destruction as well? No, how could he after what they had shared, after telling her that he loved her?

But how could she be that naive? What better way was there

for a spy to gain cooperation and information than through seduction? It was the oldest trap in the world. Until now she had ever been too canny to fall into it.

Yet no lover had ever so been as skillful as Sinclair, the caress of his eyes, that look of soul-deep understanding even more potent than the magic of his body. She had always had such scorn for women who let themselves be used, taken in, wondering how they could be such fools! It seemed she was about to discover how for herself.

She stared at the question mark by her name. Was she then fated to be the next to die? The thought sent a dull lancing of pain through her. She felt so weary of this life, the constant danger, the distrust, the suspicion, so weary of struggling with it. With Sinclair she thought she had escaped much of that for a time, at least having a partner she thoroughly trusted to share it all.

Her one honest relationship, she thought with a bitter sneer. She leaned against the bedpost, feeling suddenly drained. If it was her life he wanted, he could have it.

The thought didn't last for long. Her survival instincts were too strong, part of her yet clinging to the belief that there had to be another explanation. She must be wrong, jumping to conclusions. But she could take no chances with such a risky mission in the balance and other lives dependent upon her own.

Wearily she trudged back to her room, deciding what she had to do. She needed to know the truth about Sinclair and she needed to know it now, no matter how ruthless the measures it took to gain it.

Sinclair allowed his throbbing head to pillow against the cushions, wincing at the pain shooting through his rib cage when he moved too suddenly. He felt as though he had been dragged on a hurdle, yet he could not afford to pamper his much battered body too much longer. The fact remained that he had allowed Paulette to escape.

What was the wench doing now? Would she make all haste to

get her message to Bonaparte, or would she panic and flee? Either way he had to warn Belle. Likely, they might all have to flee Paris tonight.

He heard the door open when Belle returned to the room, but his eyelids felt too weighted to open.

"Angel?" he called.

"I shall be right with you," she said. He heard her rustling about the chamber, the sound of a drawer sliding open. Sinclair did not relish the upcoming confrontation with Belle when she had believed in his honesty. How would she react to his deceit, the destruction of the plan she seemed to so cherish?

Already he could imagine what she must be thinking at discovering he had slipped off to a brothel. Her silence seemed to send a chill through the room.

"Angel?" he called again. "Did you find the sticking plaster?"

He received no answer. He didn't know how, but he sensed her standing over him.

He flicked his eyes open.

She appeared no ministering angel this time. With a hard light in those blue eyes, she towered over him, aiming a pistol straight at his heart.

Sixteen

Belle watched Sinclair's eyes widen in astonishment. Even as his gaze fixed upon the pistol, he registered not so much alarm as confusion, a half-amused uncertainty.

"You don't seem to have found the sticking plaster, Angel." But all traces of his amusement vanished as he stared into her eyes.

"No," she said, "but I did find this." She held up the list she had found inside his umbrella.

He struggled into a sitting position. "Oh," he said in a flat voice. The single guilty syllable was as good as a confession. Stark pain ripped through Belle. Until that moment she did not know exactly how much she had been praying for a denial, some logical explanation of the damning evidence against him.

It cost her great effort to keep her grip steady upon the pistol handle. "I want to know what is going on. Who are you, Sinclair Carrington?"

He sighed. "I knew this moment had to come, but I had hoped not like this. I had been waiting for the right time to tell you the complete truth. Believe it or not, tonight I had resolved—"

"That doesn't matter now," Belle said sharply. "No more

attempts at evasion, if you please. I want naught but direct answers, and I want them now."

"And you will have them, but that pistol is not necessary. I can guess, unfortunately, what you must be thinking, and I don't blame you. But I can explain everything to your satisfaction." He made a movement as though to rise from the bed.

"No! Stay where you are." Belle drew in a steadying breath. "We played a game similar to this one time before." She felt her throat constrict as she recalled that rainy afternoon their romp had nearly ended by making love. Why did it all seem so long ago?

"I feel more at ease with you as you are," she concluded. "I don't trust you."

"Right," he said, leaning back. There was no bitterness or anger in his voice, only a deep sorrow. He half-closed his eyes. "Where would you like me to begin?"

"You can start by telling me, Mr. Carrington—if that is your real name—exactly who you are working for, for I have a strong notion it is not Victor Merchant."

"My name?" he said wearily. "My name is Daniel Anthony Sinclair Carr. I am a spy for the British army."

Sinclair continued, telling his story from the beginning when he had first infiltrated Merchant's organization until the happenings of this evening, catching Paulette and then becoming involved in the brothel fight. Belle did not interrupt, even to interject a question.

When he had finished, he studied her face for her reaction. The hand holding the pistol had relaxed, although a certain amount of skepticism remained in her eyes.

"You don't believe me?" he asked. He had been prepared for many things, but not that she would still doubt him after he had told her the truth.

"I am not sure. The fact still remains that two of the agents marked through on this list met with violent ends."

"I marked them off as suspects when I learned of their deaths.

You said the man Coterin was a fool, more than likely the sort who would be shot in a botched escape attempt. And as for Feydeau, as illogical as it sounds, you must accept the fact that for once the man did not control his drinking. People all have breaking points, times when they do the unexpected."

"And the question mark by my name?"

"I made the mark absentmindedly when I was—" He broke off, realization flashing through him. "You thought I had arranged the death of those two men and you were to be next!" Sinclair's hurt was tempered with a sorrowful understanding. They led similar lives, he and Belle. He knew too well the suspicion, the caution that kept one alive.

He explained patiently, "The question mark meant that, considering your cleverness and daring, I was paying you the compliment of believing you my most likely suspect."

"*Merci, monsieur,*" she said bitterly. "That sheds entire new light upon your assiduousness in my bedchamber."

"No! Belle, damn it!" As he lurched forward, all his battered muscles seemed to stiffen in protest. Tired of the awkwardness of his situation, he said, "I am getting up now. If you intend to fire, go ahead."

Not sparing her another glance, he forced himself to his feet. With a show of deliberate nonchalance, he limped over to examine his face in the mirror. His temple had stopped bleeding, but with his eye nearly swollen shut, the bruises discoloring his jaw, he looked like a prizefighter down for the count.

When he turned back to Belle, she had laid the pistol on the dressing table and sagged down upon a stool before the hearth with her arms wrapped about herself. She reminded him of the way he had found her that night down by the window, looking so alone, so lost. He wanted to go to her, pull her into his arms, but he knew he couldn't. Likely he would never be able to do so again.

He approached as close as he dared, saying in a gentle voice, "I won't have you believing that I bedded you in order to get you to betray yourself, to give information. This assignment has been pure hell for me. I have wanted you from the first with my blasted conscience getting in the way."

"How inconvenient for you."

"I never made love to you until I was certain you were not the spy."

"Why didn't you tell me the truth then? When were you planning to do so? On the way to the theater? Oh, by the bye, Angel, one of your members is a Napoleonic agent, so tonight you are likely leading your people into a trap."

"I was planning to tell you this evening, would have told you days ago except—"

"Except for what?"

Except that he had been afraid of losing her. No, how could he tell her that? How did one lose what one had truly never had? He started to rake his hand through his hair and winced when he grazed his wound. "Even though I was certain you were not the spy, you have told me more than once you have no strong interests on either side. What loyalties you have belong to individual people. If I had ferreted out the spy and it turned out to be someone like Baptiste ..." He let the suggestion speak for itself.

"Baptiste, of course," she murmured. "All that time I thought you were being kind to my old friend, spending so much time with him, you were merely seeking information."

"No! And yes," Sinclair admitted reluctantly. "I have grown to like and respect Baptiste, as much as I have grown to hate this assignment. But I don't know if I could have behaved any differently. Too much was at stake, too many lives at risk because of the information Paulette was passing, the lives of British soldiers, even my own brother."

Sinclair's voice trailed off as he searched Belle's eyes for some sign that she understood. But with a sinking heart all he noted were the lines of her face becoming more rigid, all her old barriers being slammed into place.

"What I find most unforgivable," she said at last, "is the way you let me rattle on and on about honesty, about how there was no pretense or deceit between us."

"God, Belle, you don't know how much I wished that had been true. I was wrong to let you go on believing in me, but it seemed like the one edge that I had over your memories of Jean-Claude—the freedom from pretense, that you and I are so much alike. We share the same world while—"

He was interrupted by her expression of blazing scorn. "Still trying to deceive me, Mr. Carr? It won't serve. You see, I take great pains to keep myself current with the world. Not only do I read the military dispatches in the paper, but the society columns as well.

"That stiff-necked old martinet you described as your father, he is General Daniel Carr, is he not?"

"You have heard of him?"

"Who has not heard of the famous general, the youngest son of the Duke of Berkstead? That, I believe, makes you the Honorable Mr. Daniel Sinclair Carr." She pronounced his title with a kind of savage sarcasm.

"I don't hold your birth against you, Belle," he said. "Don't hold mine against me."

The quiet reproof in his eyes defused some of her anger, causing her to look away. She rubbed the back of her neck, wishing Sinclair would stop talking, simply leave her be. Never had she felt such a weight of emptiness settling over her heart, not even during those dread days immediately after Jean-Claude had left her. She was so tired. She wished she could just let go of everything, yet even now she was forced to act.

Somehow she got to her feet. "None of this disagreement between you and me is of any importance. What I have to do now is try to think."

"There is not much to think about," Sinclair said. "Paulette has escaped. She may even now be relaying her information. We all must be out of Paris by first light."

"You may go. Paulette cannot be any danger to your precious army now. You have accomplished what you came for."

Sinclair flinched at her harsh words, but he said, "I go nowhere without you."

"I intend to stay. My business here in Paris is not finished."

"You cannot possibly still be thinking of going ahead with the abduction—"

"No, Mr. Carrington. I am not that big of a fool. But I cannot leave without making some attempt to discover what has become of Paulette. If there is any chance at all she has not yet gone to Bonaparte, I must try to stop her."

"Are you mad? Do you have any idea how dangerous that would be?" He took a step toward her almost as though he wished to shake sense into her head. Belle drew herself erect, defying him to touch her. He stopped just short, but she read the steely determination in his eyes.

"You are coming with me now, Belle, even if I have to take you by force."

"Don't you understand anything?" she cried. "Oh, certainly, it would be easy for you and me to flee this disaster. Our lives are not centered here. But what about Crecy and Baptiste?"

Although the set of his jaw remained stubborn, she could tell her words were giving Sinclair pause.

"Baptiste has already risked enough with nothing but a failed plot to show for it," she continued passionately. "To be exiled from Paris—I believe it would kill him. I won't see him make such a sacrifice. Not without making some attempt to prevent it."

She and Sinclair squared off for a long moment. He was the first to concede. "All right, Angel, what do you want to do?"

"Find Paulette." She was gathering up her cloak. "I intend to start by going back to that brothel—if you haven't burned it to the ground—and ask some questions."

"I will go with you."

"I doubt you will be welcome there. I will have a much better chance if I go alone. Paulette may even still be hiding there."

Sinclair regarded her with folded arms. "And what do you expect me to do?"

In his condition Belle thought the best he could do was gain a few hours' rest, but she knew he was unlikely to do so. After thinking a moment, she asked, "Is it possible you could contact your friend Warburton at this hour? If he and your other agent keep as close a watch upon that guardhouse as you say, it is possible they will know if Paulette has been there."

Sinclair appeared to turn this possibility over in his mind, and nodded in agreement. He seemed far from pleased at the prospect of letting her venture off on her own, but after gruffly ordering her to take care, he turned to go.

Yet as he stalked toward the door, he paused to look back. "I only want to tell you one more thing, Belle. I did not lie when I said I love you."

She froze, trying to steel herself against the low-spoken words, yet they stirred her all the same, touching upon a memory. Her heart constricted when she recalled what it was. Sinclair's words were almost an echo of her plea to Jean-Claude so long ago.

She turned away, not wanting to understand the misery her rejection was inflicting upon Sinclair at this moment, not wanting to, but understanding it all too well.

She heard the door open behind her, and somehow she could not let him go like that. She whipped about. "Sinclair?"

He stopped. She could almost hear his breath still. "Yes?"

She drew in a deep breath, but her pain at his deception was yet too raw for her to do more than confess, "About the pistol. It wasn't loaded."

He offered her a sad smile before exiting. "I never really thought it was, Angel."

. . .

Dawn found Belle's eyes gritty from lack of sleep, her limbs aching from exhaustion, and she had accomplished nothing. Paulette appeared to have vanished off the face of the earth. Some judicious bribes at the brothel to the sleepy-eyed femmes earned her only the knowledge that Paulette had slipped out during the fight and had never come back.

Most of Belle's time had been wasted listening to Madame Margot bemoaning the recent events. "One of our best chambers ruined by fire," the elderly dame had wailed, "to say nothing of the brutes we had tromping through here, wild-eyed Englishmen, loutish soldiers, scarred rogues—"

"*Oui*, Madame," Belle said soothingly, making her escape from these vapid outpourings as soon as she could. The visit to the brothel having proved useless, she made her way to Crecy's. At least she could alert him to the danger and solicit some of his servants to join in the search.

The morning had considerably advanced by the time she made her way back to the apartment. Gray and overcast, the day was an accurate reflection of her spirits. Dragging herself down to the apartment's tiny kitchen, she brewed a cup of tea while she attempted to decide what to do next.

She had just sagged down at the wooden table when a footfall alerted her to Sinclair's return.

"Belle?" he called.

"In here," she replied wearily.

He appeared shortly in the doorway, looking as exhausted as she, a stubble of beard rimming his jaw, a heavy circle under his one eye, the other now darkened to a shade of purple. At least the swelling had gone down. His dark hair spilled over his brow, concealing the cut on his forehead. When he collapsed down on the chair opposite her, the instinct to reach across and reach for his hand was strong. With great difficulty, she hardened herself against the impulse.

"Any luck?" she asked, although his downcast expression gave her the answer.

He shook his head. "Neither Warburton nor the other agent has seen any trace of her. Not that she couldn't have somehow slipped past them and already be inside the Tuileries. But they promise to keep as close a watch as they can and intercept her if they see her."

Sighing, Belle stared into her teacup, but she made no move to taste the bitter brew, merely warming her hands upon the steaming china. After long thought she said, "I doubt if Paulette made it to the Tuileries. If she had, we would likely have soldiers thundering at our door by now."

"Then where do you think she has gone? Does she have other friends in Paris?"

"I have no idea. It should be rather obvious I didn't know the woman that well. But Crecy's men are searching the vicinity of the Palais-Royal. I told Marcellus to do nothing more until he hears from me."

Sinclair nodded. He shifted upon the chair as though seeking a more comfortable position. Belle did not miss the way he flinched, one hand going surreptitiously toward his ribs. Despite her lingering anger with him, she could not help feeling a stab of remorse and empathy. He had taken the devil of a beating last night with no chance to rest and recover.

Silently she pushed her cup of tea across the table to him. He flashed a grateful look, but said, "No, thank you, Angel, I am not that close to death's door as to be drinking that."

"I'd offer you something stronger, but there's not much here. Thinking that we would be gone, I told Paulette to clear most everything out."

The mention of the woman's name brought them back to the problem.

"So what do we do now?" Sinclair asked. "I gather you learned nothing of any use at Madame Margot's?"

"Only that she will never let an Englishman cross her threshold again," Belle said, forcing down a swallow of the tea. "Nor any soldiers or men with—"

She broke off, startled by the recollection of some of the elderly woman's meanderings. Had her mind simply been too numb at the time to take heed, or was she reading too much significance into a certain fact now?

"Men with scars," Belle mused aloud.

"What was that?" Sinclair asked.

"Madame Margot. She said something about a man with a scar lurking in her parlor."

Some of Sinclair's fatigue appeared to be forgotten. "Lazare?" he asked eagerly.

"Lazare is certainly not the only man with a scar to be found in Paris, yet he did leave the meeting shortly after you did." Belle frowned. "But it makes no sense. Why would Lazare be there? I cannot believe he had anything to do with Paulette's business. He hates Bonaparte far too much to have had a hand in that."

"That may be true, but I have had my suspicions of Lazare all along," Sinclair said. "I never mentioned it last night, but I am almost certain those two who attacked me were the same men who nearly ran me down in the street. I think they were paid to do so."

"By Lazare?"

"I don't know, but I would wager my last farthing that he knows more about what went on in that brothel last night than anyone else does."

Belle shoved to her feet, her resolution returning. "Then perhaps it is time he shared that information with us."

Sinclair also stood, a steely look of anticipation in his eyes. "I shall be only too happy to flush the rat down from his garret for questioning."

Belle scowled, moving to intercept his retreat from the kitchen. The last thing she wished for was any more brawling. But Sinclair seemed to bear no more sense than most men in that regard.

She need not have worried, however, about the upcoming confrontation. Lazare was not in his garret apartment. The porter furnished the information that Lazare had not returned last night.

"People have a nasty habit of disappearing in this city," Sinclair grumbled. Belle did not have the energy to set off on another wild chase, so she persuaded Sinclair to wait awhile for Lazare's return.

In the meantime, it occurred to her she had yet to warn Baptiste what had transpired. Again, she met with frustration. She had forgotten that after Baptiste closed up shop the night before, he had told her he meant to spend the day with an old friend.

She knew well what he meant by that. Likely Baptiste was out strolling the streets of his Paris, visiting all his old haunts as though this might be the final time. Belle prayed that it was not. Since she had no way of tracing him, she had to content herself with slipping a carefully worded note under his door, warning him not to go to the theater that night.

Then she returned upstairs to keep her vigil with Sinclair. By early afternoon their nerves were stretched wire taut.

"I can't believe Lazare won't be back," Belle said. "It would not be like him to abandon the plot. He despises Bonaparte too much."

"Well, I am going mad, simply waiting here," Sinclair said, fairly pacing a hole in the drawing room carpet. Indeed, this inaction was making Belle nigh insane herself.

"Is there nowhere you can think of that we could find the blasted rogue?" Sinclair asked.

Belle rubbed her temples in an effort at memory. "Well, I do know Lazare does not usually stay here above the fan shop when he comes to Paris. He once mentioned other lodgings."

Sinclair tensed "It would not happen to be above a chocolate shop, would it?"

"Yes, I think he did say something about a confectioner's, but why—"

"Because I have an idea where it is, if I can only find the shop again." Sinclair tugged at her hand, dragging her after him.

It took some doing to locate the shop, but from bits and pieces of what Sinclair remembered, Belle managed to guess at the address. They retraced the route he had taken the day he had followed Lazare, arriving at last to the narrow street with its tumbledown buildings.

"This is it," Sinclair said, glancing up at the rusted signpost.

"It appears to be closed." Belle tried the door and peered through the grimy window into the empty shop.

"That should prove no problem." Sinclair gave a furtive glance about him. The street was nearly empty of pedestrians, those who did pass by looking far too occupied with their own affairs to pay much heed. "Have you got a hairpin?"

Although Belle was astonished by the request, she groped beneath her poke-front bonnet and produced the requested article.

"Stand in front of me to cover my movements," Sinclair said. Belle did as he asked. In a matter of minutes he had picked the lock.

"Is that something you learned at Eton, Mr. Carrington?" she could not refrain from asking.

"Good lord, no. The only thing of practical value I learned there was how to wield a cricket bat." He grinned at her and she could not help giving him a half-smile. It was the closest to their usual banter as they had come since his grim confession.

Even that slight relieving of tension seemed to help as they crept cautiously into the shop.

"I hope we are not caught," Belle murmured. "I would find it rather ironic to end my career being charged with stealing sweetmeats."

"Believe me, Angel," he whispered back, closing the door behind them, "no one would steal this shop's wares. Vilest march-pane I have ever tasted."

Sinclair indicated a curtained doorway behind the counter. "I believe Lazare must have disappeared through there that day. He met someone that I almost mistook to be—" He broke off, casting an easy sidewise glance at her.

"To be who?" she prompted.

"No one of importance. Come on."

Belle had the feeling that was not what Sinclair had intended to say, but she had no chance to question him, exerting herself to keep up with his long strides.

Cautiously Sinclair led the way past the curtain. A pair of rickety stairs wound upward to a landing above. They climbed up them stealthily to find a solitary door at the top.

Belle started to knock, but Sinclair stayed her hand. "If Lazare does happen to be out for my blood," Sinclair said, "I would just as soon not announce our arrival."

Grasping the hairpin, he set to work on the lock and soon set the door to creaking open. Belle tensed, catching her breath, but she peered past Sinclair's shoulder into an empty room.

"This may not even be Lazare's room," she started to say, then stopped as she recognized Lazare's trunk shoved against one chipped plaster wall, the familiar battered portmanteau held closed with a length of thick rope.

The room showed signs of recent habitation. Two dusty glasses along with a bottle drained to the dregs stood propped on an upended crate. The fireplace held a thick coating of ashes.

Sinclair's interest fixed itself upon the trunk. Striding forward, he struggled to remove the rope and began to paw through the contents. It appeared to be nothing more than Lazare's clothing.

"What do you expect to find?" Belle demanded.

"I don't exactly know."

She watched him for a moment, beginning to feel that this was all but another waste of time. Noting another door, she said, "Well, I suppose I can at least see what is in there."

"Just be careful, Angel," Sinclair replied.

As she slipped through the door, Sinclair tapped the lid of the trunk. It had a strangely hollow sound. Using his pocket knife, he began to pick at the wood. It splintered easily, revealing a compartment behind.

Excitedly, he slipped his hand inside and drew out a packet of papers. Straightening, he carried them over to one of the apartment's narrow windows, taking advantage of what meager light filtered past the filthy panes.

The first document appeared to be some sort of communication Lazare had been in the process of writing to Merchant.

"When you read this, you will know your orders have been carried out. I have already disposed of Carrington. Tonight will see the finish of the rest of it. Isabelle Varens ..."

As Sinclair scanned down the rest of the page, he drew in his breath with a sharp hiss.

"Angel, I found something you had better look at right now. Belle?"

From within the next room Belle groped through the near darkness of what she guessed to be a bedchamber. The heavy curtains had been pulled so tightly closed as to render the room but a mass of shadows.

Banging into the end of the iron bedstead Belle moved carefully toward the window. The curtains smelled of mildew and damp. When she flung them back, a flood of dim gray light entered the room. Turning, she prepared to better examine her surroundings, her gaze focusing upon the bed.

She let out a strangled gasp. A woman lay upon the bare mattress, her dark curls tumbled over the pillow. She fixed Belle with a vacant glassy-eyed stare, a bright slash of red about her neck.

But it was not Paulette's familiar red ribbon. It was blood.

Dimly Belle was aware of Sinclair calling her name from the other room but she could not seem to avert her gaze from Paulette. The French woman's features were frozen in a waxen image of horror. Involuntarily Belle's hand crept to her own throat.

Steeling herself, she stepped closer. There was no doubt that Paulette was dead. Her throat had been slit from ear to ear.

Lazare's signature, Belle thought grimly. Staring down at the woman who would have betrayed them all, Belle supposed she should have felt a righteous satisfaction. But after her initial horror, she experienced nothing but pity. Poor foolish, greedy Paulette.

Sinclair's voice came more insistently. "Belle? Are you all right in there?"

She slowly pulled the sheet over Paulette's face. Then she turned to rejoin Sinclair.

He stood just inside the door, frowning as he perused a document in his hand. He did not see the shadow that stealthily slipped into the room, creeping up behind him.

"Sinclair?" Belle cried. "Look out. Behind you!"

Her warning cry came too late. Sinclair turned, but not in time to escape the full force of Lazare's cudgel crashing down on his head.

Seventeen

Belle rushed across the room, flinging herself in Sinclair's path to prevent him from falling headlong and smashing against the hard edge of the window ledge. The papers he had been clutching in his hands fluttered to the ground.

The weight of his inert form crashed against her, dragging her with him to the floor. His head lolled back against her shoulder, his features so white, so still, a terrible fear slashed through Belle. She had seen men killed outright by such a blow as Lazare had dealt Sinclair.

Struggling, she eased herself from beneath Sinclair's unconscious form, lowering him as gently as she could.

"Sinclair?" she breathed. She was aware that Lazare towered over her. Cursing, he kicked aside the papers that Sinclair had been reading. Belle ignored him, concern for her own safety forgotten. With trembling fingers, she explored the base of Sinclair's throat. As she felt the faint but steady threading of his pulse, relief coursed through her.

"Still alive?" said Lazare. "What does it take to rid me of this English dog?"

With a furious hiss Belle turned, starting to rise, but she was stopped cold by the barrel of Lazare's pistol pointing into her eyes.

"Don't." He growled a low warning. "You have never been a stupid woman, Isabelle. Now is not the time to begin."

She froze, glaring up at him. "Damn you, Lazare. What sort of game are you playing?"

"My own and the prying Monsieur Carrington is very much in my way. Those fools, Giles and Auguste! Twice they had the chance to dispose of him. Twice! And they failed me both times. Now I must attend to the matter myself."

A surge of panic rose in Belle. She had seen that nigh-crazed look in Lazare's eyes before. Instinctively, she moved to position herself in between him and Sinclair's helpless form.

"Stay still!" His hand tightened upon the pistol.

"Why do you want to kill Sinclair?" she asked, making a futile attempt to reason with him. "He is one of us. He—"

"He's an English spy."

"How do you know that?"

Lazare's lips curved into a taut secretive smile. "That doesn't concern you. All you need understand is that I don't like being spied upon. Though I suppose I should thank the British pig for one thing. Without him, I would never have known of the Beauvais slut's treachery."

"Yes," Belle whispered, a sickening image of Paulette's mutilated body rising to her mind. "I have seen what you did with her."

"It was necessary. Someone had to stop her, although I never desired to have the slut in my bed. But I've had no time to do aught else with her."

His eyes glazed over and some of the tension seemed to go out of him. Belle tried to gauge her chances of leaping at him, disarming him. No, she would never have the strength to subdue him without a weapon.

"Get that rope over there from off the trunk," he suddenly commanded. "I want you to truss up Carrington."

"I don't see the necessity of that," she snapped. "You've made quite sure in your cowardly fashion that he will be of no threat to you."

Lazare shifted the pistol to the region of Sinclair's heart. "I can make sure in far more permanent fashion unless you do as I tell you."

"You may intend to kill us both anyway," she flung back, desperately trying to avoid carrying out the command, scarce breathing for fear her defiance would drive Lazare over the brink.

"Oh, no, *ma chére amie*, Carrington may live for the present. And as for you and me, we must go."

"Go?" she repeated numbly. "Go where?"

He shot her a mocking look. "How short your memory has grown. You must make all haste to array yourself for your assignation with Bonaparte."

Belle stared at him. Was he mad enough to think she intended to go on with the plot after all of this, indeed that she would go anywhere in his company?

He appeared to read some of her thoughts, for he said, "We will not abandon our mission now, will we, Isabelle? Not with Carrington and Mademoiselle Beauvais so nicely taken care of."

"And if I refuse?" Belle asked quietly.

"Then I will show you how large a hole can be made in a man's chest at this range. Now go get that rope."

Belle hesitated, but only for a moment. She had no choice but to obey. Lazare stood far too close to Sinclair to risk further defiance. She must think, try to play for time.

Slowly she edged toward the rope Lazare indicated, the length of hemp that had held closed his battered trunk. Keeping close watch upon her, Lazare bent long enough to scoop up the papers Sinclair had dropped. He stuffed them in the pocket of his greatcoat.

They looked like letters, Belle thought. What had Sinclair read in them that had made him call out to her with such urgency only moments before Lazare had entered the apartment? Did they hold the key to why Lazare so desperately wanted to destroy Sinclair? Belle did not believe his simple explanation that he hated being spied upon. That should not bother a man who had nothing to conceal from the rest of their society.

Lazare continued to stare down at Sinclair with such a look of contempt and hatred, Belle feared anything she might do would prove of no avail. But Lazare appeared able to keep his more turbulent emotions in check, merely saying, "Hurry. Make haste. And make sure you do a thorough job."

Belle picked up the rope, no longer able to delay returning to Sinclair's side to carry out the order. Her gaze flicked to the cudgel Lazare had dropped, but she rejected the notion almost immediately. She might not be able to move quick enough in these cramped quarters. Her best chance of saving Sinclair was to pretend to cooperate with Lazare and draw him away from these lodgings.

As Belle handled the thick length of rope, she could almost hear Sinclair's voice that long-ago rainy afternoon in the apartment, his laughing comment, "Never let your captive dictate his own bindings. The thick heavy kind is easiest undone."

A hope stirred inside her. If she could get Lazare away from here, if Sinclair regained consciousness, she had no doubt he would be able to free himself. It was a forlorn hope, but all that she had.

As she struggled to pull Sinclair's hand behind his back, she noticed a scrap of white trapped beneath his body—one of the letters that he had been reading. It had escaped Lazare's notice. As she wound the rope about Sinclair's hands, she deftly slipped the scrap of vellum up her sleeve.

Looping the rope about Sinclair's wrists, she tried to make it as loose as she dared.

"Tighter," Lazare snarled. "I know you can do better than that."

Gritting her teeth, she complied. Sinclair seemed so cold, so still, but she had to pull the knots snug with Lazare's narrowed eyes tracking her every move. With his free hand, Lazare tugged a dirty tricolor scarf from around his neck and flung it down at her.

"Gag him with this."

"He won't be able to breathe," Belle protested.

"He'll breathe less easy with a pistol ball through his lungs. Gag him, Isabelle. Now!"

With a heavy sigh, Belle forced the scarf between Sinclair's lips. As she did so, she detected a slight fluttering of his eyes. Dear God, he showed signs of stirring to life. Relief mingled with terror. She had no idea what action that might provoke from Lazare. She risked an anxious glance up at the Frenchman, but he appeared to have noticed nothing.

She stood slowly, trying to shield Sinclair's face from Lazare's sight as much as possible. But he shoved her aside.

"Adequate," Lazare said, regarding Belle's handiwork with a satisfied grunt. "Now let us be going. I understand the first consul does not like to be kept waiting."

He grabbed her roughly by the arm, pressing the muzzle of his weapon against the base of her spine. "I trust there need be no reminders of what will happen if you are tempted to call out for help once we gain the street."

"I am as eager to get on with our mission as you," she lied. Her chief desire was to get Lazare from this room. She had seen Sinclair shift his head.

As she marched toward the door, it occurred to her that this might be the last time she ever saw Sinclair, and she dared not even glance back. Her anger and her unwillingness to forgive his deception now seemed so incredibly foolish, so petty. Why did one always see matters with such appalling clarity when it might be too late?

As Lazare shoved her out onto the landing, it was as though he sensed some of her feelings, for he taunted her, "This is so touching, Isabelle. All this concern you have shown for Carrington. One might suppose you had fallen in love with the man."

One might indeed suppose that, Belle thought, a lump rising to her throat.

But then Lazare smiled and said something that drove all other thoughts out of her head.

You have proved to be distressingly inconstant, ma there. What about Jean-Claude?"

THE DARKNESS THAT SEEMED TO BE SUFFOCATING Sinclair's senses was lifting, bringing forth a throbbing pain that felt likely to split his head in twain.

He would have been grateful to sink back into the peaceful realms of oblivion, but some sense of urgency nagged at him, denying him the release.

And then there were the voices, Belle's and Lazare's. But what they were saying seemed to make little sense:

"... be going ... first consul kept waiting ... as eager to get this mission over as you."

Belle was going somewhere with Lazare. Sinclair needed to cry out a warning, to tell her she should not. Yet when he moved his lips to speak, something thick and dry pressed against his tongue, felt like it was choking him.

He heard a click as though a door had been closed. With great effort he forced his eyes to open. Even that caused his head to swim with pain, made him feel as though he would be ill. He fought down the sensation of nausea, fought to stop the room around him from continuing in a dizzying whirl.

Gradually he could bring the room into focus, but he stared blankly at the fading plaster walls, unable to place his surroundings. If only the throbbing in his head would cease so he could think. If only he could move. He realized with another sharp stabbing pain that his arms were bound behind his back and the thickness suffocating him was a gag.

What the devil had happened! Although the pain shooting through his head threatened to spin him back into blackness, Sinclair forced himself to concentrate.

He and Belle had gone to find Lazare. Yes, that was where he was—Lazare's lodgings above the confectioner's shop. He and Belle had been searching the place. Belle had gone into the other room while he had examined the trunk and found the letters.

The letters! Memory came back to Sinclair in a searing flood. Those writings that had clearly revealed to him Lazare's treachery —even worse, the treachery of that damned Merchant, who had sent them on this mission. And Jean-Claude Varens! Sinclair's suspicions about the fool had been right all along. Lazare had the idiot duped, was using him in an effort to destroy Belle.

Sinclair had to warn her. He groaned softly, remembering that had been what he had been about to do when she had cried out to him. He had caught the barest glimpse of Lazare when—Sinclair flinched, the dull pain in his head telling him clearly what had happened next.

But where were Belle and Lazare now? Despite the fading light in the apartment, he could see that he had been left alone. Dimly he recalled the shadowy figures, the voices that had seemed to be part of a dream.

"The first consul does not like to be kept waiting."

No, that had been no dream. Lazare had said that. He was forcing Belle to keep that appointment at the theater. The man had invested far too much in his plan to give up now. And Belle had no idea of what awaited her.

How long had they been gone? Sinclair strained backward, his gaze flashing up toward the window. Even through the dingy panes, he could see twilight settling over the city. Raw panic threatened to consume him.

Yet he could not afford to panic. Forcing himself to remain

calm, he tested his bonds. Tight, he thought, but not impossible, and the gag already felt a little loose. Given time, he was sure he could free himself. But time was in precious short supply. Sweat beading his forehead, Sinclair set to work.

THE FIACRE LURCHED THROUGH THE DARKENED streets, the seats creaking out a rhythm that rasped at Belle's already raw nerves. She faced Lazare across the ancient cab's shadowy interior. He held the pistol negligently, no longer guarding her with such care. But he did not need to. She had no intention of trying to escape until she obtained an answer to the question tormenting her.

"What do you know of Jean-Claude?" she demanded again.

Lazare merely smiled. "Poor Isabelle. Tell me, Do you still have those dreadful nightmares? The ones about returning to the Conciergerie, about Jean-Claude parting with his head in the company of Madame Guillotine?"

Belle strove not to reveal how his words startled her. How could Lazare possibly know about her nightmares? He had never been near her while she slept except—except, she realized with a jolt, that time he had nursed her through her delirium. Dear God, what weaknesses had she inadvertently revealed to this madman, and what use did he intend to make of them?

He leaned back against the seat, balancing the pistol upon his knee. His soft laugh chilled her blood. "I often wondered about this man Jean-Claude, who so haunted your dreams. I rather hoped to meet him one day. I finally had my chance in London last summer. It was most enlightening. We became close companions."

"Liar," she said hotly. "The Comte de Egremont would never have anything to do with the likes of ..." But her voice faded along with her conviction. Had she not made a similar declaration once to Sinclair? He had tried to warn her then that there might be a link between Lazare and Jean-Claude. But she had not wanted to listen.

Her mind drifted back to that afternoon with Jean-Claude, when they had walked together upon the Pont Neuf. She had sensed then he might be in some sort of trouble, or may have fallen under the influence of some intriguer. The possibility that it was Lazare made her blood run cold.

"So you met Jean-Claude by chance," she asked, trying to make some sense of all this.

"Not by chance, by design. Once I knew of his existence, I took great pains to track him down."

She did not need to ask Lazare why. The answer was obvious in the way he deliberately tipped his head so that moonlight filtering through the coach window played across his scar, reminding her, ever reminding her. So he did want his vengeance, had come for it at last, striking at her in a way she would never have expected.

"Where is Jean-Claude now?" she demanded hoarsely. "Have you seen him? Have you done something to him?"

"Not at all." Lazare's feigned expression of innocence mocked her. "The noble comte is most hale, and as to where, you know he is right here in Paris. Have you not enjoyed seeing him again? You have me to thank for that. It was I who convinced him to return to France, that only he can be the avenger, the restorer of the French people."

"What lies have you been telling him?" Belle cried.

"Only what he wanted to hear. I discovered a long time ago, you can inspire people to do the most incredible feats, even against their own nature, by simply telling them what they want to hear."

Belle drew in a shuddery breath. She could bear no more of Lazare's taunts, the hints of some dark plot unfolding just beyond her comprehension. Damn the villain! She would force the truth from him.

With a quick movement she lunged for his pistol, but Lazare was quicker still. He had not lowered his guard as much as she had thought. Once more he snatched up the weapon, holding it inches from her eyes, forcing her back.

"I think not, Isabelle," he said. "We will see my little game through to the end. Who knows? You may guess the solution in time and thwart me yet."

At that moment the fiacre jerked to a halt. Belle's heart pounded with dread as she realized they had drawn up outside the theater, the dark street that stretched before it bobbing with lantern bearers escorting pedestrians to the door. Other coaches rattled past theirs, disgorging their occupants.

"We have arrived in good time," Lazare said. "Soon the performance begins."

She feared he did not mean what would happen on stage. She tried one last desperate gambit. "You know Crecy's men will not be here. I told Marcellus not to proceed with anything until he heard from me."

"We will not need them. I have made my own arrangements."

"But we have no carriage. How will we manage the abduction and our escape?"

Lazare's only answer was his devil's smile. She knew in that instant that whatever took place here tonight, escape formed no part of Lazare's plans for her.

Whatever hellish plot he was weaving, maybe she could best put a stop to it by refusing to enter the theater. Let him shoot her if he would. It would be better than this tormenting uncertainty. Yet she thought of Sinclair, captive in Lazare's lodgings, and Jean-Claude, also in danger, but in what manner she did not know. Possibly the survival of both men depended upon herself.

"That is right, Isabelle." With what uncanny ease Lazare seemed able to read her mind. "Think about the men you love. The question is which do you love the more? If you could save only one, I wonder which you would choose."

She cast him a glare filled with loathing, but his taunting words fired her determination. She would never have such a choice forced upon her. She would cut through this dark web of Lazare's weaving, save both Sinclair and Jean-Claude, see Lazare in hell.

She pushed open the door to the fiacre herself, leaping down. Lazare followed close behind. The cool night breeze felt bracing against her heated cheeks. She hoped it would help to clear her mind, help her to think.

Some sort of bizarre trap awaited her within the confines of that theater, she was certain, something that involved Jean-Claude. Yet she saw no other course than to see this nightmare through. Her head whirled, her fears as intangible as phantoms in the dark, the truth of this situation eluding her like a nagging puzzle whose solution is obvious at once when it is revealed, but always too late.

As they approached the theater doors, observing the other silk-clad women, an absurd thought flitted into Belle's mind.

"I am not dressed for this," she said, gesturing to her plain gray woolen gown. "The first consul will be less than charmed."

"I am sure he will find, as so many men do, that your beauty needs no silken trappings." Lazare's cold fingers stroked her cheek. "Your unblemished beauty."

She felt his suppressed quiver of rage, the hatred long held in check. It would be so easy to goad him to violence, finish this right here and now. But that would not tell her what the man plotted.

Suppressing a shudder at his touch, she preceded him into the brightly lit theater salon. All around them gaiety and laughter spilled forth, jewels and silks mingling with the coarse dress of the common man. Everyone anticipated the play, taking no notice of lesser drama in their midst. Lazare had the pistol concealed beneath his cloak, but he no longer had need of it to control her.

He whispered in her ear, "We must separate now, Isabelle. I will watch until you enter the box. Then I will be below you in the pit. My eyes will be upon your every move. One false start, one hint of anything strange, and remember I can find my way back to Carrington much faster than you can."

She didn't give him the satisfaction of a reply. She stalked away toward the door to the box where she knew the first consul awaited her.

As she slipped inside, she cherished the wild hope that perhaps Bonaparte would fail to come. It would make this tense situation so much easier.

But he was there. He arose from his seat at her approach. He was garbed simply in the uniform of a sub-lieutenant. Here in the shadows of the box, she doubted if many in the theater were even aware of the first consul's presence.

His greeting smile was stiff. "You are late, madame. I had begun to fear you meant to disappoint me."

Belle took a deep breath, hoping her nervousness did not show. Never had she felt less capable of coolly playing out a role. "I beg your pardon, sir. I have never been very punctual."

"Like most women. Yet why did I have a feeling you would prove different?" He stared at her. Was it her imagination that he looked at her differently than he had at their first meeting? He appeared to have taken no notice how she looked, yet she knew she must appear an astonishing sight. She could feel disheveled wisps of her hair clinging to her cheeks. She knew she must be pale. Did her eyes reveal her desperation?

His own gray ones appeared too shrewd, not quite as warm as she remembered, even perhaps a little wary.

No, it must all be attributed to her own nervousness, for he stepped closer. Carrying her hand to his lips, he said, "You need not look so worried. I will not have you shot."

Belle jerked away, unable to conceal the tremor that coursed through her at his words. "What?"

"For being late." He arched one brow. "I am only teasing you." His voice gentled somewhat. "Do I frighten you? I assure you I hold nothing but admiration for you."

His hands reached up to help her off with her cloak. Belle struggled to find some measure of her old composure. When she saw him stare at her gown, she said hastily, "You must forgive my appearance, sir. It was most difficult to escape here tonight without arousing my husband's suspicion. He is a most jealous man."

"You must not apologize. You look lovely." He held out the chair himself for her to sit down. Belle started to ease herself down when he added, "Quite like an angel."

She froze, her startled gaze flying back at him. It seemed even the most innocent remarks were flinging her off balance tonight, but Bonaparte had clearly meant nothing other than a compliment. His smile disarmed her.

She was beset by a sudden urge to confide in him. But what would she say? "I beg your pardon, sir. I meant to abduct you tonight, but I would as soon call the whole thing off since one of my fellow conspirators has run mad."

The thought nearly caused her to break into hysterical laughter. Instead, she turned to stare into the theater. Bonaparte offered her the use of his opera glass. She accepted it, pleased to note that her hand was somewhat steadier.

The box she shared with Bonaparte was the closest to the right side of the stage. She had but to reach out and she could have touched the heavy velvet curtain. It afforded her an excellent vantage point of the rest of the theater. The blazing chandeliers lit the interior as bright as the day. Although the occupants of most of the boxes were lost in shadow, Belle could make out clearly the faces of those filing in to fill the benches of the pit.

Lazare had ensconced himself in the first row; directly behind the orchestra pit. She could see quite clearly that his gaze was not trained upon the stage but directed toward where she sat.

Hastily she began to inspect the other seats, fearing she would find Jean-Claude present. The vague idea occurred to her that Lazare's revenge might well consist of a scheme to abduct Napoleon himself and see that both she and Jean-Claude were implicated, left to the mercy of the mob. Yet she did not quite see how Lazare could carry out such a plan. In any event, Jean-Claude was not present. She scarce knew whether to find that a cause for relief or not.

She tensed when she did spy a familiar face near the last row of the pit. Baptiste. Her heart sank. He must have never seen her note warning him not to go to the theater. He had assumed his place, faithfully preparing to enact his part in stirring up the riot, believing that all was going according to plan, and she had no way to let him know any different.

Belle saw only one course open to her. If Jean-Claude did not put in an appearance, she would act. When the riot did begin, the theater would be in a state of confusion. She might be able to slip away, alert Baptiste, and the two of them exit the theater before Lazare could get out.

Vaguely she became aware that Bonaparte addressed her. "I despise comedy," he said. "Tragedy is the only true art. Do you not agree, madame?"

She hardly knew what she replied, nervously rubbing her hands together. Something crinkled beneath the fabric of her gown, and it was then she remembered the note she had stuffed up her sleeve.

She cherished little hope that it might be of any use to her, but as the curtain parted and the stage claimed Bonaparte's full attention, she drew out the note to examine it.

It was difficult to make out the words, but she recognized it as Lazare's handwriting at once, laboriously crude. It appeared to be a message Lazare had begun to Merchant.

"When you read this, you will know your orders have been carried out. I have already disposed of Carrington.

Belle sucked in her breath. Merchant had ordered Sinclair's death before they ever left England. She strained to see the rest of the writing.

"And tonight will see the end of the business, Isabelle Varens arrested, Paris in chaos, and Bonaparte ..."

Belle gasped, the last words blurring before her eyes. She nearly dropped the paper.

Bonaparte dead.

The plot flashed into place for her with alarming clarity. This was no abduction she had arranged for tonight, but an assassination that had been planned all along by Lazare and Victor Merchant, knowing she would never consent to commit murder. They had effectively used her as their tool, their dupe.

Belle's gaze flickered frantically to the man at her side. Bonaparte leaned forward in his seat, his gaze rapt upon the stage, oblivious to the danger. Lazare had to be the assassin. And he would act, she felt sure, when the riot began. But how had he planned to involve Jean-Claude, or had Lazare only held out such a possibility to torment her?

Belle focused on the stage, realizing they were nearing the point when Monsieur Georges would be expected to make his entrance. As soon as the wrong actor appeared on stage, the uproar would start.

Yes, there he was. The male lead strode out, his nervousness apparent even beneath the elaborate powdered wig and layer of white and red lead paint coating his cheeks. Already the hisses had begun as some of the audience realized the substitution. Lazare said nothing, but Baptiste, on cue, shouted out, "Bah! We did not pay to see this clown. Does the manager think to cheat us?"

As the rumblings in the theater grew, Belle saw Lazare start to rise. No matter what the cost, she had to do something. She could not sit by and see murder done.

She grasped Napoleon by the elbow. "Your Excellency. You are in danger. You must—"

But he shook her off impatiently, staring at the stage with a frown. "What is going on? I know that man. He is no actor,"

"Please," Belle said.

"It is, I think- yes, it is the Comte de Egremont."

"What!" Belle whipped toward the stage as she too stared at

the fake actor. It took her stunned eyes but a moment to recognize Jean-Claude clearly outlined in the glow of the candles that composed the footlights.

As though in some horrible dream, she watched him pace toward the end of the stage, so close to their box she could tell that his eyes glittered like pieces of glass. He reached beneath the dark purple cloak of his costume and drew forth a pistol.

"No! Jean-Claude, no!" But her cry was lost in the din.

The hubbub of excited and angry voices in the theater sounded in Belle's ears like a dull roar. The stage, the lights, the actors all became a blur of color. Belle saw no one but Jean-Claude leveling his pistol at Bonaparte. The first consul met the prospect of death unflinching, staring deep into Jean-Claude's face, his expression slightly contemptuous.

They seemed frozen in this horrible tableau, time itself having come to a standstill. Jean-Claude blinked, his hand beginning to tremble.

"Fire! Damn you!" Belle heard Lazare's enraged scream.

Jean-Claude braced his arm, but he could not stop the shaking. Sweat trickled down his brow, and with a strangled sob he lowered the weapon.

Belle sagged back in her seat with relief. But the next instant she saw Lazare. She knew not how he had managed to clamber past the orchestra pit or gain the stage so swiftly. With a bellow of rage, he leaped at Jean-Claude, wrestling the pistol from his grasp.

With a hate-filled snarl, Lazare whirled to fire into the box, but Belle found herself released from the daze that had taken possession of her. She dove at Bonaparte, carrying him, chair and all, to the floor of the box. The sound of the pistol shot blazed above their heads.

A moment of breathless silence descended over the theater, then the voices that had seemed so distant crashed over Belle. She could hear screams and curses as total confusion erupted upon the stage and the pit below.

Glancing up, she met Napoleon's gaze. Their eyes locked for a second, and she felt as though he read the entire contents of her mind.

But he said nothing as he struggled to his feet, helping her to do the same. Upon the stage she saw no sign of Lazare but at that moment a familiar figure emerged from the wings.

Sinclair. A glad cry choked her. Somehow it did not astonish her to see him. He charged across the stage, trying to reach her through the mill of terrified actors who gaped at Jean-Claude.

The comte stood immobile, staring off into the lights, seeming oblivious to the storm erupting around him.

"Who was the fellow shooting at?" someone demanded.

Lazare's voice unmistakably shouted out. "Look in the box. It's Bonaparte. That actor plotted to kill Bonaparte."

Astonishment rippled through the crowd, swelling to outrage. As Sinclair drew nearer, there was no way Belle could make her voice heard above the crowd. She only hoped that somehow Sinclair would understand her silent plea for him to help Jean-Claude.

Sinclair pulled up short; the understanding that had ever existed between them did not fail her. When the first man made an effort to lay hands upon the comte, Sinclair felled the one howling for vengeance with his fist.

Before any more of the audience could gain the stage, Sinclair yanked at Jean-Claude, thrusting the dazed man through one of the trapdoors in the floor of the stage and disappearing after him.

Belle judged that she could not linger herself to see more. Bonaparte appeared calm, watching the proceedings with almost an air of detachment. She backed toward the door of the box, preparing to bolt.

At that moment, the door was flung open. By her prearranged cue, two guards appeared, one of them saying, "Citoyen Consul. We were alerted you were in the theater. A riot has begun. We have come to escort you to safety."

But one glance at the men's faces was enough to tell Belle that these were indeed the real guards and not Crecy's agents. Still, she prepared to bluff it out.

"There has been as assassination attempt," she said. "You must get the first consul away at once."

But when she tried to move past the guards to the freedom of the corridor beyond, she heard Bonaparte say in a level voice, "Detain that woman."

Glancing back at him she feigned a look of surprise. "I fear I don't understand."

"You understand perfectly well, Isabelle Varens," he said coldly. "You are under arrest."

Eighteen

The heavy wooden door closed upon Belle, finality in the dull slam. Beyond the iron grill of the door's narrow window, the turnkey disappeared with his torch, leaving her in darkness, that ageless darkness that had ever been so much a part of the Conciergerie. Behind the thick stonework no light penetrated, no sound of life carried from the nearby quay, not even the rush of the Seine. The proximity of the river caused the prison walls to drip with moisture, as though weeping with the tears of countless other unfortunates who had inhabited the cell before her.

Belle wrapped her arms tightly about herself, trying to still the lashings of panic as she found herself thrust back into the prison that had haunted so many of her dreams. Only this time her eyes were wide open and the darkness would not lift. This time the dawn would not find her, To have escaped this stronghold once had been a miracle. To beg such a favor a second time was more than the fates would allow.

The silence of her cell pressed down upon her until she fancied she could hear the echoes of the past, all those who had gone from here to meet their deaths. The queen Marie Antoinette, the bloody tyrant Robespierre himself, and a host of others, the innocent, the not so innocent. Impossible that so many tormented souls could pass through this place and not leave some whisperings of their existence behind. The thought sent a chill coursing through her.

She bit down upon her fist to stem her terror. To give way to it would be to allow Lazare to triumph. This is what Lazare had planned for her all along, this descent down into the world of her nightmares. She knew not where Lazare was, in hell, she hoped. But she would never accord him the satisfaction of finding that he had broken Isabelle Varens.

Belle groped her way across the brick floor until she located the cell's wooden bench. She sank upon up it, closing her eyes. The darkness was just the same, but at least it was of her choosing.

She would force herself to be calm, to think of anything but this dread place which had once been the very heart of the Revolution's terror. She concentrated instead upon her rage against Lazare and all his twisted schemes.

How clearly she now understood what he had been trying to do, but the plan struck her as incredible. To prey upon Jean-Claude, persuade him to assassinate Bonaparte, while Lazare waited calmly for Belle, in her ignorance, to make all the arrangements which would enable Lazare to carry out his bizarre plot. With Bonaparte collapsing dead at her feet, she would have had to flee, but how could she have left Jean-Claude? They both would have been arrested. As in her nightmares, she would have had to watch him die.

A madman's fantasy and yet Lazare had nearly pulled it off. He had been thwarted by two things—that core of nobility in Jean-Claude's nature which rendered him incapable of murder. And the other obstacle: Sinclair. Belle experienced a rush of gratitude when she thought of his timely arrival at the theater.

Somehow she was certain Sinclair had gotten Jean-Claude safely away. Surely Baptiste also had no difficulty slipping out of the theater amidst the chaos. These beliefs afforded her some measure of comfort, her only comfort.

She prayed that they would realize there was no way to help her and would try nothing foolish. She must count on Sinclair. He was ever a practical man. No matter what he felt for her, he would recognize that any rescue attempt was hopeless.

Such thoughts only tugged at the despair she fought to keep at bay. She clung to her anger, cursing Lazare, but even more so Merchant. Lazare, at least, bore the excuse of being half-mad, but Victor had betrayed her, plotting the assassination with Lazare behind her back, ordering her removal and Sinclair's cold-blooded fashion. When she returned to England—

A harsh laugh escaped her. When she returned to England, she mocked herself. She could not be deluded on that score. Bonaparte had known her name. Somehow he had discovered who she was. Part of Lazare's plot had succeeded. She would be the one held responsible for planning the assassination attempt. She could expect no mercy.

Shivering, she stretched out on the bench. The bell mounted between the arches many floors above her rang seldom these days to announce that the tumbril was ready. But she did not doubt but that the peal would sound again soon. Exhaustion crept over her, threatening to steal away her strength and her courage. Sweet heaven, she dared not sleep.

Not here. If any place in Paris had ever been formed to entertain nightmares, it was the Conciergerie. She whispered the name of the one man who had been able to hold those hideous dreams at bay. "*Sinclair.*"

Her need of him no longer frightened her, no longer shamed her. She sought his image in the darkness, the memory of his voice, his eyes, his caress, his arms embracing her, the fire of his kiss driving out the cold.

Only by holding fast to the recollection of every tender

moment they had shared could she at last permit herself to relax, drifting into a deep dreamless sleep.

How long she remained asleep, she could not have said. A few minutes or a few hours—it was all one inside the Conciergerie. She was startled awake by the sound of the key's scrape in the lock. The cell door was flung open. She sat up, shading her eyes from the glare of the torch.

"Isabelle Varens?" a gruff voice called.

She nodded slowly, rubbing her eyes, clearing the last webbings of sleep from her mind.

"You are summoned upstairs."

"So soon?" she began, but the protest died upon her lips. She would as soon have the ordeal over with. It had been the waiting that had nigh broken her the last time, that unending succession of days, each hour dreading to hear her name called to face that grim tribunal whose judges knew but one sentence—death.

She felt almost a sense of relief as she allowed the turnkey to lead her from her cell. The chill of the prison seemed to have seeped into her soul, bringing with it the numbness of resignation.

When the guard nudged her forward, saying, "This way, madame," she nearly smiled. She could have shown him the direction. This walk was most familiar to her. She had followed the path through the narrow dark corridors a hundred times in her nightmares.

As they approached the stairs that twisted upward, she almost expected to see them thronged with jeering spectators as they had been in the old days. But the worn stone risers stood empty now, the light of dawn casting pearly gray shadows through the small round windows.

When Belle moved toward the steps, preparing to mount to the vast hall of justice above, the turnkey caught her arm impatiently.

"Not up there," he said. "Go that way."

He shoved her in the opposite direction. Belle regarded the

THE AVENGING ANGEL AND THE SPY

man in astonishment, but his laconic expression told her nothing. But she asked no questions, fearing she understood.

This time there would not even be the mockery of a trial. She was being herded along a crosswise corridor that she remembered led to the Galerie des Prisonniers, the area where those waiting to board the tumbrils had been kept. Some of her calm began to desert her. She had expected at least a little more time to steel herself to face the guillotine.

Yet somehow she managed to keep herself erect, taking her steps with dignity. She had never had many dealings with God before, but feverishly her mind sought to recall the words of a prayer she had oft heard Baptiste utter.

"Sweet Jesus, have mercy upon my soul," she whispered below her breath.

The guard yanked her roughly to a halt. "In there," he told her as they paused before another door.

She frowned in bewilderment, knowing this was not the way that led to the courtyard where the tumbrils were loaded. But she didn't know whether to be relieved or not.

"What is all this?" she demanded, whipping about to face the turnkey.

"Inside!" the guard barked. Opening the door, he shoved her backward across the threshold. Staring at him, she saw him snap to attention with a smart salute, then retire discreetly from the room, closing the door after him.

Belle knew the salute had not been meant for her. She turned slowly, discovering that she had been led to a small office, the reception area for new prisoners. But it was not the captain of the prison guard who sat behind the battered desk.

The pale light of morning glancing through the windows only served to highlight the whiteness of a marble complexion, the chilling intensity in the blue-gray eyes.

Bonaparte.

Belle's breath snagged in her throat. So the first consul,

himself, had decided to sit in judgment of her. She had heard once that he could be sentimental, easily moved by a woman's weeping. But as she moistened her dry lips, she knew that she could not summon up a single tear, not even to save her life.

Long moments ticked by as Bonaparte sat with his head bent, his eyes fixed upon some papers before him. "Sit down, Madame Varens," he said without glancing up.

Her legs felt like stalks of wood, but she managed to ease herself down into a stiff-backed chair. The nerve-racking silence continued. At last he looked at her, but the fine-chiseled lines of his eagle's profile gave nothing away of his thoughts. He did not appear vindictive. Nor was there sign of any compassion, either. Rather, he looked impartial, like a judge.

That, Belle supposed, was an improvement over the tribunal, whose condemnation she had read even before her trial had begun. When she could endure his steady regard no longer, she asked, "How did you know my name?"

He arched one brow. "I think it is my place to ask the questions here, madame. But I will gratify your curiosity. You met an old acquaintance at my reception, did you not?"

Understanding broke over Belle. "Fouché."

"Exactly. You are quick, madame. Fouché, my former minister of police and I have one trait in common, a memory for faces, although Fouché's is not quite as excellent as mine. He did finally recollect who you were, did some ferreting out of your past and presented the facts to me."

Bonaparte tapped the papers before him. "Isabelle Varens, once wife to Jean-Claude Varens. Known by some as the Avenging Angel. You came to trial in the summer 1794 for helping people proscribed escape from Paris,"

"I was never actually condemned," she reminded him.

"Merely because you were released as were so many others with the downfall of Robespierre."

Bonaparte thrust the papers from him. "I have no desire to

retry you on ancient charges, madame. I admire you for what you did. I helped a family escape myself once when I was a young officer during the siege of Boulogne. Aristocrats were being murdered outright. I helped a family to hide in crates.

"I have no quarrel with the role you played in the Revolution." He subjected her to a hard stare. "It is your more recent activities that I find less than tolerable."

Belle drew in a deep breath. She did not know why it was suddenly important to her that he should know the truth. The abduction plot alone was more than enough reason that he should send her to her death. But she did not want Bonaparte thinking of her as a murderess.

"I know this cannot be construed as a defense," she said. "But I was not part of any assassination plot. My intent was solely to arrange your abduction."

A glimmer of humor appeared in those cool gray eyes. "*Merci, madame.*"

Belle's lips thinned as she continued, "I have never betrayed any of my comrades before. But I will give you a name—Etienne Lazare. He was the man with the scar who fired on you. He alone is responsible for the attempt on your life."

Although Bonaparte dipped his quill into the ink and made note of the name, he said, "That may well be true, madame. But the fact remains that the pistol was first in the hands of your former husband. He had me dead in his sights. I am only alive because he lost his courage."

"It was not a loss of courage! Jean-Claude stopped because it is not in his nature to commit murder. It was only that Lazare had filled his head with so many lies. He manipulated Jean-Claude into making the attempt."

Belle saw with despair that her plea was having little effect in erasing Bonaparte's contemptuous frown. There was no way to make a strong-willed man like the general ever understand the weakness, the confusion of a broken¬hearted dreamer like

Jean-Claude. She asked the question whose answer she most dreaded.

"Has Jean-Claude been arrested?"

"No," Bonaparte said. "But it is only a matter of time. He will not get out of Paris, nor will this Lazare, nor Mr. Carrington, whom I assume also shares some part in all of this."

Despite Bonaparte's aura of confidence, Belle felt a surge of relief. No mention had been made of Baptiste or Crecy. Their part in the plot had gone undetected. They would find a way to help Sinclair and Jean-Claude escape.

She became aware of Bonaparte's thoughtful gaze upon her. "You puzzle me, Madame Varens. You obviously would have gone to great lengths to arrange my abduction. Yet this Lazare person was in the right of it. It is easier to kill than to abduct. Why did you save my life?"

"Because I too have my own code." A slight smile curved her lips. "I will admit that I am more rogue than lady. I do a great many things respectable women would frown upon. But assassination does not fall within that realm."

Bonaparte leaned back in his chair, lapsing once more into a frowning silence. As he stared out the window into the court beyond, Belle could tell that he strove to reach some sort of decision. For all that had happened, Belle sensed a grudging admiration in him. One thing yet puzzled her, and she made bold enough to interrupt him by asking, "So you did know my real name, something of my past, before you came to the theater last night?"

Bonaparte nodded. "Fouché provided me with that much, although he could not discover what you might presently be doing in Paris. Fouché, you see, would like me to believe he is indispensable for ferreting out plots, but I preferred to see what I could do on my own. I confess I was still struck by your beauty, intrigued by you."

"But you took a dreadful risk."

He gave a fatalistic shrug. "I take a risk every time I ride through the streets. This was not the first assassination attempt, nor will it be the last, I fear. When it is my time to die, there is nothing I will be able to do about it. It is a philosophy I imagine that you share, the difference between a brave man and a coward, *n'est-ce pas?*"

He didn't seem to expect an answer. Turning purposefully back to the desk, he reached for a blank sheet of vellum and his quill. From the rapidity of his ink strokes, Belle realized he had arrived at his verdict. She felt her heartbeat quicken. He was either remanding her to spend the rest of her days within the dank walls of this prison or signing the order for her death.

He stood up with his characteristic abruptness. Coming round the desk, he took her hand with a stiff bow. "This must be our farewell, madame." He handed her the papers. "Present this to the guard."

She stared down at the document, unable to focus upon those bold ink strokes. "Is it now the custom for the condemned to carry their own execution orders?"

He gave a short laugh, and then regarded her impatiently. "You are free, madame. Free to go."

She stared at him, unable to comprehend what he was saying, hardly daring to believe she had heard him right.

"You saved my life," he said. "I am returning the favor. That makes us even, does it not?"

"Y-yes," she managed to stammer. Blinding relief weakened her in a way fear had not been able to manage, causing her hands to tremble so that she nearly dropped the precious pardon. Freed a second time, a second miracle offered her, another chance to begin her life again.

She tried to voice her thanks, but Bonaparte strode toward the door. He paused to glance back with his hand upon the knob.

"One word more, madame. As gracious and beautiful as your presence is, I would make one thing clear. I would not care ever to find you in France again."

Belle recovered enough to offer him an elusive smile. "Believe me, Monsieur le General. You won't."

THE FINAL SET OF PRISON GATES OPENED TO ALLOW Belle to pass. The last time she had hurled herself through them with but one thought, to flee Paris. She was older now, she mused with an inward smile, and perhaps not as wise.

She stepped slowly past the guard, taking the time to revel in the freshness of the air after the dank odors of the prison, to feel the bite of the cold wind against her cheeks. Her younger self would never have allowed a moment to consider how good it was to be alive. It had taken Sinclair to teach her to do that.

The young guard who released Belle was far more courteous than the gruff turnkey. Her bedraggled appearance did nothing to daunt the admiring gleam in the youth's eye. He followed her through the gate into the bustling street beyond the prison's outer walls.

"Is madame all alone?" he asked sympathetically. "Have you no friends to meet you?"

Oh, she had friends all right, Belle thought, but none, she trusted, so fool as to come seeking her here. Aloud she thanked the guard for his concern, saying, "I will manage well enough on my own."

Her words seemed belied the next instant. She was jostled off balance, nearly tumbled into the mud. The culprit was one of the city's wood peddlers, his hat brim pulled so far down over his long straggling gray hair that it was a wonder he could see a thing.

"Watch where you are going, you old—" But the young guard had no opportunity to complete the insult. With a movement remarkably spry for one of his years, the old man straightened, leveling the guard with one blow of his powerful fist.

Belle gaped in astonishment. She had barely recovered from her surprise when she was seized roughly about the waist. The wood peddler flung her into the back of a passing hay cart. Leaping up beside her, he growled out a command to the driver.

"*Allez! Allez! Vite.*"

More startled than hurt, Belle struggled to sit up, but as the cart lurched into movement, she was slammed back down again. She heard outcries and curses from the startled pedestrians as the cart began a wild plunge through the streets.

The wood peddler tumbled down beside her. Belle met him, ready to defend herself as best she could. Nails bared, she went for the man's face hidden beneath its layering of beard. He caught her wrists in a strong grip, forcing them down.

"Be still, Angel. It's me."

Shorn of its French accent, the resonant voice was achingly familiar. The next instant the peddler boldly crushed his mouth against hers, all lingering doubts of his identity melting away before the heated fury of his kiss.

Belle ceased her struggles, clinging to Sinclair, returning his embrace, his graying wig coming away in her hand.

When he drew back, the beard had gone askew as well, Sinclair's hunter-green eyes twinkling wickedly at her. "Now do you know me?"

"Mr. Carrington," she murmured. "And to think I was beginning to feel as if I had not paid enough heed to the wood peddlers of Paris."

But the teasing words caught in her throat, her heart too full as she drank in the sight of him. The cart rattled on at a wild pace, jolting and bruising her with every bump, but she did not care enough to even ask where they were going, content to hold Sinclair fast, to feel the reassuring strength of his arms around her.

She buried her face against his shoulder. "Sinclair, I thought I would never see you again."

"There was no chance that I would allow you to be rid of me that easily, Angel."

He sought her lips again. At that moment the cart careened

around a corner, slamming them against the side and nearly dumping the load of straw atop them.

Belle groaned. "What madman is driving this thing?"

Sinclair struggled to a sitting position and called out, "Baptiste. I don't believe we are being followed. Draw rein."

It took several shouts for the old man to hear him, but he sawed back on the harness at last, settling the horse into a respectable trot. Baptiste risked one look back at Belle, his crooked smile beaming from beneath his own battered hat.

"What on earth?" A half-choked laugh escaped her. Sinclair settled back beside her, pulling off what remained of his disguise. "Sinclair, what is all this? What were you and Baptiste doing outside the prison?"

"Trying to get in, of course. Something a little more subtle than being arrested. I figured that even a prison must require wood for fires in the guardroom, and then once inside—"

"You thought to rescue me from the Conciergerie? Have both you and Baptiste run mad? And to think it was my one consolation that at least you had better sense than that."

"Not where you are concerned, Angel." The warmth of his gaze caused her heart to race. "I will admit I was not looking forward to the challenge. It was most convenient when they brought you out to the gate. By the way, what were you doing out there?"

"I was being set free."

"What!"

"I have an official pardon from Bonaparte for saving his life."

Sinclair looked considerably chagrined. "You mean I hit that innocent-looking guard and nearly broke our bones in this cart for nothing?"

"Not precisely," Belle said. "I have a feeling that even Bonaparte cannot be that generous. I think he hoped that I would lead him to the rest of you."

"A hope we seem to have thwarted for the moment," Sinclair said cheerfully.

He appeared content to draw her back into his arms, but Belle forestalled the gesture, saying anxiously, "And Jean-Claude?"

Some of the light went out of Sinclair's eyes. He stiffened. "He is safe in Crecy's lodgings behind the gaming house, where we are headed now."

The mention of Jean-Claude drew an element of constraint between them as it always did. Nothing more was said until the cart lumbered into the shadows behind the Palais-Royal.

Baptiste motioned them both to lie low. Then he returned shortly, signaling that all was clear. He moved to help Belle down from the cart, her weight almost too much for the old man's strength. He said nothing. Tears gathered in his eyes, and he expressed his gladness at her safe return with a fierce hug.

As she and Sinclair slipped up the back stairs normally reserved for the workers at the gaining house, Baptiste returned to attend to the horses and hide the cart. In the parlor of the lodgings, Belle discovered Crecy nervously pacing. Never one to wax sentimental, the urbane Marcellus let out a joyous cry at the sight of her. He pressed exuberant kisses upon both of Belle's hands.

"I confess, I never believed your rescue would be possible." Crecy glanced from her to Sinclair. "You are formidable, monsieur. However did you manage it?"

"We will explain all later, Marcellus," Belle said. "Right now, I must see Jean-Claude. Where is he?"

"In Crecy's bedchamber," Sinclair spoke up. Reluctantly he led the way. He gave a fleeting thought to the hellish night he had just spent, worrying, despairing and feverishly plotting some way to rescue Belle. It had seemed like a miracle to see her outside the prison gates, to clasp her once more in his arms. How passionately she had returned his kisses. But almost in the next breath she had asked about Jean-Claude. Sinclair feared it was the way it would always be.

He paused outside the bedchamber door long enough to caution her. "The comte is a little dazed from the events of last night. Shock, I suppose, and he was slightly injured in the escape."

"Injured?" Her gaze snapped to his. Did he imagine it or was there a faint hint of accusation in her tone?

"I did the best I could," he said defensively. "I was lucky to get that fool out of the theater alive. He didn't want to come. I think he wished the mob to overtake him. I had to hit him."

"I am not blaming you, Sinclair. You risked your life to save him. You cannot begin to imagine my gratitude."

Her gratitude felt like a knife thrust to his heart. Turning away from her, he shoved the bedchamber door open. Varens was no longer in bed. He sat in a chair, huddled before the fire, staring into the flames, a vacant shell of a man. Only when he saw Belle did some spark of animation appear in those empty eyes.

"Isabelle. You are safe!"

"Yes," she said quietly.

"Thank God." Jean-Claude started to rise, but his legs were weak. He wobbled and would have fallen if Belle had not caught him, easing him back into the chair.

"Sit still," she commanded. Jean-Claude's face was so pale his only color came from the streaks of purple along his jaw where Sinclair had clipped him. "I will fetch you a glass of brandy.

"No." Jean-Claude caught desperately at her hand. "Do not leave me. *Mon Dieu*, how I have needed you. Promise you will not go."

Belle hesitated, glancing back at Sinclair. The rigid set of his countenance could not quite disguise what he was feeling. He probed her with his eyes as though he awaited her answer. Yet Jean-Claude clung to her, all his pride crumbled to dust. How could she simply shake him off?

Casting Sinclair a look that pleaded for his understanding, she murmured to Jean-Claude, "No, I will not leave you."

Sinclair compressed his lips. Without another word he turned and left the room. Never had Belle felt so torn in two. She wanted to go after him, but Jean-Claude had begun to tremble, shaking so hard as though seized by an ague.

Sighing, she pried herself away long enough to fetch brandy and force it between his chattering teeth. He refused to climb back into bed, so she took a coverlet to him, tucking it about his legs.

His shivering finally stopped and he gratefully caressed back a stray lock of her hair. She must look like a woman who had been carted to hell and back. But Jean-Claude noticed no signs of her own fatigue and mental distress. He never had, she thought with an unexpected stab of resentment.

Grabbing up the brandy, she sloshed some of it into the glass for herself, downing it in one gulp. That Jean-Claude noticed. He watched her with pained surprise.

This was not the time for accusation, Belle knew, but she could not refrain. "How could you do it, Jean-Claude? How could you permit someone like Lazare to drag you down to such depths, persuade you to attempt something so against everything you have ever believed in?"

"I don't know." He gripped his hands tightly together, bowing his head. "It is only that all my life I have ever talked, never acted. I thought with that monster Bonaparte gone, I could restore France, somehow make amends, and Lazare offered me the opportunity. It was only as I stood there upon the stage looking straight into Bonaparte's eyes that I realized I couldn't do it."

Silent tears tracked down Jean-Claude's cheeks. "I failed, Isabelle. I failed again." He covered his face with his hands. "I am so ashamed, I can scarce bear to have you look at me. How you must despise me for the coward that I am."

Belle stared at his bowed head. She almost wished she could despise him when she thought of the disaster that his cooperation with Lazare had brought crashing down upon all of them. Yet even now her heart flooded with pity for this poor, desperate man.

Putting her arms about him, she cradled his head against her.

"Hush. Hush, my dear. You failed only because you are a gentle man, far too gentle for the madness of this world."

Soothing him as though he were a child, she calmed him again. By the time she had managed to restore some measure of his dignity, she felt ready to drop with exhaustion.

"What shall we do now, Isabelle?" he asked at last, looking up at her.

"Crecy will help us to flee Paris—" she began.

"I don't mean that. I mean afterward. I feel so lost, now, without a purpose. How shall I continue on with my life?"

"I don't know," Belle said, drawing away, unable to offer him any further comfort. The dramatic events of the past few days were beginning at last to take their toll upon her. She felt so drained.

"Is there any hope that you and I—"

"Please, Jean-Claude," she said wearily. "I can give no thought to the future just now. I am so tired."

"Of course. I am an inconsiderate fool." He managed to rise to his feet. "You too must rest."

Belle nodded. She wanted nothing more than to seek out Sinclair, but she feared he might be angry with her for remaining with Jean-Claude. She bore not the strength to deal with that just now. Allowing Jean-Claude to lead her to the bed, Belle collapsed onto it. He drew the coverlet over her.

"I should go. It is not proper for me to be here like this with you. Since we are no longer married."

His words caused a ripple of genuine amusement to course through her, an amusement, she thought with a pang, that only the irreverent Mr. Carrington could have appreciated.

"Do as you think best," she mumbled to Jean-Claude, burrowing her head beneath the covers.

DRAWN UP TO THE TABLE IN THE PARLOR, CRECY AND Baptiste plotted the details of smuggling Sinclair and Jean-Claude out of Paris. Moodily, Sinclair stared out the window, wishing he could be gone now. It was raining again. Belle was right. It was forever raining in this bloody city.

"We shall keep to the original plan," Crecy said. "The route through the Rouvray Forest. Instead of Bonaparte hidden in the false compartment beneath the seat, we shall have Monsieur Varens. Sinclair can disguise himself as a postilion, and Isabelle we shall garb as a boy. She makes a most attractive youth. At the cross-roads I will have my men meet you with fresh horses."

Baptiste nodded, frowning slightly. "My only concern is that Lazare also knew of this plan."

"Bah!" Crecy snorted. "We have seen the last of that villain. You may be sure he is miles from Paris by now. He ever had a knack for preserving his own skin."

"That is true." Baptiste looked reassured. He turned to Sinclair. "You approve of this plan, monsieur?"

"It sounds fine to me," Sinclair said with little interest. He hardly noticed when the two men left the salon to alert Crecy's staff as to the time of the upcoming departure.

Sinclair tried to think no longer of what might be passing between Belle and Jean-Claude in that bedchamber. It seemed a long time before anyone emerged, and then it was the comte.

He still looked worn, but his features were composed. What soothing words had Belle uttered, what promises had she made to restore Jean-Claude? It tormented Sinclair to imagine the scene.

"Isabelle is resting," Varens said. "She is exhausted."

I daresay she would be after pouring out all her strength into you. But Sinclair choked back the sneering words.

He kept facing the window, hoping Varens would possess the sense to leave him alone, but it seemed the comte had a short supply of that commodity.

Varens spoke slowly, as though he had no wish to address Sinclair, but felt compelled. "I needs must express my thanks, monsieur, for your rescue of Isabelle."

The Frenchman spoke as though she belonged to him. Perhaps that was the harsh truth Sinclair had to face. She did, always had and always would.

"Your thanks are unnecessary," he snapped. "She didn't need to be rescued."

"The fact remains that while I lay helpless, you hazarded your life to see that she was safe."

"I still don't want your thanks," Sinclair said. "I didn't do it for you."

"I am aware of that," Jean-Claude said stiffly. "You must at least accept my gratitude for what you did for me at the theater. I would be a dead man now but for you."

"Don't remind me," Sinclair said through gritted teeth. Blast the man. Could he not stop these heroic speeches and go away before Sinclair hit him again? "I could not care less whether you live or die. If I helped you for any reason, it was because of a little boy named John-Jack, whom I took great pains to convince that his Papa would come home. I don't like lying to children."

Jean-Claude looked rather humbled by the mention of his son.

"As to any other motive—" Sinclair broke off, seeing no reason why he had to confess that he had also done it for Belle, that he could not bear to see that haunting look of unhappiness return to her eyes, even if it meant surrendering her to Jean-Claude.

"Whatever your motives," Jean-Claude persisted, "I could not rest easily until I discharged my debt of gratitude." As though it cost him great effort, Jean-Claude extended his hand toward Sinclair.

Sinclair supposed he should be equally magnanimous and take it. But was it not enough he had rescued the man likely to take Belle away from him? He was damned if he could endure being thanked for it into the bargain!

"Go to the devil, Varens," he said. Ignoring the comte's outstretched hand, Sinclair strode from the room.

Nineteen

Moonlight spilled down upon the crossroads, its silvery light silhouetting the coach and four halted where the paths met. Belle alighted from the carriage's interior, her breath coming in a cloud of steam. Crossing her arms over her breast, she burrowed her hands beneath the cape of her garrick. Her masculine attire with its layering of coat, waistcoat, shirt, and breeches afforded her more protection from the chill than any of her gowns, yet she still felt the sting of the cold. The damp whisperings of autumn hung in the air tonight, the promise of winter not far behind.

All about her the Rouvray Forest loomed, acres of woodland, thick with trees, the rustling leaves like sinister voices on the night wind. Belle had never liked the place, with its legends of highwaymen, robbers, and dark ancient deeds. Not far from the carriage stood the Croix Catelan, a weatherworn and mutilated pyramid, a memorial to the poet Arnauld de Catelan, who had been savagely murdered on this spot centuries ago. A dying oak hovered nearby, its gnarled branches like skeletal fingers stretched out in a plea for mercy, the soughing of the trees a whisper of despair.

Belle shivered. This rendezvous point was bad enough in the

daytime. The thick underbrush afforded far too many places for concealment, leaving one always with the feeling of being watched by unseen eyes. But this was where she and Baptiste had always met over the course of the years when involved in a mission together, it being the farthest he would venture from Paris, the closest she would come.

Glancing about her, she saw that both Baptiste and Sinclair had leaped down from the coach and gone round to the horses' heads. Baptiste stood soothing the restive leader while Sinclair talked to him. Sinclair fell silent as she approached, her steps made a little awkward by the unaccustomed stiffness of the Hessian boots she wore.

"No sign of Crecy's men?" she asked.

Sinclair backed up to consult his pocket watch by the light of one of the carriage lanterns. "It is too early yet."

"We arrived in good time," Baptiste said, stroking the leader's nose. "We came through the barrier much more easily than I had expected. The customs officer did not even ask to search the coach. It was much more difficult during the Revolution, I promise you."

Baptiste smiled at Belle. "I daresay it was all because of you, Monsieur Gordon. You make such a fierce-looking gentleman."

Belle pulled a wry face at him, whipping off her tricorne hat and wig. Her hair tumbled about her shoulders.

She glanced at Sinclair, half-expecting some teasing remark from him as well. He remained unusually quiet even as he had ever since leaving Paris.

"Has Monsieur le Comte survived his uncomfortable journey?" Baptiste asked.

"He is a little stiff," Belle said. The place of concealment beneath the false seat had been cramped quarters. Jean-Claude had been most grateful to be released from it. Bruised from the jolts of the road, he had at last dozed off in a corner of the carriage.

Belle sensed a tension in Sinclair as soon as Jean¬Claude's name was introduced. He paced off down the road, the gravel road crunching beneath his boots, and pretended to be scanning the horizon for some sign of approaching riders.

Belle sighed. She had had no chance to speak to Sinclair alone since leaving Crecy's apartment. She had slept as one dead for the better part of the afternoon, only awakening to be told it was time to make ready for their escape.

She trailed after Sinclair. She knew he was aware of her presence, although he did not look round at her. As she stepped in place beside him, she observed with dismay the unyielding set to his shoulders. He was deliberately attempting to hold her at a distance because of Jean-Claude.

She wanted to beg Sinclair to understand why she had had to go to Jean-Claude this afternoon, but she feared that was unnecessary. Sinclair did understand, and it engendered a kind of sad resignation in him.

"It is a clear night," she remarked at last. She stamped her feet in an effort to set the blood circulating through her numbed toes. She cursed the awkwardness of her tongue. Even at the worst of their troubled times together, she and Sinclair had never had difficulty finding words.

He seemed to share her problem. After a pause he replied, "I trust Crecy's men will be able to find us."

"You need not worry about that. All of us are most familiar with this rendezvous. Baptiste and I held our meetings here after I left Paris. Our partings have always taken place on the edge of this forest."

Silence lapsed between them again, the air unbearably quiet but for the Rouvray with all its mysterious night sounds, some nocturnal creature scurrying through underbrush, the hoot of an owl, the crackling of some twigs.

"We will be back in England after two days," Belle ventured. "I suppose you will have to make haste to London to report to your superiors."

"I shall first pay a call on Victor Merchant," Sinclair said grimly.

"And I would only be too pleased to accompany you."

Their eyes met, fired with the steel of a shared determination to settle accounts with the treacherous nobleman, their thoughts as ever marching the same. Sinclair smiled and Belle felt some of the ice begin to melt between them.

"And after that, Angel—" he began softly.

"Isabelle." An anxious voice called out from the interior of the carriage. With a sinking heart, Belle realized that Jean-Claude must have awakened to find her gone.

She tried to ignore the call for the moment. Blowing on her hands, she waited for Sinclair to continue.

But he had already stiffened, saying, "You had best go back to the carriage, Belle. You are getting cold."

She started to protest, but Sinclair strode back to help Baptiste with the restless horses. Belle had little choice but to return to the coach.

Sinclair was aware of Baptiste's shrewd stare as he rejoined the little Frenchman. "I can manage the horses," Baptiste said. "Perhaps you ought to warm yourself awhile inside the coach."

"It is a little too cramped in there to suit me," Sinclair replied tersely.

Baptiste looked at him and shook his head. "Young imbecile. You should not be leaving Belle alone so much with Monsieur le Comte."

"I don't see that as my concern." Sinclair compressed his lips, hoping Baptiste would take the hint that he did not wish to discuss the situation. But Baptiste never took hints.

"You must not take this attitude, *mon ami*," he scolded. "A rival, even a paltry one, but adds spice to the romance. What sort of love is this you bear my Isabelle if it is not worth the fighting for?"

"Isabelle is not a bone. I don't propose to snarl over her like a dog. The lady is free to make her own choice."

"Bah, you English." Baptiste snorted with disgust. "What cold fish you are!"

Stamping about to keep warm, the little man reminded Sinclair of some sort of surly gnome who had strayed too far from his forest lair. Sinclair was sorry to quarrel with the old man, but at least his annoyance caused Baptiste to drop a subject Sinclair found increasingly more painful.

Within the confines of the coach, Belle huddled beneath a fur lap robe, restlessly drumming her fingers against the window. She wished that Crecy's men would come, so that they could be on their way. Even more so, she wished Jean-Claude had remained asleep. The wait was making him nervous, though he strove to hide it. The comte was not formed for this sort of intrigue.

"I never thought to say it," he admitted ruefully, "but I shall be glad to be back in England. I have missed Jean-Jacques."

When she made no comment, he added, "It should be a relief to you as well, to at least reach the warmth of an inn and be able to change into one of your frocks."

From the first, Jean-Claude had not appeared comfortable with her in her masculine garb. Some streak of perversity in her made her say, "I rather like being in breeches. It gives one a great deal of freedom, which I believe you men don't quite appreciate. You should try struggling along beneath a pair of skirts sometime."

As soon as the words were out of her mouth, Belle had to choke back a laugh, imagining what sort of ribald riposte she would have elicited from Sinclair. Jean-Claude merely looked shocked. She had forgotten how much she had always had to mind her tongue in his presence. After so many years she feared it was too late to get back in the habit again.

"You never told me how you came to be connected with this band of intriguers," he said.

"It is a long, tiresome story." One that she had no desire to relate to Jean-Claude.

Reaching across to her, he squeezed her hand. "You have been leading a life all these years the horrors of which I cannot begin to comprehend. It is all my fault. I abandoned you. I—"

"Please, Jean-Claude," she cut him short. "Let us make an end to all this harboring of guilt and blame on both our parts. Nothing was forced upon me. I lived my life as I chose to do so."

She faltered over her own words, a little stunned herself as to what she was saying. Yes, it was true, she realized with a jolt. Jean-Claude had left her a tidy sum of money. She could have returned to England, sought out a more respectable sort of existence then, if it had ever been what she truly wanted.

Jean-Claude raised her hand to his lips. "I ask no questions about your past, Isabelle. I have learned something from this fiasco. It is only the future that matters. I can no longer offer you a grand estate, but I do possess a most comfortable manor house. And who can say? One day I may still return to Egremont. I have not given up hope."

He seized both of her hands in a quiet, firm clasp. "I want you to come back to me, be my wife again, the mother to my son."

Belle studied his earnest face in the moonlight filtering past the window, those solemn features she had so long held dear. He offered her everything that she thought she had ever wanted, the security of a home, his love, even his child, the last being perhaps the most precious gift of all.

Yet she felt herself drawing away from him, even though she knew this gray-eyed man would ever hold some small corner of her heart, the place where memories were kept, bittersweet like faded roses pressed between the leaves of a book. His image already wavered before her eyes, replaced by another, a midnight-haired rogue with a warm smile, green eyes vivid with love, laughter, life. Set beside Sinclair, Jean-Claude paled, becoming naught but a gentle ghost from her past.

She disengaged her hands, letting him down as easily as she could. "I thank you for your offer, Jean-Claude. You cannot know how happy it makes me to know you have forgiven me at last. But we both know that I cannot possibly accept."

A soft cry of protest escaped him, but she continued. "You will realize this yourself if you search your heart. We were always ill-suited. Perhaps we might have remained happy if the Revolution had not disrupted our lives. But it did. We cannot pretend otherwise. It is useless to say that the intervening years do not matter, for we know that is not true."

"We could make all those lost years not matter," he pleaded. "Surely we could if we desired it enough."

She placed her fingers against his lips to gently silence him. "You will only give us both more pain if you try to pursue this dream. I beg you say no more. This time when we part, let it be as friends."

He slumped against his seat. Belle feared he meant to give way to despair. But the age-old dignity of the Comte de Egremont came to his rescue. "As you wish, my dear," he said quietly.

After such a discussion it seemed intolerable to both of them to remain closed together within the carriage. Jean-Claude alighted first, handing her down. Belle discovered Sinclair sitting up on the coachman's box, Baptiste pacing by the front wheels.

"I have never known Crecy's men to be late," Baptiste grumbled to her. "They would be delayed on one of the coldest nights thus far this year."

"I am sure—" Belle never finished what she had been about to say. The thud of hoofbeats carried to where they stood, the sound of a mount crashing through the brush.

"At last," Jean-Claude said, brightening.

But Belle tensed, listening. She caught Baptiste's worried frown and knew he was thinking the same thing.

"Something is not right," she muttered. "It sounds like a single rider and coming through the forest, not by the road."

She turned to call up to Sinclair, to warn him as the pounding of hooves drew nearer. The next instant a horse and rider burst through the thicket onto the road. The stallion's mane whipped back, flowing black as the cape of the man astride him, both seeming phantom-spawned of the night and that secret primeval darkness which was the depths of the Rouvray.

Belle froze with dread as the beast charged toward her. She heard Jean-Claude's gasp, and Sinclair's warning shout as he scrambled for Baptiste's blunderbuss.

But she could not tear her gaze from the rider. He sawed at the reins, dragging his horse to such a violent halt, the beast's head jerked to one side, its eyes rolling wildly. The man's hood flew back, revealing Lazare's ravaged features, his lips pulled back in a snarl of hatred. Belle caught the flash of a pistol in his hand and read her death in his eyes.

Before she could react, Baptiste dived forward, shoving her aside. The pistol went off in a blaze of blue fire. The sound rang in her ears, but she felt herself unharmed. With a savage curse, Lazare struggled to control his plunging mount.

Another shot cracked through the clearing as Sinclair leveled Baptiste's ancient weapon, but missed. The sound only served to terrify Lazare's horse. The stallion reared and threw him to the ground, where he lay stunned.

Jean-Claude tugged at her arm. "Isabelle, you must get back inside the safety of the coach."

Belle shook him off, her alarmed gaze drawn to Baptiste as he sagged against the coach wheel, his knees buckling beneath him.

"Baptiste!" she cried, breaking his fall. A cry of pain breached the old man's lips, his face drawn white as he tottered into her arms. As he sank down, Belle's hand came away, sticky with blood.

"No!" she whispered. "Oh, God. No!"

With Jean-Claude's help, she eased Baptiste to the ground, her one thought to stay the crimson flow spreading over his chest. She was oblivious to all further danger.

Although stunned by his fall, Lazare regained his feet. With a bestial snarl, he drew forth the knife from his belt, the blade glinting in the moonlight. Sinclair leapt down from the coach, flying at him.

The two men toppled to the ground, grappling for possession of the knife, Lazare fought with almost inhuman strength, his rage-crazed eyes glaring up at Sinclair. But Sinclair's heart fired with a fury of his own, a tempest of anger such as he had never felt.

"Drop the blade, maggot, before I crush your arm."

Lazare spat in his face. With a violent jerk Lazare nearly broke Sinclair's grasp. The tip of the knife glanced off Sinclair's throat. He barely deflected the deadly slice. Clenching his teeth, he forced the blade hand down, cracking Lazare's fingers against a jagged stone to the sound of splintering bone. Lazare screamed, releasing the blade.

Sinclair drew back his fist and drove it against Lazare's hate-twisted features again and again, his hand smearing with blood. Lazare's head snapped back and he was still. With great difficulty, Sinclair stopped himself from meting out the punishing blows. A low groan assured him that Lazare was still alive. Yanking off the man's own scarf, Sinclair used the silk to bind Lazare's hands behind his back.

Only then did he turn back to face the scene unfolding by the side of the coach. Belle hovered over Baptiste, his head pillowed on her garrick as she tried futilely to stop the flow of blood from the gaping wound in his chest. As Sinclair approached with halting step, he met Jean-Claude's gaze above her. Looking at Sinclair, the comte sadly shook his head.

"Damn you Baptiste," Belle cried. "What sort of trick was this to play upon me? Now I shall have to return to your wretched Paris to nurse you back to health."

Even through his pain, Baptiste managed a crooked smile. "*Non, mon ange*. Not this time."

Belle felt a lump form in her throat, hard, burning. She wanted to deny Baptiste's words, but she could feel the old man's life slipping away beneath her hands.

"You should have let him shoot me! Oh, Baptiste, what have I done to you? I should have left you alone amongst your fans to live in peace. I should have ..."

She could not go on. His hand closed round hers and squeezed, those slender, clever fingers already so cold. "No regrets," he rasped. "I have none. You forget that it was I who chose. I had brothers once, avenging to do of my own."

A spasm of pain wracked his leathery features, a pain she felt pierce her own heart. The hand clutching hers grew weaker. He tugged her closer to make her hear, his voice barely a whisper.

"One last favor. I beg you, *mon ange*."

Belle swallowed hard. "Anything, Baptiste. You have but to tell me what it is."

He tried, using the last of his strength, but he could not seem to make his lips form the words. He released her, raising his hand in a final gesture. Then his arm slumped to the ground, those clear brown eyes staring sightlessly past her into the endless depths of the night.

"Baptiste?" She breathed his name, knowing he could no longer hear her. After all the horrors she had seen, Belle had never had trouble accepting the reality of death before. Not until now. She continued to kneel beside Baptiste, frozen as though she knew any movement would disrupt the moment of numbing disbelief, allowing the pain of realization to come flooding through her.

Sinclair stooped down, gently closing the old man's eyes. Still Belle did not stir, not until she felt Jean-Claude's tentative touch on her shoulder. She wrenched away. She wanted no comfort.

Jerking herself to her feet, she glanced wildly about her until her gaze focused on the one she sought. Lazare. The murdering bastard rested but yards away, making no effort to struggle against his bonds. He was conscious. Even beneath the hideous swelling that was his face, the streaks of blood, she could see the vicious gleam in his eyes.

Her grief threatened to burst the confines of her heart, forming a fiery knot of rage, searing through her veins. Her mouth grim with purpose, she stalked forward and picked up Lazare's knife from the ground.

She heard Jean-Claude's frightened voice. "Isabelle! What are you doing?"

Ignoring him, Belle moved relentlessly closer to Lazare's tensed form. Jean-Claude stepped in front of her. "Ma *chére*, there is no need for you to—to— The villain has been rendered harmless."

"Leave her alone," Sinclair said quietly. Her gaze flashed briefly to his. He said nothing, but merely watched her intently, waiting.

She placed one hand against Jean-Claude's chest, shoving him out of her way. With three quick strides she towered over Lazare, the knife poised in her hand.

She longed to see him squirm in terror, his eyes fill with the tormenting fear of the death he had inflicted upon so many others. But his swollen lips stretched back in a sneer that was almost obscene, his eyes lighting up with insane triumph. She gripped the blade so hard, it trembled in her sweat-slickened hand, seeing nothing but the face of Lazare. In those ravaged bloodstained features seemed centered all the ugliness, the violence, the cruelty in the world, the dark side of the Revolution. Or was it her own reflection she saw at this moment, mirrored back to her in the mad depths of those piercing eyes?

The thought gave her pause. She raised the knife, but it was too late. With that brief pause came the return of her sanity. Drawing in a deep breath, she cast the blade aside with a dull thud. Lazare's vicious triumph turned first to bewilderment, then rage.

"Bitch," he panted as she turned from him. "Cowardly bitch. Come back here. Kill me. You know you want to."

As she walked slowly away, he started to sob, to curse her.

"Isabelle!" He screamed her name, the sound echoing in the vast rustling silence of the Rouvray.

Belle marched onward to the two men waiting for her by the coach. Jean-Claude looked sick with relief, but Sinclair's expression remained calm.

As she met his eyes, she realized that Sinclair had known all along she would never kill in cold blood. He knew her better than she did herself.

Slipping past him, she returned to keep vigil over Baptiste. Jean-Claude joined her, gazing sorrowfully down at him.

"A courageous man," he murmured. "It is a pity he could not tell you his final request."

"He had no need. I know what he wanted." Belle bent down beside Baptiste's still form, folding his hand across her old friend's breast, the hand that had been gesturing toward Paris.

Twenty

Belle remained calm in the hours following Baptiste's death. Too calm, Sinclair feared. Crecy's men arrived, and she had her friend wrapped in a cloak and laid inside the carriage, while making arrangements to have him transported back to the city he had so loved for his burial.

Lazare appeared all but forgotten, his cursing and sobbing finally ceased. One of Crecy's servants inquired what Belle wanted done with the miscreant. She spared Lazare only a cursory glance, saying, "See him delivered to the gates of the Tuileries, with a note —*A gift for the first consul, Napoleon Bonaparte. Receive one Etienne Lazare, the man who sought your life. With the compliments of the Avenging Angel.*"

She never seemed to hear the way Lazare damned her to hell or his continued blustering threats of vengeance as she mounted her horse and rode away.

Sinclair had feared that Belle might have insisted on risking the return, to escort Baptiste to the city herself. But she remained content to linger amongst the straggling trees on the fringe of the Rouvray Forest, watching Crecy's men drive the coach to the distant gates of the city.

If Belle had desired to go back into Paris, Sinclair would have found her a way. But when he asked her, she only said, "No, it is not necessary. Crecy will know what to do. Baptiste and I have ever said our farewells here at the edge of the forest."

Shading his eyes, Sinclair could just see the coach joining the procession of other carts awaiting admittance to the gates as dawn broke over Paris, tinting the city with hues of rose and gold. Then he, Belle, and Jean-Claude whipped their horses about, heading for the road that would take them to the coast.

Belle waxed silent most of the journey, lost in thought, her eyes dulled with sadness. She withdrew from Varens as much as from himself, Sinclair noted. It would have given him pain to see her turning to Jean-Claude, but Sinclair would have felt relieved to see Belle seek comfort of somebody, rather than retreat behind a wall of grief.

They caught the packet boat on the eve of the following day. Sinclair expected Belle to retire to the cabin, fighting off her customary bout of seasickness. Yet she did not seem to notice the white-capped waves as the boat rocked along the surface of the channel.

Sinclair drew near to where she stood alone, staring over the deck rail, fingering an ivory-handled fan, spreading out the leaves of silk. Sinclair needed no identification of the delicate strokes to recognize Baptiste's handiwork. The old man had depicted none of the usual classical motifs so popular with the ladies. Like a lover capturing the essence of his mistress upon canvas, Baptiste had painted a scene of the banks of Paris, the silver-green waters of the Seine reflecting back the soaring towers of Notre Dame, the arches of the Pont Neuf, the ducks skimming the surface. Gazing at the fan, Sinclair was flooded with the memory of the smell of the reeds, the lapping of the river waters, the laughter of the crowds thronging the bridge.

Belle closed the fan. She surprised him by glancing up with a tremulous smile. "I was just thinking about Baptiste, all those times he and I arranged those fake funerals, smuggling people out of Paris in coffins. It was rather ironic that in the end, we had to spirit him back in. Baptiste would have found that rather amusing, don't you think?"

Her voice broke unexpectedly on the last word. Her eyes filled, and slowly, the tears tracked down her cheeks. Sinclair said nothing, merely held out his arms. She cast herself into them, burying her face against his shoulder.

SEVERAL DAYS LATER BELLE DESCENDED THE STAIRS OF the Neptune's Trident. Mr. Shaw passed her with his usual beaming smile, his eyes twinkling over the rims of his glasses.

"The fire is banked high in the coffee room," the inn's host said. "Your brandy has been laid out, and the luncheon is ready to be served."

"Thank you." Belle returned Shaw's smile. Strange, she reflected, but she had never thought that returning to this familiar old inn would feel in some odd way like coming home.

Shaw added with a discreet cough, "Your gentleman friend is already waiting."

Belle's heart skipped a beat. Sinclair. She had not seen him since they had left the ship. He had been very gentle as he handed her into the carriage. He had affairs to attend to, he said, but he would call upon her soon—a promise he had not kept. And she had not even known the address of his current lodgings to find him.

Sweeping eagerly into the coffee room, she said, "At last, Mr. Carrington. For once I hoped you might have been more punct—"

The playful greeting died upon her lips. It was not Sinclair's tall form silhouetted by the fireside, but the reed-thin frame of Quentin Crawley, warming his hands at the blaze, the tufts of his sandy hair standing on end.

"Oh, Quentin," she said in a voice flat with disappointment.

He spun about, greeting her with his prim expression.

"Good afternoon, Mrs. Varens. Welcome back to England. You are well, I trust?"

Belle closed the door, in no mood for Crawley's punctiliousness or for making the pretense of a social call.

"Never mind all that," she snapped. "Where is Victor Merchant? I rode out to Mal du Coeur yesterday. The butler told me Merchant had gone. I want to know where he is hiding."

"Mr. Merchant is not hiding anywhere. He was arrested."

"Arrested!" Belle exclaimed.

"All arranged by Mr. Carrington. He is a spy for the British army, though I expect you know that." Quentin frowned reprovingly as though he suspected her of deliberately keeping secrets from him. "Carrington had Mr. Merchant charged with plotting the murder of a British agent. Mr. Merchant was taken off by a guard of soldiers, though I have a feeling he was glad to go by the time Mr. Carrington had done with him." Crawley gave an expressive shiver.

Annoyance and chagrin swept through Belle. So Sinclair had gotten to Merchant first. He might have included her in the capture, for she surely had greater complaint against Victor than he. But she supposed it mattered little as long as the traitor had been apprehended.

"I am glad Merchant has been arrested," she said, moving to pour herself a glass of brandy. "Though it is most unfortunate for you, Quentin. No more spying. You will have to be content with life as a parish clerk."

"Not at all." Excitement rippled across Crawley's bland features. He puffed up his chest with pride. "You see, Mrs. Varens, funding for our society never did come from Merchant. Madame Dumont is in truth our director. A great lady. She never was too pleased with Merchant, but she desires that our work be continued." Quentin's eyes dropped modestly down. "She has named me as Merchant's successor."

"Congratulations," Belle said dryly, saluting him with her glass. "This calls for a toast." She poured him out some brandy, biting back a smile. She never thought Crawley would accept it, but to her astonishment he did, sipping cautiously at the amber-colored liquid as though it were some foul-tasting medicine.

"I do not delude myself but what I have undertaken a difficult task," Quentin said after Belle had toasted him. "We have lost so many good agents, but I trust I may still depend upon you."

"Not a chance," Belle said, setting down her glass with a sharp click. "I am through with the society."

"My dear Mrs. Varens! I understand that your confidence in our organization has been a little bruised. But you cannot believe I would ever serve you such a trick as Merchant did."

"Of course not, Quentin. But I told you all along I would quit one day. I have had enough."

Crawley's indulgent smile was patent with disbelief. "I will not be gainsaid so easily. I also hope to recruit Mr. Carrington as well."

"Sinclair? He works for the British army."

"I can pay him much better," Crawley said confidently. "And offer him far more intriguing assignments. When you hear what I have next in mind—"

"I don't want to hear." Belle snapped.

Crawley's mouth drew down into something approaching a pout. "Well! You can at least furnish me with Mr. Carrington's present address."

"I cannot do that, either," Belle said bleakly. She wished that Crawley would simply go away and leave her in peace. To her relief, a discreet knock sounded on the coffee room door. Grateful for any interruption, Belle moved to answer it.

Mr. Shaw hovered upon the threshold. He slipped her a folded note closed with a blot of sealing wax. "A stable lad just delivered this for you, Mrs. Varens. I thought it might be important, so I brought it to you at once."

Belle thanked Shaw. As the innkeeper quit the room, she examined her name inked upon the paper. The scrawl was all but illegible and heart-stoppingly familiar. Her pulse raced as she broke open the seal. Unfolding the note, she struggled to read the brief message,

Angel, I meant to say my farewells in person, but I thought it better this way. I know how hard it has been for you with Varens and me both tugging at your heartstrings. I love you too well to put you through any more of this. I realize how much what he can offer means to you. Wishing that you find all that you desire, Sinclair.

Belle sighed mentally blotting out all the other phrases save one: *I love you too well*.

Becoming aware of the curious stare of Quentin Crawley, she hastily refolded the note.

"Good tidings?" he asked.

"Er, yes. I find I don't owe my dressmaker as much as I thought." She slipped the note behind her back with an overbright smile. "If you will excuse me, Quentin, I find it chilly in here. I will just slip upstairs to fetch my shawl."

"Indeed? I would be happy to partake of luncheon with you, Mrs. Varens, though I fear it not quite proper without a third party present to serve as chaperon."

"I'll fetch one of those, too," Belle said. If Quentin had any notion where she was bound, she feared he would follow her. For what she had in mind, Crawley would definitely be *de trop*.

Whisking out of the room, she quickened her steps and managed to locate the stable lad who had brought the message, He was down in the kitchen, gnawing on a roasted chicken leg. His eyes grew round as she held up a golden guinea.

"I will give you one of these," she said, "to furnish me with the address where this letter came from ... and another to forget it."

. . .

Sinclair opened the trunk upon his bed, commencing the nigh hopeless task of gathering his scattered belongings to stuff inside. He was retrieving his shaving brush, which somehow had rolled beneath the bed, when he thought he heard the creak of a footfall outside his room.

He paused, listening. He had nearly convinced himself that he had imagined it when he saw the knob slowly turn. A rattling sound followed. Someone was trying to pick the lock. Sinclair tensed, tiptoeing in search of a weapon. He had little time. The door had begun to open.

Sinclair snatched up the first thing to hand, the iron shovel used to clear out ashes from the grate. He stalked forward, raising it only to halt at the sight of cool blue eyes, fine-boned features framed by a halo of curls.

"Belle," he breathed, slowly lowering his arm. He half-feared he might be dreaming. His nights had been haunted with images of her that seemed all too real, as real as this apparition.

She closed the door, surveying the disorder of the room with a slight frown. "I don't think that little shovel is going to be of much help, Mr. Carrington."

Stooping down, she retrieved a stray cravat and began to fold it. No, Sinclair thought, with a wry smile. In his dreams she would not have been doing anything as practical as that. What was she doing here? He felt a wild hope thrum through him, but he forced himself to remain casual. "Why didn't you just knock?" he demanded.

"I was not sure you would not try to bolt if forewarned." Belle put the cravat in the trunk, following it up with a crumpled linen shirt, trying to keep her voice light. She wondered if Sinclair could see the way her hands trembled. How much courage it had taken her to come through that door! After all, she might have been wrong about that letter. It could have been Sinclair's kind way of ending an awkward affair.

But his eyes told her differently. He might be able to summon that raffish smile, remain at a distance, but his eyes were closing it with an intensity that made her catch her breath.

"Did you not receive my note?" he asked.

"Yes, that's how I knew where to find you." Belle gave up the pretense of calm. She walked toward him, resting her hands against his chest. She could feel the thud of his heart. Smiling up at him, she murmured, "I do so hate it when you try to be noble, Sinclair."

"I was only trying to make things easier for you," he said hoarsely. His hand came up to cover hers. "Where is Jean-Claude?"

"Well on his way home to John-Jack, I hope."

His eyes probed hers as he hovered between joy and apprehension. "You will be joining him soon?"

"No," she said. "I sent him away. And in truth, I think he was relieved."

The night in Rouvray Forest, she believed, Jean-Claude had finally come to an acceptance of who she was, an understanding of their differences. Their parting had been like the man himself, gentle, full of quiet dignity.

Sinclair expelled a deep breath. "Then it did not work out between you and Jean-Claude. I am sorry."

"Are you?" She raised one brow quizzically.

"No, damn it, I fear I am not. The question is: Are you?"

For her answer she cupped her hands behind his head, twining her fingers in the velvety masses of his dark hair, pulling him down to touch her lips to his. It took him less than a heartbeat to respond.

"Belle." His mouth crushed hers in a searing embrace. Holding her close, he breathed a feverish trail of kisses against her hair, his voice gone husky with passion. "You won't regret this choice, I promise. If it is the respectable life you want, I will find a way to get it for you, the blasted ivy-covered cottage and all. I can seek a post in government, make up the quarrel with my father—"

Belle halted this rash flow of pledges with another fervent kiss.

She gazed up at him with tender amusement. "No, Mr. Carrington. Let us take life as we have always done. One day at a time."

As he cradled her close, she cried. "Sinclair, Sinclair, I love you so. I was a fool not to have realized it sooner."

"Yes, you were, weren't you?" He swooped her up to carry her to bed, knocking the trunk and its contents heedlessly to the floor.

They tumbled down upon the mattress, longing only to become lost in each other's embrace, when they were rudely jarred by a knock on the door.

"Who is it?" Sinclair growled.

"The porter, sir. I just called to tell you that there is a gentleman below asking for you. A Mr. Crawley."

"Crawley? What the deuce does he want?"

Belle groaned. "The wretched man must have followed me here after all." She called out to the porter. "Tell him Mr. Carrington is not at home."

As the footsteps retreated, Belle scrambled from the bed and began to close the shutters.

Sinclair trailed after her, looking bewildered. "Angel, what on earth is this all about?"

"Crawley has become the new head of the society. He has some infernal mission he is trying to get us to undertake."

Belle paused in the act of bolting the last shutter to peer anxiously into the street below. "Good. He's leaving."

Sinclair craned his neck, looking over her shoulder. As they watched Crawley attempt to summon a hackney cab, Sinclair said, "Of course, we have not the slightest interest in knowing what it is all about."

"Not the slightest," Belle said firmly. She started to close the shutter, but she couldn't help herself. She stole one more speculative glance at Crawley. She caught Sinclair doing the same.

Their eyes met in guilty fashion and both erupted into laughter. Without another word, Sinclair tugged her by her hand, and tossed her back upon the bed. His lean hard frame closed over her as he claimed her mouth with the tender fury of his kiss.

No, Belle thought, feeling the fires stir between them. She and Sinclair had not the slightest interest in discovering what Crawley wanted.

At least not until tomorrow.

Also by Susan Carroll

The Redemption of Hellfire Harry

The Wooing of Miss Masters

Mistress Mischief

Miss Prentiss and the Yankee

Christmas Belles

The Valentine's Day Ball

Contemporary Paranormal

The Gumshoe and the Ghost Whisperer

Stand Alone Historical Romances

Winterbourne

The Painted Veil

About the Author

Author Susan Carroll began her career in 1986, writing historical romance and regencies, two of which were honored by Romance Writers of America with the RITA award. She has written twenty six novels to date. Her St. Leger series received much acclaim. The Bride Finder was honored with a RITA for Best Paranormal Romance in 1999 and also received the Reviewers Choice Award from Romantic Times magazine for Historical Romance of the year. Two sequels followed, The Night Drifter and Midnight Bride.

Ms. Carroll launched a new series with the publication of The Dark Queen set during the turbulent days of the French Renaissance. A blend of history, romance and intrigue, these six books relate the saga of the Cheney sisters, three women of extraordinary abilities who live in constant peril of being accused of witchcraft.

Her most recent title, Disenchanted is a humorous retelling of the Cinderella story.

Want updates when Susan has new books out, fun goodies to share, and other news? Click here. As a FREE BONUS for signing up, you will receive an Historical Romance Crossword puzzle.